BAPTISM
OF FIRE

ANDRZEJ SAPKOWSKI

Translated by David French

This paperback first published in Great Britain in 2020 by Gollancz
First published in Great Britain in 2014 by Gollancz
an imprint of The Orion Publishing Group Ltd
Carmelite House, 50 Victoria Embankment
London EC4Y 0DZ

An Hachette UK Company

16

Originally published in Polish as *Chrzest Ognia*
Published by arrangement with The Patricia Pasqualini Literary Agency

The moral right of Andrzej Sapkowski to be identified as the author of this work,
and the right of David French to be identified as the translator of this work, has
been asserted in accordance with the Copyright, Designs and Patents Act of 1988.

A CIP catalogue record for this book is
available from the British Library.

ISBN (Mass Market Paperback) 978 1 473 23110 8
ISBN (eBook) 978 0 575 09098 9

Typeset by Input Data Services Ltd, Somerset
Printed in Great Britain by Clays Ltd, Elcograf S.p.A.

www.gollancz.co.uk

Then the soothsayer spake thus to the witcher: 'This counsel I shall give you: don hobnailed boots and take an iron staff. Walk in your hobnailed boots to the end of the world, tap the road in front of you with the staff, and let your tears fall. Go through fire and water, do not stop, do not look back. And when your boots are worn out, when your iron staff is worn down, when the wind and the sun have dried your eyes such that not a single tear will fall from them, then you will find what you are searching for, what you love, at the end of the world. Perhaps.'

And the witcher walked through fire and water, never looking back. But he took neither hobnailed boots nor a staff. He took only his witcher's sword. He obeyed not the words of the soothsayer. And rightly so, for she was wicked.

Flourens Delannoy, *Tales and Legends*

CHAPTER ONE

Birds were chirping loudly in the undergrowth.

The slopes of the ravine were overgrown with a dense, tangled mass of brambles and barberry; a perfect place for nesting and feeding. Not surprisingly, it was teeming with birds. Greenfinches trilled loudly, redpolls and whitethroats twittered, and chaffinches gave out ringing 'vink-vink's every now and then. *The chaffinch's call signals rain*, thought Milva, glancing up at the sky. There were no clouds. *But chaffinches always warn of the rain. We could do with a little rain.*

Such a spot, opposite the mouth of a ravine, was a good place for a hunter, giving a decent chance of a kill – particularly here in Brokilon Forest, which was abundant with game. The dryads, who controlled extensive tracts of the forest, rarely hunted and humans dared to venture into it even less often. Here, a hunter greedy for meat or pelts became the quarry himself. The Brokilon dryads showed no mercy to intruders. Milva had once discovered that for herself.

No, Brokilon was not short of game. Nonetheless, Milva had been waiting in the undergrowth for more than two hours and nothing had crossed her line of sight. She couldn't hunt on the move; the drought which had lasted for more than a month had lined the forest floor with dry brush and leaves, which rustled and crackled at every step. In conditions like these, only standing still and unseen would lead to success, and a prize.

An admiral butterfly alighted on the nock of her bow. Milva didn't shoo it away, but watched it closing and opening its wings. She also looked at her bow, a recent acquisition which she still wasn't tired of admiring. She was a born archer and loved a good weapon. And she was holding the best of the best.

Milva had owned many bows in her life. She had learned to shoot

1

using ordinary ash and yew bows, but soon gave them up for composite reflex bows, of the type elves and dryads used. Elven bows were shorter, lighter and more manageable and, owing to the laminated composition of wood and animal sinew, much 'quicker' than yew bows. An arrow shot with them reached the target much more swiftly and along a flatter arc, which considerably reduced the possibility of its being blown off course. The best examples of such weapons, bent fourfold, bore the elven name of *zefhar*, since the bow's shape formed that rune. Milva had used zefhars for several years and couldn't imagine a bow capable of outclassing them.

But she had finally come across one. It was, of course, at the Seaside Bazaar in Cidaris, which was renowned for its diverse selection of strange and rare goods brought by sailors from the most distant corners of the world; from anywhere a frigate or galleon could reach. Whenever she could, Milva would visit the bazaar and look at the foreign bows. It was there she bought the bow she'd thought would serve her for many years. She had thought the zefhar from Zerrikania, reinforced with polished antelope horn, was perfect. For just a year. Twelve months later, at the same market stall, owned by the same trader, she had found another rare beauty.

The bow came from the Far North. It measured just over five feet, was made of mahogany, had a perfectly balanced riser and flat, laminated limbs, glued together from alternating layers of fine wood, boiled sinew and whalebone. It differed from the other composite bows in its construction and also in its price; which is what had initially caught Milva's attention. When, however, she picked up the bow and flexed it, she paid the price the trader was asking without hesitation or haggling. Four hundred Novigrad crowns. Naturally, she didn't have such a titanic sum on her; instead she had given up her Zerrikanian zefhar, a bunch of sable pelts, a small, exquisite elven-made medallion, and a coral cameo pendant on a string of river pearls.

But she didn't regret it. Not ever. The bow was incredibly light and, quite simply, perfectly accurate. Although it wasn't long it had an impressive kick to its laminated wood and sinew limbs. Equipped with a silk and hemp bowstring stretched between its precisely curved limbs, it generated fifty-five pounds of force from a twenty-four-inch draw. True enough, there were bows that could generate eighty, but Milva considered that excessive. An arrow shot from her whalebone fifty-fiver covered a distance of two hundred feet in two heartbeats, and at a hundred paces still had enough force to impale a stag, while it would pass right through an unarmoured human. Milva rarely hunted animals larger than red deer or heavily armoured men.

The butterfly flew away. The chaffinches continued to make a racket in the undergrowth. And still nothing crossed her line of sight. Milva leant against the trunk of a pine and began to think back. Simply to kill time.

Her first encounter with the Witcher had taken place in July, two weeks after the events on the Isle of Thanedd and the outbreak of war in Dol Angra. Milva had returned to Brokilon after a fortnight's absence; she was leading the remains of a Scoia'tael commando defeated in Temeria during an attempt to make their way into war-torn Aedirn. The Squirrels had wanted to join the uprising incited by the elves in Dol Blathanna. They had failed, and would have perished had it not been for Milva. But they'd found her, and refuge in Brokilon.

Immediately on her arrival, she had been informed that Aglaïs needed her urgently in Col Serrai. Milva had been a little taken aback. Aglaïs was the leader of the Brokilon healers, and the deep valley of Col Serrai, with its hot springs and caves, was where healings usually took place.

She responded to the call, convinced it concerned some elf who had been healed and needed her help to re-establish contact with his commando. But when she saw the wounded witcher and learned what it was about, she was absolutely furious. She ran from the cave with her hair streaming behind her and offloaded all her anger on Aglaïs.

'He saw me! He saw my face! Do you understand what danger that puts me in?'

'No, no I don't understand,' replied the healer coldly. 'That is

Gwynbleidd, the Witcher, a friend of Brokilon. He has been here for a fortnight, since the new moon. And more time will pass before he will be able to get up and walk normally. He craves tidings from the world; news about those close to him. Only you can supply him with that.'

'Tidings from the world? Have you lost your mind, dryad? Do you know what is happening in the world now, beyond the borders of your tranquil forest? A war is raging in Aedirn! Brugge, Temeria and Redania are reduced to havoc, hell, and much slaughter! Those who instigated the rebellion on Thanedd are being hunted high and low! There are spies and an'givare – informers – everywhere; it's sometimes sufficient to let slip a single word, make a face at the wrong moment, and you'll meet the hangman's red-hot iron in the dungeon! And you want me to creep around spying, asking questions, gathering information? Risking my neck? And for whom? For some half-dead witcher? And who is he to me? My own flesh and blood? You've truly taken leave of your senses, Aglaïs.'

'If you're going to shout,' interrupted the dryad calmly, 'let's go deeper into the forest. He needs peace and quiet.'

Despite herself, Milva looked over at the cave where she had seen the wounded witcher a moment earlier. *A strapping lad*, she had thought, *thin, yet sinewy . . . His hair's white, but his belly's as flat as a young man's; hard times have been his companion, not lard and beer . . .*

'He was on Thanedd,' she stated; she didn't ask. 'He's a rebel.'

'I know not,' said Aglaïs, shrugging. 'He's wounded. He needs help. I'm not interested in the rest.'

Milva was annoyed. The healer was known for her taciturnity. But Milva had already heard excited accounts from dryads in the eastern marches of Brokilon; she already knew the details of the events that had occurred a fortnight earlier. About the chestnut-haired sorceress who had appeared in Brokilon in a burst of magic; about the cripple with a broken arm and leg she had been dragging with her. A cripple who had turned out to be the Witcher, known to the dryads as Gwynbleidd: the White Wolf.

At first, according to the dryads, no one had known what steps to take. The mutilated witcher screamed and fainted by turns, Aglaïs

4

had applied makeshift dressings, the sorceress cursed and wept. Milva did not believe that at all: who has ever seen a sorceress weep? And later the order came from Duén Canell, from the silver-eyed Eithné, the Lady of Brokilon. Send the sorceress away, said the ruler of the Forest of the Dryads. And tend to the Witcher.

And so they did. Milva had seen as much. He was lying in a cave, in a hollow full of water from the magical Brokilon springs. His limbs, which had been held in place using splints and put in traction, were swathed in a thick layer of the healing climbing plant – conynhaela – and turfs of knitbone. His hair was as white as milk. Unusually, he was conscious: anyone being treated with conynhaela normally lay lifeless and raving as the magic spoke through them . . .

'Well?' the healer's emotionless voice tore her from her reverie. 'What is it going to be? What am I to tell him?'

'To go to hell,' snapped Milva, lifting her belt, from which hung a heavy purse and a hunting knife. 'And you can go to hell, too, Aglaïs.'

'As you wish. I shall not compel you.'

'You are right. You will not.'

She went into the forest, among the sparse pines, and didn't look back. She was angry.

Milva knew about the events which had taken place during the first July new moon on the Isle of Thanedd; the Scoia'tael talked about it endlessly. There had been a rebellion during the Mages' Conclave on the island. Blood had been spilt and heads had rolled. And, as if on a signal, the armies of Nilfgaard had attacked Aedirn and Lyria and the war had begun. And in Temeria, Redania and Kaedwen it was all blamed on the Squirrels. For one thing, because a commando of Scoia'tael had supposedly come to the aid of the rebellious mages on Thanedd. For another, because an elf or possibly half-elf had supposedly stabbed and killed Vizimir, King of Redania. So the furious humans had gone after the Squirrels with a vengeance. The fighting was raging everywhere and elven blood was flowing in rivers . . .

Ha, thought Milva, *perhaps what the priests are saying is true after all and the end of the world and the day of judgement are close at hand?*

5

The world is in flames, humans are preying not only on elves but on other humans too. Brothers are raising knives against brothers . . . And the Witcher is meddling in politics . . . and joining the rebellion. The Witcher, who is meant to roam the world and kill monsters eager to harm humans! No witcher, for as long as anyone can remember, has ever allowed himself to be drawn into politics or war. Why, there's even the tale about a foolish king who carried water in a sieve, took a hare as a messenger, and appointed a witcher as a palatine. And yet here we have the Witcher, carved up in a rebellion against the kings and forced to escape punishment in Brokilon. Perhaps it truly is the end of the world!

'Greetings, Maria.'

She started. The short dryad leaning against a pine had eyes and hair the colour of silver. The setting sun gave her head a halo against the background of the motley wall of trees. Milva dropped to one knee and bowed low.

'My greetings to you, Lady Eithné.'

The ruler of Brokilon stuck a small, crescent-shaped, golden knife into a bast girdle.

'Arise,' she said. 'Let us take a walk. I wish to talk with you.'

They walked for a long time through the shadowy forest; the delicate, silver-haired dryad and the tall, flaxen-haired girl. Neither of them broke the silence for some time.

'It is long since you were at Duén Canell, Maria.'

'There was no time, Lady Eithné. It is a long road to Duén Canell from the River Ribbon, and I . . . But of course you know.'

'That I do. Are you weary?'

'The elves need my help. I'm helping them on your orders, after all.'

'At my request.'

'Indeed. At your request.'

'And I have one more.'

'As I thought. The Witcher?'

'Help him.'

Milva stopped and turned back, breaking an overhanging twig of honeysuckle with a sharp movement, turning it over in her fingers before flinging it to the ground.

'For half a year,' she said softly, looking into the dryad's silvery eyes, 'I have risked my life guiding elves from their decimated commandos to Brokilon . . . When they are rested and their wounds healed, I lead them out again . . . Is that so little? Haven't I done enough? Every new moon, I set out on the trail in the dark of the night. I've begun to fear the sun as much as a bat or an owl does . . .'

'No one knows the forest trails better than you.'

'I will not learn anything in the greenwood. I hear that the Witcher wants me to gather news, by moving among humans. He's a rebel, the ears of the an'givare prick up at the sound of his name. I must be careful not to show myself in the cities. And what if someone recognises me? The memories still endure, the blood is not yet dry . . . for there was a lot of blood, Lady Eithné.'

'A great deal.' The silver eyes of the old dryad were alien, cold; inscrutable. 'A great deal, indeed.'

'Were they to recognise me, they would impale me.'

'You are prudent. You are cautious and vigilant.'

'In order to gather the tidings the Witcher requests, it is necessary to shed vigilance. It is necessary to ask. And now it is dangerous to demonstrate curiosity. Were they to capture me—'

'You have contacts.'

'They would torture me. Until I died. Or grind me down in Drakenborg—'

'But you are indebted to me.'

Milva turned her head away and bit her lip.

'It's true, I am,' she said bitterly. 'I have not forgotten.'

She narrowed her eyes, her face suddenly contorted, and she clenched her teeth tightly. The memory shone faintly beneath her eyelids; the ghastly moonlight of that night. The pain in her ankle suddenly returned, held tight by the leather snare, and the pain in her joints, after they had been cruelly wrenched. She heard again the soughing of leaves as the tree shot suddenly upright . . . Her screaming, moaning; the desperate, frantic, horrified struggle and the invasive sense of fear which flowed over her when she realised she couldn't free herself . . . The cry and fear, the creak of the rope, the rippling shadows; the swinging, unnatural, upturned earth, upturned sky, trees with upturned tops, pain, blood pounding in her temples . . .

And at dawn the dryads, all around her, in a ring . . . The distant silvery laughter . . . *A puppet on a string! Swing, swing, marionette, little head hanging down* . . . And her own, unnatural, wheezing cry. And then darkness.

'Indeed, I have a debt,' she said through clenched teeth. 'Indeed, for I was a hanged man cut from the noose. As long as I live, I see, I shall never pay off that debt.'

'Everyone has some kind of debt,' replied Eithné. 'Such is life, Maria Barring. Debts and liabilities, obligations, gratitude, payments . . . Doing something for someone. Or perhaps for ourselves? For in fact we are always paying ourselves back and not someone else. Each time we are indebted we pay off the debt to ourselves. In each of us lies a creditor and a debtor at once and the art is for the reckoning to tally inside us. We enter the world as a minute part of the life we are given, and from then on we are ever paying off debts. To ourselves. For ourselves. In order for the final reckoning to tally.'

'Is this human dear to your, Lady Eithné? That . . . that witcher?'

'He is. Although he knows not of it. Return to Col Serrai, Maria Barring. Go to him. And do what he asks of you.'

In the valley, the brushwood crunched and a twig snapped. A magpie gave a noisy, angry 'chacker-chacker', and some chaffinches took flight, flashing their white wing bars and tail feathers. Milva held her breath. At last.

Chacker-chacker, called the magpie. Chacker-chacker-chacker. Another twig cracked.

Milva adjusted the worn, polished leather guard on her left forearm, and placed her hand through the loop attached to her gear. She took an arrow from the flat quiver on her thigh. Out of habit, she checked the arrowhead and the fletchings. She bought shafts at the market – choosing on average one out of every dozen offered to her – but she always fletched them herself. Most ready-made arrows in circulation had too-short fletchings arranged straight along the

8

shaft, while Milva only used spirally fletched arrows, with the fletchings never shorter than five inches.

She nocked the arrow and stared at the mouth of the ravine, at a green spot of barberry among the trees, heavy with bunches of red berries.

The chaffinches had not flown far and began their trilling again. *Come on, little one*, thought Milva, raising the bow and drawing the bowstring. *Come on. I'm ready.*

But the roe deer headed along the ravine, towards the marsh and springs which fed the small streams flowing into the Ribbon. A young buck came out of the ravine. A fine specimen, weighing in – she estimated – at almost four stone. He lifted his head, pricked up his ears, and then turned back towards the bushes, nibbling leaves.

With his back toward her, he was an easy victim. Had it not been for a tree trunk obscuring part of the target, Milva would have fired without a second thought. Even if she were to hit him in the belly, the arrow would penetrate and pierce the heart, liver or lungs. Were she to hit him in the haunch, she would destroy an artery, and the animal would be sure to fall in a short time. She waited, without releasing the bowstring.

The buck raised his head again, stepped out from behind the trunk and abruptly turned round a little. Milva, holding the bow at full draw, cursed under her breath. A shot face-on was uncertain; instead of hitting the lung, the arrowhead might enter the stomach. She waited, holding her breath, aware of the salty taste of the bowstring against the corner of her mouth. That was one of the most important, quite invaluable, advantages of her bow; were she to use a heavier or inferior weapon, she would never be able to hold it fully drawn for so long without tiring or losing precision with the shot.

Fortunately, the buck lowered his head, nibbled on some grass protruding from the moss and turned to stand sideways. Milva exhaled calmly, took aim at his chest and gently released her fingers from the bowstring.

She didn't hear the expected crunch of ribs being broken by the arrow, however. For the buck leapt upwards, kicked and fled, accompanied by the crackling of dry branches and the rustle of leaves being shoved aside.

Milva stood motionless for several heartbeats, petrified like a marble statue of a forest goddess. Only when all the noises had subsided did she lift her hand from her cheek and lower the bow. Having made a mental note of the route the animal had taken as it fled, she sat down calmly, resting her back against a tree trunk. She was an experienced hunter, she had poached in the lord's forests from a child. She had brought down her first roe deer at the age of eleven, and her first fourteen-point buck on the day of her fourteenth birthday – an exceptionally favourable augury. And experience had taught that one should never rush after a shot animal. If she had aimed well, the buck would fall no further than two hundred paces from the mouth of the ravine. Should she have been off target – a possibility she actually didn't contemplate – hurrying might only make things worse. A badly injured animal, which wasn't agitated, would slow to a walk after its initial panicked flight. A frightened animal being pursued would race away at breakneck speed and would only slow down once it was over the hills and far away.

So she had at least half an hour. She plucked a blade of grass, stuck it between her teeth and drifted off in thought once again. The memories came back.

When she returned to Brokilon twelve days later, the Witcher was already up and about. He was limping somewhat and slightly dragging one hip, but he was walking. Milva was not surprised – she knew of the miraculous healing properties of the forest water and the herb conynhaela. She also knew Aglaïs's abilities and on several occasions had witnessed the astonishingly quick return to health of wounded dryads. And the rumours about the exceptional resistance and endurance of witchers were also clearly no mere myths either.

She did not go to Col Serrai immediately on her arrival, although the dryads hinted that Gwynbleidd had been impatiently awaiting her return. She delayed intentionally, still unhappy with her mission and wanting to make her feelings clear. She escorted the Squirrels back to their camp. She gave a lengthy account of the incidents on the road and warned the dryads about the plans to seal the border on the Ribbon by humans. Only when she was rebuked for the third time did Milva bathe, change and go to the Witcher.

He was waiting for her at the edge of a glade by some cedars. He was walking up and down, squatting from time to time and then straightening up with a spring. Aglaïs had clearly ordered him to exercise.

'What news?' he asked immediately after greeting her. The coldness in his voice didn't deceive her.

'The war seems to be coming to an end,' she answered, shrugging. 'Nilfgaard, they say, has crushed Lyria and Aedirn. Verden has surrendered and the King of Temeria has struck a deal with the Nilfgaardian emperor. The elves in the Valley of Flowers have established their own kingdom but the Scoia'tael from Temeria and Redania have not joined them. They are still fighting . . .'

'That isn't what I meant.'

'No?' she said, feigning surprise. 'Oh, I see. Well, I stopped in Dorian, as you asked, though it meant going considerably out of my way. And the highways are so dangerous now . . .'

She broke off, stretching. This time he didn't hurry her.

'Was Codringher,' she finally asked, 'whom you asked me to visit, a close friend of yours?'

The Witcher's face did not twitch, but Milva knew he understood at once.

'No. He wasn't.'

'That's good,' she continued easily. 'Because he's no longer with us. He went up in flames along with his chambers; probably only the chimney and half of the façade survived. The whole of Dorian is abuzz with rumours. Some say Codringher was dabbling in black magic and concocting poisons; that he had a pact with the devil, so the devil's fire consumed him. Others say he'd stuck his nose and his fingers into a crack he shouldn't have, as was his custom. And it wasn't to somebody's liking, so they bumped him off and set everything alight, to cover their tracks. What do you think?'

She didn't receive a reply, or detect any emotion on his ashen face. So she continued, in the same venomous, arrogant tone of voice.

'It's interesting that the fire and Codringher's death occurred during the first July new moon, exactly when the unrest on the Isle of Thanedd was taking place. As if someone had guessed that Codringher knew something about the disturbances and would be asked for details. As if someone wanted to stop his trap up good and proper in advance, strike him dumb. What do you say to that? Ah, I see you won't say anything. You're keeping quiet, so I'll tell you this: your activities are dangerous, and so is your spying and questioning. Perhaps someone will want to shut other traps and ears than Codringher's. That's what I think.'

'Forgive me,' he said a moment later. 'You're right. I put you at risk. It was too dangerous a task for a—'

'For a woman, you mean?' she said, jerking her head back, flicking her still wet hair from her shoulder with a sudden movement. 'Is that what you were going to say? Are you playing the gentleman all of a sudden? I may have to squat to piss, but my coat is lined with wolf skin, not coney fur! Don't call me a coward, because you don't know me!'

'I do,' he said in a calm, quiet voice, not reacting to her anger or raised voice. 'You are Milva. You lead Squirrels to safety in Brokilon, avoiding capture. Your courage is known to me. But I recklessly and selfishly put you at risk—'

'You're a fool!' she interrupted sharply. 'Worry about yourself, not about me. Worry about that young girl!'

She smiled disdainfully. Because this time his face did change. She fell silent deliberately, waiting for further questions.

'What do you know?' he finally asked. 'And from whom?'

'You had your Codringher,' she snorted, lifting her head proudly. 'And I have my own contacts. The kind with sharp eyes and ears.'

'Tell me, Milva. Please.'

'After the fighting on Thanedd,' she began, after waiting a moment, 'unrest erupted everywhere. The hunt for traitors began, particularly for any sorcerers who supported Nilfgaard and for the other turncoats. Some were captured, others vanished without trace. You don't need much nous to guess where they fled to and under

12

whose wings they're hiding. But it wasn't just sorcerers and traitors who were hunted. A Squirrel commando led by the famous Faoiltiarna also helped the mutinous sorcerers in the rebellion on Thanedd. So now he's wanted. An order has been issued that every elf captured should be tortured and interrogated about Faoiltiarna's commando.'

'Who's Faoiltiarna?'

'An elf, one of the Scoia'tael. Few have got under the humans' skin the way he has. There's a hefty bounty on his head. But they're seeking another too. A Nilfgaardian knight who was on Thanedd. And also for a . . .'

'Go on.'

'The an'givare are asking about a witcher who goes by the name of Geralt of Rivia. And about a girl named Cirilla. Those two are to be captured alive. It was ordered on pain of death: if either of you is caught, not a hair on your heads is to be harmed, not a button may be torn from her dress. Oh! You must be dear to their hearts for them to care so much about your health . . .'

She broke off, seeing the expression on his face, from which his unnatural composure had abruptly disappeared. She realised that however hard she tried, she was unable to make him afraid. At least not for his own skin. She unexpectedly felt ashamed.

'Well, that pursuit of theirs is futile,' she said gently, with just a faintly mocking smile on her lips. 'You are safe in Brokilon. And they won't catch the girl alive either. When they searched through the rubble on Thanedd, all the debris from that magical tower which collapsed— Hey, what's wrong with you?'

The Witcher staggered, leant against a cedar, and sat down heavily near the trunk. Milva leapt back, horrified by the pallor which his already whitened face had suddenly taken on.

'Aglaïs! Sirssa! Fauve! Come quickly! Damn, I think he's about to keel over! Hey, you!'

'Don't call them . . . There's nothing wrong with me. Speak. I want to know . . .'

Milva suddenly understood.

'They found nothing in the debris!' she cried, feeling herself go pale too. 'Nothing! Although they examined every stone and cast spells, they didn't find . . .'

She wiped the sweat from her forehead and held back with a gesture the dryads running towards them. She seized the Witcher by his shoulders and leant over him so that her long hair tumbled over his pale face.

'You misunderstood me,' she said quickly, incoherently; it was difficult to find the right words among the mass which were trying to tumble out. 'I only meant— You understood me wrongly. Because I . . . How was I to know she is so . . . No . . . I didn't mean to. I only wanted to say that the girl . . . That they won't find her, because she disappeared without a trace, like those mages. Forgive me.'

He didn't answer. He looked away. Milva bit her lip and clenched her fists.

'I'm leaving Brokilon again in three days,' she said gently after a long, very long, silence. 'The moon must wane a little and the nights become a little darker. I shall return within ten days, perhaps sooner. Shortly after Lammas, in the first days of August. Worry not. I shall move earth and water, but I shall find out everything. If anyone knows anything about that maiden, you'll know it too.'

'Thank you, Milva.'

'I'll see you in ten days . . . Gwynbleidd.'

'Call me Geralt,' he said, holding out a hand. She took it without a second thought. And squeezed it very hard.

'And I'm Maria Barring.'

A nod of the head and the flicker of a smile thanked her for her sincerity. She knew he appreciated it.

'Be careful, please. When you ask questions, be careful who you ask.'

'Don't worry about me.'

'Your informers . . . Do you trust them?'

'I don't trust anyone.'

'The Witcher is in Brokilon. Among the dryads.'

'As I thought,' Dijkstra said, folding his arms on his chest. 'But I'm glad it's been confirmed.'

He remained silent for a moment. Lennep licked his lips. And waited.

'I'm glad it's been confirmed,' repeated the head of the secret service of the Kingdom of Redania, pensively, as though he were talking to himself. 'It's always better to be certain. If only Yennefer were with him . . . There isn't a witch with him, is there, Lennep?'

'I beg your pardon?' the spy started. 'No, Your Lordship. There isn't. What are your orders? If you want him alive, I'll lure him out of Brokilon. But if you'd prefer him dead . . .'

'Lennep,' said Dijkstra, raising his cold, pale blue eyes towards the agent. 'Don't be overzealous. In our trade, officiousness never pays and should always be viewed with suspicion.'

'Sire,' said Lennep, blanching somewhat. 'I only—'

'I know. You only asked about my orders. Well, here they are: leave the Witcher alone.'

'Yes, sire. And what about Milva?'

'Leave her alone, too. For now.'

'Yes, sire. May I go?'

'You may.'

The agent left, cautiously and silently closing the oak door behind him. Dijkstra remained silent for a long time, staring at the towering pile of maps, letters, denunciations, interrogation reports and death sentences in front of him.

'Ori.'

The secretary raised his head and cleared his throat. He said nothing.

'The Witcher is in Brokilon.'

Ori Reuven cleared his throat again, involuntarily glancing under the table, towards his boss's leg. Dijkstra noticed the look.

'That's right. I won't let him get away with that,' he barked. 'I couldn't walk for two weeks because of him. I lost face with Philippa, forced to whimper like a dog and beg her for a bloody spell, otherwise I'd still be hobbling. I can't blame anyone but myself; I underestimated him. But the worst thing is that I can't get my own back and tan his witcher's hide! I don't have the time, and anyway, I can't use my own men to settle private scores! That's right isn't it, Ori?'

15

'Ahem . . .'

'Don't grunt at me. I know. But, hell, power tempts! How it beguiles, invites to be made use of! How easy it is to forget, when one has it! But if you forget once, there's no end to it . . . Is Philippa Eilhart still in Montecalvo?'

'Yes.'

'Take a quill and an inkwell. I'll dictate a letter to her. I shall begin . . . Damn it, I can't concentrate. What's that bloody racket, Ori? What's happening in the square?'

'Some students are throwing stones at the Nilfgaardian envoy's residence. We paid them to do so, hem, hem, if I'm not mistaken.'

'Oh. Very well. Close the window. And have the lads throw stones at the dwarf Giancardi's bank, tomorrow. He refused to reveal the details of some accounts.'

'Giancardi, hem, hem, donated a considerable sum of money to the military fund.'

'Ha. Then have them throw stones at the banks that didn't donate.'

'They all did.'

'Oh, you're boring me, Ori. Write, I said. Darling Phil, the sun of my . . . Blast, I keep forgetting. Take a new sheet of paper. Ready?'

'Of course, hem, hem.'

'Dear Philippa. Mistress Triss Merigold is sure to be worried about the witcher she teleported from Thanedd to Brokilon, which she kept so secret that even I didn't know anything. It hurt me terribly. Please reassure her: the Witcher is doing well now. He has even begun to send female emissaries from Brokilon to search for traces of Princess Cirilla, the young girl you're so interested in. Our good friend Geralt clearly doesn't know Cirilla is in Nilfgaard, where she's preparing for her wedding to Imperator Emhyr. It's important to me that the Witcher lies low in Brokilon, which is why I'll do my best to ensure the news reaches him. Have you got that?'

'Hem, hem . . . the news reaches him.'

'New paragraph! It puzzles me . . . Ori, wipe the bloody quill! We're writing to Philippa, not to the royal council. The letter must look neat! New paragraph. It puzzles me why the Witcher hasn't tried to make contact with Yennefer. I refuse to believe that his passion, which was verging on obsession, has petered out so suddenly, irrespective of learning his darling's political objectives. On the other hand, if Yennefer is the one who handed Cirilla over to Emhyr, and if there's proof of it, I would gladly make sure the Witcher was furnished with it. The problem would solve itself, I'm certain, and the faithless, black-haired beauty would be on very shaky ground. The Witcher doesn't like it when anyone touches his little girl, as Artaud Terranova discovered on Thanedd in no uncertain terms. I would like to think, Phil, that you don't have any evidence of Yennefer's betrayal and you don't know where she is hiding. It would hurt me greatly to discover this is the latest secret being concealed from me. I have no secrets from you . . . What are you sniggering about, Ori?'

'Oh, nothing, hem, hem.'

'Write! I have no secrets from you, Phil, and I count on reciprocity. With my deepest respect, et cetera, et cetera. Give it here, I'll sign it.'

Ori Reuven sprinkled the letter with sand. Dijkstra made himself more comfortable, interlacing his fingers over his stomach and twiddling his thumbs.

'That Milva, the Witcher's spy,' he asked. 'What can you tell me about her?'

'She is engaged at present, hem, hem' – his secretary coughed – 'in escorting the remnants of Scoia'tael units defeated by the Temerian Army to Brokilon. She rescues elves from hunts and traps, enabling them to rest and regroup into combat commandos . . .'

'Refrain from supplying me with common knowledge,' interrupted Dijkstra. 'I'm familiar with Milva's activities, and will eventually make use of them. Otherwise I would have sold her out to the Temerians long since. What can you tell me about Milva herself? As a person?'

'She comes, if I'm not mistaken, from some godforsaken village in Upper Sodden. Her true name is Maria Barring. Milva is a nickname the dryads gave her. In the Elder Speech it means—'

'Red Kite,' interrupted Dijkstra. 'I know.'

'Her family have been hunters for generations. They are forest dwellers, and feel most comfortable in the greenwood. When old

17

Barring's son was trampled to death by an elk, the old man taught his daughter the forest crafts. After he passed away, her mother married again. Hem, hem . . . Maria didn't get on with her stepfather and ran away from home. She was sixteen at the time, if I'm not mistaken. She headed north, living from hunting, but the lords' gamekeepers didn't make her life easy, hunting and harrying her as though she were fair game. So she began to poach in Brokilon and it was there, hem, hem, that the dryads got hold of her.'

'And instead of finishing her off, they took her in,' Dijkstra muttered. 'Adopted her, if you will . . . And she repaid their kindness. She struck a pact with the Hag of Brokilon, old silver-eyed Eithné. Maria Barring is dead; long live Milva . . . How many human expeditions had come unstuck by the time the forces in Verden and Kerack cottoned on? Three?'

'Hem, hem . . . Four, if I'm not mistaken . . .' Ori Reuven was always hoping he wasn't mistaken, although in fact his memory was infallible. 'All together, it was about five score humans, those who'd gone after dryad scalps most savagely. And it took them a long time to catch on, because Milva occasionally carried someone out of the slaughter on her own back, and whoever she'd rescued would praise her courage to the skies. It was only after the fourth time, in Verden, if I'm not mistaken, that someone caught on. "Why is it?" the shout suddenly went up, hem, hem, "that the guide who bands humans together to fight the dryads always gets out in one piece?" And the cat was out of the bag. The guide *was* leading them. But into a trap, right into the shooting range of the dryads waiting in ambush . . .'

Dijkstra slid an interrogation report to the edge of his desk, because the parchment still seemed to reek of the torture chamber.

'And then,' he concluded, 'Milva vanished into Brokilon like the morning mist. And it's still difficult to find volunteers for expeditions against the dryads in Verden. Old Eithné and young Red Kite were carrying out pretty effective purges. And they dare say that we, humans, invented all the dirty tricks. On the other hand . . .'

'Hem, hem?' coughed Ori Reuven, surprised by his boss's sudden – and then continuing – silence.

18

'On the other hand, they may have finally begun to learn from us,' said the spy coldly, looking down at the denunciations, interrogation reports and death sentences.

Milva grew anxious when she couldn't see blood anywhere near where the buck had disappeared. She suddenly recalled that he had jumped just as she had fired her arrow. Had jumped or was about to; it amounted to the same thing. He had moved and the arrow might have hit him in the belly. Milva cursed. A shot to the belly was a disgrace for any hunter! Urgh, the very thought of it!

She quickly ran over to the slope of the ravine, looking carefully among the brambles, moss and ferns. She was hunting for her arrow. It was equipped with four blades so sharp they could shave the hairs on your forearm. Fired from a distance of fifty paces the arrow must have passed right through the animal.

She searched, she found it and sighed in relief, then spat three times, happy with her luck. She needn't have worried; it was better than she had imagined. The arrow was not covered in sticky, foul-smelling stomach contents. Neither did it bear traces of bright, pink, frothy blood from the lungs. What covered the shaft was dark red and viscous. The arrow had gone through the heart. Milva didn't have to creep or stalk; she had been spared a long walk following the deer's tracks. The buck had to be lying in the undergrowth, no more than a hundred paces from the clearing, in a spot that would be surely indicated by the blood. And after being shot through the heart, he would have started bleeding after a few paces, so she knew she would easily find the trail.

She picked it up after ten paces and followed it, once again losing herself in her reverie.

She kept the promise she had given the Witcher. She returned to Brokilon five days after the Harvest Festival – five days after the new moon – which marked the beginning of the month of August for people, and for elves, Lammas, the seventh and penultimate savaed of the year.

She crossed the Ribbon at daybreak with five elves. The

19

commando she was leading had initially numbered nine riders, but the soldiers from Brugge were following them the whole time. Three furlongs before the river they were hot on their trail, pressing hard, and only abandoned their efforts when they reached the Ribbon, with Brokilon looming up in the dawn mists on the far bank. The soldiers were afraid of Brokilon and that alone saved the commando. They made it across. Exhausted and wounded. But not all of them.

She had news for the Witcher, but thought that Gwynbleidd was still in Col Serrai. She had intended to see him around noon, after a good long sleep so she was astonished when he suddenly emerged from the fog like a ghost. He sat down beside her without a word, watching as she made herself a makeshift bed by spreading a blanket over a heap of branches.

'You're in a hurry, Witcher,' she scoffed. 'I'm ready to drop. I've been in the saddle all day and all night, my backside's numb, and my trousers are soaked up to my belt, for we crept our way through the wetlands at dawn like a pack of wolves . . .'

'Please. Did you learn anything?'

'Yes I did,' she snorted, unlacing and pulling off her drenched, clinging boots. 'Without much difficulty, because everybody's talking about it. You never told me your young girl was such a per-sonage! I'd thought she was your stepdaughter, some sort of waif and stray, a star-crossed orphan. And who does she turn out to be? A Cintran princess! Well! And perhaps you're a prince in disguise?'

'Tell me, please.'

'The kings won't get their hands on her now, for your Cirilla, it turns out, fled straight from Thanedd to Nilfgaard; probably with those treacherous mages. And Imperator Emhyr received her there with all ceremony. And do you know what? He's said to be thinking of marrying her. Now let me rest. We can talk after I've slept, if you want.'

The Witcher said nothing. Milva hung her wet footwraps on a forked branch, positioned so that the rising sun's rays would fall on them, and tugged at her belt buckle.

'I want to get undressed,' she growled. 'Why are you still hanging about? You can't have expected happier news, can you? You're in no danger; no one's asking after you, the spies have stopped being interested in you. And your wench has escaped from the clutches of the kings and will be declared Imperatoress . . .'

'Is that information reliable?'

'Nothing is certain these days,' she yawned, sitting down on her bed, 'apart from the fact that the sun journeys across the heavens from the east to the west. But what people are saying about the Nilfgaardian Imperator and the Princess of Cintra seems to be true. It's all anyone's talking about.'

'Why this sudden interest?'

'You really don't know? She's said to be bringing Emhyr a goodly acreage of land in her dowry! And not just Cintra, but land on this side of the Yaruga too! Ha, and she'll be my Lady as well, for I'm from Upper Sodden, and the whole of Sodden, it turns out, is her fiefdom! So if I bring down a buck in her forests and they lay hands on me, I can be hung on her orders . . . Oh, what a rotten world! And a pox on it, I can't keep my eyes open . . .'

'Just one more question. Did they capture any sorceresses— I mean did they capture anyone from that pack of treacherous sorcerers?'

'No. But one enchantress, they say, took her own life. Soon after Vengerberg fell and the Kaedwen Army entered Aedirn. No doubt out of distress, or fear of torture—'

'There were riderless horses in the commando you brought here. Would the elves give me one?'

'Oh, in a hurry, I see,' she muttered, wrapping herself in the blanket. 'I think I know where you're planning to . . .'

She fell silent, astonished by the expression on his face before she realised that the news she had brought was not at all happy. She saw that she understood nothing, nothing at all. Suddenly, unexpectedly, unawares, she felt the urge to sit down by his side, bombard him with questions, listen to him, learn more, perhaps offer counsel . . . She urgently ground her knuckles into the corners of her eyes. *I'm exhausted*, she thought, *death was breathing down my neck all night. I have to rest. And anyway, why should I be bothered by his sorrows and cares? What does he matter to me? And that wench? To hell with him and with her! A pox on it, all this has driven the sleep from me . . .*

The Witcher stood up.

'Will the elves give me a horse?' he repeated.

'Take whichever you please,' she said a moment later. 'But don't let them see you. They gave us a good hiding by the ford, blood was spilt . . . And don't touch the black; he's mine . . . What are you waiting for?'

'Thank you for your help. For everything.'

She didn't answer.

'I'm indebted to you. How shall I pay you back?'

'How? By getting out of my sight!' she cried, raising herself on an elbow and tugging sharply at the blanket. 'I . . . I have to sleep! Take a horse . . . and go . . . To Nilfgaard, to hell, to all the devils. Makes no difference to me! Go away and leave me in peace!'

'I'll pay back what I owe,' he said quietly. 'I won't forget. It may happen that one day you'll be in need of help. Or support. A shoulder to lean on. Then call out, call out in the night. And I'll come.'

The buck lay on the edge of the slope, which was spongy from gushing springs and densely overgrown with ferns, his neck contorted, with a glassy eye staring up at the sky. Milva saw several large ticks bored into his light brown belly.

'You'll have to find yourselves some other blood, vermin,' she muttered, rolling up her sleeves and drawing a knife. 'Because this is going cold.'

With a swift and practised movement, she slit the skin from sternum to anus, adroitly running the blade around the genitalia. She cautiously separated the layer of fat, up to her elbows in blood. She severed the gullet and pulled the entrails out. She cut open the stomach and gall bladder, hunting for bezoars. She didn't believe in their magical qualities, but there was no shortage of fools who did and would pay well for them.

She lifted the buck and laid him on a nearby log, his slit belly pointing downwards, letting the blood drain out. She wiped her hands on a bunch of ferns.

She sat down by her quarry.

'Possessed, insane Witcher,' she said softly, staring at the crowns of the Brokilon pines looming a hundred feet above her. 'You're heading for Nilfgaard to get your wench. You're heading to the end of the world, which is all in flames, and you haven't even thought about supplying yourself with victuals. I know you have someone to live for. But do you have anything to live on?'

Naturally enough, the pines didn't comment or interrupt her monologue.

'I don't think,' Milva said, using her knife to scrape the blood out from beneath her fingernails, 'you have the slightest chance of getting your young girl back. You won't make it to the Yaruga, never mind Nilfgaard. I don't think you'll even make it to Sodden. I think you're fated to die. It's written on your fierce face, it's staring through your hideous eyes. Death will catch up with you, O mad Witcher, it'll catch up with you soon. But thanks to this little buck at least it won't be death by starvation. It may not be much, but it's something. That's what I think.'

Dijkstra sighed to himself at the sight of the Nilfgaardian ambassador entering the audience chamber. Shilard Fitz-Oesterlen, Imperator Emhyr var Emreis's envoy, was accustomed to conducting conversations in diplomatic language, and adored larding his sentences with pompous linguistic oddities, comprehensible only to diplomats and scholars. Dijkstra had studied at the Academy of Oxenfurt, and although he had not been awarded the title of Master of Letters, he knew the basics of bombastic scholarly jargon. However, he was reluctant to use it, since he hated with a vengeance pomposity and all forms of pretentious ceremony.

'Greetings, Your Excellency.'

'Your Lordship,' Shilard Fitz-Oesterlen said, bowing ceremoniously. 'Ah, please forgive me. Perhaps I ought to say: Your Grace the Duke? Your Highness the Regent? Secretary of State? 'Pon my word, offices are falling on you like hailstones, such that I really don't know how to address you so as not to breach protocol.'

'"Your Majesty" would be best,' Dijkstra replied modestly. 'You are aware after all, Your Excellency, that the king is judged by his court. And you are probably aware that when I shout: "Jump!" the court in Tretogor asks: "How high?"'

The ambassador knew that Dijkstra was exaggerating, but not inordinately. Prince Radovid was still a minor, Queen Hedwig distraught by her husband's tragic death, and the aristocracy intimidated, stupefied, at variance and divided into factions. Dijkstra was the *de facto* governor of Redania and could have taken any rank he pleased with no difficulty. But Dijkstra had no desire to do so.

'Your Lordship deigned to summon me,' the ambassador said a moment later. 'Passing over the Foreign Minister. To what do I owe this honour?'

'The minister,' Dijkstra said, looking up at the ceiling, 'resigned from the post owing to his poor state of health.'

The ambassador nodded gravely. He knew perfectly well that the Foreign Minister was languishing in a dungeon and, being a coward and a fool, had doubtless told Dijkstra everything about his collusion with the Nilfgaardian secret service during the demonstration of torture instruments preceding his interrogation. He knew that the network established by Vattier de Rideaux, head of the imperial secret service, had been crushed, and all its threads were in Dijkstra's hands. He also knew that those threads led directly to his person. But his person was protected by immunity and protocol forced them to play this game to the bitter end. Particularly following the curious, encoded instructions recently sent to the embassy by Vattier and Coroner Stephan Skellen, the imperial agent for special affairs.

'Since his successor has not yet been named,' Dijkstra continued, 'it is my unpleasant duty to inform you that Your Excellency is now deemed *persona non grata* in the Kingdom of Redania.'

The ambassador bowed.

'I regret,' he said, 'that the distrust that resulted in the mutual recall of ambassadors are the consequence of matters which, after all, directly concern neither the Kingdom of Redania nor the Nilfgaardian Empire. The Empire has not undertaken any hostile measures against Redania.'

'Apart from a blockade against our ships and goods at the mouth of the Yaruga and the Skellige Islands. And apart from arming and supporting gangs of Scoia'tael.'

'Those are insinuations.'

'And the concentration of imperial forces in Verden and Cintra? The raids on Sodden and Brugge by armed gangs? Sodden and Brugge are under Temerian protection; we in turn are in alliance with Temeria, Your Excellency, which makes an attack on Temeria an attack on us. In addition, there are matters which directly concern Redania: the rebellion on the Isle of Thanedd and the criminal assassination of King Vizimir. And the question of the role the Empire played in those incidents.'

'*Quod attinet* the incident on Thanedd,' the ambassador said, spreading his arms, 'I have not been empowered to express an opinion. His Imperial Highness Emhyr var Emreis is unaware of the substance of the private feuds of your mages. I regret the fact that our protests are achieving minimal success in the face of the propaganda which seeks to suggest something else. Propaganda disseminated, I dare say, not without the support of the highest authorities of the Kingdom of Redania.'

'Your protests greatly astonish and surprise me,' Dijkstra said, smiling faintly. 'Since the Imperator in no way conceals the presence of the Cintran princess at his court, after she was abducted from the very same Thanedd.'

'Cirilla, *Queen* of Cintra,' Shilard Fitz-Oesterlen corrected him with emphasis, 'was not abducted, but sought asylum in the Empire. That has nothing to do with the incident on Thanedd.'

'Indeed?'

'The incident on Thanedd,' the ambassador continued, his countenance stony, 'aroused the Imperator's horror. And the murderous attack on the life of King Vizimir, carried out by a madman, evoked his sincere and intense abomination. However, the vile rumour being disseminated among the common people is an even greater abomination, which dares to search for the instigators of these crimes in the Empire.'

'The capture of the actual instigators,' Dijkstra said slowly, 'will put an end to the rumours, one would hope. And their capture and the meting out of justice to them is purely a matter of time.'

'*Justitia fundamentum regnorum*,' admitted Shilard Fitz-Oesterlen gravely. 'And *crimen horribilis non potest non esse punibile*. I affirm that His Imperial Majesty also wishes this to happen.'

'The Imperator has it in his power to fulfil that wish,' Dijkstra threw in casually, folding his arms. 'One of the leaders of the conspiracy, Enid an Gleanna, until recently the sorceress Francesca Findabair, is playing at being queen of the elven puppet state in Dol Blathanna, by the imperial grace.'

'His Imperial Majesty,' said the ambassador, bowing stiffly, 'cannot interfere in the doings of Dol Blathanna, recognised by all its neighbouring powers as an independent kingdom.'

'But not by Redania. For Redania, Dol Blathanna remains part of the Kingdom of Aedirn. Although together with the elves and Kaedwen you have dismantled Aedirn – although not a stone remains of Lyria – you are striking those kingdoms too swiftly from the map of the world. It's too soon, Your Excellency. However, this is neither the time nor the place to discuss it. Let Francesca Findabair play at reigning for now; she'll get her comeuppance. And what of the other rebels and King Vizimir's assassins? What about Vilgefortz of Roggeveen, what about Yennefer of Vengerberg? There are grounds to believe they both fled to Nilfgaard following the collapse of the rebellion.'

'I assure you that is not so,' said the ambassador, raising his head. 'But were it true, they would not escape punishment.'

'They did not wrong you, thus their punishment does not rest with you. Imperator Emhyr would prove his sincere desire for justice, which after all is *fundamentum regnorum*, by handing the criminals over to us.'

'One may not deny the validity of your request,' admitted Shilard Fitz-Oesterlen, feigning an embarrassed smile. 'However, *primo*, those individuals are not in the Empire. And *secundo*, had they even reached it, there exists an impediment. Extradition is carried out on the basis of a judgment of the law, each case decided upon by the Imperial Council. Bear in mind, Your Lordship, that the breaking of diplomatic ties by Redania is a hostile act; it would be difficult to expect the Council to vote in favour of the extradition of persons seeking asylum, were a hostile country to demand that extradition. It would be an unprecedented matter . . . Unless . . .'

'Unless what?'

'A precedent were established.'

'I do not understand.'

'Were the Kingdom of Redania prepared to hand one of his subjects to the Imperator, a common criminal who had been captured here, the Imperator and his Council would have grounds to reciprocate this gesture of good will.'

Dijkstra said nothing for a long time, giving the impression he was either dozing or thinking.

'Whom do you have in mind?'

'The name of the criminal . . .' said the ambassador, pretending to recall it. He finally searched for a document in his saffian portfolio. 'Forgive me, *memoria fragilis est*. Here it is. A certain Cahir Mawr Dyffryn aep Ceallach. Serious gravamina weigh on him. He is being sought for murder, desertion, *raptus puellae*, rape, theft and forging documents. Fleeing from the Imperator's wrath, he escaped abroad.'

'To Redania? He chose a long route.'

'Your Lordship,' said Shilard Fitz-Oesterlen, smiling faintly, 'does not limit his interests only to Redania, after all. There is not a shadow of doubt in my mind that were the criminal to be seized in any of the allied kingdoms, Your Lordship would hear of it from the reports of numerous . . . friends.'

'What did you say the name of the felon was?'

'Cahir Mawr Dyffryn aep Ceallach.'

Dijkstra fell silent again, pretending to be searching in his memory.

'No,' he said finally. 'No one of that name has been apprehended.'

'Indeed?'

'Regrettably, my *memoria* is not *fragilis* in such cases, Your Excellency.'

'I regret it too,' Shilard Fitz-Oesterlen responded icily. 'Particularly since the mutual extradition of criminals seems to be impossible to carry out in such circumstances. I shall not weary Your Lordship any longer. I wish you good health and good fortune.'

'Likewise. Farewell, Your Excellency.'

The ambassador left, after several elaborate, ceremonial bows.

'You can kiss *sempiternum meam*, you sly old devil,' Dijkstra muttered, folding his arms. 'Ori!'

His secretary, red in the face from suppressing his cough, emerged from behind a curtain.

'Is Philippa still in Montecalvo?'

'Yes, hem, hem. Mistresses Laux-Antille, Merigold and Metz are with her.'

'War may break out in a day or two, the border on the Yaruga will soon go up in flames, and they've hidden themselves in some godforsaken castle! Take a quill and write. Darling Phil . . . Oh, bugger!'

'I've written: "Dear Philippa".'

'Good. Continue. It may interest you that the freak in the plumed helmet, who disappeared from Thanedd as mysteriously as he appeared, is called Cahir Mawr Dyffryn and is the son of Seneschal Ceallach. This strange individual is being sought not only by us, but also, it would appear, by the secret service of Vattier de Rideaux and the men of that son-of-a-bitch . . .'

'Mistress Philippa, hem, hem, does not like expressions of that kind. I have written: "that scoundrel".'

'Let it be: that scoundrel Stephan Skellen. You know as well as I do, dear Phil, that the imperial secret service is urgently hunting only those agents and emissaries who got under Emhyr's skin. Those who, instead of carrying out their orders or dying, betrayed him and their orders alike. The case thus appears quite curious, since we were certain that this Cahir's orders concerned the capture of Princess Cirilla and her delivery to Nilfgaard.

'New paragraph: I would like to discuss in person the strange, but well-founded suspicions this matter has evoked in me, and the somewhat astonishing, but reasonable theories I have arrived at. With my deepest respect et cetera, et cetera.'

*

Milva rode south, as the crow flies, first along the banks of the Ribbon, through Burn Stump, and then, having crossed the river, through marshy gorges covered in a soft, bright green carpet of hair-cap moss. She guessed that the Witcher, not knowing the terrain as well as she did, would not risk crossing onto the human-controlled bank. Taking a short cut across a huge bend in the river, which curved towards Brokilon, there was a chance she might catch up with him in the region of the Ceann Treise Falls. Were she to ride hard and not take a break, she even stood a chance of overtaking him.

The chirruping chaffinches hadn't been mistaken. The sky had clouded over considerably to the south. The air had become dense and heavy, and the mosquitoes and horseflies extremely annoying.

When she rode into the wetlands, thick with hazel hung with still-green nuts and leafless, blackish buckthorn, she felt a presence. She didn't hear it. She felt it. And so she knew it must be elves.

She reined in her horse, so the bowmen concealed in the under-growth could have a good look at her. She also held her breath. In the hope that she hadn't happened upon quick-tempered ones.

A fly buzzed over the buck, which was slung over the horse's rump.

A rustling. A soft whistling. She whistled back. The Scoia'tael emerged from the brush soundlessly and only then did Milva breathe freely again. She knew them. They belonged to Coinneach Dá Reo's commando.

'Hael,' she said, dismounting. 'Que'ss va?'

'Ne'ss,' an elf whose name she couldn't recall replied coldly. 'Caemm.'

Other elves were encamped in the nearby clearing. There were at least thirty of them, more than there should be in Coinneach's commando. This surprised Milva; in recent times, Squirrel units were more likely to shrink than grow in size. In recent times, commandos had become groups of bloodied, nervy ragamuffins who could barely stand or stay upright in the saddle. This commando was different.

'Cead, Coinneach,' she greeted the approaching commander.

'Ceadmil, sor'ca.'

Sor'ca. Little sister. It's how she was addressed by those she was friendly with, when they wanted to express their respect and affection. And that they were indeed many, many more winters older than she. At first, she had only been Dh'oine – human – to the elves. Later, when she had begun helping them regularly, they called her Aen Woedbeanna, 'woman of the forest'. Still later, when they knew her better, they called her – following the dryads' example – Milva, or Red Kite. Her real name, which she only revealed to those she was closest to, responding to similar gestures received from them, didn't suit the elves – they pronounced it Mear'ya, with a hint of a grimace, as though in their speech it carried negative connotations. Then they would immediately switch to 'sor'ca'.

'Where are you headed?' asked Milva, looking around more intently, but still not seeing any wounded or ill elves. 'To Eight-Mile? To Brokilon?'

'No.'

She refrained from further questions; she knew them too well. It was enough to glance several times at their motionless, hardened faces, at the exaggerated, pointed calm with which they were preparing their tackle and weapons. One close look into their deep, fathomless eyes was enough. She knew they were going into battle.

To the south the sky was darkening, becoming overcast.

'And where are you headed, sor'ca?' asked Coinneach, then quickly glanced at the buck slung over her horse and smiled faintly.

'South,' she said coldly, putting him right. 'Towards Drieschot.'

The elf stopped smiling.

'Along the human bank?'

'At least as far as Ceann Treise,' she said, shrugging. 'When I reach the falls I'll definitely go back over to the Brokilon side, because . . .'

She turned around, hearing the snorting of horses. Fresh Scoia'tael were joining the already unusually large commando. Milva knew these new ones even better.

'Ciaran!' she shouted softly, without attempting to hide her astonishment. 'Toruviel! What are you doing here? I've only just led you to Brokilon, and you're already—'

30

'Ess'creasa, sor'ca,' Ciaran aep Dearbh said gravely. The bandage swathed around his head was stained with oozing blood.

'We have no choice,' Toruviel repeated. She dismounted cautiously using one arm, in order to protect the other one, which was still bent in a sling. 'News has come. We may not remain in Brokilon, when every bow counts.'

'If I had known,' Milva said, pouting, 'I wouldn't have bothered. I wouldn't have risked my neck at the ford.'

'News came last night,' explained Toruviel quietly. 'We could not . . . We cannot leave our comrades in arms at a time like this. We cannot. Understand that, sor'ca.'

The sky had darkened even more. This time Milva clearly heard thunder in the distance.

'Don't ride south, sor'ca,' Coinneach Dá Reo pleaded. 'There's a storm coming.'

'What can a storm do to. . . ?' She broke off and looked at him intently. 'Ah! So that kind of tidings have reached you, have they? It's Nilfgaard, is it? They are crossing the Yaruga in Sodden? They are striking Brugge? And that's why you're marching?'

He did not answer.

'Yes, just like it was in Dol Angra,' she said, looking into his dark eyes. 'Once again the Nilfgaardian Imperator has you sowing mayhem with fire and sword on the humans' rear lines. And then he will make peace with the kings and they will slaughter you all. You will burn in the very fire you are starting.'

'Fire purges. And hardens. It must be passed through. Aenyell'hael, ell'ea, sor'ca? In your tongue: a baptism of fire.'

'I prefer another kind of fire,' Milva said, untying the buck and throwing it down onto the ground at the feet of the elves. 'The kind that crackles under the spit. Have it, so you won't fall from hunger on the march. It's of no use to me now.'

'Aren't you riding south?'

'I am.'

I'm going south, she thought, *and quickly. I have to warn that fool of a witcher, I have to warn him about what kind of a turmoil he's getting himself into. I have to make him turn back.*

31

'Don't go, sor'ca.'

'Give me a break, Coinneach.'

'A storm is coming from the south,' the elf repeated. 'A great tempest is coming. And a great fire. Hide in Brokilon, little sister, don't ride south. You've done enough for us, you cannot do any more now. And you do not have to. We have to. Ess'tedd, esse creasa! It is time we left. Farewell.'

The air around them was heavy and dense.

The teleprojective spell was complicated; they had to cast it together, joining their hands and thoughts. Even then, it turned out to be a devilishly great effort. Because the distance was considerable too.

Philippa Eilhart's tightly closed eyelids twitched, Triss Merigold panted and there were beads of sweat on Keira Metz's high forehead. Only on Margarita Laux-Antille's face was there no sign of fatigue.

It suddenly became very bright in the poorly lit chamber and a mosaic of flashes danced across the dark wood panelling. A sphere glowing with a milky light was suspended over the round table. Philippa Eilhart chanted the end of the spell and the sphere descended away from her onto one of the twelve chairs positioned around the table. A vague shape appeared inside the sphere. The image shimmered, as the projection was not very stable. But it quickly became more defined.

'Bloody hell,' Keira muttered, wiping her forehead. 'Haven't they heard of glamarye or beautifying spells down in Nilfgaard?'

'Apparently not,' said Triss out of the corner of her mouth. 'They don't seem to have heard of fashion either.'

'Or of make-up,' Philippa said softly. 'But now hush. And don't stare at her. We must stabilise the projection and welcome our guest. Intensify me, Rita.'

Margarita Laux-Antille repeated the spell's formula and Philippa's movements. The image shimmered several times, lost its foggy vagueness and unnatural gleam, and its contours and colours sharpened. The sorceresses could now look at the shape on the other side of the table even more closely. Triss bit her lip and winked at Keira conspiratorially.

The woman in the projection had a pale face with poor complexion, dull, expressionless eyes, thin bluish lips and a somewhat hooked nose. She was wearing a strange, conical and slightly crumpled hat. Dark, not very fresh-looking hair fell from beneath the soft brim. The impressions of unattractiveness and seediness were complemented by her shapeless, black, baggy robes, embroidered on the shoulders with frayed silver thread. The embroidery depicted a half-moon within a circle of stars. It was the only decoration worn by the Nilfgaardian sorceress.

Philippa Eilhart stood up, trying not display her jewellery, lace or cleavage too ostentatiously.

'Mistress Assire,' she said. 'Welcome to Montecalvo. We are immensely pleased that you have agreed to accept our invitation.'

'I did it out of curiosity,' the sorceress from Nilfgaard said, in an unexpectedly pleasant and melodious voice, straightening her hat involuntarily. Her hand was slim, marked by yellow spots, her fingernails broken and uneven, and clearly bitten.

'Only out of curiosity,' she repeated. 'The consequences of which may yet prove catastrophic for me. I would ask for an explanation.'

'I shall provide one forthwith,' Philippa nodded, giving a sign to the other sorceresses. 'But first, however, allow me to call forth projections of the other participants of this gathering and make some introductions. Please be patient for a moment.'

The sorceresses linked hands again and together began the incantations once more. The air in the chamber hummed like a taut wire as a glowing fog flowed down from behind the panels on the ceiling, filling the room with a shimmer of shadows. Spheres of pulsing light hung above three of the unoccupied chairs and the outlines of shapes became visible. The first one to appear was Sabrina Glevissig, in a turquoise dress with a provocatively plunging neckline and a large, lace, standing-up collar, beautifully framing her coiffured hair, which was held in a diamond tiara. Next to her Sheala de Tancarville emerged from the hazy light of the projection, dressed in black velvet sewn with pearls and with her neck draped with silver fox furs. The enchantress from Nilfgaard nervously licked her thin lips.

Just you wait for Francesca, thought Triss. *When you see Francesca, you black rat, your eyes will pop out of your head.*

Francesca Findabair did not disappoint. Not by her lavish dress, the colour of bull's blood, nor with her majestic hairstyle, nor her ruby necklace, nor her doe eyes ringed with provocative elven make-up.

'Welcome, ladies,' Philippa said, 'to Montecalvo Castle, whither I have invited you to discuss certain issues of considerable importance. I bemoan the fact that we are meeting in the form of teleprojection. But neither the time, nor the distances dividing us, nor the situation we all find ourselves in permitted a face-to-face meeting. I am Philippa Eilhart, the lady of this castle. As the initiator of this meeting and the hostess, I shall perform the introductions. On my right is Margarita Laux-Antille, the rectoress of the academy in Aretuza. On my left is Triss Merigold of Maribor and Keira Metz of Carreras. Continuing, Sabrina Glevissig of Ard Carraigh. Sheala de Tancarville of Creyden in Kovir. Francesca Findabair, also known as Enid an Gleanna, the present queen of the Valley of Flowers. And finally Assire var Anahid of Vicovaro the Nilfgaardian Empire. And now—'

'And now I bid farewell!' Sabrina Glevissig screamed, pointing a heavily beringed hand at Francesca. 'You have gone too far, Philippa! I have no intention of sitting at the same table as that bloody elf – even as an illusion! The blood on the walls and floors of Garstang has not even faded! And she spilt that blood! She and Vilgefortz!'

'I would request you observe etiquette,' Philippa said, gripping the edge of the table with both hands. 'And keep calm. Listen to what I have to say, I ask for nothing more. When I finish, each of you shall decide whether to stay or leave. The projection is voluntary, it may be interrupted at any moment. All I ask is that those who decide to leave keep this meeting secret.'

'I knew it!' Sabrina jumped up so suddenly that for a moment she moved out of the projection. 'A secret meeting! Clandestine arrangements! To put it bluntly: a conspiracy! And it's quite clear against whom it is directed. Are you mocking us, Philippa? You demand that we keep a secret from our kings and comrades, whom you did not condescend to invite. And there sits Enid Findabair – reigning in Dol Blathanna by the grace of Emhyr var Emreis – the queen of the elves, who are actively providing Nilfgaard with armed support. If that were not enough, I notice with astonishment that we are joined by a Nilfgaardian sorceress. Since when did the mages of Nilfgaard stop professing blind obedience and slavish servility to imperial rule? Secrets? What secrets, I am asking! If she is here, it is with the permission of Emhyr! By his order! As his eyes and ears!'

'I repudiate that,' Assire var Anahid said calmly. 'No one knows that I am taking part in this meeting. I was asked to keep it secret, which I have done and will continue to do. For my own sake, as much as yours. For were it to come to light, I would not survive. That's the servility of the Empire's mages for you. We have the choice of servility or the scaffold. I took a risk. I did not come here as a spy. I can only prove it in one way: through my own death. It would be sufficient for the secrecy that our hostess is appealing for to be broken. It would be sufficient for news of our meeting to go beyond these walls, for me to lose my life.'

'Betrayal of the secret could have unpleasant consequences for me, too,' Francesca said, smiling charmingly. 'You have a wonderful opportunity for revenge, Sabrina.'

'My revenge will come about in other ways, elf,' said Sabrina, and her black eyes flashed ominously. 'Should the secret come to light, it won't be through my fault or through my carelessness. By no means mine!'

'Are you suggesting something?'

'Of course,' interrupted Philippa Eilhart. 'Of course Sabrina is. She is subtly reminding you about my collaboration with Sigismund Dijkstra. As though she didn't have any contact with King Henselt's spies!'

'There is a difference,' Sabrina barked. 'I wasn't Henselt's lover for three years! Nor that of his spies, for that matter!'

'Enough of this! Be quiet!'

'I concur,' Sheala de Tancarville suddenly said in a loud voice. 'Be quiet, Sabrina. That's enough about Thanedd, enough about spying and extramarital affairs. I did not come here to take part in arguments

35

or to listen to old grudges and insults being bandied about. Nor am I interested in being your mediator. And if I was invited with that intention, I declare that those efforts were in vain. Indeed, I have my suspicions that I am participating in vain and without purpose, that I am wasting time, which I only wrested with difficulty from my scholarly work. I shall, however, refrain from presuppositions. I propose that we give the floor to Philippa Eilhart. Let us discover the aim of this gathering. Let us learn the roles we are expected to play here. Then we shall decide – without unnecessary emotion – whether to continue with the performance or let the curtain fall. The discretion we have been asked for binds us all. Along with the measures that I, Sheala de Tancarville, will personally take against the indiscreet.'

None of the sorceresses moved or spoke. Triss did not doubt Sheala's warning for a second. The recluse from Kovir was not one to make hollow threats.

'We give you the floor, Philippa. And I ask the honourable assembly to remain quiet until she indicates that she has finished.'

Philippa Eilhart stood up, her dress rustling.

'Distinguished sisters,' she said. 'Our situation is grave. Magic is under threat. The tragic events on Thanedd, to which my thoughts return with regret and reluctance, proved that the effects of hundreds of years of apparently peaceful cooperation could be laid waste in an instant, as self-interest and inflated ambitions came to the fore. We now have discord, disorder, mutual hostility and mistrust. Events are beginning to get out of control. In order to regain control, in order to prevent a cataclysm happening, the helm of this storm-tossed ship must be grasped by strong hands. Mistress Laux-Antille, Mistress Merigold, Mistress Metz and I have discussed the matter and we are in agreement. It is not enough to re-establish the Chapter and the Council, which were destroyed on Thanedd. In any case, there is no one left to rebuild the two institutions, no guarantee that should they be rebuilt they would not be infected with the disease that destroyed the previous ones. An utterly new, secret organisation should be founded which will exclusively serve matters of magic. Which will do everything to prevent a cataclysm. For if magic were to perish, our world would perish with it. Just as happened many centuries ago, the world without magic and the progress it brings with it will be plunged into chaos and darkness; will drown in blood and barbarity. We invite the ladies present here to take part in our initiative: to actively participate in the work proposed by this secret assembly. We took the decision to summon you here in order to hear your opinions on this matter. With this, I have finished.'

'Thank you,' Sheala de Tancarville said, nodding. 'If you will allow, ladies, I shall begin. My first question, dear Philippa, is: why me? Why have I been summoned here? Many times have I refused to have my candidature to the Chapter put forward, and I resigned my seat on the Council. Firstly, my work absorbs me. Secondly, I am ever of the opinion that there are others in Kovir, Poviss and Hengfors more worthy of these honours. So I ask why *I* have been invited here, and not Carduin. Not Istredd of Aedd Gynvael, not Tugdual or Zangenis?'

'Because they are men,' replied Philippa. 'This organisation will consist exclusively of women. Mistress Assire?'

'I withdraw my question,' the Nilfgaardian enchantress smiled. 'It was coincident with the substance of Mistress De Tancarville's. The answer satisfies me.'

'It smacks to me of female chauvinism,' Sabrina Glevissig said with a sneer. 'Particularly coming from your lips, Philippa, after your change in . . . sexual orientation. I have nothing against men. I'd go further; I adore men and I cannot imagine life without them. But . . . after a moment's reflection . . . Yours is actually a reasonable proposal. Men are psychologically unstable, too prone to emotions; not to be relied upon in moments of crisis.'

'That's right,' Margarita Laux-Antille admitted calmly. 'I often compare the results of the novices from Aretuza with those of the boys from the school in Ban Ard, and the comparisons are invariably to the girls' credit. Magic requires patience, delicacy, intelligence, prudence, and perseverance, not to mention the humble, but calm, endurance of defeat and failure. Ambition is the undoing of men. They always want what they know to be impossible and unattainable. And they are unaware of the attainable.'

'Enough, enough, enough,' Sheala interrupted her, making no effort to hide a smile. 'There is nothing worse than chauvinism underpinned by scholarship. You ought to be ashamed, Rita. Nonetheless . . . Yes, I also consider the proposed single-sex structure of this . . . convent or perhaps, if you will, this lodge, justified. As we have heard, it concerns the future of magic, and magic is too important a matter to entrust its fate to men.'

'If I may,' came the melodious voice of Francesca Findabair, 'I should like to cut these digressions about the natural and undeniable domination of our sex short for a moment, and focus on matters concerning the proposed initiative, the goal of which is still not entirely clear to me. For the moment chosen is not accidental and gives food for thought. A war is being waged. Nilfgaard has crushed the northern kingdoms and nailed them down. Is there not then, concealed beneath the vague slogans I have heard here, the understandable desire to reverse that state of affairs? To crush and nail down Nilfgaard? And then to tan the hides of the insolent elves? If that is so, my dear Philippa, we shall not find common grounds for agreement.'

'Is that the reason I have been invited here?' Assire var Anahid asked. 'I do not pay much attention to politics, but I know that the imperial army is seizing the advantage over your armies in this war. Apart from Mistresses Francesca and de Tancarville, who represents a neutral kingdom, all of you ladies represent kingdoms which are hostile to the Nilfgaardian Empire. How am I to understand these words of magical solidarity? As an incitement to treachery? I'm sorry, but I cannot see myself in such a role.'

On finishing her speech, Assire leant forward, as though touching something which was outside the frame of the projection. It seemed to Triss she could hear miaowing.

'She's even got a cat,' Keira Metz whispered. 'And I bet it's black . . .'

'Quiet,' hissed Philippa. 'My dear Francesca, most esteemed Mistress Assire. Our initiative is intended to be utterly apolitical; that is its fundamental premise. We shall not be guided by interests of race, kingdoms, kings or imperators, but by the interests of magic and its future.'

'While putting magic first,' Sabrina Glevissig said and smiled sneeringly, 'I hope we will not forget, though, about the interests of sorceresses. We know, after all, how sorcerers are treated in Nilfgaard. We can sit here chatting away apolitically, but when Nilfgaard triumphs and we end up under imperial rule, we shall all look like . . .'

Triss shifted anxiously, Philippa sighed almost inaudibly. Keira lowered her head, Sheala pretended to be straightening her boa. Francesca bit her lip. Assire var Anahid's face did not twitch, but a faint blush appeared on it.

'It will be bad for all of us, is what I meant to say,' Sabrina finished quickly. 'Philippa, Triss and I, all three of us were on Sodden Hill. Emhyr will seek revenge for that defeat, for Thanedd, for all our activities. But that is only one of the reservations that the declared political neutrality of this convent arouses in me. Does participation in it mean immediate resignation from the active – and indeed polit-ical – service we presently offer to our kings? Or are we to remain in that service and serve two masters: magic and kingly rule?'

'When someone tells me he is politically neutral,' Francesca smiled, 'I always ask which politics he specifically has in mind.'

'And I know he definitely isn't thinking about the one he engages in,' Assire var Anahid added, looking at Philippa.

'I am politically neutral,' Margarita Laux-Antille chimed in, lift-ing her head, 'and my school is politically neutral. I have in mind every type, kind and class of politics which exists!'

'Dear ladies,' Sheala said, having remained silent for some time. 'Remember you are the dominant sex. So don't behave like little girls, fighting over a tray of sweetmeats. The principium proposed by Philippa is clear, at least to me, and I still have too little cause to consider you any less intelligent. Outside this chamber be who you want, serve who you wish, as faithfully as you want. But when the convent meets, we shall focus exclusively on magic and its future.'

'That is precisely how I imagine it,' Philippa Eilhart agreed. 'I know there are many problems, and that there are doubts and uncer-tainties. We shall discuss them during the next meeting, in which we shall all participate; not in the form of projections or illusions,

39

but in person. Your presence will be treated not as a formal act of accession to the convent, but as a gesture of good will. We shall decide together whether a convent of this kind will be founded at all, then. Together. All of us. With equal rights.'

'All of us?' Sheala repeated. 'I see empty seats and I presume they were not put here inadvertently.'

'The convent ought to number twelve sorceresses. I would like the candidate for one of those empty seats to be proposed and presented to us at our next meeting by Mistress Assire. There must be at least one more worthy sorceress in the Nilfgaardian Empire. I leave the second place for you to fill, Francesca, so that you will not feel alone as the only pureblood elf. The third . . .'

Enid an Gleanna raised her head.

'I would like two places. I have two candidates.'

'Do any of you have any objections to this request? If not, then I concur. Today is the fifth day of August, the fifth day after the new moon. We shall meet again on the second day after the full moon, sisters dear, in fourteen days.'

'Just a moment,' Sheala de Tancarville interrupted. 'One place still remains empty. Who is to be the twelfth sorceress?'

'That is precisely the first problem the lodge will have to solve,' Philippa said, smiling mysteriously. 'In two weeks' time I shall tell you who ought to take their place in the twelfth seat. And then we shall ponder over how to get that person to take it up. My choice will astonish you. Because it is not an ordinary person, most esteemed sisters. It is death or life, destruction or rebirth, chaos or order. Depending on how you look at it.'

The entire village had poured out of their houses to watch the gang pass through. Tuzik also joined them. He had work to do, but he couldn't resist it. In recent days, people had been talking a great deal about the Rats. A rumour was even going around that they had all been caught and hanged. The rumour had been false, though, the evidence of which was ostentatiously and unhurriedly parading in front of the whole village at this very moment.

'Impudent scoundrels,' someone behind Tuzik whispered, and it was a whisper full of admiration. 'Ambling down the main street . . .'

'Decked out like wedding guests . . .'

'And what horses! You don't even see Nilfgaardians with horses like that!'

'Ha, they're nicked. Nobody's horses are safe from them. And you can offload them everywhere nowadays. But they keep the best for 'emselves . . .'

'That one up the front, look, that's Giselher . . . Their leader.'

'And next to him, on the chestnut, it's that she-elf . . . they call her Iskra . . .'

A cur came scuttling out from behind a fence, barking furiously, scurrying around near the fore hooves of Iskra's mare. The elf shook her luxurious mane of dark hair, turned her horse around, leant down to the ground and lashed the dog with a knout. The cur howled and spun on the spot three times, as Iskra spat on it. Tuzik muttered a curse between clenched teeth.

The people standing close by continued to whisper, discreetly pointing out the various Rats as they passed through the village. Tuzik listened, because he had to. He knew the gossip and tales as well as the others, and easily recognised the one with the long, tousled, straw-coloured hair, eating an apple, as Kayleigh, the broad-shouldered one as Asse, and the one in the embroidered sheepskin jerkin as Reef.

Two girls, riding side by side and holding hands, brought up the rear of the procession. The taller of the two, riding a bay, had her hair shorn as though recovering from the typhus, her jacket was unbuttoned, her lacy blouse gleamed white beneath it, and her necklace, bracelets and earrings flashed brightly.

'That shaven-headed one is Mistle . . .' someone near Tuzik said. 'Dripping with trinkets, just like a Yule tree.'

'They say she's killed more people than she's seen springs . . .'

'And the other one? On the roan? With the sword across her back?'

'Falka, they call her. She's been riding with the Rats since the summer. She also s'pposed to be a nasty piece of work . . .'

That nasty piece of work, Tuzik guessed, wasn't much older than

41

his daughter, Milena. The flaxen hair of the young bandit tumbled from beneath her velvet beret decorated with an impudently jiggling bunch of pheasant feathers. Around her neck glowed a poppy-red silk kerchief, tied up in a fanciful bow.

A sudden commotion had broken out among the villagers who had poured out in front of their cottages. For Giselher, the one riding at the head of the gang, had reined in his horse, and with a careless gesture thrown a clinking purse at the foot of Granny Mykita, who was standing leaning on a cane.

'May the Gods protect you, gracious youth!' wailed Granny Mykita. 'May you enjoy good health, O our benefactor, may you—'

A peal of laughter from Iskra drowned out the crone's mumbling. The elf threw a jaunty leg over her pommel, reached into a pouch and vigorously scattered a handful of coins among the crowd. Reef and Asse followed her lead, a veritable silver rain showering down on the dusty road. Kayleigh, giggling, threw his apple core into the figures scrambling to gather up the money.

'Our benefactors!'

'Our bold young hawks!'

'May fate be kind to you!'

Tuzik didn't run after the others, didn't drop to his knees to scrabble in the sand and chicken shit for coins. He stood by the fence, watching the girls pass slowly by.

The younger of the two, the one with the flaxen hair, noticed his gaze and expression. She let go of the short-haired girl's hand, spurred her horse and rode straight for him, pressing him against the fence and almost getting her stirrup caught. Her green eyes flashed and he shuddered, seeing so much evil and cold hatred in them.

'Let him be, Falka,' the other girl called, needlessly.

The green-eyed bandit settled for pushing Tuzik against the fence, and rode off after the Rats, without even looking back.

'Our benefactors!'

'Young hawks!'

Tuzik spat.

In the early evening, men in black uniforms arrived in the village. They were forbidding-looking horsemen from the fort near Fen

42

Aspra. Their hooves thudded, their horses neighed and their weapons clanked. When asked, the village headman and other peasants lied through their teeth, and sent the pursuers on a false trail. No one asked Tuzik. Fortunately.

When he returned from the pasture and went into his garden, he heard voices. He recognised the twittering of Zgarba the carter's twin girls, the cracking falsettos of his neighbour's adolescent boys. And Milena's voice. *They're playing*, he thought. He turned the corner beyond the woodshed. And froze in his tracks.

'Milena!'

Milena, his only surviving daughter, the apple of his eye, had hung a piece of wood across her back on a string, like a sword. She'd let her hair down, attached a cockerel's feather to her woollen hat, and tied her mother's kerchief around her neck. In a bizarre, fanciful bow.

Her eyes were green.

Tuzik had never beaten his daughter before, never raised his hand against her.

That was the first time.

Lightning flashed on the horizon and thunder rumbled. A gust of wind raked across the surface of the Ribbon.

There's going to be a storm, thought Milva, *and after the storm the rain will set in. The chaffinches weren't mistaken.*

She urged her horse on. She would have to hurry if she wanted to catch up with the Witcher before the storm broke.

I have met many military men in my life. I have known marshals, generals, commanders and governors, the victors of numerous campaigns and battles. I've listened to their stories and recollections. I've seen them poring over maps, drawing lines of various colours on them, making plans, thinking up strategies. In those paper wars everything worked, everything functioned, everything was clear and everything was in exemplary order. That's how it has to be, explained the military men. The army represents discipline and order above all. The army cannot exist without discipline and order.

So it is all the stranger that real wars – and I have seen several real wars – have as much in common with discipline and order as a whorehouse with a fire raging through it.

Dandelion, *Half a Century of Poetry*

CHAPTER TWO

The crystalline clear water of the Ribbon brimmed over the edge of the drop in a smooth, gentle arc, falling in a soughing and frothing cascade among boulders as black as onyx. It broke up on them and vanished in a white foam, from where it spilt into a wide pool which was so transparent that every pebble and every green strand of waterweed swaying in the current could be seen in the variegated mosaic of the riverbed.

Both banks were overgrown with carpets of knotgrass, through which dippers bustled, proudly flashing the white ruffles on their throats. Above the knotgrass, bushes shimmered green, brown and ochre against spruce trees which looked as though they had been sprinkled with silver.

'Indeed,' Dandelion sighed. 'It's beautiful here.'

A large, dark bull trout attempted to jump the lip of the waterfall. For a moment it hung in the air, flexing its fins and flicking its tail, and then fell heavily into the seething foam.

The darkening sky to the south was split by a forked ribbon of lightning and the dull echo of distant thunder rumbled over the wall of trees. The Witcher's bay mare danced, jerked her head and bared her teeth, trying to spit out the bit. Geralt tugged the reins hard and the mare skittered backwards, dancing hooves clattering on the stones.

'Whoa! Whoaaa! Do you see her, Dandelion? Damned ballerina! I'm getting rid of this bloody beast the first chance I get! Strike me down, if I don't swap her for a donkey!'

'See that happening anytime soon?' said the poet, scratching the itching mosquito bites on the nape of his neck. 'This valley's savage landscape indeed offers unparalleled aesthetic impressions, but for a change I'd be happy to gaze on a less aesthetic tavern. I've spent almost a week admiring nothing but romantic nature, breathtaking panoramas and distant horizons. I miss the indoors. Particularly the kind where they serve warm victuals and cold beer.'

'You'll have to carry on missing them a bit longer,' said the Witcher, turning around in the saddle. 'That I miss civilisation a little too may alleviate your suffering. As you know, I was stuck in Brokilon for exactly thirty-six days . . . and nights too, when romantic nature was freezing my arse, crawling across my back and sprinkling dew on my nose— Whoaaa! Pox on you! Will you stop sulking, you bloody nag?'

'It's the horseflies biting her. The bugs are getting vicious and bloodthirsty, because a storm's approaching. The thunder and lightning's getting more frequent to the south.'

'So I see,' the Witcher said, looking at the sky and reining in his skittish horse. 'And the wind's coming from a different direction, too. It smells of the sea. The weather's changing, without a doubt. Let's ride. Urge on that fat gelding of yours, Dandelion.'

'My steed is called Pegasus.'

'Of course, what else? Know what? Let's think up a name for my elven nag. Mmm . . .'

'Why not Roach?' mocked the troubadour.

'Roach,' agreed the Witcher. 'Nice.'

'Geralt?'

'Yes.'

'Have you ever had a horse that wasn't called Roach?'

'No,' answered the Witcher after a moment's thought. 'I haven't. Spur on that castrated Pegasus of yours, Dandelion. We've a long road ahead of us.'

'Indeed,' grunted the poet. 'Nilfgaard . . . How many miles away, do you reckon?'

'Plenty.'

'Will we make it before winter?'

'We'll ride to Verden first. We have to discuss . . . certain matters there.'

'What matters? You'll neither discourage me nor get rid of me. I'm coming along! That is my last word.'

48

'We shall see. As I said, we ride to Verden.'

'Is it far? Do you know these lands?'

'Yes I do. We are at Ceann Treise Falls and in front of us there's a place called Seventh Mile. Those are the Owl Hills beyond the river.'

'And we're heading south, downriver? The Ribbon joins the Yaruga near the stronghold at Bodrog . . .'

'We're heading south, but along the other bank. The Ribbon bends towards the west and we'll go through the forest. I want to get to a place called Drieschot, or the Triangle. The borders of Verden, Brugge and Brokilon meet there.'

'And from there?'

'Along the Yaruga. To the mouth. And to Cintra.'

'And then?'

'And then we'll see. If at all possible, force that idle Pegasus of yours to go a little quicker.'

A downpour caught them as they were crossing, right in the middle of the river. First a strong wind got up, with hurricane-force gusts blowing their hair and mantles around and lashing their faces with leaves and branches torn from the trees along the banks. They urged on their horses with shouts and kicks of their heels, stirring up the water as they headed for the bank. Then the wind suddenly dropped and they saw a grey curtain of rain gliding towards them. The surface of the Ribbon turned white and boiling, as though someone were hurling great handfuls of gravel at the river.

Having reached the bank, drenched to the skin, they hurried to hide in the forest. The branches created a dense, green roof over their heads, but it was not a roof capable of protecting them from such a downpour. The rain lashed intensely and forced down the leaves, and was soon pouring on them almost as hard as it had in the open.

They wrapped themselves up in their mantles, put up their hoods and kept moving. It became dark among the trees, the only light coming from the increasingly frequent flashes of lightning. The thunder followed, with long, deafening crashes. Roach shied, stamped her hooves and skittered around. Pegasus remained utterly calm.

'Geralt!' Dandelion yelled, trying to outshout a peal of thunder which was crashing through the forest like a gigantic wagon. 'We have to stop! Let's shelter somewhere!'

'Where?' he shouted back. 'Ride on!'

And they rode on.

After some time the rain visibly eased off, the strong wind once again soughed in the branches, and the crashes of thunder stopped boring into their ears. They rode out onto a track among a dense alder grove, then into a clearing. A towering beech tree stood in the middle. Beneath its boughs, on a thick, wide carpet of brown leaves and beechnuts, stood a wagon harnessed to a pair of mules. A wagoner sat on the coachman's seat pointing a crossbow at them. Geralt swore. His curse was drowned out by a clap of thunder.

'Put the bow down, Kolda,' said a short man in a straw hat, turning from the trunk of a beech tree, hopping on one leg and fastening his trousers. 'They're not the ones we're waiting for. But they are customers. Don't frighten away customers. We don't have much time, but there's always time to trade!'

'What the bloody hell?' muttered Dandelion behind Geralt's back.

'Over here, Master Elves!' the man in the hat called over. 'Don't you worry, no harm will come your way. N'ess a tearth! Va, Seidhe. Ceadmil! We're mates, right? Want to trade? Come on, over here, under this tree, out of the rain!'

Geralt wasn't surprised by the wagoner's mistake. Both he and Dandelion were wrapped in grey elven mantels. He was also wearing a jerkin decorated with the kind of leafy pattern elves favoured, given to him by the dryads, was riding a horse with typical elven trappings and a decorated bridle. His face was partially hidden by his hood. As far as the foppish Dandelion was concerned, he was regularly mistaken for an elf or half-elf, particularly since he had begun wearing his hair shoulder-length and taken up the habit of occasionally curling it with tongs.

'Careful,' Geralt muttered, dismounting. 'You're an elf. So don't open your trap if you don't have to.'

'Why?'

'Because they're hawkers.'

Dandelion hissed softly. He knew what that meant.

Money made the world go round, and supply was driven by demand. The Scoia'tael roaming the forests gathered saleable booty that was useless to them, while suffering from a shortage of equipment and weapons themselves. That was how forest trading began. And how a class of humans who earned their living from this kind of trade sprang up. The wagons of profiteers who traded with the Squirrels began appearing clandestinely on forest tracks, paths, glades and clearings. The elves called them *hav'caaren*, an untranslatable word, but one which was associated with rapacious greed. Among humans the term 'hawker' became widespread, and the connotations were even more hideous than usual, because the traders themselves were so awful. Cruel and ruthless, they stopped at nothing, not even killing. A hawker caught by the army could not count on mercy. Hence he was not in the habit of showing it himself. If they came across anyone who might turn them in, hawkers would reach for a crossbow or a knife without a second thought.

So they were out of luck. It was fortunate the hawkers had taken them for elves. Geralt pulled his hood down over his eyes and began to wonder what would happen if the hav'caaren saw through the masquerade.

'What foul weather,' said the trader, rubbing his hands. 'It's pouring like the sky was leaking! Awful tedd, ell'ea? But what to do, there's no bad weather for doing business. There's only bad goods and bad money, innit! You know what I'm saying?'

Geralt nodded. Dandelion grunted something from under his hood. Luckily for them, the elves' contemptuous dislike of conversing with humans was generally known and came as no surprise. The wagoner did not put the crossbow down, however, which was not a good sign.

'Who are you with? Whose commando?' the hawker asked, unconcerned, as any serious trader would be, by the reticence of his customers. 'Coinneach Dá Reo's? Or Angus Bri-Cri's? Or maybe Riordain's? I heard Riordain put some royal bailiffs to the sword.

They were travelling home after they'd done their duty, collecting a levy. And they had it in coinage, not grain. I don't take wood tar nor grain in payment, nor blood-stained clothing, and if we're talking furs, only mink, sable or ermine. But what I like most is common coinage, precious stones and trinkets! If you have them we can trade! I only have first-class goods! Evelienn; vara en ard scedde, ell'ea, you know what I mean? I've got everything. Take a look.'

The trader went over to the wagon and pulled back the edge of the wet tarpaulin. They saw swords, bows, bunches of arrows and saddles. The hawker rooted around among them and took out an arrow. The arrowhead was serrated and sawn through.

'You won't find any other traders selling this,' he said boastfully. 'They'd shit themselves if they were to touch 'em. You'd be torn apart by horses if you were caught with arrows like that. But I know what you Squirrels like. Customer comes first, and you've got to take a risk when you barter, as long as there's a profit from it! I've got barbed arrowheads at . . . nine orens a dozen. Naev'de aen tvedeane, ell'ea, got it, Seidhe? I swear I'm not fleecing you, I don't make much myself, I swear on my little children's heads. And if you take three dozen straight away, I'll knock a bit off the price. It's a bargain, I swear, a sheer bargain— Hey, Seidhe, hands off my wagon!'

Dandelion nervously withdrew his hand from the tarpaulin and pulled his hood further down over his face. Once again, Geralt quietly cursed the bard's irrepressible curiosity.

'Mir'me vara,' mumbled Dandelion, raising his hand in a gesture of apology. 'Squaess'me.'

'No harm done,' said the hawker, grinning. 'But no looking in there, because there's other goods in the wagon too. Not for sale, those, not for Seidhe. A special order, ha, ha. But that's enough rabbiting . . . Show us the colour of your money.'

Here we go, thought Geralt, looking at the wagoner's nocked crossbow. He had reason to believe the quarrel's tip was barbed too – just like the arrows he'd been so proudly shown moments before – and would, after entering the belly, exit through the back in three or sometimes four places, turning the victim's internal organs into a very messy goulash.

'N'ess tedd,' he said, trying to speak in a singsong way. 'Tearde. Mireann vara, va'en vort. We'll trade when we return from the commando. Ell'ea? Understood, Dh'oine?'

'Understood,' the hawker said, spitting. 'Understood that you're skint. You'd like the goods, you just don't have the readies. Be off with you! And don't come back, because I'm meeting important parties here. It'll be safer if they don't clap eyes on you. Go to—'

He broke off, hearing the snorting of a horse.

'Damn it!' he snarled. 'It's too late! They're here! Hoods down, elves! Don't move and button your lips! Kolda, you ass, put that crossbow down and fast!'

The heavy rain, thunder and the carpet of leaves had dampened the thudding of hooves, which meant the riders had been able to ride up undetected and surround the beech tree in an instant. They weren't Scoia'tael. Squirrels didn't wear armour, and the metal helmets, spaulders and hauberks of the eight horsemen surrounding the tree were glistening in the rain.

One of the horsemen approached at a walk and towered over the hawker like a mountain. He was of impressive height and was mounted on a powerful warhorse. A wolf skin was draped over his armoured shoulders and his face was obscured by a helmet with a broad, protruding nose-guard reaching down to his lower lip. The stranger was holding a menacing-looking war hammer.

'Rideaux!' he called huskily.

'Faoiltiarna!' replied the trader in a slightly quavering voice.

The horseman came even closer and leant forward. Water poured down from his steel nose-guard straight onto his vambrace and the balefully glistening point of the hammer.

'Faoiltiarna!' the hawker repeated, bowing low. He removed his hat and the rain immediately plastered his thinning hair to his head. 'Faoiltiarna! I'm your man; I know the password and the countersign . . . I've been with Faoiltiarna, Your Lordship . . . Here I am, as arranged . . .'

'And those men, who are they?'

'My escort,' the hawker said, bowing even lower. 'You know, elves . . .'

'The prisoner?'

'On the wagon. In a coffin.'

'In a coffin?' The thunder partially drowned the furious roar of the horseman. 'You won't get away with this! Viscount de Rideaux gave clear instructions that the prisoner was to be handed over alive!'

'He's alive, he's alive,' the trader gibbered hurriedly. 'As per orders . . . Shoved into a coffin, but alive . . . The coffin wasn't my idea, Your Lordship. It was Faoiltiarna's . . .'

The horseman rapped the hammer against his stirrup, as a sign. Three other horsemen dismounted and pulled the tarpaulin off the wagon. When they had thrown various saddles, blankets and bunches of harnesses onto the ground, Geralt actually saw a coffin made of fresh pine, lit by a flash of lightning. He didn't look too closely, however. He felt a tingling in the tips of his fingers. He knew what was about to happen.

'What's all this, Your Lordship?' the hawker said, looking at the goods lying on the wet leaves. 'You're chucking all my gear out of the wagon.'

'I'll buy it all. Along with the horse and cart.'

'Aaah,' a repulsive grin crept over the trader's bristly face. 'Now you're talking. That'll be . . . Let me think . . . Five hundred, if you'll excuse me, Your Nobleness, if we're talking Temerian currency. If it's your florins, then it'll be forty-five.'

'That's cheap,' snorted the horseman, smiling eerily behind his nose-guard. 'Come closer.'

'Watch out, Dandelion,' hissed the Witcher, imperceptibly unfastening the buckle of his mantle. It thundered once more.

The hawker approached the horseman, naively counting on the deal of his life. And in a way it was the deal of his life, not the best, perhaps, but certainly the last. The horseman stood in his stirrups and drove the point of the hammer down with great force onto the hawker's bald crown. The trader dropped without a sound, shuddered, flapped his arms and scraped the wet carpet of leaves with his heels. One of the men rummaging around on the wagon threw a leather strap around the wagoner's neck and pulled it tight; the other leapt forward and stabbed him with a dagger.

One of the horsemen raised his crossbow quickly to his shoulder and took aim at Dandelion. But Geralt already had a sword – one of those thrown from the wagon – in his hand. Seizing the weapon halfway down the blade, he flung it like a javelin and hit the crossbowman, who fell off the horse with an expression of utter astonishment on his face.

'Run, Dandelion!'

Dandelion caught up with Pegasus and leapt for the saddle with a desperate bound. The jump was a tad too desperate, however, and the poet was a tad too inexperienced. He didn't hang onto the pommel and tumbled to the ground on the other side of the horse. And that saved his life, as the blade of the attacking horseman's sword cut through the air above Pegasus's ears with a hiss. The gelding shied, jerked, and collided with the attacker's horse.

'They aren't elves!' yelled the horseman in the helmet with the nose-guard, drawing his sword. 'Take them alive! Alive!'

One of the men who had jumped down from the wagon hesitated on hearing the order. Geralt, however, had already drawn his own sword and didn't hesitate for a second. The fervour of the other two men was somewhat cooled by the fountain of blood which spurted over them. He took advantage of the situation and cut one of them down. But the horsemen were already charging at him. He ducked under their swords, parried their blows, dodged aside and suddenly felt a piercing pain in his right knee. He could feel himself keeling over. He wasn't hurt; the injured leg, which had been treated in Brokilon, had simply crumpled under him without warning.

The foot soldier aiming for him with the butt of a battle-axe suddenly groaned and lurched forward, as though someone had shoved him hard in the back. Before he fell, the Witcher saw an arrow with long fletchings sticking out of his assailant's side, driven in to halfway up the shaft. Dandelion yelled; a thunderclap drowned out his cry.

Geralt, who was hanging on to one of the cartwheels, saw a fair-haired girl with a drawn bow dashing out of an alder grove. The horsemen saw her too. They couldn't fail to see her, because at that moment one of them tumbled backwards over his horse's croup, his throat transformed into a scarlet pulp by an arrow. The remaining three, including the leader in the helmet with the nose-guard, assessed the danger immediately and galloped towards the archer, hiding behind their horses' necks. They thought the horses' necks represented sufficient protection against the arrows. They were mistaken.

Maria Barring, also known as Milva, drew her bow. She took aim calmly, the bowstring pressed against her cheek.

The first of her attackers screamed and slid off his horse. One foot caught in the stirrup and he was trampled beneath the horse's iron-shod hooves. Another arrow hurled the second from his saddle. The third man, the leader, who was already close, stood in the saddle and raised his sword to strike. Milva did not even flinch. Fearlessly looking straight at her attacker, she bent her bow and shot an arrow right into his face from a distance of five paces, striking just to the side of the steel nose-guard and jumping aside as she shot. The arrow passed right through his skull, knocking off his helmet. The horse did not slow its gallop. The horseman, now lacking a helmet and a considerable part of his skull, remained in the saddle for a few seconds, then slowly tipped over and crashed into a puddle. The horse neighed and ran on.

Geralt struggled to his feet and massaged his leg which, though painful, for a wonder seemed to be functioning normally. He could stand on it without difficulty and walk. Next to him, Dandelion hauled himself up, throwing off the corpse with a mutilated throat which was weighing down on him. The poet's face was the colour of quicklime.

Milva came closer, pulling an arrow from a dead man as she approached.

'Thank you,' the Witcher said. 'Dandelion, say thank you. This is Maria Barring, or Milva. It's thanks to her we're alive.'

Milva yanked an arrow from another of the dead bodies and examined the bloody arrowhead. Dandelion mumbled incoherently, bent over in a courtly – but somewhat quavering – bow, then dropped to his knees and vomited.

'Who's that?' the archer asked, wiping the arrowhead on some wet leaves and replacing it in her quiver. 'A comrade of yours, Witcher?'

'Yes. His name's Dandelion. He's a poet.'

'A poet,' Milva watched the troubadour wracked by attacks of dry retching and then looked up. 'That I can understand. But I don't quite understand why he's puking here, instead of writing rhymes in a quiet spot somewhere. But I suppose that's none of my business.'

'It is yours, in a sense. You saved his skin. And mine too.'

Milva wiped her rain-splashed face, with the imprint of the bow-string still visible on it. Although she had shot several arrows, there was only one imprint; the bowstring pressed against the same place each time.

'I was already in the alder grove when you started talking to the hawker,' she said. 'I didn't want the scoundrel to see me, for there was no need. And then those others arrived and the slaughter began. You messed a few of them up very nicely. You know how to swing a sword, I'll give you that. Even if you are a cripple. You should have stayed in Brokilon till your peg healed instead of making it worse. You might limp for the rest of your life. You realise that, don't you?'

'I'll survive.'

'I reckon you will, too. I followed you to warn you, and to make you turn back. Your quest won't come to anything. There's a war raging in the south. The Nilfgaardian Army are marching on Brugge from Drieschot.'

'How do you know?'

'Just look at them,' the girl said, making a sweeping gesture and pointing at the bodies and the horses. 'I mean, they're Nilfgaardians! Can't you see the suns on their helmets? The embroidery on their saddlecloths? Pack up your things, and we'll take to our heels; more of them may arrive any moment. These were mounted scouts.'

'I don't think they were just scouts,' he said, shaking his head. 'They were after something.'

'What might that be, just out of interest?'

'That,' he said, pointing at the pinewood coffin lying in the wagon, now darkened from the rain. It wasn't raining as hard as it had been during the short battle, and it had stopped thundering. The storm was moving north. The Witcher picked up his sword from among the leaves and jumped onto the wagon, quietly cursing because his knee still hurt.

'Help me get it open.'

'What do you want with a stiff . . . ?' Milva broke off, seeing the holes bored into the lid. 'Bloody hell! Was the hawker lugging a live person around in here?'

'It's some kind of prisoner,' Geralt said, levering the lid open. 'The trader was waiting for these Nilfgaardians, to hand him over to them. They exchanged passwords and countersigns . . .'

The lid tore off with the sound of splitting wood, revealing a man with a gag over his mouth, his arms and legs fastened to the sides of the coffin by leather straps. The Witcher leant over. He took a good look. And again, this time more intently. And swore.

'Well I never,' he drawled. 'What a surprise. Who would have thought it?'

'Do you know him, Witcher?'

'By sight.' He smiled hideously. 'Put the knife away, Milva. Don't cut his bonds. It seems this is an internal Nilfgaardian matter. We shouldn't get involved. Let's leave him as he is.'

'Am I hearing right?' Dandelion asked, joining in from behind. He was still pale, but curiosity had overcome his other emotions. 'Are you planning to leave him tied up in the forest? I'm guessing you've recognised someone you have a bone to pick with, but he's a prisoner, by the Gods! He was the prisoner of the men who jumped us and almost killed us. And the enemy of our enemy . . .'

He broke off, seeing the Witcher removing a knife from his boot-top. Milva coughed quietly. The captive's dark blue eyes, previously screwed up against the rain, widened. Geralt leant over and cut the strap fastened around the prisoner's left arm.

'Look, Dandelion,' he said, seizing the captive's wrist and raising his now-free arm. 'Do you see the scar on his hand? Ciri did that. On the Isle of Thanedd, a month ago. He's a Nilfgaardian. He came to Thanedd specifically to abduct Ciri and she wounded him, defending herself from being captured.'

'But it all came to nothing anyway,' muttered Milva. 'I sense something doesn't add up here. If he kidnapped your Ciri for Nilfgaard, how did he end up in this coffin? Why was that hawker handing him over to the Nilfgaardians? Take that gag off him, Witcher. Perhaps he'll tell us something.'

'I have no desire to listen to him,' he said flatly. 'My hand is itching to stab him through the heart, with him lying there looking at me. It's all I can do to restrain myself. And if he opens his mouth, I know I won't be able to hold back. I haven't told you everything.'

'Don't hold back then.' Milva shrugged her shoulders. 'Stick him, if he's such a villain. But do it quickly, because time's getting on. As I said, the Nilfgaardians will be here soon. I'm going to get my horse.'

Geralt straightened up and released the captive's hand. The man immediately loosened the gag and spat it out of his mouth. But he said nothing. The Witcher threw his knife onto the man's chest.

'I don't know what sins you committed for them to trap you in this chest, Nilfgaardian,' he said. 'And I don't care. I'll leave you this blade. Free yourself. Wait here for your own people, or escape into the forest, it's up to you.'

The captive said nothing. Tied up and lying in that wooden crate, he looked even more miserable and defenceless than he had on Thanedd – and Geralt had seen him there on his knees, wounded and trembling with fear in a pool of blood. He also looked considerably younger now. The Witcher wouldn't have put him at more than twenty-five.

'I spared your life on the island,' he said. 'And I'm doing it again. But it's the last time. The next time we meet I'll kill you like a dog. Remember that. If you persuade your comrades to pursue us, take the coffin with you. It'll come in useful. Let's go, Dandelion.'

'Make haste!' Milva shouted, turning away at full gallop from the westward track. 'But not that way! Into the trees, by thunder, into the trees!'

'What's going on?'

'A large group of riders are heading towards us from the Ribbon! It's Nilfgaard! What are you staring at? To horse, before they're upon us!'

The battle for the village had been going on for an hour and wasn't showing any signs of finishing soon. The infantry, holding out behind stone walls, fences and upturned wagons, had repulsed three attacks by the cavalry, who came charging at them from the causeway. The width of the causeway did not permit the horsemen to gain enough momentum for a frontal attack, but allowed the foot soldiers to concentrate their defence. As a result, waves of cavalry repeatedly foundered on the barricades, behind which the desperate but fierce soldiers were shooting a hail of quarrels and arrows into the mounted throng. The cavalry seethed and teemed under this assault, and then the defenders rushed out at them in a rapid counter-attack, fighting furiously with battle-axes, guisarmes and studded flails. The cavalry retreated to the ponds, leaving human and equine corpses behind, while the infantry concealed themselves among the barricades and hurled filthy insults at the enemy. After a while, the cavalry formed up and attacked once again.

And again.

'Who do you think's fighting whom?' Dandelion asked once more, but indistinctly, as he was trying to soften and chew a piece of hard tack he had scrounged from Milva.

They were sitting on the very edge of the cliff, well hidden among juniper shrubs. They were able to watch the battle without being afraid anyone would notice them. Actually, they could do nothing but watch. They had no choice: a battle was raging in front of them and a forest fire was raging behind them.

'It's easy to identify them,' Geralt said, reluctantly responding to Dandelion's question. 'They're Nilfgaardian horsemen.'

'And the infantry?'

'The infantry aren't Nilfgaardian.'

'The horsemen are regular cavalrymen from Verden,' said Milva, until then sombre and strangely taciturn. 'They have the Verdenian checkerboard emblem sewn onto their tunics. And the ones in the village are the Bruggian regular infantry. You can tell by their banners.'

Indeed, encouraged by another small victory, the infantrymen raised their green standard – with a white cross moline – above the entrenchment. Geralt had been watching intently, but hadn't noticed the standard before. It must have gone missing at the start of the battle.

'Are we staying here for much longer?' Dandelion asked.

'Oh dear,' muttered Milva 'Here he goes. Take a look around! Whichever way you turn, it looks pretty shitty, doesn't it?

Dandelion didn't have to look or turn around. The entire horizon was striped with columns of smoke. It was thickest to the north and the west, where the armies had set fire to the forests. Smoke was also rising into the sky in many places to the south, where they had been heading when the battle had barred their way. And during the hour they had spent on the hill, smoke had also started rising to the east.

'However,' the archer began a moment later, looking at Geralt, 'I'd really like to know what you intend doing now, Witcher. Behind us we've got Nilfgaard and a burning forest, and you can see for yourself what's in front of us. So what are your plans?'

'My plans haven't changed. I'll wait for this scrap to finish and then I'll head south. Towards the Yaruga.'

'I think you've lost your mind.' Milva scowled. 'Can't you see what's happening? It's as clear as the nose on your face that it's not some leaderless band of mercenaries, but something called war. Nilfgaard and Verden are on the march. They're sure to have crossed the Yaruga in the south and probably the whole of Brugge and possibly Sodden are in flames—'

'I have to get to the Yaruga.'

'Excellent. And what then?'

'I'll find a boat, I'll sail downstream and try to make it to the delta. Then a ship— I mean, hell, some ships must still sail from there—'

'To Nilfgaard?' she snorted. 'So the plans haven't changed?'

'You don't have to go with me.'

'No, I don't. And praise the Gods for that, because I don't have a death wish. I'm not afraid, but mind you: getting yourself killed is no claim to fame.'

'I know,' he replied calmly. 'I know from experience. I wouldn't be heading that way if I didn't have to. But I have to, so I'm going. Nothing's going to stop me.'

'Ah,' she said, looking him up and down. 'Listen to this hero, his voice like someone scraping a sword across a shield. If Imperator Emhyr could hear you, I'm sure he'd be shitting his britches in terror. "To my side, guards, to my side, my imperial regiments, oh woe is me, the Witcher's heading for Nilfgaard in a rowing boat, soon he'll be here to take my crown and life from me! I'm doomed!"'

'Give over, Milva.'

'I won't! It's time someone finally told you the truth to your face. Fuck me with a mangy rabbit if I've ever seen a stupider clod! You're going to snatch your maid from Emhyr? The same maid Emhyr has got lined up as his Imperatoress? The girl he snatched from Thanedd? Emhyr's got long hands. They don't let go of what they seize. The kings stand no chance against him, but still you fancy yours?'

He didn't answer.

'You're heading for Nilfgaard,' Milva repeated, shaking her head in mock sympathy. 'To fight the Imperator and rescue his fiancée. But have you thought about what might happen? When you get there, when you find Ciri in her imperial apartments, all dressed in gold and silk, what will you say to her? Follow me, my darling. What do you want with an imperial throne? We'll live together in a shack and eat bark during the lean season. Look at yourself, you lame scruff. You even got your coat and boots from the dryads, stripped from some elf who died of his wounds in Brokilon. And do you know what'll happen when your maid sees you? She'll spit in your eye and scorn you. She'll order the imperial guard to throw you out on your ear and set the dogs on you!'

Milva was speaking louder and louder and she was almost shouting by the end of her tirade. Not only from anger, but also to be heard over the intensifying noise of battle. Down below, scores – or even hundreds – of throats were roaring. Another attack descended on the Bruggian infantry. But this time from two sides simultaneously. Verdenians dressed in greyish-blue tunics adorned with a chequered pattern galloped along the causeway, while a powerful cavalry force in black cloaks dashed out from behind the ponds, striking the defenders' flank.

'Nilfgaard,' said Milva tersely.

This time the Bruggian infantry had no chance. The cavalry forced their way through the barricades and ripped the defenders apart with their swords. The standard with the cross fell. Some of the infantrymen laid down their arms and surrendered; others tried to escape towards the trees. But as they ran a third unit emerged from the trees and attacked; a mixed band of light cavalry.

'The Scoia'tael,' Milva said, getting to her feet. 'Now do you understand what's going on, Witcher? Do you get it? Nilfgaard, Verden and the Squirrels all at once. War. Like it was in Aedirn a month ago.'

'It's a raid,' Geralt said, shaking his head. 'A plundering raid. Only horsemen, no infantry . . .'

'The infantry are capturing forts and their garrisons. Where do you think those plumes of smoke are coming from? Smokehouses?'

The bestial, dreadful screams of people fleeing only to be caught and slaughtered by the Squirrels drifted up from the village. Smoke and flames belched from the roofs of the cottages. A strong wind was swiftly spreading the fire from one thatched roof to another.

'Look at that village going up in smoke,' muttered Milva. 'And they'd only just finished rebuilding it after the last war. They sweated for two years to put up the foundations and it'll burn down in a few seconds. That's a lesson to be learned!'

'What lesson would that be?' asked Geralt brusquely.

She didn't answer. The smoke from the burning village rose up to the top of the cliff, stung their eyes and made them water. They could hear the screams from the inferno. Dandelion suddenly went as white as a sheet.

The captives were driven into a huddle, surrounded by a ring of soldiers. On the order of a knight in a black-plumed helmet the horsemen began to slash and stab the unarmed villagers. They were trampled by horses as they fell. The ring tightened. The screams which reached the cliff top no longer resembled sounds made by humans.

'And you want to travel south?' asked the poet, looking meaningfully at the Witcher. 'Through these fires? Where these butchers come from?'

'Seems to me,' Geralt replied reluctantly, 'that we don't have a choice.'

'Yes, we do,' Milva said. 'I can lead you through the forests to the Owl Hills and back to Ceann Treise. And Brokilon.'

'Through those burning forests? Through more skirmishes like this?'

'It's safer than the road south. It's no more than fourteen miles to Ceann Treise and I know which paths to take.'

The Witcher looked down at the village perishing in the flames. The Nilfgaardians had dealt with the captives and the cavalry had formed up in marching order. The motley band of Scoia'tael set off along the highway leading east.

'I'm not going back,' he retorted. 'But you can escort Dandelion to Brokilon.'

'No!' the poet protested, although he still hadn't regained his normal colour. 'I'm going with you.'

Milva shrugged, picked up her quiver and bow, took a step towards the horses and then suddenly turned around.

'Devil take it!' she snapped. 'I've been saving elves from death for too long. I can't just let someone go to his death! I'll lead you to the Yaruga, you crazy fools. But by the eastern route, not the southern one.'

'The forests are burning there too.'

'I'll lead you through the fire. I'm used to it.'

'You don't have to, Milva.'

'Too right I don't. Now to horse! And get a bloody move on!'

They didn't get far. The horses had difficulty moving through the undergrowth and along the overgrown tracks, and they didn't dare use roads; the hoofbeats and clanking could be heard everywhere, betraying the presence of armed forces. Dusk surprised them among brush-covered ravines, so they stopped for the night. It wasn't raining and the sky was bright from the glow of fires.

They found a fairly dry place, wrapped themselves in their mantles and blankets and sat down. Milva went off to search the surrounding area. As soon as she moved away, Dandelion gave vent to the long-suppressed curiosity that the Brokilonian archer had aroused in him.

'That's a comely girl if ever there was one,' he murmured. 'You're lucky when it comes to the female of the species, Geralt. She's tall and curvaceous, and walks as though she were dancing. A little too slim in the hips for my taste, and a little too sturdy in the shoulders, but she's very womanly . . . And those two little apples in the front, ho, ho . . . Almost bursting out of her blouse—'

'Shut it, Dandelion.'

'I happened to bump against her by accident on the road,' the poet dreamed on. 'A thigh, I tell you, like marble. Methinks you weren't bored during that month in Brokilon—'

Milva, who had just returned from her patrol, heard his theatrical whispering and noticed their expressions.

'Are you talking about me, poet? What are you staring at as soon as my back's turned? Has a bird shat on me?'

'We're amazed by your archery skills.' Dandelion grinned. 'You wouldn't find much competition at an archery tournament.'

'Yes, yes, I've heard it all before, and the rest.'

'I've read,' Dandelion said, winking tellingly at Geralt, 'that the best archeresses can be found among the Zerrikanian steppe clans. I gather that some even cut off their left breast, so it won't interfere when they draw the bow. Their breast, they say, gets in the way of the bowstring.'

'Some poet must have dreamed that up,' Milva snorted. 'He sits down and writes twaddle like that, dipping his quill in a chamber pot, and foolish people believe it. Think I use my tits to shoot with, do you? You pull the bowstring back to your kisser, standing side on, like this. Nothing snags on the bowstring. All that talk of cutting off a tit is hogwash, thought up by some layabout with nothing but women's bodies on the brain.'

'Thank you for your kind words about poets and poetry. And the archery lesson. Good weapon, a bow. You know what? I think the arts of war will develop in that direction. People are going to fight at a distance in the wars of the future. They'll invent a weapon with such a long range that the two sides will be able to kill each other while completely out of eyeshot.'

'Twaddle,' Milva said bluntly. 'A bow's a good thing, but war's all about man against man, a sword's length apart, the stouter one smashing the weaker one's head in. That's how it's always been and that's how it'll always be. And once that finishes, all wars will finish. But for now, you've seen how wars are fought. You saw it in that village, by the causeway. And that's enough idle talk. I'm going to have another look around. The horses are snorting as though a wolf was sniffing around . . .'

'Comely, oh yes.' Dandelion followed her with his gaze. 'Mmm . . . Going back to the village by the causeway and what she told you when we were sitting on the cliff— Don't you think there's something in what she says?'

'About?'

'About . . . Ciri,' the poet stammered slightly. 'Our beautiful, sharp-shooting wench seems not to understand the relationship between you and Ciri, and thinks, it seems to me, that you intend to woo her away from the Nilfgaardian Imperator. That that's the real motive behind your expedition to Nilfgaard.'

'So in that regard she's totally wrong. But what's she right about?'

'Take it easy, keep your cool. Nonetheless stare the truth in the face. You took Ciri under your wing and consider yourself her guardian, but she's no ordinary girl. She's a princess, Geralt. Without beating about the bush, she's in line for the throne. For the palace. And the crown. Maybe not necessarily the Nilfgaardian crown. I don't know if Emhyr is the best husband for her—'

'Precisely. You don't know.'

'And do *you*?'

The Witcher wrapped himself up in a blanket.

'You're heading, quite naturally, towards a conclusion,' he said. 'But don't bother; I know what you're thinking. "There's no point saving Ciri from a fate she's been doomed to since the day of her birth. Because Ciri, who doesn't need saving at all, will be quite ready to order the imperial guard to throw us down the stairs. Let's forget about her." Right?'

Dandelion opened his mouth, but Geralt didn't let him speak.

'"After all,' he continued in an even harsher voice, 'the girl wasn't abducted by a dragon or an evil wizard, nor did pirates seize her for the ransom money. She's not locked in a tower, a dungeon or a cage; she's not being tortured or starved. Quite the opposite; she sleeps on damask, eats from silverware, wears silks and lace, is bedecked with jewellery and is just waiting to be crowned. In short, she's happy. Meanwhile some witcher who, by some unfortunate fate happened upon her, has taken it upon himself to disrupt, spoil, destroy and crush that happiness beneath the rotten old boots he pulled off some dead elf." Right?'

'That's not what I was thinking,' Dandelion muttered.

'He wasn't talking to you,' Milva said, suddenly looming up from the darkness and after a moment's hesitation sitting down beside the Witcher. 'That was for me. It was my words that upset him. I spoke in anger, without thinking . . . Forgive me, Geralt. I know what it's like when a claw scratches an open wound. Come on, don't fret. I won't do it any more. Do you forgive me? Or should I say sorry by kissing you?'

Not waiting either for an answer or permission she grabbed him powerfully by the neck and kissed him on the cheek. He squeezed her shoulder hard.

'Slide nearer.' He coughed. 'And you too, Dandelion. We'll be warmer together.'

They said nothing for a long time. Clouds scudded across a sky bright with firelight, obscuring the twinkling stars.

'I want to tell you something,' Geralt said at last. 'But promise you won't laugh.'

'Out with it.'

'I had some strange dreams. In Brokilon. At first I thought they were ravings; something wrong with my head. You know, I got a good beating on Thanedd. But I keep having the same dream. Always the same one.'

Dandelion and Milva said nothing.

'Ciri,' he began a moment later, 'isn't sleeping in a palace beneath a brocade canopy. She's riding a horse through a dusty village . . . the villagers are pointing at her. They're calling her by a name I don't recognise. Dogs are barking. She's not alone. There are others with her. There's a crop-haired girl, who's holding Ciri's hand . . . and Ciri's smiling at her but I don't like that smile. I don't like her heavy make-up . . . But the thing I like least is that she leaves a trail of death.'

'So where is the girl?' Milva mused, snuggling up to him like a cat. 'Not in Nilfgaard?'

'I don't know,' he said with difficulty. 'But I've had the same dream several times. The problem is I don't believe in dreams like that.'

'Well, you're a fool. I do.'

'I don't *know* it,' he repeated. 'But I can *feel* it. There's fire ahead of her and death behind her. I have to make haste.'

It began to rain at dawn. Not like the previous day, when the storm had been accompanied by a brief but strong downpour. The sky turned grey and took on a leaden patina. It began to spit with rain; a fine, even and drenching drizzle.

They rode east. Milva led the way. When Geralt pointed out to her that the Yaruga was to the south, the archer growled and reminded him she was the guide and knew what she was doing. He said nothing after that. After all, the most important thing was that they were under way. The direction wasn't so important.

They rode in silence, wet, chilled to the bone, and hunched over their saddles. They kept to footpaths, stole along forest tracks, cut across highways. They disappeared into the undergrowth at the sound of thudding hooves of cavalry tramping along the roads. They gave a wide berth to the uproar of battle. They rode past villages engulfed in flames, past smoking and glowing rubble, and past settlements and hamlets which had been razed to black squares of burnt earth and the acrid stench of rain-soaked charred embers. They startled flocks of crows feeding on corpses. They passed groups and columns of peasants bent beneath bundles, fleeing from war and conflagration, dazed, responding to questions with nothing but a fearful, uncomprehending and mute raising of their eyes, emptied by misfortune and horror.

They rode east, amidst fire and smoke, amidst drizzle and fog, and the tapestry of war unfolded in front of their eyes. So many sights.

There was a black silhouette of a crane projecting among the ruins of a burnt-out village, with a naked corpse dangling from it head downwards. Blood from the mutilated crotch and belly dripped down onto its chest and face, to hang like icicles from its hair. The Rune of Ard was visible on its back. Carved with a knife.

'An'givare,' Milva said, throwing her wet hair off her neck. 'The Squirrels were here.'

'What does an'givare mean?'

'Informer.'

There was a grey horse, saddled in a black caparison. It was walking unsteadily around the edge of the battlefield, wandering between piles of corpses and broken spears stuck into the ground, whinnying quietly and pitifully, dragging its entrails behind it, dangling from its mutilated belly. They couldn't finish it off, for on the battlefield – apart from the horse – there were also marauders robbing corpses.

There was a spread-eagled girl, lying near a burnt-out farmyard, naked, bloody, staring at the sky with glazed eyes.

'They say war's a male thing,' Milva growled. 'But they have no mercy on women; they have to have their fun. Fucking heroes; damn them all.'

'You're right. But you won't change it.'

'I already have. I ran away from home. I didn't want to sweep the cottage and scrub the floors. I wasn't going to wait until they arrived and put the cottage to the torch, spread me out on the very same floor and . . .' She broke off, and spurred her horse forward.

And later there was a tar house. Here Dandelion puked up everything he'd eaten that day: some hard tack and half a stockfish.

In the tar house some Nilfgaardians – or perhaps Scoia'tael – had dealt with a group of captives. It was impossible even to guess at the exact size of the group. Because during the carnage they had not only used arrows, swords and lances, but also woodmen's tools they'd found there: axes, drawknives and crosscut saws.

There were other scenes of war, but Geralt, Dandelion and Milva didn't remember them. They had discarded them from their memories.

They had become indifferent.

Over the next two days they didn't even cover twenty miles. It continued to rain. The earth, absorbent after the summer drought, sucked up water like a sponge, and the forest tracks were transformed into muddy slides. Fog and haze prevented them from spotting the smoke from fires, but the stench of burning buildings told them the armies were still close at hand and were still setting light to anything that would catch fire.

They didn't see any fugitives. They were alone in the forest. Or so they thought.

Geralt was the first to hear the snorting of the horse following in their tracks. With a stony countenance, he turned Roach back. Dandelion opened his mouth, but Milva gestured him to remain silent, and removed her bow from where it hung by her saddle.

The rider following them emerged from the brush. He saw they were waiting for him and reined back his horse, a chestnut colt. They stood in a silence broken only by the beating of the rain.

'I forbade you from riding after us,' the Witcher finally said.

The Nilfgaardian, whom Dandelion had last seen lying in a coffin, looked down at his horse's wet mane. The poet barely recognised him, as he was now dressed in a hauberk, leather tunic and cloak, no doubt stripped from one of the horsemen killed by the wagon. However, he remembered the young face, which hadn't grown much more stubble since the adventure under the beech tree.

'I forbade it,' the Witcher repeated.

'You did,' the young man finally agreed. He spoke without a Nilfgaardian accent. 'But I must.'

Geralt dismounted, handing the reins to the poet. And drew his sword.

'Get down,' he said calmly. 'You've equipped yourself with some hardware, I see. Good. There was no way I could kill you then, while you were unarmed. Now it's different. Dismount.'

'I'm not fighting you. I don't want to.'

'So I imagine. Like all your fellow countrymen, you prefer another kind of fight. Like in that tar house, which you must have ridden past, following our trail. Dismount, I said.'

'I am Cahir Mawr Dyffryn aep Ceallach.'

'I didn't ask you to introduce yourself. I ordered you to dismount.'

'I will not. I don't want to fight you.'

'Milva.' The Witcher nodded at the archer. 'Be so kind as to shoot his horse from under him.'

'No!' the Nilfgaardian raised an arm, before Milva had time to nock her arrow. 'Please don't. I'm dismounting.'

'That's better. Now draw your sword, son.'

The young man folded his arms across his chest.

'Kill me, if you want. If you prefer, order the she-elf to shoot me. I'm not fighting you. I am Cahir Mawr Dyffryn . . . son of Ceallach. I want . . . I want to join you.'

'I must have misheard. Say that again.'

'I want to join you. You're riding to search for the girl. I want to help you. I have to help you.'

'He's a madman.' Geralt turned to Milva and Dandelion. 'He's taken leave of his senses. We're dealing with a madman.'

'He'd suit the company,' muttered Milva. 'He'd suit it perfectly.'

'Think his proposition over, Geralt,' Dandelion mocked. 'After all, he's a Nilfgaardian nobleman. Perhaps with his help it'll be easier for us to get to—'

'Keep your tongue in check,' the Witcher interrupted the poet sharply. 'As I said, draw your sword, Nilfgaardian.'

'I am not going to fight. And I am not a Nilfgaardian. I come from Vicovaro, and my name is—'

'I'm not interested in your name. Draw your weapon.'

'No.'

'Witcher.' Milva leant down from the saddle and spat on the ground. 'Time's flying and the rain's falling. The Nilfgaardian doesn't want to fight, and although you're pulling a stern face, you won't cut him to pieces in cold blood. Do we have to hang about here all fucking day? I'll stick an arrow in his chestnut's underbelly and let's be on our way. He won't catch up on foot.'

Cahir, son of Ceallach, was by his chestnut colt in one bound, jumped into the saddle and galloped back the way he'd come, yelling at his steed to go faster. The Witcher watched him riding off for a moment then mounted Roach. In silence. Without looking back.

'I'm getting old,' he mumbled some time later, after Roach had caught up with Milva's black. 'I'm starting to develop scruples.'

'Aye, it can happen with old 'uns,' said the archer, looking at him in sympathy. 'A decoction of lungwort can help. But for now put a cushion on your saddle.'

'Scruples,' Dandelion explained gravely, 'are not the same as piles, Milva. You're confusing the terms.'

'Who could understand your smart-arsed chatter? You never stop jabbering, it's the only thing you know! Come on, let's ride!'

'Milva,' the Witcher asked a moment later, protecting his face from the rain, which stabbed against it as they galloped. 'Would you have killed the horse under him?'

'No,' she confessed reluctantly. 'The horse hadn't done anything. But that Nilfgaardian— Why in hell is he stalking us? Why does he say he has to?'

'Devil take me if I know.'

It was still raining when the forest suddenly came to an end and they rode onto a highway winding between the hills from the south to the north. Or the other way around, depending on your point of view. What they saw on the highway didn't surprise them. They had already seen similar sights. Overturned and gutted wagons, dead horses, scattered bundles, saddlebags and baskets. And ragged shapes, which not long before had been people, frozen into strange poses.

They rode closer, without fear, because it was apparent that the slaughter had not taken place that day. They had come to recognise such things; or perhaps to sense them with a purely animalistic instinct, which the last days had awoken and sharpened in them.

They had also learned to search through battlefields, because occasionally – though not often – they had managed to find a little food or a sack of fodder among the scattered objects.

They stopped by the last wagon of a devastated column. It had been pushed into the ditch, and was resting on the hub of a shattered wheel. Beneath the wagon lay a stout woman with an unnaturally twisted neck. The collar of her tunic was covered with rain-washed streaks of coagulated blood from her torn ear, from which an earring had been ripped. The sign on the tarpaulin pulled over the wagon read: 'Vera Loewenhaupt and Sons'. There was no sign of the sons.

'They weren't peasants,' Milva said through pursed lips. 'They were traders. They came from the south, wending from Dillingen towards Brugge, and were caught here. It's not good, Witcher. I thought we could turn south at this point, but now I truly have no idea what to do. Dillingen and the whole of Brugge is sure to be in Nilfgaardian hands, so we won't make it to the Yaruga this way. We'll have to go east, through Turlough. There are forests and wildernesses there, the army won't go that way.'

'I'm not going any further east,' Geralt protested. 'I have to get to the Yaruga.'

'You'll get there,' she replied, unexpectedly calm. 'But by a safer route. If we head south from here, you'll fall right into the Nilfgaardians' jaws. You won't gain anything.'

'I'll gain time,' he snapped, 'by heading east I'm just wasting it. I told you, I can't afford to—'

'Quiet,' Dandelion said suddenly, steering his horse around. 'Be quiet for a moment.'

'What is it?'

'I can hear . . . singing.'

The Witcher shook his head. Milva snorted.

'You're hearing things, poet.'

'Quiet! Shut up! I'm telling you, someone's singing! Can't you hear it?'

Geralt lowered his hood; Milva also strained to listen and a moment later glanced at the Witcher and nodded silently.

The troubadour's musical ear hadn't let him down. What had

73

seemed impossible turned out to be true. Here they were, standing in the middle of a forest, in the drizzle, on a road strewn with corpses, and they could hear singing. Someone was approaching from the south, singing jauntily and gaily.

Milva tugged the reins of her black, ready to flee, but the Witcher gestured to her to wait. He was curious. Because the singing they could hear wasn't the menacing, rhythmic, booming, massed singing of marching infantry, nor a swaggering cavalry song. The singing, which was becoming louder all the time, didn't arouse any anxiety.

Quite the opposite.

The rain drummed on the foliage. They began to make out the words of the song. It was a merry song, which seemed strange, unnatural and totally out of place in this landscape of death and war.

Look how the wolf dances in the holt.
Teeth bared, tail waving, leaping like a colt.
Oh, why does he prance like one bewitched?
The frolicking beast simply hasn't been hitched!
Oom-pah, oom-pah, oom-pah-pah!

Dandelion suddenly laughed, took his lute from under his wet mantle, and – ignoring the hissing from the Witcher and Milva – strummed the strings and joined in at the top of his voice:

Look how the wolf is dragging his paws.
Head drooping, tail hanging, clenching his jaws.
Oh, why is the beast in such a sorry state?
He's either proposed or he's married his mate!

'Ooh-hoo-ha!' came the roared response from many voices close by.

Thunderous laughter burst out, then someone whistled piercingly through their fingers, after which a strange but colourful company came walking around a bend in the highway, marching in single file, splashing mud with rhythmic steps of their heavy boots.

'Dwarves,' Milva said under her breath. 'But they aren't Scoia'tael. They don't have plaited beards.'

There were six of them, dressed in short, hooded capes, shimmering with countless shades of grey and brown, the kind which were usually worn by dwarves in foul weather. Capes like that, as Geralt knew, had the quality of being totally waterproof, which was achieved by the impregnation of wood tar over many years, not to mention dust from the highway and the remains of greasy food. These practical garments passed from fathers to oldest sons; as a result they were used exclusively by mature dwarves. And a dwarf attains maturity when his beard reaches his waist, which usually occurs at the age of fifty-five.

None of the approaching dwarves looked young. But none looked old either.

'They're leading some humans,' muttered Milva, indicating to Geralt with a movement of her head a small group emerging from the forest behind the company of dwarves, 'who must be fugitives, because they're laden down with goods and chattels.'

'The dwarves aren't exactly travelling light themselves,' Dandelion added.

Indeed, each dwarf was heaving a load that many humans and horses would soon have collapsed under. In addition to the ordinary sacks and saddlebags, Geralt noticed iron-bound chests, a large copper cauldron and something that looked like a small chest of drawers. One of them was even carrying a cartwheel on his back.

The one walking at the front wasn't carrying anything. He had a small battle-axe in his belt, on his back was a long sword in a scabbard wrapped in tabby cat skins, and on his shoulder sat a green parrot with wet, ruffled feathers. The dwarf addressed them.

'Greetings!' he roared, after coming to a halt in the middle of the road and putting his hands on his hips. 'These days it's better to meet a wolf in the forest than a human. And if you do have such bad luck, you're more likely to be greeted with an arrow in the chest than a kind word! But whoever greets someone with a song or music must be a sound fellow! Or a sound wench; my apologies to the good lady! Greetings. I'm Zoltan Chivay.'

'I'm Geralt,' the Witcher introduced himself after a moment's hesitation. 'The singer is Dandelion. And this is Milva.'

''Kin' 'ell!' the parrot squawked.

'Shut your beak,' Zoltan Chivay growled at the bird. 'Excuse me. This foreign bird is clever but vulgar. I paid ten thalers for the freak. He's called Field Marshal Windbag. And while I'm at it, this is the rest of my party. Munro Bruys, Yazon Varda, Caleb Stratton, Figgis Merluzzo and Percival Schuttenbach.'

Percival Schuttenbach wasn't a dwarf. From beneath his wet hood, instead of a matted beard, stuck out a long, pointed nose, unerringly identifying its owner as one of the old and noble race of gnomes.

'And those,' Zoltan Chivay said, pointing at the small group of humans, who had stopped and were huddled together, 'are fugitives from Kernow. As you can see, they're women and children. There were more, but Nilfgaard seized them and their fellows three days ago, put some of them to the sword and scattered the others. We came across them in the forest and now we're travelling together.'

'It's bold of you,' the Witcher ventured, 'to be marching along the highway, singing as you go.'

'I don't reckon,' the dwarf said, wiggling his beard, 'that weeping as we go would be any better. We've been marching through the woods since Dillingen, quietly and out of sight, and after the army passed we joined the highway to make up time.' He broke off and looked around the battlefield.

'We've grown accustomed to sights like this,' he said, pointing at the corpses. 'Beyond Dillingen and the Yaruga there's nothing but dead bodies on the roads . . . Were you with this lot?'

'No. Nilfgaard put some traders to the sword.'

'Not Nilfgaard,' said the dwarf, shaking his head and looking at the dead with an indifferent expression. 'Scoia'tael. The regular army don't bother pulling arrows out of corpses. And a good arrowhead costs half a crown.'

'He knows his prices,' Milva muttered.

'Where are you headed?'

'South,' Geralt answered immediately.

'I advise you against it,' Zoltan Chivay said, and shook his head again. 'It's sheer hell, fire and slaughter there. Dillingen is taken for sure, the Nilfgaardians are crossing the Yaruga in greater and greater numbers; any moment now they'll flood the whole valley on the right bank. As you see, they're also in front of us, to the north. They're heading for the city of Brugge. So the only sensible direction to escape is east.'

Milva glanced knowingly at the Witcher, who refrained from comment.

'And that's where we're headed; east,' Zoltan Chivay continued. 'The only chance is to hide behind the frontline, and wait until the Temerian Army finally start out from the River Ina in the east. Then we plan to march along forest tracks until we reach the hills. Turlough, then the Old Road to the River Chotla in Sodden, which flows into the Ina. We can travel together, if you wish. If it doesn't bother you that we make slow progress. You're mounted and I realise our refugees slow the pace down.'

'It doesn't seem to bother you, though,' Milva said, looking at him intently. 'A dwarf, even fully laden, can march thirty miles a day. Almost the same as a mounted human. I know the Old Road. Without those refugees you'd reach the Chotla in about three days.'

'They are women and children,' Zoltan Chivay said, sticking out his beard and his belly. 'We won't leave them to their fate. Would you suggest we do anything else, eh?'

'No,' the Witcher said. 'No, we wouldn't.'

'I'm pleased to hear it. That means my first impressions didn't deceive me. So what's it to be? Do we march as one company?'

Geralt looked at Milva and the archer nodded.

'Very well,' Zoltan Chivay said, noticing the nod. 'So let's head off, before some raiding party chances upon us on the highway. But first— Yazon, Munro, search the wagons. If you find anything useful there, get it stowed away, and pronto. Figgis, check if our wheel fits that little wagon, it'll be just right for us.'

'It fits!' yelled the one who'd been lugging the cartwheel. 'Like it was made for it!'

'You see, muttonhead? And you were so surprised when I made you take that wheel and carry it! Put it on! Help him, Caleb!'

In an impressively short time the wagon of the dead Vera Loewenhaupt had been equipped with a new wheel, stripped of its tarpaulin and inessential elements, and pulled out of the ditch and onto the road. All their goods were heaved onto it in an instant. After some thought, Zoltan Chivay also ordered the children to be loaded onto the wagon. The instruction was carried out reluctantly; Geralt noticed that the children's mothers scowled at the dwarves and tried to keep their distance from them.

With visible distaste, Dandelion watched two dwarves trying on articles of clothing removed from some corpses. The remaining dwarves rummaged around among the wagons, but didn't consider anything to be worth taking. Zoltan Chivay whistled through his fingers, signalling that the time for looting was over, and then he looked over Roach, Pegasus and Milva's black with an expert eye.

'Saddle horses,' he said, wrinkling his nose in disapproval. 'In other words: useless. Figgis and Caleb, to the shaft. We'll be hauling in turn. Maaaaarch!'

Geralt was certain the dwarves would quickly discard the wagon the moment it got well and truly stuck in soft, boggy ground, but he was mistaken. They were as strong as oxen, and the forest tracks leading east turned out to be grassy and not too swampy, even though it continued to rain without letting up. Milva became gloomy and grumpy, and only broke her silence to express the conviction that the horses' softened hooves would split at any moment. Zoltan Chivay licked his lips in reply, examined the hooves in question and declared himself a master at roasting horsemeat, which infuriated Milva.

They kept to the same formation, the core of which was formed by the wagon hauled on a shift system. Zoltan marched in front of the wagon. Next to him, on Pegasus, rode Dandelion, bantering with the parrot. Geralt and Milva rode behind them, and at the back trudged the six women from Kernow.

The leader was usually Percival Schuttenbach, the long-nosed gnome. No match for the dwarves in terms of height or strength, he was their equal in stamina and considerably superior in agility. During the march he never stopped roaming around and rummaging in bushes; then he would pull ahead and disappear, only to appear and with nervous, monkey-like gestures signal from a considerable distance away that everything was in order and that they could continue. Occasionally he would return and give a rapid report about the obstacles on the track. Whenever he did, he would have a handful of blackberries, nuts or strange – but clearly tasty – roots for the four children sitting on the wagon.

Their pace was frightfully slow and they spent three days marching along forest tracks. They didn't happen upon any soldiers; they saw no smoke or the glow of fires. They were not alone, however. Every so often Percival spotted groups of fugitives hiding in the forests. They passed several such groups, hurriedly, because the expressions of the peasants armed with pitchforks and stakes didn't encourage them to try to make friends. There was nonetheless a suggestion to try to negotiate and leave the women from Kernow with one of the groups, but Zoltan was against it and Milva backed him up. The women were in no hurry at all to leave the company either. This was all the stranger since they treated the dwarves with such obvious, fearful aversion and reserve, hardly ever spoke, and kept out of the way during every stop.

Geralt ascribed the women's behaviour to the tragedy they had experienced a short time before, although he suspected that their aversion may have been due to the dwarves' casual ways. Zoltan and his company cursed just as filthily and frequently as the parrot called Field Marshal Windbag, but had a wider repertoire. They sang dirty songs, which Dandelion enthusiastically joined in with. They spat, blew their noses on their fingers and gave thunderous farts, which usually prompted laughs, jokes and competition. They only went into the bushes for major bodily needs; with the minor ones they didn't even bother moving very far away. This finally enraged Milva, who gave Zoltan a good telling-off when one morning he pissed on the still warm ashes of the campfire, totally oblivious to his audience. Having been dressed down, Zoltan was unperturbed and announced that shamefully concealing that kind of activity was only common among two-faced, perfidious people who were likely to be informers, and could be identified as such by doing just that.

This eloquent explanation made no impression on the archer. The dwarves were treated to a rich torrent of abuse, with several very specific threats, which was effective, since they all obediently began to go into the bushes. To avoid laying themselves open to the appellation of 'perfidious informers', however, they went in a group.

The new company, nevertheless, changed Dandelion utterly. He got on famously with the dwarves, particularly when it turned out that some of them had heard of him and even knew his ballads and couplets. Dandelion dogged Zoltan's company. He wore a quilted jacket he had weaselled out of the dwarves, and his crumpled hat with a feather was replaced by a swashbuckling marten-fur cap. He sported a broad belt with brass studs, into which he had stuck a cruel-looking knife he had been given. This knife pricked him in the side each time he tried to lean over. Fortunately, he quickly mislaid it and wasn't given another.

They wandered through the dense forests covering the hillsides of Turlough. The forests seemed deserted; there were no traces of any wild animals, for they had apparently been frightened away by the armies and fugitives. There was nothing to hunt, but they weren't immediately threatened by hunger. The dwarves were lugging along a large quantity of provisions. As soon as they were finished, however – and that occurred quickly, because there were many mouths to feed – Yazon Varda and Munro Bruys vanished soon after dark, taking an empty sack with them. When they returned at dawn, they had two sacks, both full. In one was fodder for the horses, in the other barley groats, flour, beef jerky, an almost entire cheese, and even a huge haggis: a delicacy in the form of a pig's stomach stuffed with offal and pressed between two slats, the whole resembling a pair of bellows.

Geralt guessed where the haul had come from. He didn't comment right away, but bided his time until a moment when he was alone with Zoltan, and then asked him politely if he saw nothing indecent in robbing other fugitives, who were no less hungry than them, after all, and fighting for survival just like them. The dwarf answered gravely that indeed, he was very ashamed of it, but unfortunately, such was his character.

'Unbridled altruism is a huge vice of mine,' he explained. 'I simply have to do good. I am a sensible dwarf, however, and know that I'm unable to do everyone good. Were I to attempt to be good to everyone, to the entire world and to all the creatures living in it, it would be a drop of fresh water in the salt sea. In other words, a wasted effort. Thus, I decided to do specific good; good which would not go to waste. I'm good to myself and my immediate circle.'

Geralt asked no further questions.

At one of the camps, Geralt and Milva chatted at length with Zoltan Chivay, the incorrigible and compulsive altruist. The dwarf was well informed about how the military activities were proceeding. At least, he gave that impression.

'The attack,' he said, frequently quietening down Field Marshal Windbag, who was screeching obscenities, 'came from Drieschot, and began at dawn on the seventh day after Lammas. Nilfgaard marched with its allies, the Verdenian Army, since Verden, as you know, is now an imperial protectorate. They moved swiftly, putting all the villages beyond Drieschot to the torch and wiping out the Bruggian Army which was garrisoned there. The Nilfgaardian infantry marched on the fortress in Dillingen from the other side of the Yaruga. They crossed the river in a totally unexpected place. They built a pontoon bridge. Only took them half a day, can you believe it?'

'It's possible to believe anything,' muttered Milva. 'Were you in Dillingen when it started?'

'Thereabouts,' the dwarf replied evasively. 'When news of the attack reached us, we were already on the way to the city of Brugge. The highway was an awful shambles, it was teeming with fugitives, some of them fleeing from the south to the north, others from the north to the south. They jammed up the highway, so we got stuck. And Nilfgaard, as it turned out, were both behind us and in front of us. The forces that had left Drieschot must have split up. I reckon a large cavalry troop had headed north-east, towards Brugge.'

'So the Nilfgaardians are already north of Turlough. It appears we're stuck between two forces, right in the middle. And safe.'

'Right in the middle, yes,' the dwarf agreed. 'But not safe. The imperial troops are flanked by the Squirrels, Verdenian volunteers and various mercenaries, who are even worse than the Nilfgaardians. It was them as burnt down Kernow and almost seized us later; we barely managed to leg it into the woods. So we shouldn't poke our noses out of the forest. And we should remain on guard. We'll make it to the Old Road, then downstream by the River Chotla to the Ina, and at the Ina we're sure to bump into the Temerian Army. King Foltest's men must have shaken off their surprise and begun standing up to the Nilfgaardians.'

'If only,' Milva said, looking at the Witcher. 'But the problem is that urgent and important matters are driving us on to the south. We pondered heading south from Turlough, towards the Yaruga.'

'I don't know what matters are driving you to those parts,' Zoltan said, glowering suspiciously at them. 'They must indeed be greatly urgent and important to risk your necks for them.'

He paused and waited, but neither of them was in a hurry to explain. The dwarf scratched his backside, hawked and spat.

'It wouldn't surprise me,' he said finally, 'if Nilfgaard had both banks of the Yaruga right up to the mouth of the Ina in their grasp. And where exactly on the Yaruga do you need to be?'

'Nowhere specific,' Geralt decided to reply. 'As long as we reach the river. I want to take a boat up to the delta.'

Zoltan looked at him and laughed. Then stopped immediately when he realised it hadn't been a joke.

'I have to admit,' he said a moment later, 'you've got quite some route in mind. But get rid of those pipe dreams. The whole of south Brugge is in flames. They'll impale you before you reach the Yaruga, or drive you to Nilfgaard in fetters. However, were you by some miracle to reach the river, there'd be no chance of sailing to the delta. That pontoon bridge spanning the river from Cintra to the Bruggian bank? They guard it day and night; nothing could get through that part of the river, except perhaps a salmon. Your urgent and important matters will have to lose their urgency and importance. You haven't got a prayer. That's how I see it.'

Milva's glance testified that she shared his opinion. Geralt didn't comment. He felt terrible. The slowly healing bone in his left forearm and his right knee still gnawed with the invisible fangs of a dull, nagging pain, made worse by effort and the constant damp. He was also being troubled by overwhelming, disheartening, exceptionally unpleasant feelings, alien feelings he had never experienced before and was unable to deal with.

Helplessness and resignation.

After two days, it stopped raining and the sun came out. The forests breathed forth mists and quickly dissipating fog, and birds began to vigorously make up for the silence forced on them by the constant rain. Zoltan cheered up and ordered a long break, after which he promised a quicker march and that they would reach the Old Road in a day at most.

The women from Kernow draped all the surrounding branches with the black and grey of drying clothing, and then, dressed only in their shifts, hid shamefacedly in the bushes and prepared food. The children charged around naked, disturbing the dignified calm of the steaming forest in elaborate ways. Dandelion slept off his tiredness. Milva vanished.

The dwarves took their rest seriously. Figgis Merluzzo and Munro Bruys went off hunting mushrooms. Zoltan, Yazon Varda, Caleb Stratton and Percival Schuttenbach sat down near the wagon and without taking a breather played Barrel, their favourite card game, which they devoted every spare minute to, including the previous wet evenings.

The Witcher occasionally sat down to join them and watch them play, as he did during this break. He was still unable to understand the complicated rules of this typical dwarven game, but was fascinated by the amazing, intricate workmanship of the cards and the drawings of the figures. Compared to the cards humans played with, the dwarves' cards were genuine works of art. Geralt was once again convinced that the advanced technology of the bearded folk was not limited to the fields of mining and metallurgy. The fact that in this specific, card-playing field the dwarves' talents hadn't helped them to monopolise the market was because cards were still less popular among humans than dice, and human gamblers attached little importance to aesthetics. Human card players, whom the Witcher had had several opportunities to observe, always played with greasy cards, so dirty that before cards were placed on the table they had to be laboriously peeled away from the fingers. The court cards were painted so carelessly that distinguishing the lady from the knave was only possible because the knave was mounted on a horse. Which actually looked more like a crippled weasel.

Mistakes of that kind were impossible with the dwarves' cards. The crowned king was really regal, the lady comely and curvaceous, and the halberd-wielding knave jauntily moustachioed. The colour cards were called, in Dwarven Speech, the *hraval*, *vaina* and *ballet*, but Zoltan and company used the Common Speech and human names when they played.

The sun shone warmly, the forest steamed, and Geralt watched.

The fundamental principle of dwarven Barrel was something resembling an auction at a horse fair, both in its intensity and the volume of the bidders' voices. The pair declaring the highest 'price' would endeavour to win as many tricks as possible, which the rival pair had to impede at all costs. The game was played noisily and heatedly, and a sturdy staff lay beside each player. These staffs were seldom used to beat an opponent, but were often brandished.

'Look what you've done! You plonker! You bonehead! Why did you open with spades instead of hearts? Think I was leading hearts just for the fun of it? Why, I ought to take my staff and knock some sense into you!'

'I had four spades up to the knave, so I was planning to make a good contract!'

'Four spades, 'course you did! Including your own member, which you counted when you looked down at your cards. Use your loaf, Stratton, we're not at university! We're playing cards here! And remember that when the fool has the cards and doesn't blunder, he'll even beat the sage, by thunder. Deal, Varda.'

'Contract in diamonds.'

'A small slam in diamonds!'

'The king led diamonds, but lost his crown, fled the kingdom with his trousers down. A double in spades!'

'Barrel!'

'Wake up, Caleb. That was a double with a Barrel! What are you bidding?'

'A big slam in diamonds!'

'No bid. Aaagh! What now? No one's Barrelling? Chickened out, laddies? You're leading, Varda. Percival, if you wink at him again, I'll whack you so hard in the kisser your eyes'll be screwed up till next winter.'

'Knave.'

'Lady!'

'And the king on the lady! The lady's shafted! I'll take her and, ha, ha, I've got another heart, kept for a rainy day! Knave, a ten and another—'

'And a trump! If you can't play a trump, you'd better take a dump. And diamonds! Zoltan? Grabbed you where it hurts!'

'Do you see him, fucking gnome. Pshaw, I'm gonna take my staff to him . . .'

Before Zoltan could use his stick, a piercing cry was heard from the forest.

Geralt was the first to his feet. He swore as he ran, pain shooting through his knee. Zoltan Chivay rushed after him, seizing his sword wrapped in tabby cat skins from the wagon. Percival Schuttenbach and the rest of the dwarves ran after them, armed with sticks, while Dandelion, who'd been woken by the screaming, brought up the rear. Figgis and Munro leapt out of the forest from one side. Throwing down their baskets of mushrooms, the two dwarves gathered up the scattering children and pulled them away. Milva appeared from nowhere, drawing an arrow from her quiver while running and showing the Witcher where the scream had come from. There was no need. Geralt saw and heard, and now knew what it was all about.

One of the children was screaming. She was a freckled, little girl with plaits, aged about nine. She stood petrified, a few paces from a pile of rotten logs. Geralt was with her in an instant. He seized her under the arms, interrupting her terrified shrieking, and watched the movement among the logs out of the corner of his eye. He quickly withdrew and bumped into Zoltan and his dwarves. Milva, who had also seen something moving, nocked her arrow and took aim.

'Don't shoot,' Geralt hissed. 'Get this kid out of here, fast. And you, get back. But nice and easy. Don't make any sudden movements.'

At first it seemed to them that the movement had come from one of the rotten logs, as though it was intending to crawl out of the sunlit woodpile and look for shade among the trees. It was only when they looked closer that they saw features which were atypical for a log: in particular, four pairs of thin legs with knobbly joints sticking up from the furrowed, speckled, segmented crayfish-like shell.

'Easy does it,' Geralt said quietly. 'Don't provoke it. Don't let its apparent sluggishness deceive you. It isn't aggressive, but it moves like lightning. If it feels threatened it may attack and there's no antidote for its venom.'

The creature slowly crawled onto a log. It looked at the humans and the dwarves, slowly turning its eyes, which were set on stalks. It was barely moving. It cleaned the ends of its legs, lifting them up one by one and carefully nibbling them with its impressive-looking, sharp mandibles.

'There was such an uproar,' Zoltan declared emotionlessly, appearing beside the Witcher, 'I thought it was something really worrying. Like a cavalryman from a Verdenian reserve troop. Or a military prosecutor. And what is it? Just an overgrown creepy-crawly. You have to admit, nature takes on some pretty curious forms.'

'Not any longer,' Geralt replied. 'The thing that's sitting there is an eyehead. A creature of Chaos. A dying, post-conjunction relic, if you know what I'm talking about.'

'Of course I do,' the dwarf said, looking him in the eyes. 'Although I'm not a witcher, nor an authority on Chaos and creatures like that. Well, I'm very curious to see what the Witcher will do with this post-conjunction relic. Or to be more precise, I'm wondering *how* the Witcher will do it. Will you use your sword or do you prefer my sihil?'

'Nice weapon,' Geralt said, glancing at the sword, which Zoltan

86

had drawn from its lacquered scabbard wrapped in tabby cat skins. 'But it won't be necessary.'

'Interesting,' Zoltan repeated. 'So are we just going to stand here looking at each other? Just wait until that relic feels threatened? Or should we withdraw and ask some Nilfgaardians for help? What do you suggest, monster slayer?'

'Fetch the ladle and the cauldron lid from the wagon.'

'What?'

'Don't question his authority, Zoltan,' Dandelion chipped in.

Percival Schuttenbach scurried off to the wagon and soon returned with the requested objects. The Witcher winked at the company and then began to beat the ladle against the lid with all his strength.

'Stop it! Stop it!' Zoltan Chivay screamed a moment later, covering his ears with his hands. 'You'll break the fucking ladle! The beast's run off! He's gone, for pox's sake!'

'Oh yes,' Percival said, delighted. 'Did you see him? On my life, he showed a clean pair of heels! Not that he has any!'

'The eyehead,' Geralt explained calmly, handing back the slightly dented kitchen utensils to the dwarves, 'has remarkably delicate, sensitive hearing. It doesn't have any ears, but hears, so to speak, with its entire body. In particular it can't bear metallic noises. It feels them as a pain . . .'

'Even in the arse,' Zoltan interrupted. 'I know, because it pained me too when you started whacking that lid. If the monster has more sensitive hearing than I do, he has my sympathy. Sure he won't be back? He won't rustle up some mates?'

'I don't imagine many of its mates are left on this earth. That specimen is certain not to be back in these parts for a long time. There's nothing to be afraid of.'

'I'm not going to talk about monsters,' the dwarf said, looking glum. 'But your concerto for brass instruments must have been heard as far away as the Skellige Islands, so it's possible some music lovers might be heading this way. And we'd better not be around when they come. Strike camp, boys! Hey, ladies, get clad and count up the children! We're moving out, and quickly!'

*

87

When they stopped for the night, Geralt decided to clear up a few issues. This time Zoltan Chivay hadn't sat down to play Barrel, so there was no difficulty leading him away to a secluded place for a frank, man-to-man conversation. He got straight to the point.

'Out with it. How do you know I'm a witcher?'

The dwarf winked at him and smiled slyly.

'I might boast about my perspicacity. I could say I noticed your eyes changing after dusk and in full sunlight. I could show that I'm a dwarf-of-the-world and that I've heard this and that about Geralt of Rivia. But the truth is much more banal. Don't scowl. You can keep things to yourself, but your friend the bard sings and jabbers; he never shuts his trap. That's how I know about your profession.'

Geralt refrained from asking another question. And rightly so.

'It's like this,' Zoltan continued. 'Dandelion told me everything. He must have sensed we value sincerity, and, after all, he didn't have to sense our friendly disposition to you, because we don't hide our dispositions. So in short: I know why you're in a hurry to go south. I know what important and urgent matters are taking you to Nilfgaard. I know who you're planning to seek. And not just from the poet's gossip. I lived in Cintra before the war and I heard tales of the Child of Destiny and the white-haired witcher to whom the child was granted.'

Geralt did not respond this time either.

'The rest,' the dwarf said, 'is just a question of observation. You let that crusty monstrosity go, even though you're a witcher and it's your professional duty to exterminate monsters like that. But the beast didn't do your Surprise any harm, so you spared it and just drove it away by banging on a cauldron lid. Because you're no longer a witcher; you're a valiant knight, who is hastening to rescue his kidnapped and oppressed maiden.

'Why don't you stop glaring at me,' he added, still not hearing an answer or an explanation. 'You're constantly sniffing out treachery; fearful of how this secret – now it's out – may turn against you. Don't fret. We're all going to the Ina, helping each other, supporting each other. The challenge you have in front of you is the same one we face: to survive and stay alive. In order for this noble mission to continue. Or live an ordinary life, but so as not to be ashamed at the hour of death. You think you've changed. That the world has changed. But look; the world's the same as it's always been. Quite the same. And you're the same as you used to be. Don't fret.

'But drop your idea about heading off alone,' Zoltan continued his monologue, unperturbed by the Witcher's silence, 'and about a solo journey south, through Brugge and Sodden to the Yaruga. You'll have to search for another way to Nilfgaard. If you want, I can advise you—'

'Don't bother,' Geralt said, rubbing his knee, which had been hurting incessantly for several days. 'Don't bother, Zoltan.'

He found Dandelion watching the Barrel-playing dwarves. He took the poet by the sleeve and led him off to the forest. Dandelion realised at once what it was all about; one glance at the Witcher's face was enough.

'Babbler,' Geralt said quietly. 'Windbag. Bigmouth. I ought to shove your tongue in a vice, you blockhead. Or put a bit between your teeth.'

The troubadour said nothing, but his expression was haughty.

'When news got out that I'd started to associate with you,' the Witcher continued, 'some sensible people were surprised by our friendship. It astonished them that I let you travel with me. They advised me to abandon you in a desert, to rob you, strangle you, throw you into a pit and bury you in dung. Indeed, I regret I didn't follow their advice.'

'Is it such a secret who you are and what you're planning to do?' Dandelion suddenly said, losing his temper. 'Are we to keep the truth from everybody and pretend all the time? Those dwarves . . . We're all one company now . . .'

'I don't have a company,' the Witcher snapped. 'I don't have one, and I don't want to have one. I don't need one. Do you get it?'

'Of course he gets it,' Milva said from behind him. 'And I get it too. You don't need anyone, Witcher. You show it often enough.'

'I'm not fighting a private war,' he said, turning around suddenly. 'I don't need a company of daredevils, because I'm not going to Nilfgaard to save the world or to bring down an evil empire. I'm going to get Ciri. And that's why I can go alone. Forgive me if that sounds unkind, but the rest of it doesn't concern me. And now leave me. I want to be alone.'

When he turned around a moment later, he discovered that only Dandelion had walked away.

'I had that dream again,' he said abruptly. 'Milva, I'm wasting time. I'm wasting time! She needs me. She needs help.'

'Talk,' she said softly. 'Get it out. No matter how frightening it is, get it out.'

'It wasn't frightening. In my dream . . . She was dancing. She was dancing in some smoky barn. And she was – hell's bells – happy. There was music playing, someone was yelling . . . The entire barn was shaking from shouting and music . . . And she was dancing, dancing, clicking her heels . . . And on the roof of that bloody barn, in the cold, night air . . . death was dancing too. Milva . . . Maria . . . She needs me.'

Milva turned her face away.

'Not just her,' she whispered. Quietly, so he wouldn't hear.

At the next stop, the Witcher demonstrated his interest in Zoltan's sword, the sihil, which he had glanced at during the adventure with the eyehead. Without hesitation, the dwarf unwrapped the weapon from its catskins and drew it from its lacquered scabbard.

The sword measured a little over three feet, but didn't weigh much more than two pounds. The blade, which was decorated along much of its length with mysterious runes, had a bluish hue and was as sharp as a razor. In the right hands, it could have been used to shave with. The twelve-inch hilt, wound around with criss-crossed strips of lizard skin, had a cylindrical brass cap instead of a spherical pommel and its crossguard was very small and finely crafted.

'A fine piece of work,' Geralt said, making a quick, hissing moulinet followed by a thrust from the left and then a lightning transition to a high seconde parry and then laterally into prime. 'Indeed, a nice bit of ironmongery.'

'Phew!' Percival Schuttenbach snorted. 'Bit of ironmongery! Take a better look at it, because you'll be calling it a horseradish root next.'

'I had a better sword once.'

'I don't dispute that,' Zoltan said, shrugging his shoulders. 'Because it was sure to have come from our forges. You witchers know how to wield a sword, but you don't make them yourselves. Swords like that are only forged by dwarves, in Mahakam under Mount Carbon.'

'Dwarves smelt the steel,' Percival added, 'and forge the laminated blades. But it's us, the gnomes, who do the finishing touches and the sharpening. In our workshops. Using our own, gnomish technology, as we once made our gwyhyrs, the best swords in the world.'

'The sword I wield now,' Geralt said, baring the blade, 'comes from the catacombs of Craag An in Brokilon. It was given to me by the dryads. It's a first-class weapon, but it's neither dwarven nor gnomish. It's an elven blade, at least one or maybe two hundred years old.'

'He doesn't know what he's talking about!' the gnome called, picking up the sword and running his fingers over it. 'The details are elven, I give you that. The hilt, crossguard and pommel. The etching, engraving, chasing and other decorative elements. But the blade was forged and sharpened in Mahakam. And it's true that it was made several centuries ago, because it's obvious that the steel is mediocre and the workmanship primitive. Now, hold Zoltan's sihil against it; do you see the difference?'

'Yes I do. And I have the impression mine's just as well made.'

The gnome snorted and waved a hand. Zoltan smiled superciliously.

'The blade,' he explained in a patronising voice, 'should cut, not make an impression, and it shouldn't be judged on first impressions either. The point is that your sword is a typical composition of steel and iron, while my sihil's blade was forged from a refined alloy containing graphite and borax . . .'

'It's a modern technique!' Percival burst out, a little excited, since the conversation was moving inevitably towards his field of expertise. 'The blade's construction and composition, numerous laminates in its soft core, edged with hard – not soft – steel . . .'

'Take it easy,' the dwarf said, reining him in. 'You won't make a metallurgist out of him, Schuttenbach, so don't bore him with details. I'll explain it in simple terms. It's incredibly difficult to sharpen good, hard, magnetite steel, Witcher. Why? Because it's hard! If you don't have the technology, as we dwarves once did not, and you humans still don't have, but you want a sharp sword, you forge soft steel edges, which are more malleable, onto a hardened core. Your Brokilonian sword is made using just such a simplified method. Modern dwarven blades are made the opposite way around: with a soft core and hard edges. The process is time-consuming and, as I said, demands advanced technology. But as a result you get a blade which will cut a batiste scarf tossed up in the air.'

'Is your sihil capable of a trick like that?'

'No' The dwarf smiled. 'The swords sharpened to that degree are few and far between, and not many of them ever left Mahakam. But I guarantee that the shell of that knobbly old crab wouldn't have put up much resistance against it. You could have sliced him up without breaking a sweat.'

The discussion about swords and metallurgy continued for some time. Geralt listened with interest, shared his own experiences, added some extra information, asked about this and that and then examined and tried out Zoltan's sihil. He had no idea that the following day he would have the opportunity to add practice to the theory he had acquired.

The first indication that humans were living in the area was the neatly stacked cord of firewood standing among woodchips and tree bark by the track, spotted by Percival Schuttenbach, who was walking at the head of the column.

Zoltan stopped the procession and sent the gnome ahead to scout. Percival vanished and after half an hour hurried back, excited and out of breath and gesticulating from a long way off. He reached them, but instead of giving his report, grabbed his long nose in his fingers and blew it powerfully, making a sound resembling a shepherd's horn.

'Don't frighten away the game,' Zoltan Chivay barked. 'And talk. What lies ahead of us?'

'A settlement,' the gnome panted, wiping his fingers on the tails of his many-pocketed kaftan. 'In a clearing. Three cottages, a barn, a few mud and straw huts . . . There's a dog running around in the farmyard and the chimney's smoking. Someone's preparing food there. Porridge. And made with milk.'

'You mean you went into the kitchen?' Dandelion laughed. 'And peered into the pot? How do you know it's porridge?'

The gnome looked at him with an air of superiority and Zoltan snarled angrily.

'Don't insult him, poet. He can sniff out grub a mile away. If he says it's porridge, it's porridge. Still, I don't like the sound of this.'

'Why's that? I like the sound of porridge. I'd be happy to try some.'

'Zoltan's right,' Milva said. 'And you keep quiet, Dandelion, because this isn't poetry. If the porridge is made with milk that means there's a cow. And a peasant who sees fires burning will take his cow and disappear into the forest. Why didn't this one? Let's duck into the forest and give it a wide berth. There's something fishy about this.'

'Not so fast, not so fast,' the dwarf muttered. 'There'll be plenty of time to flee. Perhaps the war's over. Perhaps the Temerian Army has finally moved out. What do we know, stuck in this forest? Perhaps the decisive battle's over, perhaps Nilfgaard's been repulsed, perhaps the front's already behind us, and the peasants are returning home with their cows. We ought to examine this and find out what's behind it. Figgis and Munro; you two stay here and keep your eyes peeled. We'll do a bit of reconnaissance. If it's safe, I'll make a call like a sparrow hawk.'

'Like a sparrow hawk?' said Munro Bruys, anxiously moving his chin. 'Since when did you know anything about mimicking bird calls, Zoltan?'

'That's the whole point. If you hear a strange, unrecognisable sound, you'll know it's me. Percival, lead on. Geralt, will you come with us?'

'We'll all go,' Dandelion said, dismounting. 'If it's a trap we'll be safer in a bigger group.'

'I'll leave you the Field Marshal,' Zoltan said, removing the parrot from his shoulder and passing him to Figgis Merluzzo. 'This ugly bird might suddenly start effing and blinding at the top of his voice and then our silent approach will go to fuck. Let's go.'

Percival quickly led them to the edge of the forest, into dense elder shrubs. The ground fell away slightly beyond the shrubs, where they saw a large pile of uprooted tree stumps. Beyond them there was a broad clearing. They peered out cautiously.

The gnome's account had been accurate. There really were three cottages, a barn and several sod-roofed mud and straw huts in the middle of the clearing. A huge puddle of muck glistened in the farm-yard. The buildings and a small, untended plot were surrounded by a low, partly fallen down fence, on the other side of which a scruffy dog was barking. Smoke was rising from the roof of one of the cot-tages, creeping lazily over the sunken turfs.

'Indeed,' Zoltan whispered, sniffing, 'that smoke smells good. Particularly since my nostrils are used to the stench of burnt-down houses. There are no horses or guards around, which is good, because I bore in mind that some rabble might be resting up and cooking a meal here. Mmm, I'd say it's safe.'

'I'll take a look,' volunteered Milva.

'No,' the dwarf protested. 'You look too much like a Squirrel. If they see you they might get frit, and humans can be unpredictable when they're startled. Yazon and Caleb will go. But keep your bow at the ready; you can cover them if needs be. Percival, leg it over to the others. You lot be prepared, in case we have to sound the retreat.'

Yazon Varda and Caleb Stratton cautiously left the thicket and headed towards the buildings. They walked slowly, looking around intently.

The dog smelled them right away, started barking furiously, then ran around the farmyard, not reacting to the dwarves' clucking and whistling. The door to the cottage opened. Milva raised her bow and drew back the bowstring in a single movement. And then immedi-ately slackened it.

A short, stout girl with long plaits came rushing out. She shouted something, waving her arms. Yazon Varda spread his arms and shouted something back. The girl continued to bawl something. They could hear the sound but were unable to make out what she was saying.

But the words must have reached Yazon and Caleb, who made an about-turn and hurried back towards the elder shrubs. Milva drew her bow again and swept around with the arrowhead, searching for a target.

'What the devil's going on?' Zoltan rasped. 'What's happening? What are they running away from? Milva?'

'Shut your trap,' the archer hissed, still taking aim at each cottage and hut in turn. But she couldn't find anyone to shoot. The girl with the plaits disappeared into her cottage and shut the door behind her.

The dwarves were sprinting as though the Grim Reaper was on their heels. Yazon yelled something – or possibly cursed. Dandelion suddenly blanched.

'He's saying . . . Oh, Gods!'

'What . . .' Zoltan broke off, for Yazon and Caleb had made it back, red in the face. 'What is it? Spit it out!'

'The plague . . .' Caleb gasped. 'Smallpox . . .'

'Did you touch anything?' Zoltan Chivay asked, stepping back nervously and almost knocking Dandelion over. 'Did you touch anything in the farmyard?'

'No . . . The dog wouldn't let us near . . .'

'May the fucking mutt be praised,' Zoltan said, raising his eyes heavenwards. 'May the Gods give it a long life and a heap of bones higher than Mount Carbon. That girl, the plump one, did she have blisters?'

'No. She's healthy. The infected ones are in the last cottage, her in-laws. And a lot of people have already died, she said. Blimey, Zoltan, the wind was blowing right towards us!'

'That's enough teeth chattering,' Milva said, lowering her bow. 'If you didn't touch any infected people, you've got nothing to worry about. If it's true what she says about the pox. Maybe the girl just wanted to scare you away.'

'No,' Yazon replied, still breathing heavily. 'There was a pit behind the hut . . . with bodies in it. The girl doesn't have the strength to bury the dead, so she throws them into the pit . . .'

'Well,' Zoltan said, sniffing. 'That's your porridge, Dandelion. But I've slightly lost my appetite for it. Let's get out of here; and fast.'

The dog in the farmyard began barking again.

'Get down,' the Witcher hissed, dropping into a crouch.

A group of horsemen came riding out from a gap in the trees on the other side of the clearing. Whistling and whooping, they circled the farmstead at a gallop and then burst into the yard. The riders were armed, but weren't in identical uniforms. Quite the contrary, in fact – they were all dressed differently and haphazardly, and their weaponry and tackle gave the impression of being assembled at random. And not in an armoury, but on a battlefield.

'Thirteen,' Percival Schuttenbach said, making a quick tally.

'Who are they?'

'Neither Nilfgaard, nor any other regulars,' came Zoltan's assessment. 'Not Scoia'tael. I think they're volunteers. A random mob.'

'Or marauders.'

The horsemen were yelling and cavorting around the farmyard. One of them hit the dog with a spear shaft and it bolted. The girl with the plaits ran outside, shouting. But this time her warning had no effect or wasn't taken seriously. One of the horseman galloped up, seized the girl by one of her plaits, pulled her away from the doorway and dragged her through the puddle of muck. The others jumped off their horses to assist the first, dragging the girl to the end of the farmyard. They tore her shift off her and threw her down onto a pile of rotten straw. The girl fought back ferociously, but she had no chance. Only one of the marauders didn't join in the fun; he guarded the horses, which were tied to the fence. The girl gave a long, piercing scream. Then a short, pained one. They heard nothing after that.

'Warriors!' Milva said, jumping to her feet. 'Fucking heroes!'

'They aren't afraid of the pox,' Yazon Varda said, shaking his head.

'Fear,' Dandelion muttered, 'is a human quality. There's nothing human in them any longer.'

'Apart from their innards,' Milva rasped, carefully nocking an arrow, 'which I shall now prick.'

'Thirteen,' Zoltan Chivay repeated gravely. 'And they're all mounted. You'll knock off one or two and the rest will have us surrounded. And anyway, it might be an advance party. The devil knows what kind of bigger force they belong to.'

'Do you expect me to stand by and watch?'

'No,' Geralt said, straightening his headband and the sword on his back. 'I've had enough of standing by and watching. I'm fed up with my own helplessness. But first we have to stop them from getting away. See the one holding the horses? When I get there, knock him out of the saddle. And if you can, take out another. But only when I get down there.'

'That leaves eleven,' the archer said, turning to face him.

'I can count.'

'You've forgotten about the smallpox,' Zoltan Chivay muttered. 'If you go down there, you'll come back infected . . . Bollocks to that, Witcher! You're putting us all at risk . . . For fuck's sake, *she's* not the girl you're looking for!'

'Shut up, Zoltan. Go back to the wagon and hide in the forest.'

'I'm coming with you,' Milva declared hoarsely.

'No. Cover me from here, you'll be helping more if you do that.'

'What about me?' Dandelion asked. 'What should I do?'

'The same as usual. Nothing.'

'You're insane . . .' Zoltan snarled. 'Taking on the entire band? What's got into you? Want to play the hero, rescuing fair maidens?'

'Shut up.'

'Go to hell! No, wait. Leave your sword. There's a whole bunch of them, so it'd be better if you didn't have to swing twice. Take my sihil. One blow is enough.'

The Witcher took the dwarf's weapon without a word or a moment's hesitation. He pointed out the marauder guarding the horses one more time. And then hopped over the tree stumps and moved quickly towards the cottages.

The sun was shining. Grasshoppers scattered in front of him.

The man guarding the horses saw him and pulled a spear from its place by his saddle. He had very long, unkempt hair, falling onto a torn hauberk, patched up with rusty wire. He was wearing brand-new – clearly stolen – boots with shiny buckles.

The guard yelled and another marauder appeared from behind the fence. He was carrying a sword slung from a belt around his neck and was just buttoning his britches. Geralt was quite close by now. He could hear the guffawing of the men amusing themselves with the girl on the pile of straw. He took some deep breaths and each one intensified his blood lust. He could have calmed himself down, but didn't want to. He wanted to have some fun himself.

'And who might you be? Stop!' the long-haired man shouted, hefting the spear in his hand. 'What do you want here?'

'I've done enough standing and watching.'

'Whaaat?'

'Does the name Ciri mean anything to you?'

'I'll—'

The marauder was unable to finish his sentence. A grey-fletched arrow hit him in the middle of his chest and threw him from the saddle. Before he hit the ground, Geralt could hear the next arrow whistling. The second soldier caught the arrowhead in the abdomen, low, right between the hands buttoning up his fly. He howled like an animal, bent double and lurched back against the fence, knocking over and breaking some of the pickets.

Before the others had managed to come to their senses and pick up their weapons, the Witcher was among them. The dwarven blade glittered and sang. There was a savage craving for blood in the song of the feather-light, razor-sharp steel. The bodies and limbs offered almost no resistance. Blood splashed onto his face; he had no time to wipe it off.

Even if the marauders were thinking about putting up a fight, the sight of falling corpses and blood gushing in streams effectively discouraged them. One of them, who had his trousers around his knees since he hadn't even had time to pull them up, was slashed in the carotid artery and tumbled onto his back, comically swinging his still unsatisfied manhood. The second, nothing but a stripling, covered his head with both hands, which the sihil severed at the

98

wrists. The remaining men took flight, dispersing in various directions. The Witcher pursued them, softly cursing the pain that was once again pulsing through his knee. He hoped the leg wouldn't buckle under him.

He managed to pin two of them against the fence. They tried to defend themselves by holding up their swords. Paralysed by terror, their defence was woeful. The Witcher's face was once again spattered with blood from arteries slashed open by the dwarven blade. But the remaining men made use of the time and managed to get away; they were already mounted. One of then fell, however, hit by an arrow, wriggling and squirming like a fish emptied from a net. The last two spurred their horses into a gallop. But only one of them managed to escape, because Zoltan Chivay had suddenly appeared in the farmyard. The dwarf swung his axe around his head and threw it, hitting one of the fleeing men in the centre of the back. The marauder screamed and tumbled from the saddle, legs kicking. The last one pressed himself tight to his horse's neck, cleared the pit full of dead bodies and galloped towards the gap in the trees.

'Milva!' the Witcher and the dwarf both yelled.

The archer was already running towards them. Now she stopped, frozen, with legs apart. She let her nocked bow fall and then began to lift it up slowly, higher and higher. They didn't hear the twang of the bowstring, neither did Milva change her position or even twitch. They only saw the arrow when it dipped and hurtled downwards. The horseman lurched sideways out of the saddle, the feathered shaft protruding from a shoulder. But he didn't fall. He straightened up and with a cry urged his horse into a faster gallop.

'What a bow,' Zoltan Chivay grunted in awe. 'What a shot!'

'What a shot, my arse,' the Witcher said, wiping blood from his face. 'The whoreson's got away and he'll be back with a bunch of his mates.'

'She hit him! And it must have been two hundred paces!'

'She could have aimed at the horse.'

'The horse isn't guilty of anything,' Milva panted with anger, walking over to them. She spat and watched the horseman disappear into the forest. 'I missed the good-for-nothing, because I was a mite out of breath . . . Ugh, you rat, running away with my arrow! I hope it brings you bad luck!'

The neighing of a horse could be heard from the gap in the trees, and immediately afterwards the dreadful cry of a man being killed.

'Ho, ho!' Zoltan said, looking at the archer in awe. 'He didn't get very far! Your arrows are damned effective! Poisoned? Or enchanted perhaps? Because even if the good-for-nothing had caught the small-pox, the plague wouldn't have taken its toll so quickly!'

'It wasn't me,' Milva said, looking knowingly at the Witcher. 'Nor the smallpox. But I think I know who it was.'

'I think I do too,' the dwarf said, chewing his moustache with a canny smile on his face. 'I've noticed you keep looking back, and I know someone's secretly following us. On a chestnut colt. I don't know who he is, but since it doesn't bother you . . . It's none of my business.'

'Particularly since a rearguard can have its uses,' Milva said, looking at Geralt meaningfully. 'Are you certain that Cahir's your enemy?'

The Witcher didn't reply. He gave Zoltan his sword back.

'Thanks. It cuts nicely.'

'In the right hands,' the dwarf said, grinning. 'I've heard tales about witchers, but to fell eight in less than two minutes . . .'

'It's nothing to brag about. They didn't know how to defend themselves.'

The girl with the plaits raised herself onto her hands and knees, stood up, staggered, and then tried ineffectually to pull down her torn shift with trembling hands. The Witcher was astonished to see that she was in no way similar to Ciri, when a moment earlier he would have sworn they were twins. The girl wiped her face with an uncoordinated movement, and moved unsteadily towards the cottage. Straight through the puddle of muck.

'Hey, wait,' Milva called. 'Hey, you . . . Need any help? Hey!'

The girl didn't even look towards her. She stumbled over the threshold, almost falling, then grabbed the door jamb. And slammed the door behind her.

'Human gratitude knows no boundaries,' the dwarf commented. Milva jerked around, her face hardened.

'What does she have to be grateful for?'

'Exactly,' the Witcher added. 'What for?'

'For the marauders' horses,' Zoltan said, not lowering his gaze. 'She can slaughter them for their meat; she won't have to kill the cow. She's clearly resistant to smallpox and now she doesn't have to fear hunger. She'll survive. And in a few days, when she gathers her thoughts, she'll understand that thanks to you she avoided a longer frolic and these cottages being burnt to the ground. Let's get out of here before the plague blows our way . . . Hey, Witcher, where are you going? To get a token of gratitude?'

'To get a pair of boots,' Geralt said coldly, stooping down over the long-haired marauder, whose dead eyes stared heavenwards. 'These look right for me.'

They ate horsemeat for several days. The boots with the shiny buckles were quite comfortable. The Nilfgaardian called Cahir was still riding in their tracks on his chestnut colt, but the Witcher had stopped looking back.

He had finally fathomed the arcana of Barrel and even played a hand with the dwarves. He lost.

They didn't speak about the incident in the forest clearing. There was nothing to say.

Mandrake, or Love Apple, is a class of plant from the Mandragora *or nightshade family, a group including herbaceous, stemless plants with parsnip-like roots, in which a similarity to the human form may be observed; the leaves are arranged in a rosette.* **M.** *autumnalis or officinalis, is cultivated on a small scale in Vicovaro, Rowan and Ymlac, rarely found in the wild. Its berries, which are green and later turn yellow, are eaten with vinegar and pepper, while its leaves are consumed raw. The root of the* **m.**, *which is a valued ingredient in medicine and herb lore, long ago had great import in superstitions, particularly among the Nordlings; human effigies (called alruniks or alraunes) were carved from it and kept in homes as revered talismans. They were believed to offer protection from illnesses, to bring good fortune during trials, and to ensure fertility and uncomplicated births. The effigies were clad in dresses which were changed at each new moon.* **M.** *roots were bought and sold, with prices reaching as much as sixty florins. Bryony roots (q.v.) were used as substitutes. According to superstition,* **m.** *was used for making spells, magical philtres and poisons. This belief returned during the period of the witch hunts. The charge of the criminal use of* **m.** *was made, for example, during the trial of Lucretia Vigo (q.v.). The legendary Philippa Alhard (q.v.) was also said to have used* **m.** *as a poison.*

Effenberg and Talbot, *Encyclopaedia Maxima Mundi,*
Volume IX

CHAPTER THREE

The Old Road had changed somewhat since the last time the Witcher had travelled along it. Once a level highway paved with slabs of basalt, built by elves and dwarves centuries before, it had now become a potholed ruin. In some places the holes were so deep that they resembled small quarries. The pace of the march dropped since the dwarves' wagon wove between the potholes with extreme difficulty, frequently becoming stuck.

Zoltan Chivay knew the reason for the road's desperate state of disrepair. Following the last war with Nilfgaard, he explained, the need for building materials had increased tremendously. People had recalled that the Old Road was an almost inexhaustible source of dressed stone. And since the neglected road, built in the middle of nowhere and leading nowhere, had long ago lost its importance for transport and served few people, it was vandalised without mercy or restraint.

'Your great cities,' the dwarf complained, accompanied by the parrot's screeched expletives, 'were without exception built on dwarven and elven foundations. You built your own foundations for your smaller castles and towns, but you still use our stones for the walls. And yet you never stop repeating that it's thanks to you – humans – that the world progresses and develops.'

Geralt did not comment.

'But you don't even know how to destroy things wisely,' Zoltan griped, ordering yet another attempt to pull a wheel out of a hole. 'Why can't you remove the stones gradually, from the edges of the road? You're like children! Instead of eating a doughnut systematically, you gouge the jam out with a finger and then throw away the rest because it's not sweet any more.'

Geralt explained patiently that political geography was to blame

105

for everything. The Old Road's western end lay in Brugge, the eastern end in Temeria and the centre in Sodden, so each kingdom destroyed its own section at its own discretion. In response, Zoltan obscenely stated where he'd happily shove all the kings and listed some imaginative indecencies he would commit regarding their politics, while Field Marshal Windbag added his own contribution to the subject of the kings' mothers.

The further they went, the worse it became. Zoltan's comparison with a jam doughnut turned out to be less than apt; the road was coming to resemble a suet pudding with all the raisins gouged out. It looked as though the inevitable moment was approaching when the wagon would shatter or become totally and irreversibly stuck. They were saved, however, by the same thing that had destroyed the road. They happened upon a track heading towards the southeast, worn down and compacted by the heavy wagons which had been used to transport the pillaged stone. Zoltan brightened up, for he recognised that the track led unerringly to one of the forts on the Ina, on whose bank he was hoping to meet the Temerian Army. The dwarf solemnly believed that, as during the previous war, a crushing counter-attack by the northern kingdoms would be launched from Sodden on the far side of the Ina, following which the survivors of Nilfgaard's thoroughly decimated forces would scurry back across the Yaruga.

And indeed, the change in their trek's direction once again brought them closer to the war. During the night a great light suddenly flared up in front of them, while during the day they saw columns of smoke marking the horizon to the south and the east. Since they were still uncertain who was attacking and burning and who was being attacked and burnt they proceeded cautiously, sending Percival Schuttenbach far ahead to reconnoitre.

They were astonished one morning to be overtaken by a riderless horse, the chestnut colt. The green saddlecloth embroidered with Nilfgaardian symbols was stained with dark streaks of blood. There was no way of knowing if it was the blood of the horseman who had been killed near the hawker's wagon or if it had been spilt later, when the horse had acquired a new owner.

'Well, that takes care of the problem,' Milva said, glancing at Geralt. 'If it ever really was a problem.'

'The biggest problem is we don't know who knocked the rider from the saddle,' Zoltan muttered. 'And whether that someone is following our trail and the trail of our erstwhile, unusual rearguard.'

'He was a Nilfgaardian,' Geralt said between clenched teeth. 'He spoke almost without an accent, but runaway peasants could have recognised it . . .'

Milva turned to face him.

'You ought to have finished him off, Witcher,' she said softly. 'He would have had a kinder death.'

'He got out of that coffin,' Dandelion said, nodding, looking meaningfully at Geralt, 'just to rot in some ditch.'

And that was the epitaph for Cahir, son of Ceallach, the Nilfgaardian who insisted he wasn't a Nilfgaardian. He was not talked about any longer. Since Geralt – in spite of repeated threats – seemed to be in no hurry to part with the skittish Roach, Zoltan Chivay mounted the chestnut. The dwarf's feet didn't reach the stirrups, but the colt was mild-mannered and let himself be ridden.

During the night the horizon was bright with the glow of fires and during the day ribbons of smoke rose into the sky, soiling the blue. They soon came upon some burnt-out buildings, with flames still creeping over the charred beams and ridges. Alongside the smouldering timbers sat eight ragged figures and five dogs, all busily gnawing the remains of the flesh from a bloated, partly charred horse carcass. At the sight of the dwarves the feasters fled in a panic. Only one man and one dog remained, who no threats were capable of tearing away from the carrion on the arched spine and ribs. Zoltan and Percival tried to question the man, but learned nothing. He only whimpered, trembled, tucked his head into his shoulders and choked on the scraps torn from the bones. The dog snarled and bared its teeth up to its gums. The horse's carcass stank repulsively.

They took a risk and didn't leave the road, and soon reached the next smouldering remains. A sizeable village had been burnt down and a skirmish must have taken place nearby, because they saw a fresh burial mound directly behind the smoking ruins. And at a certain distance beyond the mound a huge oak tree stood by the crossroads. The tree was hung with acorns.

And human corpses.

'We ought to take a look,' Zoltan Chivay decided, putting an end to the discussion about the risks and the danger. 'Let's go closer.'

'Why the bloody hell,' Dandelion asked, losing his temper, 'do you want to look at those corpses, Zoltan? To despoil them? I can see from here they don't even have boots.'

'Fool. It's not their boots I'm interested in but the military situation. I want to know of the developments in the theatre of war. What's so funny? You're just a poet, and you don't know what strategy is.'

'You're in for a surprise. I do.'

'Nonsense. You wouldn't know strategy from your own arse, even if your life depended on it.'

'Indeed, I wouldn't. I'll leave half-arsed strategies to dwarves. The same applies to strategies dangling from oak trees.'

Zoltan dismissed him with a wave and tramped over to the tree. Dandelion, who had never been able to rein in his curiosity, urged Pegasus on and trotted after him. A moment later Geralt decided to follow them. And then noticed that Milva was riding behind him.

The crows feeding on the carcasses took flight, cawing and flapping their wings noisily. Some of them flew off towards the forest, while others merely alighted on the mighty tree's higher branches, intently observing Field Marshal Windbag, who was coarsely defaming their mothers from the dwarf's shoulder.

The first of the seven hanged humans had a sign on his chest reading: 'Traitor'. The second was described as a 'Collaborator', the third as an 'Elven Nark' and the fourth as a 'Deserter'. The fifth was a woman in a torn and bloodied shift, described as a 'Nilfgaardian Whore'. Two of the corpses weren't bearing signs, which suggested at least some of the victims had been hanged by chance.

'Look,' Zoltan Chivay said cheerfully, pointing at the signs. 'Our army passed by this way. Our brave boys have taken the initiative

108

and repulsed the enemy. And they had time, as we can see, for relaxation and wartime entertainment.'

'And what does that mean for us?'

'That the front has moved and the Temerian Army are between us and the Nilfgaardians. We're safe.'

'And the smoke ahead of us?'

'That's our boys,' the dwarf declared confidently. 'They're burning down villages where Squirrels were given rest or vittles. We're behind the front line now, I'm telling you. The southern way heads from the crossroads to Armeria, a fortress lying in a fork of the Chotla and the Ina. The road looks decent, we can take it. We needn't be afraid of Nilfgaardians now.'

'Where there's smoke, there's fire,' Milva said. 'And where there's fire you can get your fingers burnt. I reckon it's stupid to head towards the flames. It's also stupid to travel along a road, when the cavalry could be on us in an instant. Let's disappear into the trees.'

'The Temerians or an army from Sodden passed through here,' the dwarf insisted. 'We're behind the front line. We can march along the highway without fear; if we come across an army it'll be ours.'

'Risky,' said the archer, shaking her head. 'If you're such an old hand, Zoltan, you must know that Nilfgaard usually sends advance parties a long way ahead. Perhaps the Temerians were here. But we have no idea what's in front of us. The sky's black from smoke to the south. That fortress of yours in Armeria is probably burning right now. Which means we aren't behind the front line, but right on it. We may run into the army, marauders, leaderless bands of rogues, or Squirrels. Let's head for the Chotla, but along forest tracks.'

'She's right,' Dandelion concurred. 'I don't like the look of that smoke either. And even if Temeria is on the offensive, there may still be advance Nilfgaardian squadrons in front of us. The Nilfgaardians are fond of long-distance raids. They attack the rear lines, link up with the Scoia'tael, wreak havoc and ride back. I remember what happened in Upper Sodden during the last war. I'm also in favour of travelling through the forest. We have nothing to fear there.'

'I wouldn't be so sure,' Geralt said, pointing to the last corpse who, although he was dangling high up, had bloody stumps instead of feet. They looked like they had been raked by talons until all that was left was protruding bones. 'Look. That's the work of ghouls.'

'Ghouls?' Zoltan Chivay said, retreating and spitting on the ground. 'Flesh-eaters?'

'Naturally. We have to beware in the forest at night.'

'Fuuuckiiin' 'ell!' Field Marshal Windbag screeched.

'You took the words right out of my mouth, birdie,' Zoltan Chivay said, frowning. 'Well, we're in a pretty pickle. What's it to be, then? Into the forest, where there's ghouls, or along the road, where there's armies and marauders?'

'Into the forest,' Milva said with conviction. 'The denser the better. I prefer ghouls to humans.'

They marched through the forest, at first cautious, on edge, reacting with alarm to every rustle in the undergrowth. Soon, however, they regained their poise, their good humour and their previous speed. They didn't see any ghouls, or the slightest trace of their presence. Zoltan joked that spectres and any other demons must have heard about the approaching armies, and if the fiends had happened to see the marauders and Verdenian volunteers in action, then – seized with terror – they would have hidden in their most remote and inaccessible lairs, where they were now cowering and trembling, fangs chattering.

'And they're guarding the she-ghouls, their wives and their daughters,' Milva snapped. 'The monsters know that a soldier on the march won't even pass up a sheep. And if you hung a woman's shift on a willow tree, a knothole would be enough for those heroes.' She looked pointedly at the women and children from Kernow, who were still with the group.

Dandelion, who had been full of vigour and good humour for quite some time, tuned his lute and began to compose a fitting couplet about willows, knotholes and lascivious warriors, and the dwarves and the parrot outdid each other in supplying ideas for rhymes.

*

'O,' Zoltan stated.

'What? Where?' Dandelion asked, standing up in his stirrups and looking down into the ravine in the direction the dwarf was pointing. 'I can't see anything!'

'O.'

'Don't drivel like your parrot! What do you mean "oh"?'

'It's a stream,' Zoltan calmly explained. 'A right-bank tributary of the Chotla. It's called the O.'

'Ey . . .'

'Not a bit of it!' Percival Schuttenbach laughed. 'The A joins the Chotla upstream, some way from here. That's the O, not the A.'

The ravine, along the bottom of which flowed the stream with the uncomplicated name, was overgrown with nettles taller than the marching dwarves, smelled intensively of mint and rotten wood and resounded with the unremitting croaking of frogs. It also had steep sides, which turned out to be fatal. Vera Loewenhaupt's wagon, which from the beginning of the journey had valiantly born the adversities of fate and overcome every obstacle, lost out in its clash with the stream by the name of 'O'. It slipped from the hands of the dwarves leading it downwards, bounced on down to the very bottom of the ravine and was smashed to matchwood.

''Kin' . . . 'ell!' Field Marshal Windbag squawked, a counterpoint to the massed cry of Zoltan and his company.

'To tell the truth,' Dandelion concluded, scrutinising the remains of the vehicle and the scattered possessions, 'perhaps it's for the best. That bloody wagon of yours only slowed down the march. There were constant problems with it. Look at it realistically, Zoltan. We were just lucky that no one was following us. If we'd had to suddenly run for it we'd have had to abandon the wagon along with all of your belongings, which we can now at least salvage.'

The dwarf seethed and grunted angrily into his beard, but Percival Schuttenbach unexpectedly backed up the troubadour. The support, as the Witcher observed, was accompanied by several conspiratorial winks. The winks were meant to be surreptitious, but the lively expression of the gnome's little face revealed everything.

'The poet's right,' Percival repeated, contorting his face and winking. 'We're a muddy stone's throw from the Chotla and the Ina. Fen Carn's in front of us; not a road to be seen. It would have been arduous with a wagon. And should we meet the Temerian Army by the Ina, with our load . . . we might be in trouble.'

Zoltan pondered this, sniffing.

'Very well,' he said finally, looking at the remains of the wagon being washed by the O's lazy current. 'We'll split up. Munro, Figgis, Yazon and Caleb will stay here. The rest of us will continue on our way. We'll have to saddle the horses with our sacks of vittles and small tackle. Munro, do you know what to do? Got spades?'

'Yes.'

'Just don't leave the merest trace! And mark the spot well and remember it!'

'Rest assured.'

'You'll catch up with us easily,' Zoltan said, throwing his rucksack and sihil over his shoulder and adjusting the battle-axe in his belt. 'We'll be heading down the O and then along the Chotla to the Ina. Farewell.'

'I wonder,' Milva mumbled to Geralt when the depleted unit had set off, sent on its way by the waving of the four dwarves who were remaining behind, 'I wonder what they have in those chests that needs burying in secret.'

'It's not our business.'

'I can't imagine,' Dandelion said, *sotto voce*, cautiously steering Pegasus between the fallen trees, 'that there were spare trousers in those chests. They're pinning their hopes on that load. I talked with them enough to work out how the land lies and what might be concealed in those coffers.'

'And what might be concealed in them, in your opinion?'

'Their future,' the poet said, looking around to check no one could hear. 'Percival's a stone polisher and cutter by trade, and wants to open his own workshop. Figgis and Yazon are smiths, they've been talking about a forge. Caleb Stratton plans to marry, but his fiancée's parents have already driven him away once as a penniless bum. And Zoltan . . .'

'That's enough, Dandelion. You're gossiping like an old woman. No offence, Milva.'

'None taken.'

The trees thinned out beyond the stream and the dark, boggy strip of ancient woodland. They rode into a clearing with low birch woods and dry meadows. In spite of that they made slow progress. Following the example of Milva, who right away had lifted the freckled girl with the plaits onto her saddle, Dandelion also put a child on Pegasus, while Zoltan put a couple on his chestnut colt and walked alongside, holding the reins. But the pace didn't increase, since the women from Kernow were unable to keep up.

It was almost evening when, after nearly an hour of roaming through ravines and gorges, Zoltan Chivay stopped, exchanged a few words with Percival Schuttenbach, and then turned to the rest of the company.

'Don't yell and don't laugh at me,' he said, 'but I reckon we're lost. I don't bloody know where we are or which way to go.'

'Don't talk drivel,' Dandelion said, irritated. 'What do you mean you don't know? After all, we're following the course of the river. And down there in the ravine is your O. Right?'

'Right. But look which way it's flowing.'

'Oh bugger. That's impossible!'

'No, it's not,' Milva said gloomily, patiently pulling dry leaves and pine needles from the hair of the freckled girl who was riding in front of her. 'We're lost among the ravines. The stream twists and turns. We're on a meander.'

'But it's still the O,' Dandelion insisted. 'If we follow the river, we can't get lost. Little rivers are known to meander, I admit, but ultimately they all invariably flow into something bigger. That is the way of the world.'

'Don't play the smart-arse, singer,' Zoltan said, wrinkling his nose. 'And shut your trap. Can't you see I'm thinking?'

'No. There's nothing to suggest it. I repeat, let's keep to the course of the stream, and then . . .'

'That'll do,' Milva snapped. 'You're a townie. Your world is bounded by walls. Perhaps your worldly wisdom is of some use there. Take a look around! The valley's furrowed by ravines with steep, overgrown banks. How do you think we'll follow the course of the stream? Down the side of a gorge into thickets and bogs, up the other side and down again and up again, pulling our horses by the reins? After two ravines you'll be so short of breath you'll be flat on your back halfway up a slope. We're leading women and children, Dandelion. And the sun'll be setting directly.'

'I noticed. Very well, I'll keep quiet. And listen to what the experienced forest trackers come up with.'

Zoltan Chivay cuffed the cursing parrot around the head, twisted a tuft of his beard around a finger and tugged it in anger.

'Percival?'

'We know the rough direction,' the gnome said, squinting up at the sun, which was suspended just above the treetops. 'So the first conception is this: blow the stream, turn back, leave these ravines for dry land and go through Fen Carn, between the rivers, all the way to the Chotla.'

'And the second conception?'

'The O's shallow. Even though it's carrying more water than usual after the recent rains, it can be forded. We'll cut off the meanders by wading through the stream each time it blocks our way. By holding a course according to the sun, we'll come right out at the fork of the Chotla and the Ina.'

'No,' the Witcher suddenly broke in. 'I suggest we drop the second idea right away. Let's not even think about it. On the far bank we'll end up in one of the Mealybug Moors sooner or later. It's a vile place, and I strongly advise we keep well away from it.'

'Do you know these parts, then? Ever been there before? Do you know how we can get out of here?'

The Witcher remained silent for a while.

'I've only been there once,' he said, wiping his forehead. 'Three years ago. But I entered from the other side. I was heading for Brugge and wanted to take a short cut. How I got out I don't remember. I was carried out on a wagon half-dead.'

The dwarf looked at him for a while, but asked no more questions.

114

They returned in silence. The women from Kernow had difficulty walking. They were stumbling and using sticks for support, but none of them uttered a word of complaint. Milva rode alongside the Witcher, holding up the girl with the plaits, who was asleep on the saddle in front of her.

'I think,' she suddenly began, 'that you got carved up in that wilderness, three years ago. By some monster, I understand. You have a dangerous job, Geralt.'

'I don't deny it.'

'I remember what happened then,' Dandelion boasted from behind. 'You were wounded, some merchant got you out and then you found Ciri in Riverdell. Yennefer told me about it.'

At the sound of that name Milva smiled faintly. It did not escape Geralt's notice. He decided to give Dandelion a good dressing down at the next camp for his untrammelled chatter. Knowing the poet, he couldn't count on any results, particularly since Dandelion had probably already blabbed everything he knew.

'Perhaps it wasn't such a good idea,' said the archer after a while, 'that we didn't cross to the far bank, towards the wilderness. If you found the girl then . . . The elves say that sometimes lightning can strike twice. They call it . . . Bugger, I've forgotten. The noose of fate?'

'The loop,' he corrected her. 'The loop of fate.'

'Uurgh!' Dandelion said, grimacing. 'Can't you stop talking about nooses and loops? A she-elf once divined that I would say farewell to this vale of tears on the scaffold, with the help of the deathsman. Admittedly I don't believe in that type of tawdry fortune-telling, but a few days ago I dreamed I was being hanged. I awoke in a muck sweat, unable to swallow or catch my breath. So I listen with reluctance to discussions about gibbets.'

'I'm not talking to you, I'm talking to the Witcher,' Milva riposted. 'So don't flap your ears and nothing horrible will fall into them. Well then, Geralt? What have you got to say about that loop of fate? If we go to the wilderness, perhaps time will repeat itself.'

'That's why it's good we've turned back,' he replied brusquely. 'I don't have the slightest desire to repeat that nightmare.'

'There's no two ways about it.' Zoltan nodded, looking around. 'You've led us to a pretty charming place, Percival.'

'Fen Carn,' the gnome muttered, scratching the tip of his long nose. 'Meadow of the Barrows . . . I've always wondered how it got its name . . .'

'Now you know.'

The broad valley in front of them was already shrouded in evening mist from which, as far as the eye could see, protruded thousands of burial mounds and moss-covered monoliths. Some of the boulders were ordinary, shapeless lumps of stone. Others, smoothly hewn, had been sculpted into obelisks and menhirs. Still others, standing closer to the centre of this stone forest, were formed into dolmens, cairns and cromlechs, in a way that ruled out any natural processes.

'Indeed,' the dwarf repeated, 'a charming place to spend the night. An elven cemetery. If my memory doesn't fail me, Witcher, some time ago you mentioned ghouls. Well, you ought to know, I can sense them among these kurgans. I bet there's everything here. Ghouls, graveirs, spectres, wights, elven spirits, wraiths, apparitions; the works. They're hunkered down there and do you know what they're whispering? "We won't have to go looking for supper, because it's come right to us."'

'Perhaps we ought to go back,' Dandelion suggested in a whisper. 'Perhaps we should get out of here, while there's still some light.'

'That's what I think too.'

'The womenfolk can't go any further,' Milva said angrily. 'The kids are ready to drop. The horses have stopped. You were the one driving us on, Zoltan. "Let's keep going, just another half a mile," you kept repeating. "Just another furlong," you said. And now what? Two more furlongs back the way we came? Crap. Cemetery or no cemetery, we're stopping for the night, the first place we find.'

'That's right,' the Witcher said in support, dismounting. 'Don't panic. Not every necropolis is crawling with monsters and apparitions. I've never been to Fen Carn before, but if it were really dangerous I'd have heard about it.'

No one, not even Field Marshal Windbag, commented. The

women from Kernow retrieved their children and sat down in a tight group, silent and visibly frightened. Percival and Dandelion tethered the horses and let them graze on the lush grass. Geralt, Zoltan and Milva approached the edge of the meadow, to look at the burial ground drowning in the fog and the gathering gloom.

'To cap it all, the moon's completely full,' the dwarf muttered. 'Oh dear, there'll be a ghastly feast tonight, I can feel it, oh, the demons will make our lives miserable . . . But what's that glow to the south? A fire?'

'What else? Of course it is,' the Witcher confirmed. 'Someone's torched someone else's roof over their head again. Know what, Zoltan? I think I feel safer here in Fen Carn.'

'I'll feel like that too, but only when the sun comes up. As long as the ghouls let us see out the night.'

Milva rummaged in her saddlebag and took out something shiny.

'A silver arrowhead,' she said. 'Kept for just such an occasion. It cost me five crowns at the market. That ought to kill a ghoul, right, Witcher?'

'I don't think there are any ghouls here.'

'You said yourself,' Zoltan snapped, 'that ghouls had been chewing that corpse on the oak tree. And where there's a cemetery, there are ghouls.'

'Not always.'

'I'll take your word for it. You're a witcher, a specialist; so you'll defend us, I hope. You chopped up those marauders pretty smartly . . . Is it harder fighting ghouls than marauders?'

'Incomparably. I said stop panicking.'

'And will it be any good for a vampire?' Milva asked, screwing the silver arrowhead onto a shaft and checking it for sharpness with her thumb. 'Or a spectre?'

'It may be.'

'An ancient dwarven incantation in ancient dwarven runes is engraved on my sihil,' Zoltan growled, drawing his sword, 'If just one ghoul approaches at a blade's length, it won't forget me. Right here, look.'

'Ah,' Dandelion, who had just joined them, said with interest. 'So

117

those are some of the famous secret runes of the dwarves. What does the engraving say?'

'"Confusion to the whores' sons!"'

'Something moved among the stones,' Percival Schuttenbach suddenly yelled. 'It's a ghoul, it's a ghoul!'

'Where?'

'Over there! It's hid itself among the boulders!'

'One?'

'I saw one!'

'He must be seriously hungry, since he's trying to get his teeth into us before nightfall,' the dwarf said, spitting on his hands and gripping the hilt of his sihil tightly. 'Ha! He'll soon find out gluttony will be his ruin! Milva, you stick an arrow in his arse and I'll cut his gizzard open!'

'I can't see anything there,' Milva hissed, with the fletchings already touching her chin. 'Not a single weed between the stones is trembling. Sure you weren't seeing things, gnome?'

'Not a chance,' Percival protested. 'Do you see that boulder that looks like a broken table? The ghoul hid behind it.'

'You lot stay here,' Geralt said, quickly drawing his sword from the scabbard on his back. 'Guard the womenfolk and keep an eye on the horses. If the ghouls attack, the animals will panic. I'll go and find out what it was.'

'You aren't going by yourself,' Zoltan firmly stated. 'Back there in the clearing I let you go alone. I chickened out because of the smallpox. And two nights running I haven't slept for shame. Never again! Percival, where are you off to? To the rear? You claim to have seen the phantom, so now you're going in the vanguard. Don't be afeared, I'm coming with you.'

They headed off cautiously between the barrows, trying not to disturb the weeds – which were knee-high to Geralt and waist-high to the dwarf and the gnome. As they approached the dolmen that Percival had pointed out they artfully split up, cutting off the ghoul's potential escape route. But the strategy turned out to be unnecessary. As Geralt had expected, his witcher medallion didn't even quiver; betrayed no sign of anything monstrous nearby.

'There's no one here,' Zoltan confirmed, looking around. 'Not a soul. You must have imagined it, Percival. It's a false alarm. You put the wind up us for no reason. You truly deserve my boot up your arse for that.'

'I saw it!' the gnome said indignantly. 'I saw it hopping about among the stones! It was skinny and dressed all in black like a tax collector . . .'

'Be quiet, you foolish gnome, or I'll . . .'

'What's that strange odour?' Geralt suddenly asked. 'Can you smell it?'

'Indeed,' the dwarf said, nose extended like a pointer. 'What a pong.'

'Herbs,' Percival said, sniffling with his sensitive, two-inch-long nose. 'Wormwood, basil, sage, aniseed . . . Cinnamon? What the blazes?'

'What do ghouls smell of, Geralt?'

'Rotting corpses,' the Witcher said, taking a quick look around and searching for footprints in the grass. Then with a few swift steps he returned to the sunken dolmen and tapped gently against the stone with the flat of his sword.

'Get out,' he said through clenched teeth. 'I know you're in there. Be quick, or I'll poke a hole in you.'

A soft scraping could be heard from a cleverly concealed cavity beneath the stones.

'Get out,' Geralt repeated. 'You're perfectly safe.'

'We won't touch a hair on your head,' Zoltan added sweetly, raising his sihil above the hollow and rolling his eyes menacingly. 'Out with you!'

Geralt shook his head and made a clear sign for the dwarf to withdraw. Once again there was a scratching from the cavity under the dolmen and once again they were aware of the intense aroma of herbs and spices. A moment later they saw a grizzled head and then a face embellished with a nobly aquiline nose, belonging by no means to a ghoul but to a slim, middle-aged man. Percival hadn't been wrong. The man did indeed somewhat resemble a tax collector.

'Is it safe to come out?' he asked, raising black eyes beneath slightly greying eyebrows towards Geralt.

'Yes, it is.'

The man scrambled out of the hole, brushed down his black robes – which were tied around the waist with some kind of apron – and straightened a linen bag, causing another wave of the herbal aroma.

'I suggest you put away your weapons, gentlemen,' he declared in a measured voice, running his eyes over the group of wanderers surrounding him. 'They won't be necessary. I, as you can see, bear no blade. I never do. Neither do I have anything on me that might be termed attractive booty. My name is Emiel Regis. I come from Dillingen. I'm a barber-surgeon.'

'Indeed,' Zoltan Chivay grimaced a little. 'A barber-surgeon, alchemist or herbalist. No offence, my dear sir, but you smell seriously like an apothecary's shop.'

Emiel Regis smiled strangely, with pursed lips, and spread his arms apologetically.

'The scent betrayed you, master barber-surgeon,' Geralt said, replacing his sword in its sheath. 'Did you have any particular reason to hide from us?'

'Any particular reason?' the man asked, turning his black eyes towards him. 'No. I was just taking general precautions. I was simply afraid of you. These are difficult times.'

'True.' The dwarf nodded and pointed towards the glow of fire lighting up the sky. 'Difficult times. I surmise that you are a fugitive, as we are. It intrigues me, however, that although you've fled far from your native Dillingen, you're hiding all alone among these kurgans. Well, people's fates are various, particularly during difficult times. We were afraid of you and you of us. Fear makes one imagine things.'

'You have nothing to fear from me,' the man who was claiming to be Emiel Regis said, without taking his eyes off them, 'I hope I can count on reciprocity.'

'My, my,' Zoltan said, grinning broadly. 'You don't take us for robbers, do you? We, master barber-surgeon, are fugitives. We are travelling to the Temerian border. You may join us if you wish. The more the merrier . . . and safer, and a physician may come in handy. We have women and children in the party. Among the stinking medicaments I can smell about you, would you have a remedy for blisters?'

'I ought to have something,' the barber-surgeon said softly. 'Glad to be of assistance. But as far as travelling together is concerned . . . Thank you for the offer, but I'm not running away, gentlemen. I wasn't fleeing from Dillingen to escape the war. I live here.'

'Come again?' the dwarf said, frowning and taking a step back. 'You live here? Here, in this burial ground?'

'In the burial ground? No. I have a cottage not far from here. Apart from my house and shop in Dillingen, you understand. But I spend my summers here every year, from June to September, from Midsummer to the Equinox. I gather healing herbs and roots, from which I distil medicines and elixirs in my cottage . . .'

'But you know about the war in spite of your reclusive solitude far from the world and people.' Geralt pointed out. 'Who do you get your news from?'

'From the refugees who pass this way. There's a large camp less than two miles from here, by the River Chotla. A good few hundred fugitives – peasants from Brugge and Sodden – are gathered there.'

'And what about the Temerian Army?' Zoltan asked with interest. 'Are they on the move?'

'I know nothing about that.'

The dwarf swore and then glowered at the barber-surgeon.

'So you simply live here, Master Regis,' he drawled, 'and stroll among the graves of an evening. Aren't you afraid?'

'What ought I to be afraid of?'

'This here gentleman,' Zoltan pointed at Geralt, 'is a witcher. He saw evidence of ghouls not long ago. Corpse eaters, get it? And you don't have to be a witcher to know that ghouls hang around in cemeteries.'

'A witcher,' the barber-surgeon said, and looked at Geralt with obvious interest. 'A monster killer. Well, well. Fascinating. Didn't you explain to your comrades, Master Witcher, that this necropolis is over five hundred years old? Ghouls aren't fussy about what they eat, but they don't chew five-hundred-year-old bones. There aren't any ghouls here.'

'I feel a lot better knowing that,' Zoltan Chivay said, looking around. 'Well, master physician, come over to our camp. We have some cold horsemeat. You won't refuse it, will you?'

Regis looked at him long and hard.

'My thanks,' he said finally. 'But I have a better idea. Come to my place. My summer abode is more of a shack than a cottage, and a small one at that. You'll have no choice but to sleep under the stars. But there's a spring nearby and a hearth where you can warm up your horsemeat.'

'We'll gladly take you up on your invitation,' the dwarf said, bowing. 'Perhaps there really aren't any ghouls here, but the thought of spending a night in the burial ground doesn't do much for me. Let's go, I'll introduce you to the rest of our company.'

When they reached the camp the horses snorted and stamped their hooves on the ground.

'Stand a little downwind, Master Regis,' Zoltan Chivay said, casting the physician a telling glance. 'The smell of sage frightens our horses, and in my case, I'm ashamed to admit, reminds me unpleasantly of teeth being pulled.'

'Geralt,' Zoltan muttered, as soon as Emiel Regis had disappeared behind the flap covering the entrance to the cottage. 'Let's keep our eyes open. There's something fishy about that stinking herbalist.'

'Anything specific?'

'I don't like it when people spend their summers near cemeteries, never mind cemeteries a long way from human dwellings. Do herbs really not grow in more pleasant surroundings? That Regis looks like a grave robber to me. Barber-surgeons, alchemists and the like exhume corpses from boneyards, in order to perform various excrements on them.'

'Experiments. But fresh corpses are needed for practices of that kind. This cemetery is very old.'

'True,' the dwarf said, scratching his chin and watching the women from Kernow making their beds under some hagberry shrubs growing by the barber-surgeon's shack. 'So perhaps he steals buried treasure from these barrows?'

'Ask him,' Geralt said, shrugging. 'You accepted the invitation to stay at his homestead at once, without hesitation, and now you've suddenly become as suspicious as an old maid being paid a compliment.'

'Er . . .' Zoltan mumbled, somewhat tongue-tied. 'There's something in that. But I'd like to have a gander at what he keeps in that hovel of his. You know, just to be on the safe side . . .'

'So follow him in and pretend you want to borrow a fork.'

'Why a fork?'

'Why not?'

The dwarf gave Geralt an old-fashioned look and finally made up his mind. He hurried over to the cottage, knocked politely on the door jamb and entered. He remained inside for some little time, and then suddenly appeared in the doorway.

'Geralt, Percival, Dandelion, step this way. Come and see something interesting. Come on, without further ado, Master Regis has invited us in.'

The interior of the cottage was dark and dominated by a warm, intoxicating aroma that made the nose tickle, mainly coming from the bunches of herbs and roots hanging from all the walls. The only items of furniture were a simple cot – also strewn with herbs – and a rickety table cluttered with innumerable glass, pottery and ceramic vials. The room was illuminated by the dim glow of burning coals in a curious, pot-bellied stove, resembling a bulging hourglass. The stove was surrounded by a spidery lattice of shining pipes of various diameters, bent into curves and spirals. Beneath one of the pipes stood a wooden pail into which a liquid was dripping.

At the sight of the stove Percival Schuttenbach first stared goggle-eyed, then gaped, and finally sighed and leapt up in the air.

'Ho, ho, ho!' he called, unable to conceal his delight. 'What do I see? That's an absolutely authentic athanor coupled to an alembic! Equipped with a rectifying column and a copper condenser! A beautiful apparatus! Did you build it yourself, master barber-surgeon?'

'Indeed,' Emiel Regis admitted modestly. 'My work involves producing elixirs, so I have to distil, extract the fifth essence, and also . . .'

He broke off, seeing Zoltan Chivay catching a drop falling from the end of the pipe and licking his finger. The dwarf sighed and a look of indescribable bliss appeared on his ruddy face.

Dandelion couldn't resist and also had a go, tasting and moaning softly.

'The fifth essence,' he confirmed, smacking his lips. 'And I suspect the sixth and even the seventh.'

'Well . . .' The barber-surgeon smiled faintly. 'As I said: a distillate.'

'Moonshine,' Zoltan corrected him gently. 'And what moonshine! Try some, Percival.'

'But I'm not an expert in organic chemistry,' the gnome answered absentmindedly, examining the details of the alchemical furnace's construction. 'It's doubtful I would be familiar with the ingredients . . .'

'It is a distillate of mandrake,' Regis said, dispelling any doubt. 'Enriched with belladonna. And fermented starch mass.'

'You mean mash?'

'One could also call it that.'

'May I request a cup of some kind?'

'Zoltan, Dandelion,' the Witcher said, folding his arms on his chest. 'Are you deaf? It's mandrake. The moonshine is made of mandrake. Leave that copper alone.'

'But dear Master Geralt,' the alchemist said, digging a small graduated flask out from between some dust-covered retorts and demijohns, and meticulously polishing it with a rag. 'There's nothing to be afraid of. The mandrake is appropriately seasoned and the proportions carefully selected and precisely weighed out. I only add five ounces of mandrake to a pound of mash, and only half a dram of belladonna . . .'

'That's not the point,' the Witcher said, looking at Zoltan. The dwarf understood at once, grew serious and cautiously withdrew from the still. 'The point is not how many drams you add, Master Regis, but how much a dram of mandrake costs. It's too dear a tipple for us.'

'Mandrake,' Dandelion whispered in awe, pointing at the small heap of sugar beet-like roots piled up in the corner of the shack. 'That's mandrake? Real mandrake?'

'The female form' – the alchemist nodded – 'grows in large clumps in the very cemetery where we chanced to meet. Which is also why I spend my summers here.'

The Witcher looked knowingly at Zoltan. The dwarf winked. Regis gave a half-suppressed smile.

'Gentlemen, please, I warmly invite you to sample it, if you wish. I appreciate your moderation, but in the current situation there's little chance of me taking the elixirs to war-torn Dillingen. It all would have gone to waste anyway, so let's not talk about the price. My apologies, but I only have one drinking vessel.'

'That should do,' Zoltan said, picking up the flask and carefully scooping up moonshine from the pail. 'Your good health, Master Regis. Ooooh . . .'

'Please forgive me,' the barber-surgeon said, smiling again. 'The quality of the distillate probably leaves a lot to be desired . . . It's actually unfinished.'

'It's the best unfinished product I've ever tasted,' Zoltan said, gasping. 'Your turn, poet.'

'Aaaah . . . Oh, mother of mine! Excellent! Have a sip, Geralt.'

'Give it to our host,' the Witcher said, bowing slightly towards Emiel Regis. 'Where are your manners, Dandelion?'

'Please forgive me, gentlemen,' the alchemist said, acknowledging the gesture, 'but I never permit myself any stimulants. My health isn't what it was. I've been forced to give up many . . . pleasures.'

'Not even a sip?'

'It's a principle,' Regis explained calmly. 'I never break any principles once I've adopted them.'

'I admire and envy you your resoluteness,' Geralt said, sipping a little from the flask and then, after a moment's hesitation, draining it in one. The tears trickling from his eyes interfered a little with the taste of the moonshine. An invigorating warmth spread through his stomach.

'I'll go and get Milva,' he offered, handing the flask to the dwarf. 'Don't polish it all off before we get back.'

Milva was sitting near the horses, bantering with the freckled girl she had been carrying on her saddle all day. When she heard about Regis's hospitality she initially shrugged, but in the end didn't need much persuading.

When they entered the shack they found the company carrying out an inspection of the stored mandrake roots.

'I've never seen it before,' Dandelion confessed, turning a bulbous root around in his fingers. 'Indeed, it does somewhat resemble a man.'

'A man twisted by lumbago, perhaps,' Zoltan added. 'And that one's the spitting image of a pregnant woman. And that one, if you'll excuse me, looks just like a couple busy bonking.'

'You lot only think of one thing,' Milva sneered, boldly drinking from the full flask and then coughing loudly into a fist. 'Bloody hell . . . Powerful stuff, that hooch! Is it really made from love apples? Ha, so we're drinking a magic potion! That doesn't happen every day. Thank you, master barber-surgeon.'

'The pleasure is all mine.'

The flask, kept topped up, circulated around the company, prompting good humour, verve and garrulousness.

'The mandrake, I hear, is a vegetable with great magical powers,' Percival Schuttenbach said with conviction.

'Yes, indeed,' Dandelion confirmed. He then emptied the flask, shuddered and resumed talking. 'There's no shortage of ballads written on the subject. It's well known that sorcerers use mandrake in elixirs, which help them preserve their eternal youth and sorceresses make an ointment, which they call glamarye. If an enchantress applies such ointment she becomes so beautiful and enchanting it makes your eyes pop out of your head. You also ought to know that mandrake is a powerful aphrodisiac and is used in love magic, particularly to break down female resistance. That's the explanation of mandrake's folk name: love apple. It's a herb used to pander lovers.'

'Blockhead,' Milva commented.

'And I heard,' the gnome said, downing the contents of the flask, 'that when mandrake root is pulled from the ground the plant cries and wails as though it were alive.'

'Why,' Zoltan said, filling the flask from the pail, 'if it only wailed! Mandrake, they say, screams so horribly it can send you up the wall, and moreover it screams out evil spells and showers curses on whoever uproots it. You can pay with your life taking a risk like that.'

'That sounds like a cloth-headed fairy-tale,' Milva said, taking the flask from him and drinking deeply. She shuddered and added: 'It's impossible for a plant to have such powers.'

'It's an infallible truth!' the dwarf called heatedly. 'But sagacious herbalists have found a way of protecting themselves. Having found a mandrake, you must tie one end of a rope to the root and the other end to a dog . . .'

'Or a pig,' the gnome broke in.

'Or a wild boar,' Dandelion added gravely.

'You're a fool, poet. The whole point is for the mutt or swine to pull the mandrake out of the ground, for then the vegetable's curses and spells fall on the said creature, while the herbalist – hiding safely, far away in the bushes – gets out in one piece. Well, Master Regis? Am I talking sense?'

'An interesting method,' the alchemist admitted, smiling mysteriously. 'Interesting mainly for its ingenuity. The disadvantage, however, is its extreme complexity. For in theory the rope ought to be enough, without the draught animal. I wouldn't suspect mandrake of having the ability of knowing who or what's pulling the rope. The spells and curses should always fall on the rope, which after all is cheaper and less problematic to use than a dog, not to mention a pig.'

'Are you jesting?'

'Wouldn't dream of it. I said I admire the ingenuity. Because although the mandrake, contrary to popular opinion, is incapable of casting spells or curses, it is – in its raw state – an extremely toxic plant, to the extent that even the earth around the root is poisonous. Sprinkling the fresh juice onto the face or on a cut hand, why, even breathing in its fumes, may all have fatal consequences. I wear a mask and gloves, which doesn't mean I have anything against the rope method.'

'Mmmm . . .' the dwarf pondered. 'But what about that horrifying scream the plucked mandrake makes? Is that true?'

'The mandrake doesn't have vocal chords,' the alchemist explained calmly, 'which is fairly typical for plants, is it not? However, the toxin secreted by the root has a powerful hallucinogenic effect. The voices, screams, whispers and other sounds are nothing more than hallucinations produced by the poisoned central nervous system.'

'Ha, I clean forgot,' Dandelion said, having just drained the flask and letting out a suppressed burp, 'that mandrake is extremely poisonous! And I was holding it! And now we're guzzling this tincture with abandon . . .'

'Only the fresh mandrake root is toxic,' Regis said, calming him down. 'Mine is seasoned and suitably prepared, and the distillate has been filtered. There is no need for alarm.'

'Of course there isn't,' Zoltan agreed. 'Moonshine will always be moonshine, you can even distil it from hemlock, nettles, fish scales and old bootlaces. Give us the glass, Dandelion, there's a queue forming here.'

The flask, kept topped up, circulated around the company. Everybody was sitting comfortably on the dirt floor. The Witcher hissed and swore, and shifted his position, because the pain shot through his knee again as he sat. He caught sight of Regis looking at him intently. 'Is that a fresh injury?'

'Not really. But it's tormenting me. Do you have any herbs capable of soothing the pain?'

'That all depends on the class of pain,' the barber-surgeon said, smiling slightly. 'And on its causes. I can detect a strange odour in your sweat, Witcher. Were you treated with magic? Were you given magic enzymes and hormones?'

'They gave me various medicaments. I had no idea they could still be smelled in my sweat. You've got a bloody sensitive nose, Regis.'

'Everybody has their good points. To even out the vices. What ailment did they use magic to treat you with?'

'I broke my arm and the shaft of my thighbone.'

'How long ago?'

'A little over a month.'

'And you're already walking? Remarkable. The dryads of Brokilon, I presume?'

'How can you tell?'

'Only the dryads have medicaments capable of rebuilding bone tissue so quickly. I can see dark marks on the backs of your hands. They're the places where the tendrils of the conynhaela and the symbiotic shoots of knitbone entered. Only dryads know how to use conynhaela, and knitbone doesn't grow outside Brokilon.'

'Well done. Admirable deduction skills. Though something else interests me. My thighbone and forearm were broken, but the strong pain is in the knee and elbow.'

'That's typical,' the barber-surgeon nodded. 'The dryads' magic reconstructed your damaged bone, but simultaneously caused a minor upheaval in your nerve trunks. It's a side effect, felt most intensely in the joints.'

'What do you advise?'

'Unfortunately, nothing. You'll continue to predict rainy weather unerringly for a long time to come. The pains will grow stronger in the winter. However, I wouldn't recommend that you take powerful painkilling drugs. Particularly steer clear of narcotics. You're a witcher and in your case it's absolutely to be avoided.'

'I'll treat myself with your mandrake, then,' the Witcher said, raising the full flask, which Milva had just handed him. He took a deep swallow and hacked until tears filled his eyes. 'Bloody hell! I'm feeling better already.'

'I'm not certain,' Regis said, smiling through pursed lips, 'that you're treating the right illness. I'd also like to remind you that one should treat causes, not symptoms.'

'Not in the case of this witcher,' Dandelion snorted, now a little flushed and eavesdropping on their conversation. 'Booze is just right for him and his worries.'

'It ought to do you good, too,' Geralt said, giving the poet a chilling stare. 'Particularly if it paralyses your tongue.'

'I wouldn't especially count on that.' The barber-surgeon smiled again. 'Belladonna is one of the preparation's ingredients, which means a large number of alkaloids, including scopolamine. Before the mandrake puts you to sleep, you're all sure to give me a display of eloquence.'

'A display of what?' Percival asked.

'Talkativeness. My apologies. Let's use simpler words.'

Geralt mouth twisted into a fake smile.

'That's right,' he said. 'It's easy to adopt an affected style and start using words like that every day. Then people take the speaker for an arrogant buffoon.'

'Or an alchemist,' Zoltan Chivay said, filling the flask from the pail once more.

'Or a witcher,' Dandelion snorted, 'who's read a lot to impress a certain enchantress. Nothing attracts enchantresses like an elaborate tale, gentlemen. Am I right, Geralt? Go on, spin us a yarn . . .'

'Sit out your turn, Dandelion,' the Witcher cut in coldly. 'The alkaloids in this hooch are acting on you too quickly. They've loosened your tongue.'

'It's time you gave up your secrets, Geralt,' Zoltan grimaced. 'Dandelion hasn't told us much we didn't know. You can't help it if you're a walking legend. They re-enact stories of your adventures in puppet theatres. Like the story about you and an enchantress by the name of Guinevere.'

'Yennefer,' Regis corrected in hushed tones. 'I saw that one. It was the story of a hunt for a genie, if my memory serves me correctly.'

'I was present during that hunt,' Dandelion boasted. 'We had some laughs, I can tell you . . .'

'Tell them all,' Geralt said, getting up. 'Tell them while you're sipping the moonshine and embellishing the story suitably. I'm taking a walk.'

'Hey,' the dwarf said, nettled. 'No need to get offended . . .'

'You misunderstand, Zoltan. I'm going to relieve my bladder. Why, it even happens to walking legends.'

The night was as cold as hell. The horses stamped and snorted, and steam belched from their nostrils. Bathed in moonlight, Regis's shack seemed utterly as if it could have come from a fairy-tale. It could have been a witch's cottage. Geralt fastened his trousers.

Milva, who had left soon after him, coughed hesitantly. Her long shadow drew level with his.

'Why are you delaying going back?' she asked. 'Did they really annoy you?'

'No,' he replied.

'Then why the hell are you standing here by yourself in the moonlight?'

'I'm counting.'

'Huh?'

'Twelve days have passed since I set out from Brokilon, during which I've travelled around sixty miles. Rumour has it that Ciri's in Nilfgaard, the capital of the Empire. Which is around two and half thousand miles from here. Simple arithmetic tells me that at this rate I'll get there in a year and four months. What do you say to that?'

'Nothing,' Milva said, shrugging and coughing again. 'I'm not as good at reckoning as you. I don't know how to read or write at all. I'm a foolish, simple country girl. No company for you. Nor someone to talk to.'

'Don't say that.'

'It's the truth, though,' she said, turning away abruptly. 'Why did you tally up the days and miles? For me to advise you? Cheer you up? Chase away your fear, suppress the remorse that torments you worse than the pain in your broken peg? I don't know how! You need another. The one Dandelion was talking about. Intelligent, educated. Your beloved.'

'Dandelion's a prattler.'

'That he is. But he occasionally prattles sense. Let's go back, I want to drink some more.'

'Milva?'

'What?'

'You never told me why you decided to ride with me.'

'You never asked.'

'I'm asking now.'

'It's too late now. I don't know any more.'

*

131

'Oh, you're back at last,' Zoltan said, pleased to see them, his voice now sounding quite different. 'And we, just imagine, have decided that Regis will continue on our journey with us.'

'Really?' The Witcher looked intently at the barber-surgeon. 'What's behind this sudden decision?'

'Master Zoltan,' Regis said, without lowering his gaze, 'has made me aware that Dillingen has been engulfed by a much more serious war than I understood from the refugees' accounts. A return to those parts is totally out of the question, and remaining in this wilderness doesn't seem wise. Or travelling alone, for that matter.'

'And we, although you don't know us at all, look like people you could travel with safely. Was one glance enough for you?'

'Two,' the barber-surgeon replied with a faint smile. 'One at the women you're looking after. And the other at their children.'

Zoltan belched loudly and scraped the flask against the bottom of the pail.

'Appearances can be deceptive,' he sneered. 'Perhaps we intend to sell the women into slavery. Percival, do something with this apparatus. Loosen a valve a little or something. We want to drink more and it's taking for ever to drip out.'

'The condenser can't keep up. The liquor will be warm.'

'Not a problem. The night's cool.'

The lukewarm moonshine greatly stimulated the conversation. Dandelion, Zoltan and Percival were all ruddy-cheeked, and their voices had altered even more – in the case of the poet and the gnome one could now say that they were almost on the verge of gibbering. Ravenous, the company were chewing cold horsemeat and nibbling horseradish roots they had found in the cottage – which made their eyes water, because the horseradish was as bracing as the hooch. And added passion to the discussion.

Regis gave an expression of astonishment when it turned out that the final destination of the trek was not the enclave of the Mahakam massif, the eternal and secure home of the dwarves. Zoltan, who had become even more garrulous than Dandelion, declared that under no circumstances would he ever return to Mahakam, and unburdened himself of his animosity to its ruling regime, particularly regarding the politics and absolute rule of Brouver Hoog, the Elder of Mahakam and all the dwarven clans.

'The old fart!' he roared, and spat into the hearth of the furnace. 'To look at him you wouldn't know if he was alive or stuffed. He almost never moves, which is just as well, because he farts every time he does. You can't understand a word he's saying because his beard and whiskers are stuck together with dried borscht. But he lords it over everyone and everything, and everyone has to dance to his tune . . .'

'It would be difficult to claim, however, that Hoog's policies are poor,' Regis interrupted. 'For, owing to his decisive measures, the dwarves distanced themselves from the elves and don't fight alongside the Scoia'tael any more. And thanks to that the pogroms have ceased. Thanks to that there have been no punitive expeditions to Mahakam. Prudence in their dealings with humans is bearing fruit.'

'Bollocks,' Zoltan said, drinking from the flask. 'In the case of the Squirrels, the old fossil wasn't interested in prudence, it was because too many youngsters were abandoning work in the mines and the forges and joining the elves to sample freedom and manly adventures in the commandos. When the phenomenon grew to the size of a problem, Brouver Hoog took the punks in hand. He couldn't care less about the humans being killed by the Squirrels, and he made light of the repression falling on the dwarves because of that – including your infamous pogroms. He didn't give a damn and doesn't give a damn about them, because he considers the dwarves who've settled in the cities apostates. And as regards punitive expeditions to Mahakam – don't make me laugh, my dears. There's no threat and never has been, because none of the kings would dare lay a finger on Mahakam. I'll go further: even the Nilfgaardians, were they to manage to take control of the valleys surrounding the massif, wouldn't dare touch Mahakam. Do you know why? I'll tell you: Mahakam is steel; and not just any old steel. There's coal there, there's magnetite ore, boundless deposits. Everywhere else it's just bog ore.'

'And they have expertise and technology in Mahakam,' Percival

Schuttenbach interposed. 'Metallurgy and smelting! Enormous furnaces, not some pathetic smelteries. Trip hammers and steam hammers . . .'

'There you go, Percival, neck that,' Zoltan said, handing the gnome the now full flask, 'before you bore us to death with your technology and engineering. Everyone knows about it. But not everyone knows Mahakam exports steel. To the kingdoms, but to Nilfgaard too. And should anyone lay a finger on us, we'll wreck the workshops and flood the mines. And then you humans will continue fighting, but with oaken staves, flint blades and asses' jawbones.'

'You say you have it in for Brouver Hoog and the regime in Mahakam,' the Witcher observed, 'but you've suddenly started saying "we".'

'I certainly have,' the dwarf confirmed heatedly. 'There is something like solidarity, isn't there? I admit that pride also plays its part, because we're cleverer than those stuck-up elves. You can't deny it, can you? For a few centuries the elves pretended there weren't any humans at all. They gazed up at the sky, smelled the flowers, and at the sight of a human averted their vulgarly bedaubed eyes. But when that strategy turned out to be ineffective they suddenly roused themselves and took up arms. They decided to kill and be killed. And we? The dwarves? We adapted. No, we didn't subordinate ourselves to you, don't get that into your heads. We subordinated you. Economically.'

'To tell the truth,' Regis chipped in, 'it was easier for you to adapt than it was for the elves. Land and territory is what integrates elves. In your case it's the clan. Wherever your clan is, that's your homeland. Even if an exceptionally short-sighted king were to attack Mahakam, you'd flood the mines and head off somewhere else without any regrets. To other, distant mountains. Or perhaps to human cities instead.'

'And why not? It's not a bad life in your cities.'

'Even in the ghettoes?' Dandelion asked, gasping after a swig of distillate.

'And what's wrong with living in a ghetto? I'd prefer to live among my own. What do I need with assimilation?'

'As long as they let us near the guilds,' Percival said, wiping his nose on his sleeve.

'They will eventually,' the dwarf said with conviction. 'And if they don't we'll just bodge our way through, or we'll found our own guilds; and healthy competition will decide.'

'So it would be safer in Mahakam than in the cities, then,' Regis observed. 'The cities could go up in flames any second. It would be more judicious to see out the war in the mountains.'

'Anyone who wishes to can do just that,' Zoltan said, replenishing the flask from the pail. 'Freedom is dearer to me, and you won't find that in Mahakam. You have no idea how the old bugger governs. He recently took it upon himself to regulate what he calls "community issues". For example: whether you can wear braces or not. Whether you should eat carp right away or wait until the jelly sets. Whether playing the ocarina is in keeping with our centuries-old dwarven traditions or is a destructive influence of rotten and decadent human culture. How many years you have to work before submitting an application for a permanent wife. Which hand you should wipe your arse with. How far away from the mines you're allowed to whistle. And other issues of vital importance. No, boys, I'm not going to return to Mount Carbon. I have no desire to spend my life at the coalface. Forty years underground, assuming firedamp doesn't blow you up first. But we've got other plans now, haven't we, Percival? We've already secured ourselves a future . . .'

'A future, a future . . .' the gnome said and emptied the graduated flask. He cleared his nose and looked at the dwarf with a now slightly glazed expression. 'Don't count our chickens, Zoltan. Because they might still nab us and then our future's the gibbet . . . Or Drakenborg.'

'Shut your trap,' the dwarf snapped, looking menacingly at him. 'You're blabbing!'

'Scopolamine,' Regis mumbled softly.

The gnome was rambling. Milva was gloomy. Zoltan, having forgotten that he'd already done so, told everyone about Hoog, the old fart and the Elder of Mahakam. Geralt listened, having forgotten he'd already heard it once. Regis also listened and even added comments, utterly unperturbed by the fact that he was the only sober individual in a now very drunk party. Dandelion strummed away on his lute and sang.

No wonder that comely ladies are all so stuck-up
For the taller the tree, the harder it is to get up.

'Idiot,' Milva commented. Dandelion was undeterred.

Simply treat a maiden as you would a tree
Whip out your chopper and one-two-three . . .

'A cup . . .' Percival Schuttenbach jabbered. 'A goblet, I mean . . . Carved from a single piece of milk opal . . . This big. I found it on the summit of Montsalvat. Its rim was set with jasper and the base was of gold. A sheer marvel . . .'

'Don't give him any more spirits,' Zoltan Chivay said.

'Hold on, hold on,' Dandelion said, becoming interested, also slurring his words somewhat. 'What happened to that legendary goblet?'

'I exchanged it for a mule. I needed a mule, in order to transport a load . . . Corundum and crystalline carbon. I had . . . Err . . . Lots of it . . . Hic . . . A load, I mean, a heavy load, couldn't have moved it without a mule . . . Why the hell did I need that goblet?'

'Corundum? Carbon?'

'Yeah, what you call rubies and diamonds. Very . . . hic . . . handy . . .'

'So I imagine.'

'. . . for drill bits and files. For bearings. I had lots of them . . .'

'Do you hear, Geralt?' Zoltan said. He waved a hand and although seated, almost fell over. 'He's little, so he got pissed quickly. He's dreaming about a shitload of diamonds. Careful now, Percival, that your dream doesn't come true! Or at least half. And I don't mean the half about diamonds!'

'Dreams, dreams,' Dandelion mumbled once more. 'And you,

Geralt? Have you dreamed of Ciri again? Because you ought to know, Regis, that Geralt has prophetic dreams! Ciri is the Child of Destiny, and Geralt is bound to her by bonds of fate, which is why he sees her in his dreams. You also ought to know that we're going to Nilfgaard to take back Ciri from Imperator Emhyr, who abducted her and wants to marry her. But he can whistle for it, the bastard, because we'll rescue her before he knows it! I'd tell you something else, boys, but it's a secret. A dreadful, deep, dark secret . . . Not a word, understood? Not one!'

'I haven't heard anything,' Zoltan assured him, looking impudently at the Witcher. 'I think an earwig crawled into my ear.'

'There's a veritable plague of earwigs,' Regis agreed, pretending to be poking around in his ear.

'We're going to Nilfgaard . . .' Dandelion said, leaning against the dwarf to keep his balance, which turned out to be a bad idea. 'Which is a secret, just like I told you. It's a secret mission!'

'And ingeniously concealed indeed,' the barber-surgeon nodded, glancing at Geralt, who was now white with rage. 'Not even the most suspicious individual would ever guess the aim of your journey by analysing the direction you are headed.'

'Milva, what is it?'

'Don't talk to me, you drunken fool.'

'Hey, she's crying! Hey, look . . .'

'Go to hell, I said!' the archer raised her voice, wiping away the tears. 'Or I'll smack you between the eyes, you fucking poetaster . . . Give me the glass, Zoltan . . .'

'I've mislaid it . . .' the dwarf mumbled. 'Oh, here it is. Thanks, master barber-surgeon . . . And where the hell is Schuttenbach?'

'He went outside. Some time ago. Dandelion, I recall you promised you'd tell me the story of the Child of Destiny.'

'All right, all right, Regis. I'll just have a swig . . . and I'll tell you everything . . . About Ciri, and about the Witcher . . . In detail . . .'

'Confusion to the whores' sons!'

'Be quiet, dwarf! You'll wake up the kids outside the cottage!'

'Calm down, archeress. There you go, drink that.'

'Ah, well.' Dandelion looked around the shack with a slightly vacant stare. 'If the Countess de Lettenhove could see me like this . . .'

'Who?'

'Never mind. Bloody hell, this moonshine really does loosen the tongue . . . Geralt, shall I pour you another one? Geralt!'

'Leave him be,' Milva said. 'Let him sleep.'

The barn on the edge of the village was pounding with music. The rhythm seized them before they arrived, filling them with excitement. They began to sway involuntarily in their saddles as their horses walked up, firstly to the rhythm of the dull boom of the drum and double bass, and then, when they were closer, to the beat of the melody being played by the fiddles and the pipes. The night was cold, the moon shone full and in its glow the barn, illuminated by the light shining through gaps in the planks, looked like a fairy-tale enchanted castle.

A clamour and a bright glow, broken up by the shadows of cavorting couples, flooded out from the doorway of the barn.

When they entered the music fell silent, dissolving in a long-drawn-out discord. The dancing, sweating peasants parted, leaving the dirt floor, and grouped together by the walls and posts. Ciri, walking alongside Mistle, saw the eyes of the young women, wide with fear; noticed the hard, determined glances of the men and lads, ready for anything. She heard the growing whispering and growling, louder than the cautious skirling of the bagpipes, than the fading insect-like droning of violins and fiddles. Whispering. The Rats . . . The Rats . . . Robbers . . .

'Fear not,' Giselher said loudly, chucking a plump and chinking purse towards the dumbstruck musicians. 'We've come here to make merry. The village fair is open to anyone, isn't it?'

'Where's the beer?' Kayleigh asked, shaking a pouch. 'And where's the hospitality?'

'And why is it so quiet here?' Iskra asked, looking around. 'We came down from the mountains for a dance. Not for a wake!'

One of the peasants finally broke the impasse, and walked over to Giselher with a clay mug overflowing with froth. Giselher took it with a bow, drank from it, and courteously and decorously thanked him. Several peasants shouted enthusiastically. But the others remained silent.

'Hey, fellows,' Iskra called again. 'I see that you need livening up!'

A heavy oak table, laden with clay mugs, stood against one wall of the barn. The she-elf clapped her hands and nimbly jumped onto it. The peasants quickly gathered up the mugs. With a vigorous kick Iskra cleared the ones they were too slow to remove.

'Very well, musicians,' she said, putting her fists on her hips and shaking her hair. 'Show me what you can do. Music!'

She quickly tapped out a rhythm with her heels. The drum repeated the rhythm and the double bass and oboe followed. The pipes and fiddles took up the tune, quickly embellishing it, challenging Iskra to adjust her steps and tempo. The she-elf, gaudily dressed and as light as a butterfly, adapted to it with ease and began moving rhythmically. The peasants began to clap.

'Falka!' Iskra called, narrowing her eyes, which were intensified by heavy make-up. 'You're swift with a sword! And in the dance? Can you keep step with me?'

Ciri freed herself from Mistle's arm, untied the scarf from around her neck and took off her beret and jacket. With a single bound she was on the table beside the she-elf. The peasants cheered enthusiastically, the drum and double bass boomed and the bagpipes wailed plaintively.

'Play, musicians!' Iskra yelled. 'With verve! And passion!'

With her hands on her hips and an upturned head, the she-elf tapped her feet, cut a caper, and beat out a quick, rhythmic staccato with her heels. Ciri, bewitched by the rhythm, copied the steps. The she-elf laughed, hopped and changed the tempo. Ciri shook her hair from her forehead with a sudden jerk of her head and copied Iskra's movements perfectly. The two girls stepped in unison, each the mirror image of the other. The peasants yelled and applauded. The fiddles and violins sang a piercing song, tearing the measured, solemn rumbling of the double bass and keening of the bagpipes to shreds.

They danced, both as straight as a poker, arms akimbo, touching each other's elbows. The iron on their heels beat out the rhythm, the table shook and trembled, and dust whirled in the light of tallow candles and torches.

'Faster!' Iskra urged on the musicians. 'Look lively!'

It was no longer music, it was a frenzy.

'Dance, Falka! Abandon yourself to it!'

Heel, toe, heel, toe, heel, step forward and jump, shoulders swinging, fists on hips, heel, heel. The table shakes, the light shimmers, the crowd sways, everything sways, the entire barn is dancing, dancing, dancing . . . The crowd yells, Giselher yells, Asse yells, Mistle laughs, claps, everyone claps and stamps, the barn shudders, the earth shudders, the world is shaken to its foundations. The world? What world? There's no world now, there's nothing, only the dance, the dance . . . Heel, toe, heel . . . Iskra's elbow . . . Fever pitch, fever pitch . . . Only the wild playing of the fiddles, pipes, double bass and bagpipes, the drummer raises and lowers his drumsticks but he is now superfluous, they beat the rhythm out by themselves. Iskra and Ciri, their heels, until the table booms and rocks, the entire barn booms and rocks . . . The rhythm, the rhythm is them, the music is them, they are the music. Iskra's dark hair flops on her forehead and shoulders. The fiddles' strings play a passionate tune, reaching fever pitch. Blood pounds in their temples.

Abandon. Oblivion.

I am Falka. I have always been Falka! Dance, Iskra! Clap, Mistle! The violins and pipes finish the melody on a strident, high chord, and Iskra and Ciri mark the end of the dance with a simultaneous bang of their heels, their elbows still touching. They are both panting, quivering, het up, they suddenly cling to each other, they hug, they share their sweat, their heat and their happiness with each other. The barn explodes with one great bellow and the clapping of dozens of hands.

'Falka, you she-devil,' Iskra pants. 'When we grow tired of robbery, we'll go out into the world and earn a living as dancers . . .'

Ciri also pants. She is unable to say a single word. She just laughs spasmodically. A tear runs down her cheek.

A sudden shout in the crowd, a disturbance. Kayleigh shoves a burly peasant hard, the peasant shoves Kayleigh back, the two of them are caught in the press, raised fists fly. Reef jumps in and a dagger flashes in the light of a torch.

'No! Stop!' Iskra cries piercingly. 'No brawling! This is a night of dance!' She takes Ciri by the hand. They drop from the table to the floor. 'Musicians, play! Whoever wants to show us their paces, join us! Well, who's feeling brave?'

The double bass booms monotonously, the long-drawn-out wailing of the bagpipes cuts in, to be joined by the high, piercing song of the fiddles. The peasants laugh, nudge one another, overcoming their reserve. One – broad-shouldered and fair-haired – seizes Iskra. A second – younger and slimmer – bows hesitantly in front of Ciri. Ciri haughtily tosses her head, but soon smiles in assent. The lad closes his hands around her waist and Ciri places her hands on his shoulders. The touch shoots through her like a flaming arrowhead, filling her with throbbing desire.

'Look lively, musicians!'

The barn shudders from the noise, vibrates with the rhythm and the melody.

Ciri dances.

*A vampire, or upir, is a dead person brought to life by Chaos. Having lost its first life, a **v.** enjoys its second life during the night hours. It leaves its grave by the light of the moon and only under its light may it act, assailing sleeping maidens or young swains, who it wakes not, but whose blood it sucks.*

Physiologus

The peasants consumed garlic in great abundance and for greater certainty hung strings of garlic around their necks. Some, women-folk in particular, stopped up their orifices with whole bulbs of garlic. The whole hamlet stank of garlic horrendus, so the peasants believed they were safe and that the vampire was incapable of doing them harm. Mighty was their astonishment, however, when the vampire who flew to their hamlet at midnight was not in the least afraid and simply began to laugh, gnashing his teeth in delight and jeering at them.

'It is good,' he said, 'that you have spiced yourselves, for I shall soon devour you and seasoned meat is more to my taste. Apply also salt and pepper to yourselves, and forget not the mustard.'

Sylvester Bugiardo, *Liber Tenebrarum,*
or The Book of Fell but Authentic Cases
never Explained by Science

The moon shines bright,
The vampire alights
Swish, swish goes his cloak . . .
Maiden, are you not afeared?

Folk song

CHAPTER FOUR

As usual, the birds filled the grey and foggy dawn with an explosion of chirruping in anticipation of the sunrise. As usual, the first members of the party ready to set off were the taciturn women from Kernow and their children. Emiel Regis turned out to be equally swift and energetic, joining the others with a travelling staff and a leather bag over one shoulder. The rest of the company, who had drained the still during the night, were not quite so lively. The cool of the morning roused and revived the revellers, but failed to thwart the effects of the mandrake moonshine. Geralt awoke in a corner of the shack with his head in Milva's lap. Zoltan and Dandelion lay in each other's arms on a pile of mandrake roots, snoring so powerfully that they were making the bundles of herbs hanging on the walls flutter. Percival was discovered outside, curled up in a ball under a hagberry bush, covered by the straw mat Regis normally used to wipe his boots on. The five of them betrayed distinct – but varied – symptoms of fatigue and they all went to soothe their raging thirst at the spring.

However, by the time the mists had dissipated and the red ball of the sun was blazing in the tops of the pines and larches of Fen Carn the company were already on their way, marching briskly among the barrows. Regis took the lead, followed by Percival and Dandelion, who kept each other's spirits up by singing a two-part ballad about three sisters and an iron wolf. After them trudged Zoltan Chivay, leading the chestnut colt by the reins. The dwarf had found a knobbly ashen staff in the barber-surgeon's yard, which he was now using to whack all the menhirs they passed and wish the long-deceased elves eternal rest, while Field Marshal Windbag – who was sitting on his shoulder – puffed up his feathers and occasionally squawked; reluctantly, indistinctly and somewhat half-heartedly.

Milva turned out to be the least tolerant to the mandrake distillate. She marched with visible difficulty, was sweaty, pale and acted like a bear with a sore head, not even responding to the twittering of the little girl with the plaits who was riding in the black's saddle. Geralt thus made no attempt to strike up a conversation, not being in the best of shape himself.

The fog and the adventures of the iron wolf sung in loud – though somewhat morning-after – voices meant that they happened upon a small group of peasants suddenly and without warning. The peasants, however, had heard them much earlier and were waiting, standing motionless among the monoliths sunk into the ground, their grey homespun coats camouflaging them perfectly. Zoltan Chivay barely avoided whacking one of them with his staff, having mistaken him for a tombstone.

'Yo-ho-ho!!' he shouted. 'Forgive me, good people! I didn't notice you. A good day to you! Greetings!'

The dozen peasants murmured an answer to his greeting in an incoherent chorus, grimly scrutinising the company. The peasants were clutching shovels, picks and six-foot pointed stakes.

'Greetings,' the dwarf repeated. 'I presume you're from the camp by the Chotla. Am I right?'

Rather than answering, one of the peasants pointed out Milva's horse to the rest of them.

'That black one,' he said. 'See it?'

'The black,' affirmed another and licked his lips. 'Oh, yes, the black. Should do the job.'

'Eh?' Zoltan said, noticing their expressions and gestures. 'Are you referring to our black steed? What about it? It's a horse, not a giraffe, there's nothing to be astonished about. What are you up to, my good fellows, in this burial ground?'

'And you?' the peasant asked, looking askance at the company. 'What are *you* doing here?'

'We've bought this land,' the dwarf said, looking him straight in the eye and hitting a menhir with his staff, 'and we're pacing it out, to check we haven't been swindled on the acreage.'

'And we're hunting a vampire!'

'What?'

'A vampire,' the oldest peasant repeated emphatically, scratching his forehead beneath a felt cap stiff with grime. 'He must have his lair somewhere here, curse him. We have sharpened these here aspen stakes, and now we shall find the scoundrel and run him through, so he will never rise again!'

'And we've holy water in a pot the priest gave us!' another peasant called cheerfully, pointing to the vessel. 'We'll sprinkle it on the bloodsucker, make things hot for him!'

'Ha, ha,' Zoltan Chivay said, with a smile. 'I see it's a proper hunt; full scale and well organised. A vampire, you say? Well, you're in luck, good fellows. We have a vampire specialist in our company, a wi . . .'

He broke off and swore under his breath, because the Witcher had kicked him hard in the ankle.

'Who saw the vampire?' Geralt asked, hushing his companions with a telling glance. 'Why do you think you should be looking for him here?'

The peasants whispered among themselves.

'No one saw him,' the peasant in the felt cap finally admitted. 'Or heard him. How can you see him when he flies at night, in the dark? How can you hear him when he flies on bat's wings, without a sound?'

'We didn't see the vampire,' added another, 'but there are signs of his ghastly practices. Ever since the moon's been full, the fiend's murdered one of our number every night. He's already torn two people apart, ripped them to shreds. A woman and a stripling. Horrors and terrors! The vampire tore the poor wretches to ribbons and drank all their blood! What are we to do? Stand idly by for a third night?'

'But who says the culprit is a vampire, and not some other predator? Whose idea was it to root around in this burial ground?'

'The venerable priest told us to. He's a learned and pious man, and thanks be to the Gods he arrived in our camp. He said at once that a vampire was plaguing us. As punishment, for we've neglected our prayers and church donations. Now he's reciting prayers and carrying out all kinds of exorcismums in the camp, and ordered us to search for the tomb where the undead fiend sleeps during the day.'

'What, here?'

'And where would a vampire's grave be, if not in a burial ground? And anyway it's an elven burial ground and every toddler knows that elves are a rotten, godless race, and every second elf is condemned to damnation after death! Elves are to blame for everything!'

'Elves and barber-surgeons,' said Zoltan, nodding his head seriously. 'That's true. Every child knows that. That camp you were talking about, is it far from here?'

'Why, no . . .'

'Don't tell them too much, Father,' said an unshaven peasant with a shaggy fringe, the one who had previously been unfriendly. 'The devil only knows who they are; they're a queer-looking band. Come on, let's get to work. Let them give us the horse and they can go on their way.'

'Right you are,' the older peasant said. 'Let's not dilly-dally, time's getting on. Hand over the horse. That black one. We need it to search for the vampire. Get that kid off the saddle, lassie.'

Milva, who had been staring at the sky with a blank expression all along, looked at the peasant and her features hardened dangerously.

'Talking to me, yokel?'

'What do you think? Give us the black, we need it.'

Milva wiped her sweaty neck and gritted her teeth, and the expression in her tired eyes became truly ferocious.

'What's this all about, good people?' the Witcher asked, smiling and trying to defuse the tense situation. 'Why do you need this horse? The one you are so politely requesting?'

'How else are we going to find the vampire's grave? Everybody knows you have to ride around a cemetery on a black colt, as it will stop by the vampire's grave and will not be budged from it. Then you have to dig up the vampire and stab him with an aspen stake. Don't argue with us, for we're desperate. It's a matter of life and death here. We have to have that black horse!'

'Will another colour do?' Dandelion asked placatingly, holding out Pegasus's reins to the peasant.

'Not a chance.'

'Pity for you, then,' Milva said through clenched teeth. 'Because I'm not giving you my horse.'

'What do you mean you won't? Didn't you hear what we said, wench? We have to have it!'

'You might. But I don't have to give it to you.'

'We can solve this amicably,' Regis said in a kind voice. 'If I understand rightly, Miss Milva is reluctant to hand over her horse to a stranger . . .'

'You could say that,' the archer said, and spat heartily. 'I cringe at the very thought.'

'Both the wolves have eaten much and the sheep have not been touched,' the barber-surgeon recited calmly. 'Let Miss Milva mount the horse herself and carry out the necessary circuit of the necropolis.'

'I'm not going to ride around the graveyard like an idiot!'

'And no one's asking you to, wench!' said the one with the shaggy fringe. 'This requires a bold and strong blade; a maid's place is in the kitchen, bustling around the stove. A wench may come in handy later, true enough, because a virgin's tears are very useful against a vampire; for if you sprinkle a vampire with them he burns up like a firebrand. But the tears must be shed by a pure and untouched wench. And you don't quite look the part, love. So you're not much use for anything.'

Milva took a quick step forward and her right fist shot out as fast as lightning. There was a crack and the peasant's head lurched backwards, which meant his bristly throat and chin created an excellent target. The girl took another step and struck straight ahead with the heel of her open hand, increasing the force of the blow with a twist of her hips and shoulders. The peasant staggered backwards, tripped over his own feet and keeled over, banging the back of his head with an audible thud against the menhir.

'Now you see what use I am,' the archer said, in a voice trembling with fury, rubbing her fist. 'Who's the blade now, and whose place is in the kitchen? Truly, there's nothing like a fist-fight, which clears everything up. The bold and strong one is still on his feet, and the pussy and the milksop is lying on the ground. Am I right, yokels?'

The peasants didn't hurry to answer, but looked at Milva with their mouths wide open. The one in the felt cap knelt down by the one on the ground and slapped him gently on his cheek. In vain.

'Killed,' he wailed, raising his head. 'Dead. How could you, wench? How could you just up and kill a man?'

'I didn't mean to,' Milva whispered, lowering her hands and blenching frightfully. And then she did something no one expected.

She turned away, staggered, rested her forehead against the menhir and vomited violently.

'What's up with him?'

'Slight concussion,' the barber-surgeon replied, standing up and fastening his bag. 'His skull's in one piece. He's already regained consciousness. He remembers what happened and he knows his own name. That's a good sign. Miss Milva's intense reaction was, fortunately, groundless.'

The Witcher looked at the archer, who was sitting at the foot of the menhir with her eyes staring into the distance.

'She isn't a delicate maiden, prone to that sort of emotion,' he muttered. 'I'd be more inclined to blame yesterday's hooch.'

'She's puked before,' Zoltan broke in softly. 'The day before yesterday, at the crack of dawn. While everyone was still asleep. I think it's because of those mushrooms we scoffed in Turlough. My guts gave me grief for two days.'

Regis looked at the Witcher from under his greying eyebrows with a strange expression on his face, smiled mysteriously, and wrapped himself in his black, woollen cloak. Geralt went over to Milva and cleared his throat.

'How do you feel?'

'Rough. How's the yokel?'

'He'll be fine. He's come round. But Regis won't let him get up. The peasants are making a cradle and we'll carry him to the camp between two horses.'

150

'Take mine.'

'We're using Pegasus and the chestnut. They're more docile. Get up, it's time we hit the road.'

The enlarged company now resembled a funeral procession and crawled along at a funereal pace.

'What do you think about this vampire of theirs?' Zoltan Chivay asked the Witcher. 'Do you believe their story?'

'I didn't see the victims. I can't comment.'

'It's a pack of lies,' Dandelion declared with conviction. 'The peasants said the dead had been torn apart. Vampires don't do that. They bite into an artery and drink the blood, leaving two clear fang marks. The victim quite often survives. I've read about it in a respectable book. There were also illustrations showing the marks of vampire bites on virgins' swanlike necks. Can you confirm that, Geralt?'

'What do you want me to confirm? I didn't see those illustrations. I'm not very clued up about virgins, either.'

'Don't scoff. You can't be a stranger to vampire bite marks. Ever come across a case of a vampire ripping its victim to shreds?'

'No. That never happens.'

'In the case of higher vampires – never, I agree,' Emiel Regis said softly. 'From what I know alpors, katakans, moolas, bruxas and nosferats don't mutilate their victims. On the other hand, fleders and ekimmas are pretty brutal with their victims' remains.'

'Bravo,' Geralt said, looking at him in genuine admiration. 'You didn't leave out a single class of vampire. Nor did you mention any of the imaginary ones, which only exist in fairy-tales. Impressive knowledge indeed. You must also know that ekimmas and fleders are never encountered in this climate.'

'What happened, then?' Zoltan snorted, swinging his ashen staff. 'Who mutilated that woman and that lad in this climate, then? Or did they mutilate themselves in a fit of desperation?'

'The list of creatures that may have been responsible is pretty long. Beginning with a pack of feral dogs, quite a common affliction during times of war. You can't imagine what dogs like that are capable of. Half the supposed victims of chaotic monsters can actually be chalked up to packs of wild farmyard curs.'

'Does that mean you rule out monsters?'

'Not in the least. It may have been a striga, a harpy, a graveir, a ghoul . . .'

'Not a vampire?'

'Unlikely.'

'The peasants mentioned some priest or other,' Percival Schuttenbach recalled. 'Do priests know much about vampires?'

'Some are expert on a range of subjects, to quite an advanced level, and their opinions are worth listening to, as a rule. Sadly, that doesn't apply to all of them.'

'Particularly the kind that roam around forests with fugitives,' the dwarf snorted. 'He's most probably some kind of hermit, an illiterate anchorite from the wilderness. He dispatched a peasant expedition to your burial ground, Regis. Have you never noticed a single vampire while you were gathering mandrake there? Not even a tiny one? A teeny-weeny one?'

'No, never,' the barber-surgeon gave a faint smile. 'But no wonder. A vampire, as you've just heard, flies in the dark on bat's wings, without making a sound. He's easy to miss.'

'And easy to see one where it isn't and has never been,' Geralt confirmed. 'When I was younger, I wasted my time and energy several times chasing after delusions and superstitions which had been seen and colourfully described by an entire village, including the headman. Once I spent two months living in a castle which was supposedly haunted by a vampire. There was no vampire. But they fed me well.'

'No doubt, however, you have experienced cases when the rumours about vampires were well founded,' Regis said, not looking at the Witcher. 'In those cases, I presume, your time and energy were not wasted. Did the monsters die by your sword?'

'It has been known.'

'In any event,' Zoltan said, 'the peasants are in luck. I think we'll wait in that camp for Munro Bruys and the lads, and a rest won't do you any harm either. Whatever killed the woman and the boy,

I don't fancy its chances when the Witcher turns up in the camp.'

'While we're at it,' Geralt said, pursing his lips, 'I'd rather you didn't bruit who I am and what my name is. That particularly applies to you, Dandelion.'

'As you wish,' the dwarf nodded. 'You must have your reasons. Lucky you've forewarned us, because I can see the camp.'

'And I can hear it,' Milva added, breaking a lengthy silence. 'They're making a fearful racket.'

'The sound we can hear,' Dandelion said, playing the wiseacre, 'is the everyday symphony of a refugee camp. As usual, scored for several hundred human throats, as well as no fewer bovine, ovine and anserine ones. The solo parts are being performed by women squabbling, children bawling, a cock crowing and, if I'm not mistaken, a donkey, who someone's poked in the backside with a thistle. The title of the symphony is: *A human community fights for survival*.'

'The symphony, as usual, can be heard *and* smelled,' Regis observed, quivering the nostrils of his noble nose. 'This community – as it fights for survival – gives off the delicious fragrance of boiled cabbage, a vegetable without which survival would apparently be impossible. The characteristic olfactory accent is also being created by the effects of bodily functions, carried out in random places, most often on the outskirts of the camp. I've never understood why the fight for survival manifests itself in a reluctance to dig latrines.'

'To hell with your smart-arsed chatter,' said Milva in annoyance. 'Three dozen fancy words when three will do: it stinks of shit and cabbage!'

'Shit and cabbage always go hand in hand,' Percival Schuttenbach said pithily. 'One drives the other. It's perpetuum mobile.'

No sooner had they set foot in the noisy and foul-smelling camp, among the campfires, wagons and shelters, than they became the centre of interest of all the fugitives gathered there, of which there must have been at least two hundred, possibly even more. The interest bore fruit quickly and remarkably; someone suddenly screamed, someone else suddenly bellowed, someone suddenly flung their arms around someone else's neck, someone began to laugh wildly, and someone else to sob wildly. There was a huge commotion. At first it was difficult to work out what was happening among the cacophony of men, women and children screaming, but finally all was explained. Two of the women from Kernow who had been travelling with them had found, respectively, a husband and a brother, whom they had believed to be dead or to missing without trace in the turmoil of war. The delight and tears seemed to be never-ending.

'Something so banal and melodramatic,' Dandelion said with conviction, indicating the moving scene, 'could only happen in real life. If I tried to end one of my ballads like that, I would be ribbed mercilessly.'

'Undoubtedly,' Zoltan confirmed. 'Nonetheless, banalities like these gladden the heart, don't they? One feels more cheerful when fortune gives one something, rather than only taking. Well, we've got rid of the womenfolk. We guided them and guided them and finally got them here. Come on, no point hanging around.'

For a moment, the Witcher felt like suggesting they delay their departure. He was counting on one of the women deciding it would be fitting to express a few words of gratitude and thanks to the dwarf. He abandoned that idea, though, when he saw no sign of it happening. The women, overjoyed at being reunited with their loved ones, had completely forgotten about Geralt and his company.

'What are you waiting for?' Zoltan said, looking at him keenly. 'To be covered in blossom out of gratitude? Or anointed with honey? Let's clear off; there's nothing for us here.'

'You're absolutely right.'

They didn't get far. A squeaky little voice stopped them in their tracks. The freckle-faced little girl with the plaits had caught them up. She was out of breath and had a large posy of wild flowers in her hand.

'Thank you,' she squeaked, 'for looking after me and my little brother and my mummy. For being kind to us and all that. I picked these flowers for you.'

'Thank you,' Zoltan Chivay said.

'You're kind,' the little girl added, sticking the end of her plait into her mouth. 'I don't believe what auntie said at all. You aren't filthy little burrowing midgets. And you aren't a grey-haired misfit from hell. And you, Uncle Dandelion, aren't a gobbling turkey. Auntie wasn't telling the truth. And you, Auntie Maria, aren't a slapper with a bow and arrow. You're Auntie Maria and I like you. I picked the prettiest flowers for you.'

'Thank you,' Milva said in a slightly altered voice.

'We all thank you,' Zoltan echoed. 'Hey, Percival, you filthy little burrowing midget, give the child some token as a farewell present. A souvenir. Have you got a spare stone in one of your pockets?'

'I have. Take this, little miss. It's beryllium aluminium cyclosilicate, popularly known as . . .'

'An emerald,' the dwarf finished off the sentence. 'Don't confuse the child, she won't remember anyway.'

'Oh, how pretty! And how green! Thank you very, very much!'

'Enjoy it and may it bring you fortune.'

'And don't lose it,' Dandelion muttered. 'Because that little pebble's worth as much as a small farm.'

'Get away,' Zoltan said, adorning his cap with the cornflowers the girl had given him. 'It's only a stone, nothing special. Take care of yourself, little miss. Let's go and sit down by the ford to wait for Bruys, Yazon Varda and the others. They ought to stroll by any time now. Strange they haven't shown up yet. I forgot to get the bloody cards off 'em. I bet they're sitting somewhere and playing Barrel!'

'The horses need feeding,' Milva said. 'And watering. Let's go towards the river.'

'Perhaps we'll happen upon some home-cooked fare,' Dandelion added. 'Percival, take a gander around the camp and put your hooter to use. We'll eat where the food is tastiest.'

To their slight amazement, the way down to the river was fenced off and under guard. The peasants guarding the watering place were demanding a farthing per horse. Milva and Zoltan were incandescent, but Geralt, hoping to avoid a scene and the publicity it would lead to, calmed them down, while Dandelion contributed a few coins he dug from the depths of his pocket.

Soon after Percival Schuttenbach showed up, dour and cross.

'Found any grub?'

The gnome cleared his nose and wiped his fingers on the fleece of a passing sheep.

'Yes. But I don't know if we can afford it. They expect to be paid for everything here and the prices will take your breath away. Flour and barley groats are a crown a pound. A plate of thin soup's two nobles. A pot of weatherfish caught in the Chotla costs the same as a pound of smoked salmon in Dillingen . . .'

'And fodder for the horses?'

'A measure of oats costs a thaler.'

'How much?' the dwarf yelled. 'How much?'

'How much, how much,' Milva snapped. 'Ask the horses how much. They'll peg it if we make them nibble grass! And there isn't any here anyway.'

There was no way of debating self-evident facts. Attempts at hard bargaining with the peasant selling oats didn't achieve anything either. He relieved Dandelion of the last of his coins, and was also treated to a few insults from Zoltan, which didn't bother him in the slightest. But the horses enthusiastically stuck their muzzles into the nosebags.

'Daylight bloody robbery!' the dwarf yelled, unloading his anger by aiming blows of his staff at the wheels of passing wagons. 'Incredible that they let us breathe here for nothing, and don't charge a ha'penny for each inhalation! Or a farthing for a dump!'

'Higher physiological needs,' Regis declared in utter seriousness, 'have a price. Do you see the tarpaulin stretched between those sticks? And the peasant standing alongside? He's peddling the charms of his own daughter. Price open to negotiation. A moment ago I saw him accepting a chicken.'

'I predict a bad end for your race, humans,' Zoltan Chivay said grimly. 'Every sentient creature on this earth, when it falls into want, poverty and misfortune, usually cleaves to his own. Because it's easier to survive the bad times in a group, helping one another. But you, humans, you just wait for a chance to make money from other people's mishaps. When there's hunger you don't share out your food, you just devour the weakest ones. This practice works among wolves, since it lets the healthiest and strongest individuals survive. But among sentient races selection of that kind usually allows the biggest bastards to survive and dominate the rest. Come to your own conclusions and make your own predictions.'

Dandelion forcefully protested, giving examples of even greater scams and self-seeking among the dwarves, but Zoltan and Percival drowned him out, simultaneously and loudly imitating with their lips the long-drawn-out sounds which accompany farting, by both races considered an expression of disdain for one's adversary's arguments in a dispute.

The sudden appearance of a small group of peasants led by their friend the vampire hunter, the old chap in the felt cap, brought an end to the quarrel.

'It's about Cloggy,' one of the peasants said.

'We aren't buying anything,' the dwarf and the gnome snapped in unison.

'The one whose head you split open,' another peasant quickly explained. 'We were planning to get him married off.'

'We've got nothing against that,' Zoltan said angrily. 'We wish him and his new bride all the best. Good health, happiness and prosperity.'

'And lots of little Cloggies,' Dandelion added.

'Just a moment,' the peasant said. 'You may laugh, but how are we to get him hitched? For ever since you whacked him in the head he's been totally dazed, and can't tell day from night.'

'It isn't that bad,' Milva grunted, eyes fixed on the ground. 'He seems to be doing better. That is, much better than he was early this morning.'

'I've got no idea how Cloggy was early this morning,' the peasant retorted. 'But I just saw him standing in front of an upright thill saying what a beauty she was. But never mind. I'll say it briefly: pay up the blood money.'

'What?'

'When a knight kills a peasant he must pay blood money. So says the law.'

'I'm not a knight!' Milva yelled.

'That's one thing,' Dandelion said in her defence. 'And for another, it was an accident. And for a third, Cloggy's alive, so blood money's out of the question. The most you can expect is compensation, namely redress. But for a fourth, we're penniless.'

'So hand over your horses.'

'Hey,' Milva said, her eyes narrowing malevolently. 'You must be out of your mind, yokel. Mind you don't go too far.'

'Motherrfuccckkerr!' Field Marshal Windbag squawked.

'Ah, the bird's hit the nail on the head,' Zoltan Chivay drawled, tapping his axe, which was stuck into his belt. 'You ought to know, tillers of the soil, that I also don't have the best opinion about the mothers of individuals who think of nothing but profit, even if they plan to make money out of their mate's cracked skull. Be off with you, people. If you go away forthwith, I promise I won't come after you.'

'If you don't want to pay, let the authorities arbitrate.'

The dwarf ground his teeth and was just reaching for his battle-axe when Geralt seized him by the elbow.

'Calm down. How do you want to solve this problem? By killing them all?'

'Why kill them right away? It's enough to cripple them good and proper.'

'That's enough, darn it,' the Witcher hissed, and then turned to the peasant. 'These authorities you were talking about; who are they?'

'Our camp elder, Hector Laabs, the headman from Breza, one of the villages that was burnt down.'

'Lead us to him, then. We'll come to some agreement.'

'He's busy at present,' the peasant announced. 'He's sitting in judgement on a witch. There, do you see that crowd by the maple? They've caught a hag who was in league with a vampire.'

'Here we go again,' Dandelion snorted, spreading his arms. 'Did you hear that? When they aren't digging up cemeteries they're hunting witches, supposedly vampires' accomplices. Folks, perhaps instead of ploughing, sowing and harvesting, you'll become witchers.'

'Joke as much as you like,' the peasant said, 'and laugh all you want, but there's a priest here and priests are more trustworthy than witchers. The priest said that vampires always carry out their practices in league with witches. The witch summons the vampire and points out the victim to him, then blinds everyone's eyes so they won't see anything.'

'And it turned out it was indeed like that,' a second one added. 'We were harbouring a treacherous hag among us. But the priest saw through her witchcraft and now we're going to burn her.'

'What else,' the Witcher muttered. 'Very well, we'll take a look at your court. And we'll talk to the elder about the accident that befell the unfortunate Cloggy. We'll think about suitable compensation. Right, Percival? I'll wager that we'll find another pebble in one of your pockets. Lead on, good people.'

The procession set off towards a spreading maple. The ground beneath it was indeed teeming with excited people. The Witcher, having purposely slowed his pace, tried to strike up a conversation with one of the peasants, who looked reasonably normal.

'Who's this witch they've captured? Was she really engaged in black magic?'

'Well, sir,' the peasant mumbled, 'I couldn't say. That wench is a waif, a stranger. To my mind, she's not quite right in the head. Grown-up, but still only plays with the nippers, as if she was a child herself; ask her something and she won't say a word. Everyone says she consorted with a vampire and hexed people.'

'Everyone except the suspect,' said Regis, who until then had been walking quietly beside the Witcher. 'Because she, if asked, wouldn't utter a word. I'm guessing.'

There was not enough time for a more detailed investigation, because they were already under the maple. They made their way through the crowd, not without the help of Zoltan and his ashen staff.

A girl of about sixteen had been tied to the rack of a wagon laden with sacks, her arms spread wide apart. The girl's toes barely reached the ground. Just as they arrived, her shift and blouse were torn away to reveal thin shoulders. The captive reacted by rolling her eyes and loosing a foolish combination of giggling and sobbing.

A fire had been started directly alongside the wagon. Someone had fanned the coals well and someone else had used pincers to place some horseshoes in the glowing embers. The excited cries of the priest rose above the crowd.

'Vile witch! Godless female! Confess the truth! Ha, just look at her, people, she's overindulged in some devilish herbs! Just look at her! Witchery is written all over her countenance!'

The priest who spoke those words was thin and his face was as dark and dry as a smoked fish. His black robes hung loosely on his skinny frame. A sacred symbol glistened on his neck. Geralt didn't recognise which deity it represented, and anyway he wasn't an expert. The pantheon, which in recent times had been growing quickly, did not interest him much. The priest must, however, have belonged to one of the newer religious sects. The older ones were concerned with more useful matters than catching girls, tying them to wagons and inciting superstitious mobs against them.

'Since the dawn of time woman has been the root of all evil! The tool of Chaos, the accomplice in a conspiracy against the world and the human race! Woman is governed only by carnal lust! That is why she so willingly serves demons, in order to slake her insatiable urges and her unnatural wantonness!'

'We'll soon learn more about women,' Regis muttered. 'This a phobia, in a pure clinical form. The devout man must often dream about a *vagina dentata*.'

'I'll wager it's worse,' Dandelion murmured. 'I'm absolutely certain that even when he's awake he dreams about a regular toothless one. And the semen has affected his brain.'

'But it's this feeble-minded girl who will have to pay for it.'

'Unless we can find someone,' Milva growled, 'who'll stop that black-robed ass.'

Dandelion looked meaningfully and hopefully at the Witcher, but Geralt avoided his gaze.

'And of what, if not female witchery, are our current calamities and misfortunes the result?' the priest continued to yell. 'For no one else but the sorceresses betrayed the kings on the Isle of Thanedd and concocted the assassination of the King of Redania! Indeed, no one else but the elven witch of Dol Blathanna is sending Squirrels after us! Now you see to what evil the familiarity with sorceresses has led us! And the tolerance of their vile practices! Turning a blind eye to their wilfulness, their impudent hubris, their wealth! And who is to blame? The kings! The vainglorious kings renounced the Gods, drove away the priests, took away their offices and seats on councils, and showered the loathsome sorceresses with honours and gold! And now we all suffer the consequences!'

'Aha! There lies the rub,' Dandelion said. 'You were wrong, Regis. It was all about politics and not vaginas.'

'And about money,' Zoltan Chivay added.

'Verily,' the priest roared, 'I say unto you, before we join battle with Nilfgaard, let us first purge our own house of these abominations! Scorch this abscess with a white-hot iron! Subject it to a baptism of fire! We shall not allow any woman who dabbles in witchcraft to live!'

'We shall not allow it! Burn her at the stake!' yelled the crowd.

The girl who was bound to the wagon laughed hysterically and rolled her eyes.

'All right, all right, easy does it,' said a lugubrious peasant of immense size who until that moment had been silent, and around whom was gathered a small group of similarly silent men and several grim-faced women. 'We've only heard squawking so far. Everyone's capable of squawking, even crows. We expect more from you, venerable father, than we would from a crow.'

'Do you refute my words, Elder Laabs? The words of a priest?'

'I'm not refitting anything,' the giant replied, then he spat on the ground and hitched up a pair of coarse britches. 'That wench is an orphan and a stray, no family of mine. If it turns out that she is in league with a vampire, take her and kill her. But while I'm the elder of this camp, only the guilty will be punished here. If you want to punish her, first establish her guilt.'

'That I shall!' the priest screamed, giving a sign to his stooges, the same ones who had previously put the horseshoes into the fire. 'I'll show you incontrovertibly! You, Laabs, and everyone else present here!'

His stooges brought out a small, blackened cauldron with a curved handle from behind the wagon and set it on the ground.

'Here is the proof!' the priest roared, kicking the cauldron over. A thin liquid spilt onto the ground, depositing some small pieces of carrots, some strips of unrecognisable greens and several small bones onto the sand. 'The witch was brewing a magic concoction! An elixir which enabled her to fly through the air to her vampire-lover. To have immoral relations with him and hatch more iniquities! I know the ways and deeds of sorcerers and I know what that decoct is made of! The witch boiled up a cat alive!'

The crowd oohed and aahed in horror.

'Ghastly,' Dandelion said, shuddering. 'Boiling a creature alive? I felt sorry for the girl, but she went a bit too far . . .'

'Shut your gob,' Milva hissed.

'Here is the proof!' the priest yelled, holding up a small bone he had removed from the steaming puddle. 'Here is the irrefutable proof! A cat's bone!'

'That's a bird's bone,' Zoltan Chivay said coldly, squinting. 'It's a jay's, I would say, or a pigeon's. The girl cooked herself some broth, and that's that!'

'Silence, you pagan imp!' the priest roared. 'Don't blaspheme, or the Gods will punish you at the hands of the pious! The brew came from a cat, I tell you!'

'From a cat! Without doubt a cat!' the peasants surrounding the priest yelled. 'The wench had a cat! A black cat! Everyone knew she did! It followed her around everywhere! And where is that cat now? It's gone! Gone into the pot!'

'Cooked! Boiled up as a potion!'

'Right you are! The witch has cooked up the cat into a potion!'

'No other proof is needed! Into the fire with the witch! But first torture her! Let her confess everything!'

''Kin' 'ell!' Field Marshal Windbag squawked.

'It's a shame about that cat,' Percival Schuttenbach suddenly said in a loud voice. 'It was a fine beast, sleek and fat. Fur shining like anthracite, eyes like two chrysoberyls, long whiskers, and a tail as thick as a mechanical's tool! Everything you could want in a cat. He must have caught plenty of mice!'

The peasants fell silent.

'And how would you know, Master Gnome?' someone asked. 'How do you know what the cat looked like?'

Percival Schuttenbach cleared his nose and wiped his fingers on a trouser leg.

'Because he's sitting over there on a cart. Right behind you.'

The peasants all turned around at once, muttering as they observed the cat sitting on a pile of bundles. The cat, meanwhile, utterly unconcerned about being the centre of attention, stuck a hind leg up in the air and got down to licking his rump.

'Thus it has turned out,' Zoltan Chivay said, breaking the silence, 'that your irrefutable proof is a load of crap, reverend. What will the next proof be? Perhaps a she-cat? That would be good. Then we'll put them together, they'll produce a litter and not a single rodent will come within half an arrow's shot of the granary.'

Several peasants snorted, and several others, including Elder Laabs, cackled openly. The priest turned purple with rage.

'I will remember you, blasphemer!' he roared, pointing a finger at the dwarf. 'O heathen kobold! O creature of darkness! How did you come to be here? Perhaps you are in collusion with the vampire? Just wait; we'll punish the witch and then we'll inter-rogate you! But first we'll try the witch! Horseshoes have already been put on the coals, so we'll see what the sinner reveals when her hideous skin starts to sizzle! I tell you she will confess to the crimes of witchcraft herself. And what more proof is there than a confession?'

'Oh, she will, she will,' Hector Laabs said. 'And were red-hot horseshoes placed against the soles of your feet, reverend, you would surely even confess to immoral coition with a mare. Ugh! You're a godly man, but you sound like a rascal!'

'Yes, I'm a godly man!' the priest bellowed, outshouting the inten-sifying murmurs of the peasants. 'I believe in divine judgement! And in a divine trial! Let the witch face trial by ordeal . . .'

'Excellent idea,' the Witcher interrupted loudly, stepping out from the crowd.

The priest glared at him. The peasants stopped muttering and stared at him with mouths agape.

'Trial by ordeal,' Geralt repeated to complete silence from the crowd, 'is utterly certain and utterly just. The verdicts of trial by ordeal are also accepted by secular courts and have their own principles. These rules say that in the case of a charge against a woman, child, old or otherwise enfeebled person a defence counsel may represent them. Am I right, Elder Laabs? So, I hereby offer myself in that role. Mark off the circle. Whomsoever is certain of the girl's guilt and is not afraid of trial of ordeal should step forward and do battle with me.'

'Ha!' the priest called, still glaring at him. 'Don't be too cunning, noble stranger. Throwing down the gauntlet? It's clear at once you are a swordsman and a killer! You wish to conduct a trial of ordeal with your criminal sword?'

'If the sword doesn't suit you, your reverence,' Zoltan Chivay announced in a drawling voice, standing alongside Geralt, 'and if you object to this gentleman, perhaps I would be more suitable. By all means, may the girl's accuser take up a battle-axe against me.'

'Or challenge me at archery,' Milva said, narrowing her eyes and also stepping forward. 'A single arrow each at a hundred paces.'

'Do you see, people, how quickly defenders of the witch are springing up?' the priest screamed, and then turned away and contorted his face into a cunning smile. 'Very well, you good-for-nothings, I invite all three of you to the trial by ordeal which will soon take place. We shall establish the hag's guilt, and test your virtue at one and the same time! But not using swords, battle-axes, lances or arrows! You know, you say, the rules? I also know them! See the horseshoes in the coals, glowing white-hot? Baptism of fire! Come, O minions of witchcraft! Whomsoever removes a horseshoe from the fire, brings it to me and betrays no marks of burning, will have proven that the witch is innocent. If, though, the trial of ordeal reveals something else, then it shall be death to all of you and to her! I have spoken!'

The hostile rumble of Elder Laabs and his group was drowned out by the enthusiastic cries of most of the people gathered behind the priest. The mob had already scented excellent sport and entertainment. Milva looked at Zoltan, Zoltan at the Witcher, and the Witcher first at the sky and then at Milva.

'Do you believe in the Gods?' he asked in hushed tones.

'Yes, I do,' the archer snapped back softly, looking at the glowing coals. 'But I don't think they'll want to be bothered by red-hot horseshoes.'

'It's no more than three paces from the fire to that bastard,' Zoltan hissed through clenched teeth. 'I'll get through it somehow, I worked in a foundry . . . But if you wouldn't mind praying to your Gods for me. . .'

'One moment,' Emiel Regis said, placing a hand on the dwarf's shoulder. 'Please withhold your prayers.'

The barber-surgeon walked over to the fire, bowed to the priest and the audience, then stooped rapidly and put his hand into the hot coals. The crowd screamed as one, Zoltan cursed and Milva dug her fingers into Geralt's arm. Regis straightened up, calmly looked down at the white-hot horseshoe he was holding, and walked unhurriedly over to the priest. The priest took a step back, bumping into the peasants standing behind him.

'This was the idea, if I'm not mistaken, your reverence.' Regis said, holding up the horseshoe. 'Baptism of fire? If so, I believe the divine judgement is unambiguous. The girl is innocent. Her defenders are innocent. And I, just imagine, am also innocent.'

'Sh . . . sh . . . show me your hand . . .' the priest mumbled. 'Is it not burnt?'

The barber-surgeon smiled his usual smile, with pursed lips, then moved the horseshoe to his left hand, and showed his right hand, totally unharmed, first to the priest, and then, holding it up high, to everyone else. The crowd roared.

'Whose horseshoe is it?' Regis asked. 'Let the owner take it back.'

No one came forward.

'It's a devilish trick!' the priest bellowed. 'You are a sorcerer yourself, or the devil incarnate!'

Regis threw the horseshoe onto the ground and turned around.

'Carry out an exorcism on me then,' he suggested coldly. 'You are free to do so. But the trial of ordeal has taken place. I have heard, though, that to question its verdict is heresy.'

'Perish. Be gone!' the priest shrieked, waving an amulet in front of the barber-surgeon's nose and tracing cabbalistic signs with his other hand. 'Be gone to the abyss of hell, devil! May the earth be riven asunder beneath you . . .'

'That is enough!' Zoltan shouted angrily. 'Hey, people! Elder Laabs! Do you intend to stand and watch this foolishness any longer? Do you intend . . . ?'

The dwarf's voice was drowned out by a piercing cry.

'Niiiilfgaaaaaard!'

'Cavalry from the west! Horsemen! Nilfgaard are attacking! Every man for himself!'

In one moment the camp was transformed into total pandemonium. The peasants charged towards their wagons and shelters, knocking each other down and trampling on each other. A single, great cry rose up into the sky.

'Our horses!' Milva yelled, making room around herself with punches and kicks. 'Our horses, Witcher! Follow me, quickly!'

'Geralt!' Dandelion shouted. 'Save me!'

The crowd separated them, scattered them like a great wave and carried Milva away in the blink of an eye. Geralt, gripping Dandelion by the collar, didn't allow himself to be swept away, for just in time he caught hold of the wagon which the girl accused of witchcraft was tied to. The wagon, however, suddenly lurched and moved off, and the Witcher and the poet fell to the ground. The girl jerked her head and began to laugh hysterically. As the wagon receded the laughter became quieter and was then lost among the uproar.

'They'll trample us!' Dandelion shouted from the ground. 'They'll crush us! Heeeelp!'

''Kiiin' 'ell!' Field Marshal Windbag squawked from somewhere out of sight.

Geralt raised his head, spat out some sand and saw a chaotic scene. Only four people did not panic, although to tell the truth one of them simply had no choice. That was the priest, unable to move owing to his neck being held in the iron grip of Hector Laabs. The two other individuals were Zoltan and Percival. The gnome lifted up the priest's robe at the back with a rapid movement, and the dwarf, armed with the pincers, seized a red-hot horseshoe from the fire and dropped it down the saintly man's long johns. Freed from Laabs's grip, the priest shot straight ahead like a comet with a smoking tail, but his screams were drowned in the roar of the crowd. Geralt saw Laabs, the gnome and the dwarf about to congratulate one another on a successful ordeal by fire when another wave of panic-stricken peasants descended upon them. Everything disappeared in clouds of dust. The Witcher could no longer see anything, though neither did he have time to watch since he was busy rescuing Dandelion, whose legs had been swept from under him again by a stampeding hog. When Geralt bent down to lift the poet up, a hay rack was thrown straight on his back from a wagon rattling past. The weight pinned him to the ground, and before he was able to throw it off a dozen people ran across it. When he finally freed himself, another wagon overturned with a bang and a crash right alongside, and three sacks of wheaten flour – costing a crown a pound in the camp – fell onto him. The sacks split open and the world vanished in a white cloud.

'Get up, Geralt!' the troubadour yelled. 'Get on your blasted feet!'

'I can't,' the Witcher groaned, blinded by the precious flour, seizing in both hands his knee, which had been shot through by an overwhelming pain. 'Save yourself. Dandelion . . .'

'I won't leave you!'

Gruesome screams could be heard from the western edge of the camp, mixed up with the thud of iron-shod hooves and the neighing of horses. The screaming and tramping of hooves intensified suddenly, and the ringing, clanging and banging of metal striking against metal joined it.

'It's a battle!' the poet shouted. 'It's war!'

'Who's fighting who?' Geralt asked, trying desperately to clean the flour and chaff from his eyes. Not far away something was on fire, and they were engulfed by a wave of heat and a cloud of foul-smelling smoke. The hoofbeats rose in their ears and the earth shuddered. The first thing he saw in the cloud of dust were dozens of horses' fetlocks crashing up and down. All around him. He fought off the pain.

'Get under the wagon! Hide under the wagon, Dandelion, or they'll trample us!'

'Let's stay still . . .' the poet whimpered, flattened against the ground. 'Let's just lie here . . . I've heard a horse will never tread on a person lying on the ground . . .'

'I'm not sure,' Geralt exhaled, 'if every horse has heard that. Under the wagon! Quickly!'

At that moment one of the horses, unaware of human proverbs, kicked him in the side of the head as it thundered by. Suddenly all the constellations of the firmament flashed red and gold in the Witcher's eyes, and a moment later the earth and the sky were engulfed in impenetrable darkness.

The Rats sprang up, awoken by a long-drawn-out scream that boomed with an intensifying echo around the walls of the cave. Asse and Reef seized their swords and Iskra swore loudly as she banged her head on a rocky protrusion.

'What is it?' Kayleigh yelled. 'What's happening?'

It was dark in the cave even though the sun was shining outside – the Rats had been sleeping off a night spent in the saddle, fleeing from pursuers. Giselher shoved a brand into the glowing embers, lit it, held it up and walked over to where Ciri and Mistle were sleeping, as usual away from the rest of the gang. Ciri was sitting with her head down and Mistle had her arm around her.

Giselher lifted the flaming brand higher. The others also approached. Mistle covered Ciri's naked shoulders with a fur.

'Listen, Mistle,' the leader of the Rats said gravely. 'I've never interfered with what you two do in a single bed. I've never said a nasty or mocking word. I always try to look the other way and not notice. It's your business and your tastes, and nobody else's, as long as you do it discreetly and quietly. But this time you went a little too far.'

'Don't be stupid,' Mistle exploded. 'Are you trying to say that . . . ? She was screaming in her sleep! It was a nightmare!'

'Don't yell. Falka?'

Ciri nodded.

'Was your dream so dreadful? What was it about?'

'Leave her in peace!'

'Give it a rest, Mistle. Falka?'

'Someone, someone I once knew,' Ciri stammered, 'was being trampled by horses. The hooves . . . I felt them crushing me . . . I felt his pain . . . In my head and knee . . . I can still feel it. I'm sorry I woke you up.'

'Don't be sorry,' Giselher said, looking at Mistle's stern expression. 'You two deserve the apology. Forgive me. And the dream? Why, anybody could have dreamed that. Anybody.'

Ciri closed her eyes. She wasn't certain if Giselher was right.

He was awoken by a kick.

He was lying with his head against a wheel of the overturned cart, with Dandelion hunched up alongside him. He had been kicked by a foot soldier in a padded jacket and a round helmet. A second stood beside him. They were both holding the reins of horses, the saddles of which were hung with crossbows and shields.

'Bloody millers or what?'

The other soldier shrugged. Geralt saw that Dandelion couldn't take his eyes off the shields. Geralt himself had already noticed that there were lilies on them. The emblem of the Kingdom of Temeria. Other mounted crossbowmen – who were swarming around nearby – also bore the same arms. Most of them were busy catching horses and stripping the dead. The latter mainly wore black Nilfgaardian cloaks.

The camp was still a smoking ruin after the attack, but peasants who had survived and hadn't fled very far were beginning to reappear. The mounted crossbowmen with Temerian lilies were rounding them up with loud shouts.

Neither Milva, Zoltan, Percival nor Regis were anywhere to be seen.

The hero of the recent witchcraft trial, the black tomcat, sat alongside the cart, dispassionately looking at Geralt with his greenish-golden eyes. The Witcher was a little surprised, since ordinary cats couldn't bear his presence. He had no time to reflect on this unusual phenomenon, since one of the soldiers was prodding him with the shaft of his lance.

'Get up, you two! Hey, the grey-haired one has a sword!'

'Drop your weapon!' the other one shouted, attracting the attention of the rest. 'Drop your sword on the ground. Right now, or I'll stick you with my glaive.'

Geralt obeyed. His head was ringing.

'Who are you?'

'Travellers,' Dandelion said.

'Sure you are,' the soldier snorted. 'Are you travelling home? After fleeing from your standard and throwing away your uniforms? There are plenty of travellers like that in this camp, who've taken fright at Nilfgaard and lost the taste for army bread! Some of them are old friends of ours. From our regiment!'

'Those travellers can expect another trip now,' his companion cackled. 'A short one! Upwards on a rope!'

'We aren't deserters!' the poet yelled.

'We'll find out who you are. When you account for yourselves to the officer.'

A unit of light horse led by several armoured cavalrymen with splendid plumes on their helmets emerged from the ring of mounted crossbowmen.

Dandelion looked closely at the knights, brushed the flour off himself and tidied up his clothing, then spat on a hand and smoothed down his dishevelled hair.

'Geralt, keep quiet,' he forewarned. 'I'll parley with them. They're Temerian knights. They defeated the Nilfgaardians. They won't do anything to us. I know how to talk to the knighthood. You have to show them they aren't dealing with commoners, but with equals.'

'Dandelion, for the love of . . .'

'Never fear, everything will be fine. I have a lot of experience in talking to the knighthood and the nobility; half of Temeria know me. Hey, out of our way, servants, step aside! I wish to speak with your superiors!'

The soldiers looked on hesitantly, and then raised their couched lances and made room. Dandelion and Geralt moved towards the knights. The poet strode proudly, bearing a lordly expression which was somewhat out of place considering his frayed and flour-soiled tunic.

'Stop!' one of the armoured men yelled at him. 'Not another step! Who are you?'

'Who should I tell?' Dandelion said, putting his hands on his hips. 'And why? Who are these well-born lords, that they oppress innocent travellers?'

'You don't ask the questions, riffraff! You answer them!'

The troubadour inclined his head and looked at the coats of arms on the knights' shields and tabards.

'Three red hearts on a golden field,' he observed. 'That means you are an Aubry. There's a three-pointed label on the shield's chief, so you must be the eldest son of Anzelm Aubry. I know your pater well, good Sir Knight. And you, strident Sir Knight, what do you have on your silver shield? A black stripe between two gryphons' heads? The Papebrock family's coat of arms, if I'm not mistaken, and I am rarely mistaken in matters of this kind. The stripe, they say, illustrates the acuity possessed by that family's members.'

'Will you bloody stop,' Geralt groaned.

'I'm the celebrated poet Dandelion!' the bard said, puffing himself up and paying no attention to the Witcher. 'No doubt you've heard of me? Lead me, then, to your commander, to the seigneur, for I'm accustomed to speaking with equals!'

The knights did not react, but their facial expressions became more and more uncongenial and their iron gloves gripped their decorated bridles more and more tightly. Dandelion clearly hadn't noticed.

'Well, what's the matter with you?' he asked haughtily. 'What are you staring at? Yes, I'm talking to you, Sir Black Stripe! Why are you making faces? Did someone tell you that if you narrow your eyes and stick your lower jaw out you look manly, doughty, dignified and menacing? Well, they deceived you. You look like someone who hasn't had a decent shit for a week!'

'Seize them!' yelled the eldest son of Anzelm Aubry – the bearer of the shield with three hearts – to the foot soldiers. The Black Stripe from the Papebrock family spurred his steed.

'Seize them! Bind the blackguards!'

They walked behind the horses, pulled by ropes attaching their wrists to the pommels. They walked and occasionally ran, because the horsemen spared neither their mounts nor their captives. Dandelion fell over twice and was dragged along on his belly, yelling pathetically. He was stood up again and urged on roughly with the lance shaft. And then driven on once more. The dust choked and blinded them, making their eyes water and their noses tingle. Thirst parched their throats.

Only one thing was encouraging; the road they were being driven along was heading south. Geralt was thus journeying in the right direction at last and pretty quickly, at that. He wasn't happy, though. Because he had imagined the journey would be altogether different.

They arrived at their destination just as Dandelion had made himself hoarse from curses peppered with cries for mercy, while the pain in Geralt's elbow and knee had become sheer torment – so severe that the Witcher had begun to consider taking radical, or even desperate measures.

They reached a military camp organised around a ruined, half-burnt stronghold.

Beyond the ring of guards, hitching bars and smoking campfires they saw knights' tents adorned with pennants, surrounding a large and bustling field beyond a ruined and charred stockade. The field marked the end of their forced trek.

Seeing a horse trough, Geralt and Dandelion strained against their bonds. The horsemen were initially disinclined to let them go anywhere near the water, but Anzelm Aubry's son evidently recalled the supposed acquaintance of Dandelion and his father and deigned to be kind. They forced their way between the horses, and drank and washed their faces using their bound hands. A tug of the ropes soon brought them back to reality.

'Who've you brought me this time?' said a tall, slim knight in enamelled, richly gilded armour, rhythmically striking a mace against an ornamented tasset. 'Don't tell me it's more spies.'

'Spies or deserters,' Anzelm Aubry's son stated. 'We captured them in the camp by the Chotla, when we wiped out the Nilfgaardian foray. Clearly a suspicious element!'

The knight in the gilded armour snorted, looked intently at Dandelion, and then his young – but austere – face suddenly lit up.

'Nonsense. Untie them.'

'They're Nilfgaardian spies!' Black Stripe of the Papebrocks said indignantly. 'Particularly this one here, as insolent as a country cur. Says he's a poet, the rogue!'

'And he speaks the truth,' the knight in the gilded armour smiled. 'It's the bard Dandelion. I know him. Remove his bonds. And free the other one too.'

'Are you sure, My Lord?'

'That was an order, Knight Papebrock.'

'Didn't realise I could come in useful, did you?' said Dandelion to Geralt, while he rubbed his wrists, which were numb from the bonds. 'So now you do. My fame goes before me, I'm known and esteemed everywhere.'

Geralt didn't comment, being busy massaging his own wrists, his sore elbow and knee.

'Please forgive the overzealousness of these youngsters,' said the knight who had been addressed as a member of the nobility. 'They see Nilfgaardian spies everywhere, bring back a few suspicious-looking types every time they're sent out. I mean anybody who in any way stands out from the fleeing rabble. And you, Master Dandelion, stand out, after all. How did you end up by the Chotla, among those fugitives?'

'I was travelling from Dillingen to Maribor,' the poet lied with ease, 'when we were caught up in this hell, me and my . . . confrere. You're sure to know him. His name is . . . Giraldus.'

'But of course I do, I've read him,' the knight bragged. 'It's an

173

honour for me, Master Giraldus. I am Daniel Etcheverry, Count of Garramone. Upon my word, Master Dandelion, much has changed since the times you sang at King Foltest's court.'

'Much indeed.'

'Who would have thought,' the count said, his face darkening, 'that it would come to this. Verden subjugated to Emhyr, Brugge practically defeated, Sodden in flames . . . And we're in retreat, in constant retreat . . . My apologies, I meant to say we are "executing tactical withdrawals". Nilfgaard are burning and pillaging everywhere. They have almost reached the banks of the Ina, have almost completed the sieges of the fortresses of Mayena and Razwan, and the Temerian Army continues its "tactical withdrawals". . .'

'When I saw the lilies on your shields by the Chotla,' Dandelion said, 'I thought the offensive was here.'

'A counter-attack,' Daniel Etcheverry corrected him, 'and reconnaissance in force. We crossed the Ina, put to the sword a few Nilfgaardian forays and Scoia'tael commandos who were lighting fires. You can see what remains of the garrison in Armeria, who we managed to free. But the forts in Carcano and Vidort were burnt to the ground . . . The entire south is soaked in blood, afire and dense with smoke . . . Oh, but I'm boring you. You know only too well what's happening in Brugge and Sodden. After all, you ended up wandering with fugitives from there. And my brave boys took you for spies! Please accept my apologies one more time. And my invitation to dinner. Some of the noblemen and officers will be delighted to meet you, Master Poets.'

'It is a genuine honour, My Lord,' said Geralt, bowing stiffly. 'But time is short. We must be away.'

'Oh, please don't be shy,' Daniel Etcheverry said, smiling. 'A standard, modest soldier's repast. Venison, grouse, sterlet, truffles . . .'

'To decline,' Dandelion said, swallowing and giving the Witcher a telling glance, 'would be a serious affront. Let us go without delay, My Lord. Is that your tent, the sumptuous one, in blue and gold?'

'No. That is the commander-in-chief's. Azure and gold are the colours of his fatherland.'

'Really?' Dandelion said in astonishment. 'I thought this was the Temerian Army. And that you were in command.'

'This is a regiment assigned to the Temerian Army. I am King Foltest's liaison officer, and a goodly number of the Temerian nobility are serving here with detachments, which bear lilies on their shields as a formality. But the main part of this corps consists of the subjects of another kingdom. Do you see the standard in front of the tent?'

'Lions,' Geralt said, stopping. 'Golden lions on a blue field. That's . . . That's the emblem . . .'

'Of Cintra,' the count averred. 'They are emigrants from the Kingdom of Cintra, at present occupied by Nilfgaard. Under the command of Marshal Vissegerd.'

Geralt turned back, intending to announce to the count that urgent matters were nonetheless compelling him to decline the venison, sterlet and truffles. He wasn't quick enough. He saw some men approaching, led by a well-built, big-bellied, grey-haired knight in a blue cloak with a gold chain over his armour.

'Here, Master Poets, is Marshal Vissegerd in person,' Daniel Etcheverry said. 'Allow me, Your Lordship, to introduce you to . . .'

'That won't be necessary,' Marshal Vissegerd interrupted hoarsely, looking piercingly at Geralt. 'We have already been introduced. In Cintra, at the court of Queen Calanthe. On the day of Princess Pavetta's betrothal. It was fifteen years ago, but I have a good memory. And you, you rogue of a witcher? Do you remember me?'

'Indeed, I do,' Geralt said nodding, obediently holding out his hands for the soldiers to bind.

Daniel Etcheverry, Count of Garramone, had tried to vouch for them when the infantrymen were sitting the trussed-up Geralt and Dandelion down on stools in the tent, and now, after the soldiers had left on the orders of Marshal Vissegerd, the count renewed his efforts.

'That is the poet and troubadour Dandelion, marshal,' he repeated. 'I know him. The whole world knows him. I consider it unfitting to treat him thus. I pledge my knightly word he is not a Nilfgaardian spy.'

'Don't make such rash pledges,' Vissegerd snarled, without taking his eyes off the captives. 'Perhaps he is a poet, but if he was captured in the company of that blackguard, the Witcher, I wouldn't vouch for him. It seems to me you still have no idea what kind of bird we've ensnared.'

'The Witcher?'

'Indeed. Geralt, also known as the Wolf. The very same good-for-nothing who claimed the right to Cirilla, the daughter of Pavetta and the granddaughter of Calanthe; the very same Ciri about whom everyone is talking at present. You are too young, My Lord, to remember the time when that scandal was being widely discussed at many courts. But I, as it happens, was an eyewitness.'

'But what could link him to Princess Cirilla?'

'That scoundrel there,' Vissegerd said, pointing at Geralt, 'played his part in giving Pavetta, the daughter of Queen Calanthe, in marriage to Duny, a totally unknown stranger from the south. From that mongrel union was subsequently born Cirilla, the subject of their reprehensible conspiracy. For you ought to know that Duny, the bastard, had promised the girl to the Witcher in advance, as payment for facilitating his marriage. The Law of Surprise, do you see?'

'Not entirely. But speak on, My Lord Marshal.'

'The Witcher,' Vissegerd said, pointing a finger at Geralt once again, 'wanted to take the girl away after Pavetta's death, but Calanthe did not permit him, and drove him away. But he waited for a timely moment. When the war with Nilfgaard broke out and Cintra fell, he kidnapped Ciri, exploiting the confusion. He kept the girl hidden, although he knew we were searching for her. And finally he grew tired of her and sold her to Emhyr!'

'Those are lies and calumny!' Dandelion yelled. 'There is not a word of truth in it!'

'Quiet, fiddler, or I'll have you gagged. Put two and two together, My Lord. The Witcher had Cirilla and now Emhyr var Emreis has her. And the Witcher gets captured in the vanguard of a Nilfgaardian raid. What does that signify?'

Daniel Etcheverry shrugged his shoulders.

'What does it signify?' Vissegerd repeated, bending over Geralt. 'Well, you rascal? Speak! How long have you been spying for Nilfgaard, cur?'

'I do not spy for anybody.'

'I'll have your hide tanned!'

'Go ahead.'

'Master Dandelion,' the Count of Garramone suddenly interjected. 'It would probably be better if you set about explaining. The sooner, the better.'

'I would have done so before,' the poet exploded, 'but My Lord Marshal here threatened to gag me! We are innocent; those are all outright fabrications and vile slanders. Cirilla was kidnapped from the Isle of Thanedd, and Geralt was seriously wounded defending her. Anybody can confirm that. Every sorcerer who was on Thanedd. And Redania's secretary of state, Sigismund Dijkstra . . .'

Dandelion suddenly fell silent, recalling that Dijkstra was in no way suitable as a defence witness in the case; and neither were references to the mages of Thanedd likely to improve the situation to any great degree.

'What utter nonsense it is,' he continued loudly and quickly, 'to accuse Geralt of kidnapping Ciri in Cintra! Geralt found the girl when she was wandering around in Riverdell after the city had been sacked, and hid her, not from you, but from the Nilfgaardian agents who were pursuing her! I myself was captured by those agents and submitted to torture so that I would betray where Ciri was concealed! But I didn't breathe a word and those agents are now six feet under. They didn't know who they were up against!'

'Your valour,' the count interrupted, 'was in vain, however. Emhyr finally has Cirilla. As we are all aware, he means to marry her and make her Imperatrice of Nilfgaard. For the moment he has proclaimed her Queen of Cintra and the surrounding lands, causing us some problems by so doing.'

'Emhyr,' the poet declared, 'could place whoever he wanted on the Cintran throne. Ciri, whichever way you look at it, has a right to the throne.'

'A right?' Vissegerd bellowed, spraying Geralt with spittle. 'What fucking right? Emhyr may marry her; that is his choice. He may give her and the children he sires with her endowments and titles according to his whims and fancies. Queen of Cintra and the Skellige Islands? Duchess of Brugge? Countess Palatine of Sodden? By all means. Let us all bow down! And why not, I humbly ask, why not the Queen of the Sun and the Suzerain of the Moon? That accursed, tainted blood has no right to the throne! The entire female line of that family is accursed, all rotten vipers, beginning with Riannon! Like Cirilla's great-grandmother, Adalia, who lay with her own cousin; like her great-great-grandmother, Muriel the Impure, who debased herself with everyone! Incestuous bastards and mongrels emerge from that family on the distaff side, one after the other!'

'Speak more softly, My Lord Marshal,' Dandelion advised haughtily. 'The standard with the golden lions flutters before your tent, and you are prepared at any moment to proclaim Ciri's grand-mother, Calanthe, the Lioness of Cintra, in whose name the majority of your soldiers shed blood at the Battles of Marnadal and Sodden, a bastard. I would not be sure of the loyalty of your army, were you to do so.'

Vissegerd covered the distance separating him from Dandelion in two paces, seized the poet by the ruff and lifted him up from his chair. The marshal's face, which a moment before had only been flecked with red spots, now assumed the colour of deep, heraldic red. Geralt was just beginning to seriously worry about his friend when luckily an aide-de-camp burst into the tent, informing the marshal in an excited voice about urgent and important news brought by the scouts. Vissegerd shoved Dandelion back down onto the stool and exited.

'Phew . . .' the poet snuffled, twisting his head and neck around. 'Much more of that and he'd have throttled me . . . Could you loosen my bonds somewhat, My Lord?'

'No, Master Dandelion. I cannot.'

'Do you give credence to this balderdash? That we are spies?'

'My credence is neither here nor there. You will remain bound.'

'Very well,' Dandelion said, clearing his throat. 'What's got into your marshal? Why did he suddenly assault me like a falcon swooping on a woodcock?'

Daniel Etcheverry smiled wryly.

'When you alluded to the soldiers' loyalty you unwittingly rubbed salt in the wound, Master Poet.'

'What do you mean? What wound?'

'These soldiers sincerely lamented Cirilla's passing, when news of her death reached them. And then new information got out. It turned out that Calanthe's granddaughter was alive. That she was in Nilfgaard, in the good graces of Imperator Emhyr. Which led to mass desertion. Bear in mind that these men left their homes and families, and fled to Sodden and Brugge, and to Temeria, because they wanted to fight for Cintra, for Calanthe's blood. They wanted to liberate their country, to drive the invader from Cintra, so that Calanthe's descendant would regain the throne. And what has happened? Calanthe's blood is returning to the Cintran throne in triumph and glory . . .'

'As a puppet in the hands of Emhyr, who kidnapped her.'

'Emhyr will marry her. He wants to place her beside him on the imperial throne and validate her titles and fiefs. Is that how puppets are treated? Cirilla was seen at the imperial court by envoys from Kovir. They maintain that she did not give the impression of someone who had been kidnapped. Cirilla, the only heiress to Cintra's throne, is returning to that throne as an ally of Nilfgaard. That is the news that has spread among the soldiery.'

'Circulated by Nilfgaardian agents.'

'I'm aware of that.' The count nodded. 'But the soldiers aren't. When we catch deserters, we stretch their necks, but I understand them a little. They're Cintrans. They want to fight for their own – not Temerian – homes. Under their own banner. Under their own command, not the command of Temeria. They see that here, in this army, their golden lions have to bow the knee before the Temerian lilies. Vissegerd had eight thousand men, of which five thousand were native Cintrans; the rest consisted of Temerian reserve units and volunteer chivalry from Brugge and Sodden. At this moment the corps numbers six thousand. And all the deserters have been from Cintra. Vissegerd's army has been decimated even before the battle has begun. Do you understand what that means for him?'

'A serious loss of face. And maybe position.'

'Precisely. Should another few hundred desert, King Foltest will deprive him of his baton. Right now it's hard to call this corps "Cintran". Vissegerd is vacillating, wanting to put an end to the defection, which is why he's spreading rumours about the doubtful – but most certainly unlawful – descent of Cirilla and her ancestors.'

'Which you,' Geralt said, unable to stop himself, 'listen to with evident distaste, My Lord.'

'Have you noticed?' Daniel Etcheverry said, smiling faintly. 'Why, Vissegerd doesn't know my lineage . . . In short, I'm related to this Cirilla. Muriel, Countess of Garramone, known as the Beautiful Impure, Cirilla's great-great-grandmother, was also my great-great-grandmother. Legends about her love affairs circulate in the family to this day. However, I listen with distaste as Vissegerd imputes incestuous tendencies and promiscuity to my ancestor. But I do not react. Because I'm a soldier. Do you understand me sufficiently, gentlemen?'

'Yes,' Geralt said.

'No,' Dandelion said.

'Vissegerd is the commander of this corps, which forms part of the Temerian Army. And Cirilla in Emhyr's hands is a threat to the corps, and thus to the army, not to mention my king and my country. I have no intention of refuting the rumours being circulated about Cirilla by Vissegerd nor of challenging my commanding officer's authority. I even intend to support him in proving that Cirilla is a bastard with no rights to the throne. Not only will I not challenge the marshal – not only will I not question his decisions or orders – I shall actually support them. And execute them when necessary.'

The Witcher's mouth contorted into a smile.

'I think you understand now, don't you, Dandelion? Not for a moment did the count consider us spies, or he would not have given us such a thorough explanation. The count knows we're innocent. But he will not lift a finger when Vissegerd sentences us.'

'You mean . . . You mean we're . . .'

The count looked away.

'Vissegerd,' he said softly, 'is furious. You were unlucky to fall into his hands. Particularly you, Master Witcher. As for Master Dandelion, I shall try to . . .'

He was interrupted by the return of Vissegerd, still red-faced and panting like a bull. The marshal walked over to the table, slammed his mace onto the maps spread over it, then turned towards Geralt and bored his eyes into him. The Witcher did not avert his gaze.

'The wounded Nilfgaardian the scouts captured,' Vissegerd drawled, 'managed to tear his dressing off and bled to death on the way. He preferred to die, rather than contribute to the defeat and death of his countrymen. We wanted to use him, but he escaped, slipped through our fingers, leaving nothing on them but blood. He'd been well schooled. It's a pity that witchers don't instil such customs in royal children when they take them to be raised.'

Geralt remained silent, but still did not lower his eyes.

'Well, you monster. You freak of nature. You hell spawn. What did you teach Cirilla after kidnapping her? How did you bring her up? Everyone can see how! That snake-in-the-grass is alive, and is lounging on the Nilfgaardian throne, as if it were nothing! And when Emhyr takes her to his bed she's sure to spread her legs willingly, as if it were nothing too, the slut!'

'Your anger is getting the better of you,' Dandelion mumbled. 'Is it chivalrous, marshal, to blame a child for everything? A child that Emhyr took by force?'

'There are also ways against force! Chivalrous ones, noble ones! Were she really of royal blood, she would have found a way! She would have found a knife! A pair of scissors, a piece of broken glass. Why, even a bodkin! The bitch could have torn open the veins in her wrists with her own teeth! Or hanged herself with her own stockings!'

'I don't want to listen to you any longer, marshal,' Geralt said softly. 'I don't want to listen to you any longer.'

Vissegerd ground his teeth audibly and leant over.

'You don't want to,' he said, in a voice trembling with fury. 'That is fortunate, because I don't have anything more to say to you. Apart

181

from one thing. Back then, in Cintra, fifteen years ago, a great deal was said about destiny. At the time I thought it was nonsense. But it turned out to be your destiny, Witcher. Ever since that night your fate has been sealed, written in black runes among the stars. Ciri, daughter of Pavetta, is your destiny. And your death. Because of Ciri, daughter of Pavetta, you shall hang.'

The Brigade joined Operation Centaur as a unit assigned to the 4th Horse Cavalry. We received reinforcements in the form of three squads of Verdenian light horse, which I assigned to the Vreemde Battle Group. Following the example of the campaign in Aedirn, I created two more battle groups from the rest of the brigade, naming them Sievers and Morteisen, each comprising four squadrons.

We set out from the concentration area near Drieschot on the night of the fourth of August. The Groups' orders ran:

> Capture the Vidort-Carcano-Armeria territory; seize the crossing over the Ina; destroy any hostile troops encountered, but avoid significant points of resistance. Start fires, particularly at night, to light the way for the 4th Horse Cavalry. Induce panic among civilians and use their flight to block all of the arterial routes to the enemy's rear. Feign encirclement to drive the retreating enemy forces towards the actual encirclements. Carry out the elimination of selected groups of the civilian population and prisoners of war to cause terror, intensify panic, and undermine the enemy's morale.

The Brigade carried out the above mission with great soldierly devotion.

Elan Trahe,
For Imperator and Fatherland. The glorious trail of fire of the 7th Daerlanian Cavalry Brigade

CHAPTER FIVE

Milva did not have time to reach the horses and save them. She was a witness to their theft, but a helpless one. First she was swept along by the frantic, panic-stricken crowd, then the road was obstructed by careering wagons, and finally she became stuck in a woolly, bleating flock of sheep, through which she had to force her way as though it were a snowdrift. Later, by the Chotla, only a leap into the tall rushes growing in the marshes by the bank saved her from the Nilfgaardians' swords as they ruthlessly cut down the fugitives crowded by the river, showing no mercy either to women or children. Milva jumped into the water and reached the other bank, partly wading and partly swimming on her back among the corpses being carried by the current.

And she took up the hunt. She remembered the direction in which the peasants who had stolen Roach, Pegasus, the chestnut colt and her own black had fled. And her priceless bow was still attached to her saddle. *Tough luck*, she thought, feet squelching in her wet boots as she ran, *the others will have to cope without me for now. I must get my damn bow and horse back!*

She freed Pegasus first. The poet's horse was ignoring the heels digging into his sides. He was paying no heed to the urgent shouts of the inexperienced rider and had no intention of galloping; instead he trotted slowly through the birch wood. The poor fellow was being left a long way behind the other horse thieves. When he heard and then saw Milva over his shoulder, he jumped off without a second thought and bolted into the undergrowth, holding up his britches with both hands. Milva did not pursue him, overcoming her seething desire to exact some serious revenge. She leapt into the saddle in full flight, landing heavily and making the strings of the lute fastened to the saddlebags twang. A skilled horsewoman, she managed to force the gelding to gallop. Or rather, to the lumbering canter that Pegasus considered a gallop.

But even this pseudo-gallop was enough, for the horse thieves' escape had been slowed by another tricky mount. The Witcher's skittish Roach, the infuriating, sulky bay mare Geralt had so often sworn he'd exchange for another steed, whether it be an ass, a mule or even a billy goat. Milva caught up with the thieves just as Roach, irritated by a clumsy tug of the reins, had thrown her rider to the ground. The rest of the peasants had dismounted and were trying to get the frisky and excitable mare under control. They were so busy they only noticed Milva when she rode among them on Pegasus and kicked one of them in the face, breaking his nose. When he fell to the ground, howling and calling upon the Gods, she recognised him. It was Cloggy. A peasant who clearly had no luck in his dealings with people. Or, more particularly, with Milva.

Unfortunately, luck deserted Milva too. To be precise, it wasn't her luck that was to blame, more her own conceit and her conviction – based on shaky practical evidence – that she could beat up any brace of peasants she happened to meet, in whatever manner she chose. When she dismounted she was punched in the eye and found herself on the ground. She drew her knife, ready to spill some guts, but was hit over the head with a stout stick so hard that it broke, blinding her with bark and rotten wood. Stunned and blinded, she still managed to grab the knee of the peasant beating her with the remains of the stick, when he unexpectedly howled and keeled over. The other yelled too, bringing both hands up to protect his head. Milva rubbed her eyes and saw that he was protecting himself from a rain of blows from a knout, dealt by a man riding a grey horse. She sprang up, dealing a powerful kick to the neck of the prostrate peasant. The rustler wheezed and flailed his legs, leaving his loins unprotected. Milva took advantage of that at once, channelling all her anger into a well-aimed kick. The peasant curled up in a ball, clamped his hands on his crotch and howled so loudly leaves fell from the birch trees.

Meanwhile, the horseman on the grey was busy with Cloggy, whose nose was streaming blood, and with the other peasant – he chased them away into the trees with blows from the knout. He returned in order to thrash the one on the ground, but reined in his horse; Milva had managed to catch her black and was holding her bow with an arrow already nocked. The bowstring was only pulled halfway back, but the arrowhead was pointing directly at the horseman's chest.

For a moment, they looked at each other: the horseman and the young woman. Then, with a slow movement, he pulled an arrow with long fletchings from his belt and threw it down at Milva's feet.

'I knew I'd have the chance to give you back your arrow, elf,' he said calmly.

'I'm not an elf, Nilfgaardian.'

'And I'm not a Nilfgaardian. Put that bow down, will you? If I wished you ill, I could have just stood by and watched those peasants kick you around.'

'The devil only knows,' she said through her teeth, 'who you are and what you wish for me. But thanks for saving me. And for my arrow. And for dealing with that good-for-nothing I didn't hit properly the other day.'

The roughed-up horse thief, still curled up in a ball, choked back his sobs, his face buried in the leaf litter. The horseman didn't even look at him. He looked at Milva.

'Catch the horses,' he said. 'We have to get away from the river, and fast too; the army's combing the forests on both banks.'

'*We* have to?' she said, grimacing and lowering her bow. 'Together? Since when were we comrades? Or a company?'

'I'll explain,' he said, steering his horse and grabbing the chestnut's reins, 'if you give me time.'

'The point is, I don't have any time. The Witcher and the others—'

'I know. But we won't save them by letting ourselves get killed or captured. Catch the horses and we'll flee into the forest. Hurry!'

His name's Cahir, Milva recalled, glancing at her companion, with whom she was now sitting in the pit left by a fallen tree. *A strange Nilfgaardian, who says he isn't a Nilfgaardian. Cahir.*

'We thought they'd killed you,' she muttered. 'The riderless chestnut came running past us . . .'

'I had a minor adventure,' he answered drily, 'with three brigands, as shaggy as werewolves. They ambushed me. The horse got away. The brigands didn't, but then they were on foot. Before I managed to get a new mount, I'd fallen far behind you. I only managed to catch up with you this morning. Right by the camp. I crossed the river down in the gully and waited on the far bank. I knew you'd head east.'

One of the horses concealed in the alder wood snorted and stamped its hooves. Dusk was falling. Mosquitoes whined annoyingly around their ears.

'It's quiet in the forest,' Cahir said. 'The armies have gone, the battle is over.'

'The slaughter's over, you mean.'

'Our cavalry . . .' he stammered and cleared his throat. 'The imperial cavalry attacked the camp, and then troops appeared from the south. I think it was the Temerian Army.'

'If the battle's over, we should go back. We should search for the Witcher, Dandelion and the others.'

'It would be better to wait until nightfall.'

'There's something horrible about this place,' she said softly, tightening her grip on the bow. 'It's such a bleak wilderness. It gives me the shivers. Apparently quiet, but there's always something rustling in the bushes . . . The Witcher said ghouls are attracted to battlefields . . . And the peasants were telling stories about a vampire . . .'

'You aren't alone,' he replied under his breath. 'It's much more frightening when you're alone.'

'Indeed.' She nodded, empathising with him. 'After all you've been following us for almost a fortnight, all alone. You've been trudging after us, while surrounded by your people— You might say you're not a Nilfgaardian, but they're still yours, aren't they. Devil take me if I understand it; instead of going back to your own you're tracking the Witcher. Why?'

'It's a long story.'

*

188

When the tall Scoia'tael leant over him Struycken, who was bound to a pole, blinked in fear. It was said there was no such thing as an ugly elf, that every single one of them was comely, that they were born beautiful. And perhaps the legendary commander of the Squirrels had been born beautiful. But now that his face was gashed by a hideous diagonal scar deforming his forehead, eyebrow, nose and cheek, nothing remained of his elven good looks.

The elf with the disfigured physiognomy sat down on a fallen tree trunk.

'I am Isengrim Faoiltiarna,' he said, leaning over the captive once again. 'I've been fighting humans for four years and leading a commando for three. I have buried my brother, who fell in combat, four cousins and more than four hundred brothers in arms. In my struggle, I treat your imperator as my ally, as I have proved several times by passing intelligence to your spies, helping your agents and eliminating individuals selected by you.'

Faoiltiarna fell silent and made a sign with his gloved hand. The Scoia'tael standing alongside picked up a small birchbark canteen. The canteen gave off a sweet aroma.

'I considered and consider Nilfgaard an ally,' the elf with the scar repeated, 'which is why I did not, initially, believe my informant when he warned that a trap was being laid for me. That I would receive instructions for a private meeting with a Nilfgaardian emissary, and that I would be captured then. I didn't believe but, being cautious by nature, I turned up for the rendezvous a little earlier than expected and not alone. Much to my surprise and dismay, instead of the said emissary, there were six thugs waiting with a fishing net, ropes, a leather mask with a gag, and a straitjacket fastened with straps and buckles. Standard equipment used by your secret service during abductions I would say. Nilfgaard wanted to capture me, Faoiltiarna, alive, and transport me somewhere, gagged and securely fastened in a straitjacket. A curious affair, I would say. And one requiring some elucidation. I'm delighted that I managed to take alive at least one of the thugs who had been set on me – no doubt their leader – who will be able to furnish me with that elucidation.'

Struycken gritted his teeth and turned his head away, in order not to look at the elf's disfigured face. He preferred to look at the birch-bark canteen, and the two wasps buzzing around it.

'And now,' Faoiltiarna continued, wiping his sweaty neck with a scarf, 'let's have a little chat, Master Kidnapper. To make the conversation flow, let me clarify a few points. There is maple syrup in the canteen. Should our little chat not proceed in a spirit of mutual understanding and complete frankness, we shall copiously anoint your head with the aforementioned syrup, paying very close attention to your eyes and ears. Then we shall place you on an anthill, this one here to be precise, over which these charming, hardworking insects are scurrying. Let me add that this method has already proved its worth in the case of several Dh'oine and an'givare who evinced great stubbornness and a lack of candour.'

'I am in the imperial service!' the spy screamed, blanching. 'I am an officer of the imperial military intelligence, a subordinate of Lord Vattier de Rideaux, Viscount of Eiddon! My name is Jan Struycken! I protest—'

'What awful luck,' the elf interrupted him, 'that these red ants, greedy for maple syrup, have never heard of the viscount. Let us begin. I shall not ask who gave the order for my abduction, because it is obvious. So my first question shall be: where was I to be taken?'

The Nilfgaardian spy struggled against the ropes and jerked his head, for it seemed to him the ants were already crawling over his cheeks. But he remained silent.

'Too bad,' Faoiltiarna said, breaking the silence and gesturing to the elf with the canteen. 'Apply the syrup.'

'I was to transport you to Nastrog Castle in Verden!' Struycken yelled. 'On the orders of Viscount de Rideaux!'

'Thank you. And what awaited me there?'

'An interrogation . . .'

'What was I to be asked about?'

'About the events on Thanedd! Untie me, I beg you! I'll tell you everything!'

'Of course you will,' the elf sighed, stretching. 'Particularly since we've already made a start, and in matters like these that's usually the most difficult part. Continue.'

'I was ordered to make you confess where Vilgefortz and Rience are hiding! And Cahir Mawr Dyffryn, son of Ceallach!'

'How comical. A trap laid to ask me about Vilgefortz and Rience? Whatever would I know about them? What could link me with them? And Cahir? That's even more comical. I sent him to you, did I not? Just as you requested. In fetters. Are you saying the package didn't arrive?'

'The unit which was sent to the designated rendezvous point was slaughtered . . . Cahir was not among the dead . . .'

'Ah. And Lord Vattier de Rideaux became suspicious? But instead of sending another emissary to the commando and asking for an explanation, he immediately laid a trap for me. And ordered me dragged to Nastrog in chains and interrogated about the incidents on Thanedd.'

The spy said nothing.

'Didn't you get it?' the elf said and bent his head, bringing his hideous face towards Struycken. 'That was a question. And it ran: what's this all about?'

'I don't know . . . I don't know, I swear . . .'

Faoiltiarna beckoned with a hand and pointed. Struycken howled, thrashed around, swore on the Great Sun, pleaded his innocence, wept, tossed his head about and spat out the syrup, which had been thickly smeared over his face. Only when he was carried over to the anthill by four Scoia'tael did he decide to talk – although the consequences of speaking were potentially more dreadful than the ants.

'Sire . . . Should anyone find out about this, I'm dead meat . . . But I shall disclose it to you . . . I've seen confidential orders. I've eavesdropped . . . I'll tell you everything . . .'

'Of course you will.' The elf nodded. 'The record on the anthill is an hour and forty minutes, and belongs to a certain officer from King Demavend's special forces. But even he talked in the end. Very well, begin. Quickly, coherently and to the point.'

'The Imperator is certain he was betrayed on Thanedd. The traitor is Vilgefortz of Roggeveen, a sorcerer, and his assistant Rience. But mostly Cahir Mawr Dyffryn aep Ceallach. Vattier . . . Viscount Vattier is not certain whether you Scoia'tael also had a hand in the treachery, if only unwittingly . . . Which is why he ordered you to be seized and delivered in secret to Nastrog Castle . . . Lord Faoiltiarna, I've been working in the secret service for twenty years . . . Vattier de Rideaux is my third boss . . .'

'More coherently, please. And stop shaking. If you're frank with me, you'll still be able to serve a few more bosses.'

'Although it was kept absolutely confidential, I knew . . . I knew who Vilgefortz and Cahir were supposed to capture on the island. And it looked like they had succeeded. Because they brought that . . . you know . . . that princess from Cintra to Loc Grim. I thought they'd pulled it off and that Cahir and Rience would become barons, and that sorcerer a count at least . . . But instead the Imperator summoned Tawny Owl – I mean, Lord Skellen – and ordered him and Lord Vattier to capture Cahir . . . And Rience, and Vilgefortz . . . Anyone who might know anything about Thanedd and that incident was to be tortured . . . Including you . . . It didn't take much to guess, you know, that it was treachery. That a sham princess had been brought to Loc Grim . . .'

The spy struggled to breathe, nervously gasping for air through lips covered with maple syrup.

'Untie him,' Faoiltiarna ordered his Squirrels. 'And let him wash his face.'

The order was carried out immediately. A moment later the mastermind of the unsuccessful ambush was standing with head lowered before the legendary Scoia'tael commander. Faoiltiarna looked at him indifferently.

'Scrape the syrup thoroughly from your ears,' he finally said. 'Then prick them up and listen carefully, as befits a spy with many years' experience. I shall give you proof of my loyalty to the Imperator. I shall give you a thorough account of the matters that interest him. And you will repeat everything, word for word, to Vattier de Rideaux.'

The spy nodded eagerly.

'In the middle of Blathe, which according to your reckoning is the beginning of June,' the elf began, 'I was contacted by Enid an Gleanna, the sorceress also known as Francesca Findabair. Soon after, on her orders, a certain Rience came to my commando. He was said to be the factotum of Vilgefortz of Roggeveen, also a sorcerer. A plan of action was drawn up in utter secrecy, with the aim of eliminating a number of mages during the conclave on the Isle of Thanedd. The plan was presented as one having the full support of Imperator Emhyr, Vattier de Rideaux and Stephan Skellen; otherwise I should not have agreed to collaborate with Dh'oine – sorcerers or not – for I have seen too many entrapments in my life. The involvement of the Empire was confirmed by the arrival of a ship at Cape Bremervoord. On board was Cahir, son of Ceallach, equipped with special authorisation and orders. According to those orders I selected a special squad from the commando, which would be answerable only to Cahir. I was aware that they were trusted to capture and remove a . . . certain individual . . . from the island.'

'We sailed to Thanedd,' Faoiltiarna began again after a pause, 'on the ship which had brought Cahir. Rience had some amulets and he used them to surround the ship with a magical fog. We sailed into the caverns beneath the island. From there we proceeded to the catacombs under Garstang. There we realised at once that something wasn't right. Rience had received some telepathic signals from Vilgefortz. We knew we'd have to start fighting any minute. Fortunately, we were ready, because the moment we left the catacombs we were plunged into hell.'

The elf contorted his mutilated face, as though the recollection pained him.

'After our initial successes, matters became complicated. We were unable to eliminate all the royal sorcerers, and we took heavy casualties. Several mages who were party to the conspiracy also perished, while others began to save their skins and teleport away. All of a sudden Vilgefortz vanished, then Rience, and Enid an Gleanna soon followed suit. I treated that final disappearance as the conclusive signal for our withdrawal. I did not, however, give the order, but waited for the return of Cahir and his squad, who had set off at once to carry out their mission. When they did not return, we began to search for them.'

'No one,' Faoiltiarna said, looking the Nilfgaardian spy in the eyes, 'survived from that squad; they were all brutally slaughtered. We found Cahir on the steps leading to Tor Lara, a tower which exploded during the battle and ended up as a heap of rubble. He was wounded and unconscious; it was clear he had not accomplished the mission he had been assigned. There was no sign of his target anywhere and royal troops were already pouring out of Aretuza and Loxia. I knew there was no way Cahir could fall into their hands, because it would have been proof of Nilfgaard's active involvement in the operation. So we took him with us and fled back to the catacombs and then the caverns. We boarded the ship and sailed away. Twelve remained of my commando, most of them wounded.'

'The wind was at our backs. We landed to the west of Hirundum and hid in the forest. Cahir was trying to tear off his bandages and was yelling something about an insane girl with green eyes, about the Lion Cub of Cintra, about a witcher who had massacred his men, about the Tower of Gulls and a mage who flew like a bird. He demanded a horse and ordered us to return him to the island, citing the imperial orders, which under the circumstances I had to treat as the ravings of a madman. As we knew, war was already raging in Aedirn, so I considered it more important to swiftly rebuild my depleted commando and resume the fight against the Dh'oine.'

'Cahir was still with us when I found your secret order in a dead drop. I was astonished. Although Cahir had clearly not completed his mission, there was nothing to suggest he was guilty of treachery. But I did not ponder over it for long, judging that it was your business and that you ought to clear it up. Cahir put up no resistance to being tied up, he was calm and resigned. I ordered him to be placed in a coffin and with the help of a hawker acquaintance delivered to the location designated in the letter. I was not, I admit, inclined to further deplete my commando by providing an escort. I don't know who murdered your men at the rendezvous point. But only I knew where it was. So if this version of the totally random extermination of your unit doesn't suit you, search for traitors among your own, because only you and I knew the time and place.'

Faoiltiarna stood up.

'That is all. All the information I have given here is true. I would

194

not supply you with anything more in the dungeons of Nastrog. The lies and confabulations with which I might try to satisfy the investigating officer and his torturers would actually do more harm than good. I do not know anything more. In particular I don't know Vilgefortz and Rience's whereabouts, and neither do I know if your suspicions of betrayal are justified. I also emphatically declare that I know nothing about the princess from Cintra, the genuine or the sham one. I have told you everything I know. I trust that neither Lord de Rideaux nor Stephan Skellen will want to set any more traps for me. The Dh'oine have been trying to capture and kill me for a long, long time, so I have adopted the custom of ruthless extermination of all trap setters. I shall not, in the future, investigate to check if one of the trap setters is, by chance, a subordinate of Vattier or Skellen. I do not have the time nor the desire to make such an investigation. Do I make myself clear?'

Struycken nodded and swallowed.

'Now take a horse, spy, and get the hell out of my forest.'

'You mean they were delivering you to the gallows?' Milva mumbled. 'Now I understand some of it, but not everything. Why, instead of holing up somewhere, are you following the Witcher? He's really got it in for you . . . And he's spared your life twice . . .'

'Three times.'

'I saw two of them. Though you weren't the one who beat the shit out of the Witcher on Thanedd, as I first thought, I don't think you ought to get in the way of his sword again. There's a lot about your feud I don't understand, but you saved me and you've got an honest face . . . So I'll tell you, Cahir, bluntly: when the Witcher talks about the men who took his Ciri to Nilfgaard, he grinds his teeth until sparks fly. And if you spat on him, he would steam.'

'Ciri,' he repeated. 'Sounds nice.'

'Didn't you know?'

'No. My people always called her Cirilla or the Lion Cub of Cintra . . . And when she was with me – for she was once . . . she didn't say a single word. Even though I saved her life.'

'Only the devil himself could grasp all this,' Milva said,

exasperated. 'Your fates are all entangled, Cahir, knotted and mixed up. It's too much for my head.'

'And what's your name?' he suddenly asked.

'Milva . . . Maria Barring. But call me Milva.'

'The Witcher's heading the wrong way, Milva,' he offered a moment later. 'Ciri isn't in Nilfgaard. The kidnappers didn't take her to Nilfgaard. If it was a kidnap at all.'

'What do you mean?'

'It's a long story.'

'By the Great Sun,' Fringilla said, standing in the doorway, tilting her head and looking in astonishment at her friend. 'What have you done to your hair, Assire?'

'I washed it,' Assire var Anahid replied coldly. 'And styled it. Come in and sit down. Get out of that chair, Merlin. Shoo!'

The sorceress sat down in the chair the black cat had reluctantly vacated, her eyes still fixed on her friend's coiffure.

'Stop staring,' Assire said, touching her bouffant and glistening curls. 'I decided to make a few changes. Why, I just took your lead.'

'I was always taken as an oddball and a rebel,' Fringilla Vigo chuckled. 'But when they see you in the academy or at court . . .'

'I'm seldom at court,' Assire cut her off, 'and the academy will have to get used to it. This is the thirteenth century. It's high time we challenged the superstition that dressing up is proof of an enchantress's flightiness and the superficiality of her mind.'

'Fingernails too,' Fringilla said, slightly narrowing her green eyes, which never, ever, missed anything. 'Whatever next, darling? I hardly recognise you.'

'A simple spell,' the enchantress replied coolly, 'ought to be enough to prove it's me and no doppelgänger. Cast the spell, if you must. And then let's move on to the matter in hand. I asked something of you . . .'

Fringilla Vigo stroked the cat, which was rubbing himself against her calf, purring and arching his back, pretending it was a gesture of friendship and not a veiled hint that the black-haired sorceress should get up from the armchair.

'The same thing Seneschal Ceallach aep Gruffyd asked of you,' she said, without raising her head.

'Indeed,' Assire confirmed in hushed tones, 'Ceallach visited me, distraught, and asked me to intercede to save his son. Emhyr has ordered him to be captured, tortured and executed. Who else could he turn to except a relative? Mawr, Ceallach's wife and Cahir's mother, is my niece, my sister's youngest daughter. In spite of all that I didn't promise him anything. Because my hands are tied. Certain circumstances took place recently which do not permit me to draw attention to myself. I shall elucidate. But only after you've given me the information I asked you to gather.'

Fringilla Vigo furtively sighed with relief. She had been afraid her friend would want to get involved in the case of Cahir, son of Ceallach, which had 'gallows' written all over it. And equally afraid she would be asked for help she couldn't refuse.

'Around the middle of July,' she began, 'the entire court at Loc Grim had the opportunity to marvel at a fifteen-year-old girl, supposedly the Princess of Cintra, whom Emhyr insisted on referring to as "Your Majesty" during the audience and was treated so kindly there were even rumours of a quick marriage.'

'So I heard,' Assire said, stroking the cat, which had given up on Fringilla and was trying to occupy her own armchair instead. 'This doubtlessly political marriage is still talked about.'

'But more discreetly and not so often. For the Cintran was moved to Darn Rowan. Prisoners of state, as you know, are often kept in Darn Rowan. Potential imperatrices much less often.'

Assire didn't comment. She waited patiently, examining her freshly filed and varnished fingernails.

'You must remember,' Fringilla Vigo continued, 'how Emhyr summoned us all three years ago and ordered us to establish the whereabouts of a certain individual. Within the Northern Kingdoms. You must also recall how furious he became when we failed. Albrich – who explained it was impossible to detect anything from such a distance, never mind bypassing protective screens – was severely reprimanded. But that's not all. A week after the aforementioned audience in Loc Grim, when victory at Aldersberg was being celebrated, Emhyr noticed myself and Albrich in the castle chamber. And graced us with his conversation. The gist of his speech, only somewhat trivialising it, was: "You're all of you leeches, spongers and idlers. Your conjuring tricks cost me a fortune and there's nothing to show for it. The task which your entire lamentable academy failed to achieve was carried out in four days by an ordinary astrologist.'

Assire var Anahid snorted disdainfully and continued to stroke the cat.

'It was easy to discover,' Fringilla Vigo went on, 'that the miracle worker was none other than the infamous astrologist Xarthisius.'

'I take it the subject of the search was the Cintran candidate for the position of Imperatrice. Xarthisius found her. And then what? Was he appointed Secretary of State? Head of the Department of Unfeasible Affairs?'

'No. He was thrown into a dungeon the following week.'

'I fear I fail to understand what this has to do with Cahir, son of Ceallach.'

'Patience. Don't make me get ahead of myself. This is crucial.'

'I beg your pardon. Go on.'

'Do you remember what Emhyr gave us when we began our search three years ago?'

'A lock of hair.'

'Precisely,' Fringilla said, reaching for a small, leather purse. 'And this is it. A few blonde hairs belonging to a six-year-old girl. I kept the remnants. And it's worth your knowing that Stella Congreve, Countess of Liddertal, is looking after the Cintran princess who is being kept in isolation in Darn Rowan. Stella happens to be indebted to me for various reasons, so it was easy for me to come by a second lock of hair. And this is it. Somewhat darker, but hair darkens with age. Nonetheless, the locks belong to two totally different people. I've examined them and there is no doubt in this respect.'

'I had expected a revelation of this kind,' Assire var Anahid admitted, 'when I heard that the Cintran had been shut up in Darn Rowan. The astrologer either fouled up completely or is implicated in a conspiracy that planned to supply Emhyr with a bogus individual. A conspiracy which will cost Cahir aep Ceallach his head. Thank you, Fringilla. Everything is clear.'

'Not everything,' the sorceress said and shook her head of black hair. 'First of all, it wasn't Xarthisius who found the Cintran or took her to Loc Grim. The astrologist started on his horoscopes and astromancy *after* Emhyr realised he had a bogus princess and begun an intensive search for the real one. And the old fool ended up in the dungeon because of a simple mistake in his art or fraud. For he had established the whereabouts of the person Emhyr sought with a radial tolerance of approximately one hundred miles. And that region turned out to be a desert, a savage wilderness somewhere beyond the Tir Tochair massif and the riverhead of the Velda. Stephan Skellen, who was sent there, found nothing but scorpions and vultures.'

'I wouldn't have expected much more from Xarthisius. But that won't affect Cahir's fate. Emhyr is quick-tempered, but he never sentences anyone to torture or death just like that, without evidence. Someone, as you said yourself, made sure the bogus princess was taken to Loc Grim in place of the real one. Someone came up with a double. So there was a conspiracy and Cahir became mixed up in it. Possibly unwittingly. Which means he was used.'

'If that was the case, he would have been used until the goal was reached. He would personally have delivered the double to Emhyr. But Cahir has vanished without a trace. Why? His disappearance was sure to have aroused suspicions. Did he fear Emhyr would notice the deception at first glance? For he did. He couldn't fail to, after all he had a—'

'A lock of hair,' Assire cut in. 'A lock of hair from a six-year-old girl. Fringilla, Emhyr hasn't been hunting for that girl for three years, but for much longer. It looks as though Cahir has become embroiled in something very nasty, something which began when he was still riding a stick horse and pretending to be a knight. Mmm . . . Leave me those strands of hair. I'd like to test them both thoroughly.'

Fringilla Vigo nodded slowly and narrowed her green eyes.

'I will. But be cautious, Assire. Don't get mixed up in any dirty business, because it might draw attention to you. And at the beginning of the conversation you hinted that attention would be inconvenient to you. And promised you'd reveal why.'

Assire var Anahid stood up, walked over to the window and stared at the spires and pinnacles of Nilfgaard – the capital of the Empire, called the City of the Golden Towers – shimmering in the setting sun.

'You once told me and I remembered it,' she said, without turning around, 'that no borders should ever divide magic. That magic should have the highest values, be above all divisions. That what was needed was some kind of . . . secret organisation . . . Something like a convent or a lodge . . .'

'I am ready,' said Fringilla Vigo, Nilfgaardian sorceress, breaking the short silence. 'My mind is made up and I am ready. Thank you for your trust and the distinction. When and where will this lodge meet, my mysterious and enigmatic friend?'

Assire var Anahid, Nilfgaardian sorceress, turned away. The hint of a smile played on her lips.

'Soon,' she said. 'I'll explain everything to you soon. But first, before I forget . . . Give me the address of your milliner, Fringilla.'

'There isn't a single fire,' Milva whispered, staring at the dark bank beyond the river, gleaming in the moonlight, 'or a living soul there, I reckon. There were two hundred refugees in the camp. Has no one got off scot-free?'

'If the imperial troops won, they took them all captive,' Cahir whispered back. 'If your boys got the upper hand, they took the refugees with them when they moved on.'

They neared the riverbank and the reeds covering the marsh. Milva trod on something and sprang back, suppressing a scream, at the sight of a stiff arm, covered in leeches, sticking out of the mud.

'It's just a dead body,' Cahir muttered, grabbing her hand. 'One of ours. A Daerlanian.'

'Who is he?'

'One of the Seventh Daerlanian Cavalry Brigade. See the silver scorpion on his sleeve . . .'

'By the Gods. . .' The girl shuddered and gripped her bow tightly in her sweating fist. 'Did you hear that noise? What was it?'

'A wolf.'

'Or a ghoul . . . Or some other hell spawn. There must be a whole load of dead bodies in the camp . . . A pox on it, I'm not crossing that river at night!'

'Fine, we'll wait until dawn . . . Milva? What's that strange . . . ?'

'Regis . . .' the archer said, stifling a shout at the scent of wormwood, sage, coriander and aniseed. 'Regis? Is that you?'

'Yes, it's me,' the barber-surgeon replied, noiselessly emerging from the gloom, 'I was worried about you. But you're not alone, I see.'

'Aye.' Milva released Cahir's arm, noticing he had already drawn his sword. 'I'm not alone and he's not alone any more. But that's a long story, as some people would say. Regis, what about the Witcher? And Dandelion? And the others? Do you know what's happened to them?'

'Indeed I do. Do you have horses?'

'Yes, they're hidden in the willows . . .'

'Then let's head southwards, down the Chotla. Without delay. We must reach Armeria before midnight.'

'What about the Witcher and the poet? Are they alive?'

'Yes. But they're in a bit of difficulty.'

'What kind of difficulty?'

'It's a long story.'

Dandelion groaned, trying to turn around and get into a slightly more comfortable position. It was, however, an impossible task for someone lying trussed up like a ham to be smoked in a pile of soft wood shavings and sawdust and.

'They didn't hang us right away,' he grunted. 'There's hope for us still. We aren't done for yet . . .'

'Would you mind shutting up?' the Witcher said, lying back calmly and looking up at the moon, visible through a hole in the roof of the woodshed. 'Do you know why Vissegerd didn't hang us right away? Because we're to be executed publicly, at dawn, while the entire corps are mustered before moving out. For propaganda purposes.'

Dandelion did not respond to that. Geralt only heard him panting with worry.

'You still have a chance of dodging the drop,' he added, trying to reassure the poet. 'Vissegerd simply wants to exact his own private revenge on me; he hasn't got anything against you. Your friend the count will get you out of trouble, you'll see.'

'That's crap,' the bard replied, to the Witcher's astonishment calmly and quite reasonably. 'Crap, crap, crap. Don't treat me like a child. For one thing, two hanged men are better for propaganda purposes than one. For another, you don't let a witness to private revenge live. No, brother, they'll stretch us both.'

'That's enough, Dandelion. Lie there quietly and think up a plan.'

'What bloody plan?'

'Any bloody plan.'

The poet's idle chatter prevented the Witcher from gathering his thoughts, and he had no time to waste. He expected that men from Temerian military intelligence – some of whom must have been present in Vissegerd's corps – would burst into the woodshed at any moment. Intelligence officers would surely be interested in asking him about various aspects of the events in Garstang on the Isle of Thanedd. Geralt hardly knew any of the details, but he was confident that he would be feeling very, very poorly indeed before the agents accepted this. All his hopes depended on Vissegerd, blinded by the lust for revenge, not having made the Witcher's capture public. Intelligence officers might want to free the captives from the clutches of the furious marshal in order to take them to headquarters. Or, to be more precise, take whatever was left of them after the first round of interrogation.

The poet, meanwhile, had come up with a plan.

'Geralt! Let's pretend we know something important. That we really are spies or something like that. Then—'

'Dandelion, please.'

'No? So we could try to bribe the sentries. I have some money hidden away. Doubloons, sewn into the lining of my boot. For a rainy day . . . We'll summon the sentries . . .'

'Who'll take all you have and then beat you up for good measure.'

The poet grumbled, but stopped talking. From the field they heard shouts, the patter of hooves and – what was worse – the smell of army pea soup. At that moment, Geralt would have given all the sterlets and truffles in the world for a bowl of it. The sentries standing outside the shed were talking lazily, chuckling and, from time to time, hawking up and spitting. The sentries were professional soldiers, which could be discerned by their remarkable ability to communicate using sentences constructed entirely of pronouns and coarse expletives.

'Geralt?'

'What?'

'I wonder what's happened to Milva . . . And Zoltan, and Percival and Regis . . . Did you see them?'

'No. We can't rule out their being hacked to death or trampled by horses during the skirmish. The camp was knee-deep in corpses.'

'I can't believe,' Dandelion declared resolutely and with a note of hope in his voice, 'I can't believe that crafty buggers like Zoltan and Percival . . . Or Milva . . .'

'Stop deluding yourself. Even if they did survive, they won't help us.'

'Why not?'

'For three reasons. Firstly, they have their own problems. Secondly, we're lying tied up in a shed in the middle of a camp of several thousand soldiers.'

'And the third reason? You mentioned three.'

'Thirdly,' the Witcher replied in a tired voice, 'the monthly quota on miracles was used up when the woman from Kernow found her missing husband.'

'Over there,' the barber-surgeon said, indicating the small dots of campfires, 'is Fort Armeria, at present the camp of the Temerian Army concentrated at Mayena.'

'Are the Witcher and Dandelion being held prisoner there?'

Milva asked, standing up in her stirrups. 'Ha, then things are bad . . . There must be hordes of armed men and guards everywhere. Won't be easy sneaking in there.'

'You won't have to,' Regis responded, dismounting from Pegasus. The gelding gave a long snort and pulled his head away, clearly disgusted by the barber-surgeon's herbal odour, which made his nostrils tingle.

'You won't have to sneak in,' he repeated. 'I'll take care of it. You'll be waiting with the horses where the river's sparkling, do you see? Beneath the brightest star in the Seven Goats. The Chotla flows into the Ina there. Once I've got the Witcher out of trouble I'll point him in that direction. And that's where you'll meet.'

'How arrogant is that?' Cahir muttered to Milva when they came close to each other, dismounting. 'He'll get them out of trouble by himself, without anyone's help. Did you hear that? Who is he?'

'In truth, I don't know,' Milva muttered back. 'But when it comes to impossible tasks, I believe him. Yesterday, in front of my very eyes, he got a red-hot horseshoe out of a fire with his bare hands . . .'

'Is he a sorcerer?'

'No,' Regis answered from behind Pegasus, demonstrating his exceptionally sensitive hearing. 'But does it really matter who I am? After all, I haven't asked for your personal details.'

'I am Cahir Mawr Dyffryn aep Ceallach.'

'I thank you and am full of admiration.' The barber-surgeon's voice had a slight note of scorn. 'I heard almost no Nilfgaardian accent when you pronounced your Nilfgaardian surname.'

'I'm not—'

'Enough!' Milva cut him off. 'This isn't the time for arguing or hesitating. Regis, the Witcher's waiting to be rescued.'

'Not before midnight,' the barber-surgeon said coldly, looking up at the moon. 'So we have some time to talk. Who is this person, Milva?'

'That person,' the archer replied, a little angry and standing up for Cahir, 'rescued me from a tight spot. That person will tell the Witcher, when he meets him, that he's going in the wrong direction. Ciri's not in Nilfgaard.'

'A revelation indeed,' the barber-surgeon said, his voice softening. 'And its source, Sir Cahir, son of Ceallach?'

'It's a long story.'

Dandelion had been silent for a long time when one of the sentries suddenly stopped talking in the middle of a curse and the other rasped, or possibly groaned. Geralt knew there had been three on guard, so he listened intently, but the third didn't utter even the slightest sound.

The Witcher waited, holding his breath, but what came to his ears a moment later was not the creaking of the door to the woodshed being opened by their rescuers. Not in the least. He heard even, soft, choral snoring. The sentries were quite simply asleep on duty.

He breathed out, swore silently, and was just about to lose himself in thoughts about Yennefer when medallion around the Witcher's neck suddenly vibrated and the air was filled with the scent of wormwood, basil, coriander, sage, aniseed, and the devil only knew what else.

'Regis?' he whispered in disbelief, ineffectually trying to lift his head from the wood shavings.

'Regis,' Dandelion whispered back, moving around and rustling. 'No one else reeks like that . . . Where are you? I can't see you—'

'Be quiet!'

The medallion stopped vibrating, Geralt heard the poet's relieved sigh and immediately after the soft hiss of a blade cutting his ropes. A moment later Dandelion gave a moan of pain as his circulation returned, but dutifully tried to suppress it by sticking his fist into his mouth.

'Geralt,' the barber-surgeon said, his vague, wavering shadow materialising at the Witcher's side, and immediately began to cut his bonds. 'You'll have to get past the camp guard yourselves. Head towards the east and the brightest star in the Seven Goats. Straight to the Ina. Milva's waiting for you there with the horses.'

'Help me get up . . .'

He stood first on one leg and then on the other, biting his fist.

Dandelion's circulation was already back to normal. A moment later the Witcher was also ready for action.

'How are we going to get out?' the poet suddenly asked. 'The sentries at the door are snoring, but they may . . .'

'No, they won't,' Regis interrupted in a whisper. 'But be careful when you leave. It's a full moon and the field's lit by campfires. In spite of it being night the entire camp is bustling, but perhaps that's a good thing. The corporals of the guard are bored of challenging the sentries. Out you go. Good luck.'

'What about you?'

'Don't worry about me. Don't wait for me and don't look back.'

'But—'

'Dandelion,' the Witcher hissed. 'You've been told not to worry about him, got it?'

'Out you go,' Regis repeated. 'Good luck. Until the next time, Geralt.'

The Witcher turned around.

'Thank you for rescuing us,' he said. 'But it would be best if we never met again. Am I making myself clear?'

'Absolutely. Don't waste time.'

The sentries were sleeping as they had fallen, snoring and smacking their lips. Not one of them even twitched when Geralt and Dandelion squeezed out through the slightly open door. Neither did any of them react when the Witcher unceremoniously pulled the thick homespun capes from two of them.

'That's no ordinary sleep,' Dandelion whispered.

'Of course it isn't,' Geralt said. Hidden in the dark of the woodshed's shadow, he looked around.

'I see.' The poet sighed. 'Is Regis a sorcerer?'

'No. No, not a sorcerer.'

'He took that horseshoe from the fire. Put the sentries to sleep . . .'

'Stop wittering and concentrate. We aren't free yet. Wrap that cape around you and let's cross the field. If anyone stops us we're pretending to be soldiers.'

'Right. If anything happens I'll say—'

'We're pretending to be stupid soldiers. Let's go.'

They crossed the field, keeping their distance from the soldiers crowded around glowing braziers and campfires. Soldiers were roaming about here and there; two more weren't conspicuous. They didn't arouse anyone's suspicions; no one questioned them or stopped them. They passed beyond the stockade quickly and without any difficulty.

Everything went smoothly; in fact, *too* smoothly. Geralt became anxious, since he instinctively sensed danger and his anxiety was growing – rather than diminishing – the further they moved from the centre of the camp. He repeated to himself that there was nothing strange in that: they hadn't drawn attention to themselves in the middle of a military camp that was busy even at night, and the only danger had been that of the alarm being raised, should someone notice the sleeping sentries at the door to the woodshed. Now, however, they were approaching the perimeter, where the sentries had – by necessity – to be vigilant. The fact that they were heading away from the centre of the camp could not be helping them. The Witcher recalled the plague of desertion in Vissegerd's corps and was certain the guards had orders to watch carefully for anyone trying to abandon the camp.

The moon was shining brightly enough for Dandelion not to have to grope his way. This amount of light meant the Witcher could see as well as during the day, which enabled them to avoid two sentry posts and wait in the bushes for a mounted patrol to pass. There was an alder grove directly in front of them, apparently outside the ring of sentry posts. Everything was still going smoothly. Too smoothly.

Their ignorance of military customs proved to be their undoing.

They were tempted by the low, dark clump of alders, because of the cover it offered. But since time immemorial there have always been soldiers who lie in the bushes when it is their turn to be on guard duty, while the ones who aren't asleep keep an eye both on the enemy and on their own bloody-minded officers, should any of the latter descend on them with an unexpected inspection.

Geralt and Dandelion had barely reached the alder grove before several dark shapes – and spear blades – loomed up in front of them.

'Password?'

'Cintra!' Dandelion blurted out without hesitation.

The soldiers chuckled as one.

'Really, boys,' one of them said, 'is that the best you can do? If only someone would come up with something original. But no, nothing but "Cintra". Missing home, are we? Well, the fee's the same as yesterday.'

Dandelion audibly ground his teeth. Geralt weighed up the situation and their chances. His assessment: decidedly crap.

'Come on,' the soldier said, hurrying them. 'If you want to get through, pay up and we'll turn a blind eye. And quickly, because the corporal of the guard will be here any second.'

''Owd on,' the poet said, changing his accent and mode of speech. 'I'll just sit down and get me boot off, because there's. . .'

He didn't manage to say anything else. Four soldiers threw him to the ground. Then two of them, each one seizing one of his legs between theirs, pulled off his boots. The one who'd asked for the password tore the lining from the inside of a bootleg. Something scattered around with a jingle.

'Gold!' the leader yelled. 'Pull the boots off the other one! And summon the corporal!'

However, there was no one to do any boot-pulling or summoning, because half the guard dropped on their knees to search for the doubloons scattered among the leaves while the other half immediately began fighting furiously over Dandelion's second boot. *It's now or never*, Geralt thought, punching the leader in the jaw and then kicking him in the side of his head as he fell. The soldiers who were searching for gold didn't even notice. Dandelion needed no encouragement to spring up and dash through the bushes, his footwraps flapping. Geralt ran after him.

'Help! Help!' the leader of the watch bellowed from the ground, his voice soon after joined by his comrades. 'Cooorporaaal!'

'You swine!' Dandelion yelled back as he fled. 'Knaves! You stole my money!'

'Save your breath, dolt! See that forest? Make for it.'

'Stop them! Stop theeem!'

They ran. Geralt swore furiously, hearing shouts, whistles, neighing and the thudding of hooves. Behind them. And in front of them. His astonishment didn't last long; one careful look was enough. What he had taken for a forest and a safe haven was an approaching wall of cavalry, surging towards them like a wave.

'Stop, Dandelion!' he shouted, then turned back to the patrol galloping in their direction and whistled piercingly through his fingers.

'Nilfgaard!' he yelled at the top of his voice. 'Nilfgaard are coming! Back to the camp! Get back to the camp, you fools! Sound the alarm! Nilfgaard!'

The leading rider of the patrol pursuing them reined his horse to a rapid stop, looked towards where Geralt had pointed, screamed in terror and was about to turn back. But Geralt decided he had already done enough for the Cintran lions and Temerian lilies. He leapt at the soldier and dragged him from the saddle with a dextrous tug.

'Jump on, Dandelion! And hold tight!'

The poet didn't need to be told twice. The horse sagged a little under the weight of an extra rider, but spurred on by two pairs of heels was soon galloping hard. The approaching swarm of Nilfgaardians now represented a much greater threat than Vissegerd and his corps, so they galloped along the ring of sentry posts, trying to escape from the area where the two armies would clash at any moment. The Nilfgaardians were close, however, and had seen them. Dandelion yelled, then Geralt looked around and saw the dark wall of Nilfgaardian troops beginning to extend black tentacles of pursuit. Without hesitating he steered the horse towards the camp, overtaking the fleeing guards. Dandelion yelled once again, but this time there was no need. The Witcher could also see the cavalry charging at them from the camp. Having been alerted, Vissegerd's corps had mounted at admirable speed. And Geralt and Dandelion were caught in a trap.

There was no way out. The Witcher changed the direction of their flight once more and urged from the horse all the speed it could muster, trying to slip out of the dangerously narrowing gap between hammer and anvil. When hope dawned that they might just make it, the night air suddenly sang with a whistle of fletchings. Dandelion yelled, this time very loudly indeed, and dug his fingers into Geralt's sides. The Witcher felt something warm dripping onto his neck.

'Hold on!' he shouted, catching the poet by his elbow and drawing him closer to his own back. 'Hold on, Dandelion!'

'They've killed me!' the poet howled, impressively loudly for a dead man. 'I'm bleeding! I'm dying!'

'Hold on!'

The hail of arrows and quarrels, which was raining down on both armies and had proved to be so disastrous for Dandelion, was also their salvation. The armies under fire seethed and lost momentum, and the gap between the front lines which had been about to draw together remained open just long enough for the heavily snorting horse to whisk the two riders out of the trap. Geralt mercilessly forced his steed to ride hard, for although the trees and safety were looming up in front of them, hooves continued to thunder behind them. The horse grunted and stumbled, but did not stop and they might have escaped had not Dandelion suddenly groaned and lurched backwards, dragging the Witcher out of the saddle with him. Geralt unintentionally tugged on the reins, the horse reared, and the two men tumbled to the ground among some very low pines. The poet thudded onto the dirt and lay still, groaning pathetically. His head and left shoulder were covered in blood, which glistened black in the moonlight.

Behind them, the armies collided with thuds, clangs and screams. But despite the raging battle, their Nilfgaardian pursuers hadn't forgotten about them. Three cavalrymen were galloping towards them.

The Witcher sprang up, feeling a swelling wave of cold fury and hatred inside him. He jumped out to meet their pursuers, drawing the horsemen's attention away from Dandelion. But not because he wanted to sacrifice himself for his friend. He wanted to kill.

The leading rider, who had pulled ahead, flew at him with a raised battle-axe, but had no way of knowing he was attacking a witcher. Geralt dodged the blow effortlessly and seized the Nilfgaardian leaning over in the saddle by his cloak, while the fingers of his other hand caught the soldier's broad belt. He pulled the rider from the saddle with a powerful wrench and fell on him, pinning him to the ground.

Only then did Geralt realise he had no weapon. He caught the man by the throat, but couldn't throttle him because of his iron gorget. The Nilfgaardian struggled, hit him with an armoured gauntlet and gashed his cheek. The Witcher smothered his opponent with his entire body, groped for the misericord in the broad belt, and jerked it out of its sheath. The man on the ground felt it and howled. Geralt fended off the arm with the silver scorpion on the sleeve that was still hitting him and raised the dagger to strike.

The Nilfgaardian screamed.

The Witcher plunged the misericord into his open mouth. Up to the hilt.

When he got to his feet, he saw horses without riders, bodies and a cavalry unit heading away towards the battle. The Cintrans from the camp had dispatched their Nilfgaardian pursuers, and had not even noticed the poet or the two men fighting on the ground in the gloom among the low pine trees.

'Dandelion! Where were you hit? Where's the arrow?'

'In my head . . . It's stuck in my head . . .'

'Don't talk nonsense! Bloody hell, you were lucky . . . It only grazed you . . .'

'I'm bleeding . . .'

Geralt removed his jerkin and tore off a shirtsleeve. The point of the quarrel had caught Dandelion above the ear, leaving a nasty-looking gash extending to his temple. The poet kept bringing his shaking hand up to the wound and then looking at the blood, which was profusely spattering his hands and cuffs. His eyes were vacant. The Witcher realised he was dealing with a person who, for the first time in his life, had been wounded and was in pain. Who, for the first time in his life, was seeing his own blood in such quantities.

'Get up,' he said, wrapping the shirtsleeve quickly and clumsily around the troubadour's head. 'It's nothing. Dandelion, it's only a scratch . . . Get up, we have to get out of here fast . . .'

The battle on the field raged on in the dark; the clatter of steel, neighing of horses and screams grew louder and louder. Geralt quickly caught two Nilfgaardian steeds, but it turned out one was sufficient. Dandelion managed to get up, but immediately sat down again, groaned and sobbed pitifully. The Witcher lifted him to his feet, shook him back to consciousness and hauled him into the saddle.

Geralt mounted behind the wounded poet and spurred the horse east, to where – above the already visible pale blue streaks of the dawn – hung the brightest star of the Seven Goats constellation.

'Dawn will be breaking soon,' Milva said, looking not at the sky but at the glistening surface of the river. 'The catfish are tormenting the small fry. But there's neither hide nor hair of the Witcher or Dandelion. Oh, I hope Regis didn't mess up—'

'Don't tempt fate,' Cahir muttered, adjusting the girth of the recovered chestnut colt.

Milva looked around for a piece of wood to knock on.

'. . . But it does seem to be like that . . . Whoever encounters your Ciri, it's as though they've put their head on the block . . . That girl brings misfortune . . . Misfortune and death.'

'Spit that out, Milva.'

She spat obediently, as superstition demanded.

'There's such a chill, I'm shivering . . . And I'm thirsty, but I saw another rotting corpse in the river near the bank. Phooey . . . I feel sick . . . I think I'm going to throw up . . .'

'There you go,' Cahir said, handing her a canteen. 'Drink that. And sit down close to me, I'll keep you warm.'

Another catfish struck a shoal of minnows in the shallows and they scattered near the surface in a silver hail. A bat or nightjar flashed past in a beam of moonlight.

'Who knows,' Milva muttered pensively, cuddling up to Cahir, 'what tomorrow will bring. Who'll cross that river and who'll perish.'

'What will be, will be. Drive those thoughts away.'

'Aren't you afraid?'

'I am. What about you?'

'I feel sick.'

There was a lengthy pause.

'Tell me, Cahir, when did you meet Ciri?'

'For the first time? Three years ago. During the fight for Cintra. I got her out of the city. I found her, beset by fire. I rode through the fire, through the flames and smoke, holding her in my arms. And she was like a flame herself.'

'And?'

'You can't hold a flame in your hands.'

'If it isn't Ciri in Nilfgaard,' she said after a long silence, 'then who is it?'

'I don't know.'

Drakenborg, the Redanian fortress converted into an internment camp for elves and other subversive elements, had some grim traditions, which had evolved during its three years of operation. One of those traditions was dawn hangings. Another was gathering all those under death sentences in a large, common cell, from which they were led out to the gallows at daybreak.

About a dozen of the condemned were grouped together in the cell, and every morning two, three – or occasionally four – of them were hanged. The others waited their turn. A long time. Sometimes as long as a week. The condemned were called Clowns. Because the mood around the death cell was always jolly. Firstly, at meals prisoners were served very thin, sour wine nicknamed 'Dijkstra Dry' in the camp, as it was no secret that they could enjoy it at the behest of the head of the Redanian secret service. Secondly, no one was dragged to the sinister, underground Wash House to be interrogated any longer, nor were the warders allowed to maltreat the convicts.

The tradition was also observed that night. It was merry in the cell being occupied by six elves, a half-elf, a halfling, two humans and a Nilfgaardian. Dijkstra Dry was poured onto a single, shared tin plate and lapped up without the use of the arms, since that method gave the greatest chance of at least some intoxication by the gnat's piss. Only one of the elves, a Scoia'tael from Iorweth's defeated commando, recently severely tortured in the Wash House, retained his composure and dignity and was busy carving the words 'Freedom Or Death' on a post. There were several hundred similar inscriptions on the posts around the cell. The remaining condemned convicts, also in keeping with tradition, sang the Clowns' Anthem over and over again, a song composed in Drakenborg by an unknown author. Every convict learned the words in the barracks, as the song drifted to them at night from the condemned cell, knowing that the day would come when they would join the choir.

> The Clowns dance on the scaffold
> Rhythmically twitching and jerking
> They sing their song
> Of sadness and beauty
> And the Clowns have all the fun
> Every corpse will recall
> When the stool's kicked away
> And his eyes roll up to the sun.

The bolt rattled, the key grated in the lock and the Clowns stopped singing. Warders entering at dawn could only mean one thing: in a moment the choir would be depleted by several voices. The only question was: whose?

The warders entered together. All were carrying ropes to tie the hands of the convicts being led to the scaffold. One sniffed, shoved his cudgel under his arm, unrolled a scroll of parchment and cleared his throat.

'Echel Trogelton!'

'Traighlethan,' the elf from Iorweth's commando corrected him softly. He looked at the carved slogan once more and struggled to his feet.

'Cosmo Baldenvegg!'

The halfling swallowed loudly. Nazarian knew Baldenvegg had been imprisoned on charges of acts of sabotage, carried out on the instructions of the Nilfgaardian secret service. However, Baldenvegg had not admitted his guilt and stubbornly maintained he had stolen both cavalry horses on his own initiative to make some money, and that Nilfgaard had nothing to do with it. He had clearly not been believed.

'Nazarian!'

Nazarian stood up obediently and held his hands out for the

warders to bind. When the three of them were being led out, the rest of the Clowns took up the song.

The Clowns dance on the scaffold
Merrily twitching and jerking
And the wind carries their song
The chorus echoing all around . . .

The dawn glowed purple and red, heralding a beautiful, sunny day.

The Clowns' Anthem, thought Nazarian, *was misleading*. They could not dance a jaunty jig, since they were not hanged from a gibbet with a cross beam, but from ordinary posts sunk into the ground. They didn't have stools kicked from under them, but practical, low birch blocks, bearing the marks of frequent use. The song's anonymous author, who had been executed the previous year, could not have known that when he composed it. Like all the other convicts, he was only acquainted with the details shortly before his death. In Drakenborg the executions were never carried out in public. They were a just punishment and not sadistic vengeance. Those words were also attributed to Dijkstra.

The elf from Iorweth's commando shook the warders' hands off, stepped onto the block without hesitation and allowed the noose to be placed around his neck.

'Long li—'

The block was kicked out from under his feet.

The halfling required two blocks, which were placed one on top of the other. The alleged saboteur did not bother with any grandiloquent cries. His short legs kicked vigorously and then sagged against the post. His head lolled slackly on his shoulder.

When the warders seized Nazarian he suddenly changed his tune.

'I'll talk!' he croaked. 'I'll testify! I have important information for Dijkstra!'

'Bit late for that,' said Vascoigne, the deputy commander for political affairs at Drakenborg, who was assisting at the execution, doubtingly. 'The sight of the noose rouses the imagination in every second one of you!'

'I'm not making it up!' Nazarian appealed, struggling in the executioners' arms. 'I've got information!'

Less than an hour later Nazarian was sitting in a seclusion cell, delighting in the beauty of life. A messenger stood at readiness beside his horse, scratching his groin vigorously, and Vascoigne was reading and checking the report which was about to be sent to Dijkstra.

I humbly inform Your Lordship, that the felon by the name of Nazarian, sentenced for an assault on a royal official, has testified to the following: that acting on the orders of a certain Ryens, on the day of the July new moon this year, with two of his accomplices, the elven half-breed Schirrú and Millet, he did take part in the murder of the jurists Codringher and Fenn in the city of Dorian. Millet was killed there, but the half-breed Schirrú murdered the two jurists and set their house on fire. The felon Nazarian shifts all the blame onto the said Schirrú, denies and refutes any suggestion that he committed the murders, but that is probably owing to fear of the gallows. What may interest Your Lordship, however, is that prior to the crime against the jurists being committed, the said malefactors (that is Nazarian, the half-elf Schirrú and Millet) were hunting a witcher, a certain Gerald of Rivia, who had been holding secret meetings with the jurist Codringher. To what end, the felon Nazarian does not know, because neither the aforementioned Ryens, nor the half-elf Schirrú, did divulge the secret to him. But when Ryens was given the report concerning their collusions, he ordered the jurists to be destroyed.

The felon Nazarian further testified that his accomplice Schirrú stole some documents from the jurists, which were later delivered to Ryens at an inn called the Sly Fox in Carreras. What Ryens and Schirrú conversed about there is not known to Nazarian, but the following day the criminal trio travelled to Brugge where, on the fourth day after the new moon, they committed the abduction of a maiden from a red-brick house, on the door of which a pair of brass shears were affixed. Ryens drugged her with a magic potion, and the malefactors Schirrú and Nazarian conveyed her in great

216

haste by carriage to the stronghold of Nastrog in Verden. And now a matter which I commend to Your Lordship's close attention: the malefactors handed the abducted maid over to the stronghold's Nilfgaardian commandant, assuring him that the said individual was Cyryla of Cintra. The commandant, as testified by the felon Nazarian, was greatly content with these tidings.

I dispatch the above in strict confidence to Your Lordship by messenger. I shall likewise send an exhaustive report of the inter-rogation, when the scribe has made a fair copy. I humbly request instructions from Your Lordship as to what to do with the felon Nazarian. Whether to order him stung with a bullwhip, so that he remembers more, or hang him according to regulations.

Your loyal servitor.

Vascoigne signed the report with a flourish, affixed a seal and sum-moned the messenger.

Dijkstra was acquainted with the contents of the report that evening; Philippa Eilhart by noon of the following day.

By the time the horse carrying the Witcher and Dandelion emerged from the riverside alders, Milva and Cahir were extremely agitated. They had heard the battle, as the water of the Ina carried the sounds a great distance.

As she helped lift the poet down from the saddle, Milva saw Geralt stiffening at the sight of the Nilfgaardian. However, she did not say anything – and neither did the Witcher – for Dandelion was moaning desperately and swooning. They laid him down on the sand, placing a folded-up cloak beneath his head. Milva had just set about changing the blood-soaked makeshift dressing when she felt a hand on her shoulder and smelled the familiar scent of wormwood, aniseed and other herbs. Regis, as was his custom, had appeared unexpectedly, out of thin air.

'Let me,' he said, pulling instruments and other paraphernalia from his sizeable medical bag, 'I'll take it from here.'

When the barber-surgeon peeled the dressing from the wound, Dandelion groaned pitifully.

'Relax,' Regis said, cleansing the wound. 'It's nothing. Only blood. Only a little blood . . . Your blood smells nice, poet.'

At precisely that moment the Witcher did something Milva would never have expected. He walked over to the horse and drew a long Nilfgaardian sword from the scabbard fastened under the saddle flap.

'Move away from him,' he snarled, standing over the barber-surgeon.

'The blood smells nice,' Regis repeated, not paying the slightest bit of attention to the Witcher. 'I can't detect in it the smell of infection, which with a head wound could have disastrous consequences. The main arteries and veins are intact . . . This will sting a little.'

Dandelion groaned and took a sharp intake of breath. The sword in the Witcher's hand vibrated and glistened with light reflected from the river.

'I'll put in a few stitches,' Regis said, continuing to ignore both the Witcher and his sword. 'Be brave, Dandelion.'

Dandelion was brave.

'Almost done here,' Regis said, setting about bandaging the victim's head. 'Don't you worry, Dandelion, you'll be right as rain. The wound's just right for a poet, Dandelion. You'll look like a war hero, with a proud bandage around your head, and the hearts of the maidens looking at you will melt like wax. Yes, a truly poetic wound. Unlike an abdominal wound for instance. Liver all cut up, kidneys and guts mangled, stomach contents and faeces pouring out, peritonitis . . . Right, that's done. Geralt, I'm all yours.'

He stood and the Witcher brought the sword up against his throat, as quick as lightning.

'Move away,' he snapped at Milva. Regis didn't twitch, even though the point of the sword was pressing gently against his neck. The archer held her breath, seeing the barber-surgeon's eyes glowing in the dark with a strange, cat-like light.

'Go on,' Regis said calmly. 'Thrust it in.'

'Geralt,' Dandelion spoke from the ground, totally alert. 'Are you utterly insane? He saved us from the gallows . . . And patched me up . . .'

'He saved us and the girl in the camp,' Milva recalled softly.

'Be quiet, all of you. You don't know what he is.'

The barber-surgeon did not move. And Milva suddenly saw what she ought to have seen long before: Regis did not cast a shadow.

'Indeed,' he said slowly. 'You don't know what I am. And it's time you did. My name is Emiel Regis Rohellec Terzieff-Godefroy. I have lived on this earth for four hundred and twenty-eight years according to your reckoning, or six hundred and forty-two years by the elven calendar. I'm the descendant of survivors, unfortunate beings imprisoned here after the cataclysm you call the Conjunction of the Spheres. I'm regarded, to put it mildly, as a monster. As a blood-sucking fiend. And now I've encountered a witcher, who earns his living eliminating creatures such as I. And that's it.'

'And that is enough,' Geralt said, lowering the sword. 'More than enough. Now scram, Emiel Regis Whatever-It-Was. Get out of here.'

'Astonishing.' Regis sneered. 'You're permitting me to leave? Me, who represents a danger to people? A witcher ought to make use of every opportunity to eliminate dangers of this kind.'

'Get lost. Make yourself scarce and do it fast.'

'To which far-flung corner should I make myself scarce?' Regis asked slowly. 'You're a witcher, after all. You know about me. When you've dealt with your problem, when you've sorted out whatever you need to sort out, you'll probably return to these parts. You know where I live, where I spend my time, how I earn my keep. Will you come after me?'

'It's possible. If there's a bounty. I am a witcher.'

'I wish you luck,' Regis said, fastening his bag and spreading his cape. 'Farewell. Ah, one more thing. How high would the price on my head have to be in order for you to bother? How high do you value me?'

'Bloody high.'

'You tickle my vanity. To be precise?'

'Fuck off, Regis.'

'I'm going. But first put a value on me. If you please.'

'I've usually taken the equivalent of a good saddle horse for an ordinary vampire. But you, after all, are not ordinary.'

'How much?'

'I doubt,' the Witcher said, his voice as cold as ice, 'I doubt whether anyone could afford it.'

'I understand and thank you,' the vampire said, smiling. This time he bared his teeth. At the sight, Milva and Cahir stepped back and Dandelion stifled a cry of horror.

'Farewell. Good luck.'

'Farewell, Regis. Same to you.'

Emiel Regis Rohellec Terzieff-Godefroy shook his cape, wrapped himself up in it with a flourish and vanished. He simply vanished.

'And now,' Geralt said, spinning around, the unsheathed sword still in his hand, 'it's your turn, Nilfgaardian . . .'

'No,' Milva interrupted angrily. 'I've had a bellyful of this. To horse, let's get out of here! Shouts carry over the water and before we know it someone will be hot on our trail!'

'I'm not going any further in his company.'

'Go on alone then!' she yelled, furious. 'The other way! I'm up to here with your moods, Witcher! You've driven Regis away, even though he saved your life, and that's your business. But Cahir saved me, so we're comrades! If he's an enemy to you, go back to Armeria. Suit yourself! Your mates are waiting for you there with a noose!'

'Stop shouting.'

'Well, don't just stand there. Help me get Dandelion onto the gelding.'

'You rescued our horses? Roach too?'

'*He* did,' she said, nodding towards Cahir. 'Let's be going.'

They forded the Ina. They rode along the right-hand bank, alongside the river, through shallow backwaters, through wetlands and old riverbeds, through swamps and marshes resounding with the croaking of frogs and the quacking of unseen mallards and garganeys. The day exploded with red sunlight, blindingly sparkling on the surfaces of small lakes overgrown with water lilies, and they turned towards a point where one of the Ina's numerous branches flowed into the Yaruga. Now they were riding through tenebrous, gloomy forests, where the trees grew straight from the marsh, green with duckweed.

Milva led the way, riding beside the Witcher, busy giving him an account of Cahir's story in hushed tones. Geralt was as silent as the grave, never once looking back at the Nilfgaardian, who was riding behind them, helping the poet. Dandelion moaned a little from time to time, swore and complained that his head was hurting, but held out bravely, without slowing down the march. His mood had improved with the recovery of Pegasus and the lute fastened to the saddle.

Around noon they rode out once more into sunny wetlands, beyond which the broad, calm waters of the Great Yaruga stretched out. They forced their way through dried-up riverbeds and waded through shallows and backwaters. And happened upon an island, a dry spot among the marshes and tussocks of grass between the river's numerous offshoots. The island was overgrown with bushes and willows, and there were a few taller trees growing on it, bare, withered and white from cormorants' guano.

Milva was the first to notice a boat among the reeds, which must have been deposited there by the current. She was also the first to spot a clearing among the osiers, which was a perfect place for a rest.

They stopped, and the Witcher decided it was time to talk to the Nilfgaardian. Face to face and without witnesses.

'I spared your life on Thanedd. I felt sorry for you, whippersnapper. It's the biggest mistake I've ever made. Early this morning I let a higher vampire go, even though he is certain to have several human lives on his conscience. I ought to have killed him. But I couldn't be bothered with him, for I'm preoccupied with one thought: to get my hands on the people who harmed Ciri. I've sworn that those who've harmed her will pay for it with their blood.'

Cahir did not speak.

'Your revelations, which Milva has told me about, don't change anything. There's only one conclusion: you were unable to abduct

221

Ciri on Thanedd, despite your best efforts. Now you're trailing me, so that I can lead you to her. So that you can get your hands on her again, because then your imperator might spare you and not send you to the scaffold.'

Cahir said nothing. Geralt felt bad. Very bad.

'She cried out in the night because of you,' he snapped. 'You grew to nightmarish proportions in her child's eyes. But actually, you were – and are – only a tool, a wretched minion of your imperator. I don't know what you did to become a nightmare for her. And the worst thing is I don't understand why in spite of everything I can't kill you. I don't understand what's holding me back.'

'Perhaps,' Cahir said softly, 'that despite all the circumstances and appearances we have something in common, you and I.'

'You reckon?'

'Like you, I want to rescue Ciri. Like you, I don't care if that surprises or astonishes anybody. Like you, I have no intention of justifying my motives to anybody.'

'Is that all?'

'No.'

'Very well, go on.'

'Ciri,' the Nilfgaardian began slowly, 'is riding a horse through a dusty village. With six other young people. Among those people is a girl with close-cropped hair. Ciri is dancing on a table in a barn and is happy . . .'

'Milva has told you about my dreams.'

'No. She hasn't told me anything. Do you believe me?'

'No.'

Cahir lowered his head and ground his heel in the sand.

'I'd forgotten,' he said, 'that you can't believe me, can't trust me. I understand that. But like you I had one more dream. A dream you haven't told anyone about. Because I seriously doubt that you'd want to tell anyone about it.'

It could be said that Servadio was simply in luck. He had come to Loredo without intending to spy on anyone in particular. But the village wasn't called the Bandits' Lair for no reason. Loredo lay on the Bandits' Trail, and brigands and thieves from all the regions of the Upper Velda called in there, met up to sell or barter loot, to stock up with provisions and tackle, and relax and enjoy themselves in the select company of fellow criminals. The village had been burnt down several times, but the few permanent and more numerous temporary residents would rebuild it each time. They lived off the bandits, and did very well, thank you. And snoopers and narks like Servadio always had the opportunity to pick up some information there, which might be worth a few florins to the prefect.

This time Servadio was counting on more than just a few. Because the Rats were riding into the village.

They were led by Giselher and flanked by Iskra and Kayleigh. Behind them rode Mistle and the new, flaxen-haired girl they called Falka. Asse and Reef brought up the rear, pulling some riderless horses, doubtlessly stolen with intent to sell. The Rats were tired and dust-covered but bore themselves briskly in the saddle, enthusiastically responding to greetings from the various comrades and acquaintances they happened to see. After dismounting and being given beer, they immediately entered noisy negotiations with traders and fences. All of them except Mistle and the new, flaxen-haired one, who wore a sword slung across her back. These two set off among the stalls, which, as usual, covered the village green. Loredo had its market days and the range of goods on offer (with the visiting bandits in mind) was especially rich and varied then. Today was such a day.

Servadio cautiously followed the girls. In order to make any money, he had to have information, and in order to have information he had to eavesdrop.

The girls looked at colourful scarves, beads, embroidered blouses, saddlecloths and ornate browbands for their horses. They sifted through the goods, but didn't buy anything. Mistle kept a hand on the fair-haired girl's shoulder almost the whole time.

The snooper cautiously moved closer, pretending to be looking at the straps and belts on a leatherworker's stall. The girls were talking, but quietly. He couldn't hear them and was too afraid to approach them any closer. They might have noticed, grown suspicious.

Candyfloss was being sold at one of the stalls. The girls walked over, Mistle bought two sticks wrapped round with the snow-white sweetmeat and handed one to the flaxen-haired girl. She nibbled it delicately. A white strand stuck to her lip. Mistle wiped it off with a careful, tender movement. The flaxen-haired girl opened her emerald-green eyes widely, slowly licked her lips and smiled, cocking her head playfully. Servadio felt a shudder, a cold trickle running between his shoulder blades. He recalled the rumours going around about the two female bandits.

He was going to withdraw stealthily, since it was clear he wouldn't pick up any useful information. The girls weren't talking about anything important. However, not far away, where the senior members of various bandit gangs were gathered, Giselher, Kayleigh and the others were noisily quarrelling, haggling, and yelling, every now and then holding mugs under the tap of a small cask. Servadio was likely to learn more from them. One of the Rats might let something slip, if only a single word, betraying the gang's current plans, their route or their destination. Should he manage to eavesdrop and supply the information in time to the prefect's soldiers or the Nilfgaardian spies who showed a lively interest in the Rats, the reward was practically his for the taking. And were the prefect to set a successful trap thanks to his information, Servadio could count on a considerable injection of funds. *I'll buy the old lady a sheepskin coat*, he thought feverishly. *I'll finally get the kids some shoes and maybe some toys . . . And for me . . .*

The girls wandered between the stalls, licking and nibbling the candyfloss from the sticks. Servadio suddenly noticed they were being watched. And pointed at. He knew who was doing the pointing; footpads and horse thieves from the gang of Pinta, also known as Otterpelt.

The thieves exchanged several provocatively loud comments and cackled with glee. Mistle squinted and placed her hand on the flaxen-haired girl's shoulder.

'Turtle doves!' one of the thieves snorted. He was a beanpole with a moustache like a bunch of oakum. 'Look, they'll be billing and cooing next!' Servadio saw the flaxen-haired girl tense up and noticed that Mistle's grip on her shoulder tightened. The thieves all chuckled. Mistle turned around slowly and several of them stopped laughing. But the one with the oakum moustache was either too drunk or too lacking in imagination to take the hint.

'Maybe one of you needs a man?' he said, moving closer and making obscene, suggestive movements. 'All you need is a good shag, and you'll cure that kink in a flash! Hey! I'm talking to you, you—'

He didn't manage to touch her. The flaxen-haired girl coiled up like an attacking adder, and her sword flashed and struck before the candyfloss she released had hit the ground. The moustachioed thief staggered and gobbled like a turkey, the blood from his butchered neck gushing in a long stream. The girl coiled up again, was on him in two nimble steps and struck once more, a wave of gore splashing the stalls. The corpse toppled over, the sand around it immediately turning red. Someone screamed. A second thief leant over and drew a knife from his bootleg, but at the same moment slumped, struck by Giselher with the metal handle of his knout.

'One stiff's enough!' the Rats' leader yelled. 'That one's only got himself to blame; he didn't know who he was crossing! Back off, Falka!'

Only then did the flaxen-haired girl lower her sword. Giselher took out a purse and shook it.

'According to the laws of our brotherhood, I'm paying for the man who was killed. Fairly, according to his weight, a thaler for every pound of the lousy cadaver! And that'll put an end to the feud! Am I right, comrades? Pinto, what do you say?'

Iskra, Kayleigh, Reef and Asse stood behind their leader. They had faces of stone and held their hands on their sword hilts.

'That's fair,' Otterpelt replied, surrounded by his gang. He was a short, bow-legged man in a leather tunic. 'You're right, Giselher. The feud's over.'

Servadio swallowed, trying to melt into the crowd now gathering at the scene. He swiftly lost all interest in stalking the Rats or the flaxen-haired girl they called Falka. He decided that the reward promised by the prefect was not nearly as high as he'd thought.

Falka calmly sheathed her sword and looked around. Servadio was dumbstruck at the sudden change in her expression.

'My candyfloss,' the girl whined miserably, looking at her treat lying soiled in the sand. 'I dropped my candyfloss . . .'

Mistle hugged her.

'I'll buy you another.'

The Witcher sat on the sand among the willows, gloomy, angry and lost in thought. He was looking at the cormorants sitting on the shit-covered tree.

After their conversation, Cahir had vanished into the bushes and had not reappeared. Milva and Dandelion were looking for something to eat. They had managed to find a copper cauldron and a trug of vegetables under some nets in the boat which had been washed up by the current. They set a wicker trap they had found in the boat in a riverside channel, then waded near to the bank and began hitting the rushes with sticks in order to drive fish into it. The poet was now feeling better and was strutting around as proud as a peacock with his heroically bandaged head.

Geralt continued to brood and sulk.

Milva and Dandelion hauled the fish pot out and began to swear, for instead of the catfish and carp they had expected, all they saw was silvery fry wriggling around inside.

The Witcher stood up.

'Come over here, you two! Leave that trap and come here. I've got something to tell you.

'You're returning home,' he began bluntly when they came over, wet and stinking of fish. 'Head north, towards Mahakam. I'm going on by myself.'

'What?'

'Now we must go our separate ways. The party's over, Dandelion. You're going home to write poems. Milva will lead you through the forests . . . What's the matter?'

'Nothing's the matter,' Milva said, tossing her hair from her shoulder with a sudden movement. 'Nothing. Speak, Witcher. I'd like to hear what you're going to say.'

'I don't have anything else to say. I'll go south, crossing to the Yaruga's far bank. Through Nilfgaardian territory. It'll be a dangerous and long journey. And there's no time to waste. Which is why I'm going by myself.'

'Having got rid of the inconvenient baggage.' Dandelion nodded. 'The ball and chain slowing down your march and causing so many problems. In other words: me.'

'And me,' Milva added, glancing to one side.

'Listen,' Geralt said, now much more calmly. 'This is my own private matter. None of this concerns you. I don't want you to risk your necks for something that only concerns me.'

'It only concerns you,' Dandelion repeated slowly. 'You don't need anybody. Company impedes you and slows down your journey. You don't expect help from anybody and you have no intention of relying on anybody. Furthermore, you love solitude. Have I forgotten anything?'

'Naturally,' Geralt replied angrily. 'You've forgotten to swap your empty head for one with a brain. Had that arrow passed an inch to the right, you idiot, the rooks would be pecking out your eyes now. You're a poet and you've got an imagination; so try imagining a scene like that. I repeat: you're returning north, and I'm heading in the opposite direction. By myself.'

'Go on then,' Milva said, and sprang to her feet. 'I'm not going to plead with you. Go to hell, Witcher. Come on, Dandelion, let's cook something. I'm starving and listening to him makes me sick.'

Geralt turned his head away. He watched the green-eyed cormorants hanging their wings out to dry on the limbs of the guano-covered tree. He smelled the intense scent of herbs and swore furiously.

'You're trying my patience, Regis.'

The vampire, who had suddenly appeared out of thin air, was unconcerned, and sat down alongside the furious witcher.

'I have to change the poet's dressing,' he said calmly.

'Then go to him. But stay well away from me.'

Regis heaved a sigh, showing no intention of moving away.

'I was listening to your conversation with Dandelion and the archer,' he said, not without a hint of mockery in his voice. 'I have to admit you've got a real talent for winning people over. Though the entire world seems to be out to get you, you disregard the comrades and allies wanting to help you.'

'The world turned upside down. A vampire's teaching me how to deal with humans. What do you know about humans, Regis? The only thing you know is the taste of their blood. Why am I still talking to you?'

'The world turned upside down,' the vampire admitted, deadpan. 'You are talking to me indeed. Perhaps you'd also like to listen to some advice?'

'No. No, I wouldn't. I don't need to.'

'True, I'd forgotten. Advice is superfluous to you, allies are superfluous, you'll get by without any travelling companions. The goal of your expedition is, after all, personal and private. More than that, the nature of the goal demands that you accomplish it alone, in person. The risks, dangers, hardships and constant struggle with doubt must only burden you. For, after all, they are components of the penance, the expiation of guilt you want to earn. A baptism of fire, I'd say. You'll pass through fire, which burns, but also purges. And you'll do it alone. For were someone to support you in this, help you, take on even a scrap of that baptism of fire, that pain, that penance, they would, by the same token, impoverish you. They would deprive you of part of the expiation you desire, which would be owed to them for their involvement. After all, it should be your exclusive expiation. Only *you* have a debt to pay off, and you don't want to run up debts with other creditors at the same time. Is my logic correct?'

'Surprisingly so, considering you're sober. Your presence annoys me, vampire. Leave me alone with my expiation, please. And with my debt.'

'As you wish,' Regis said, arising. 'Sit and think. But I will give you some advice anyway. A sense of guilt, as well as the need for expiation, for a cleansing baptism of fire, aren't things you can claim an exclusive right to. Life differs from banking because it has debts which are paid off by running up debts with others.'

'Go away, please.'

'As you wish.'

The vampire walked off and joined Dandelion and Milva. While Regis changed the dressing the trio debated what to eat. Milva shook the fry from the fish pot and examined the catch critically.

'There's nothing for it,' she said. 'We'll have to skewer the little tiddlers on twigs and grill them over the embers.'

'No,' Dandelion demurred, shaking his freshly bandaged head, 'that isn't a good idea. There are too few of them, and they won't fill us up. I suggest we make soup.'

'Fish soup?'

'By all means. We have enough of these tiddlers and we have salt,' Dandelion said, counting out the list of ingredients on his fingers. 'We've acquired onions, carrots, parsley root and celery. And a cauldron. If we put it all together we end up with soup.'

'Some seasoning would come in handy.'

'Oh.' Regis smiled, reaching into his bag. 'No problem there. Basil, pimento, pepper, bay leaves, sage . . .'

'Enough, enough.' Dandelion raised his hand, stopping him. 'That'll do. We don't need mandrake in the soup. Right, let's get to work. Clean the fish, Milva.'

'Clean them yourself! Ha! Just because you've got a woman in the company, it doesn't mean she'll slave for you in the kitchen! I'll bring the water and start the fire. And you can get yourself covered in guts with those weatherfish.'

'They aren't weatherfish,' Regis said. 'They're chub, roach, ruff and silver bream.'

'Ah,' Dandelion said, unable to keep quiet. 'I see you know your fish.'

'I know lots of things,' Regis replied neutrally, without boasting. 'I've picked up this and that along the way.'

'If you're such a scholar,' Milva said, blowing on the fire again and getting to her feet, 'use your brain to get these tiddlers gutted. I'm getting the water.'

'Can you manage a full cauldron? Geralt, help her.'

'Course I can.' Milva snorted. 'And I don't need his help. He has his own – personal – issues. No one's to disturb him!'

Geralt turned his head away, pretending not to hear. Dandelion and the vampire skilfully prepared the small fry.

'This soup's going to be thin,' Dandelion said, hanging the cauldron over the fire. 'We could do with a bigger fish.'

'Will this do?' Cahir said, suddenly emerging from the willows carrying a three-pound pike by the gills. It was still flexing its tail and opening and closing its mouth.

'Oh! What a beauty! Where did you come by that, Nilfgaardian?'

'I'm not a Nilfgaardian. I come from Vicovaro and my name is Cahir—'

'All right, all right, we know all that. Now where did you get the pike?'

'I knocked up a tip-up using a frog as bait. I cast it into a hollow under the bank. The pike took it right away.'

'Experts to a man,' Dandelion said, shaking his bandaged head. 'Pity I didn't suggest steak, you would have conjured up a cow. But let's make a start on what we've got. Regis, chuck all the fry into the cauldron, heads and tails and all. And the pike needs to be nicely dressed. Know how to, Nilf— Cahir?'

'Yes.'

'Get to work then. Geralt, dammit, do you plan to sit there sulking for much longer? Peel the vegetables!'

The Witcher got up obediently and joined them, but stayed ostentatiously well away from Cahir. Before he had time to complain that there wasn't a knife, the Nilfgaardian – or possibly the Vicovarian – gave him his, taking another from his bootleg. Geralt took it, grunting his thanks.

The teamwork was carried out efficiently. The cauldron full of fingerlings and vegetables was soon bubbling and frothing. The vampire dextrously skimmed off the froth using a spoon Milva had whittled. Once Cahir had dressed and divided up the pike, Dandelion threw the predator's tail, fins, spine and toothed head into the cauldron and stirred.

'Mmm, it smells delicious. Once it's all boiled down, we'll strain off the waste.'

'What, through our footwraps?' Milva said with a grimace, as she whittled another spoon. 'How can we strain it without a sieve?'

'But my dear Milva,' smiled Regis. 'Don't say that! We can easily replace what we don't have with what we do. It's purely a matter of invention and positive thinking.'

'Go to hell with your smart-arsed chatter, vampire.'

'We'll sieve it through my hauberk,' Cahir said. 'Not a problem, it can be rinsed out afterwards.'

'It should be rinsed out before, too,' Milva declared, 'or I won't eat it.'

The sieving was carried out efficiently.

'Now throw the pike into the broth, Cahir,' Dandelion instructed. 'Smells delicious. Don't add any more wood, it just needs to simmer. Geralt, where are you shoving that spoon! You don't stir it now!'

'Don't yell. I didn't know.'

'Ignorance' – Regis smiled – 'is no justification for ill-conceived actions. When one doesn't know or has doubts it's best to seek advice . . .'

'Shut up, vampire!' Geralt said, stood up and turned his back on them. Dandelion snorted.

'He's taken offence, look at him.'

'That's him all over,' Milva said, pouting. 'He's all talk. If he doesn't know what to do, he just talks and gets offended. Haven't you lot caught on yet?'

'A long time ago,' Cahir said softly.

'Add pepper,' Dandelion said, licking the spoon and smacking his lips. 'And some more salt. Ah, now it's just right. Take the cauldron off the heat. By thunder, it's hot! I don't have any gloves . . .'

'I have,' Cahir said.

'And I,' Regis said, seizing the cauldron from the other side, 'don't need any.'

'Right,' said the poet, wiping the spoon on his trousers. 'Well, company, be seated. Enjoy! Geralt, are you waiting for a special invitation? For a herald and a fanfare?'

They sat crowded around the cauldron on the sand and for a long time all that could be heard was dignified slurping, interrupted by blowing on spoons. After half of the broth had been eaten, the cautious fishing out of pieces of pike began, until finally their spoons were scraping against the bottom of the cauldron.

'Oh, I'm stuffed,' Milva groaned. 'It wasn't a bad idea with that soup, Dandelion.'

'Indeed,' Regis agreed. 'What do you say, Geralt?'

'I say "thank you",' the Witcher said, getting up with difficulty and rubbing his knee, which had begun to torment him again. 'Will that do? Or do you want a fanfare?'

'He's always like that,' the poet said, waving a hand. 'Take no notice of him. You're lucky, anyway. I was around when he was fighting with that Yennefer of his; the wan beauty with ebony hair.'

'Be discreet,' the vampire admonished Dandelion, 'and don't forget he has problems.'

'Problems,' said Cahir, stifling a burp, 'are there to be solved.'

'Of course they are,' Dandelion replied. 'But how?'

Milva snorted, making herself more comfortable on the hot sand. 'The vampire is a scholar. He's sure to know.'

'It's not about knowledge, but about the skilful examination of the circumstances,' Regis said calmly. 'And when the circumstances are examined, we come to the conclusion that we are facing an insoluble problem. The entire undertaking has no chance of success. The likelihood of finding Ciri amounts to zero.'

'But you can't say that,' Milva jibed. 'We should think positively and use inventigation. It's like it was with that sieve. If we don't have something, we find a replacement. That's how I see it.'

'Until recently,' the vampire continued, 'we thought Ciri was in Nilfgaard. Reaching the destination and rescuing her – or abducting her – seemed beyond our powers. Now, after hearing Cahir's revelations, we have no idea where Ciri is. It's hard to talk about invention when we have no idea where we should be directing it.'

'What are we to do, then?' Milva said, bridling. 'The Witcher insists on going south . . .'

'For him' – Regis laughed – 'the points of the compass have no great importance. It's all the same to him which one he chooses, as long as he's not idle. That is truly a witcher's principium. The world is full of evil, so it's sufficient to stride ahead, and destroy the Evil encountered on the way, in that way rendering a service to Good. The rest takes care of itself. To put it another way: being in motion is everything, the goal is nothing.'

'Baloney,' Milva commented. 'I mean, Ciri's his goal. How can you say she's nothing?'

'I was joking,' the vampire admitted, winking at Geralt's back, which was still turned away from them. 'And not very tactfully. I apologise. You're right, dear Milva. Ciri is our goal. And since we don't know where she is, it would make sense to find that out and direct our activities accordingly. The case of the Child of Destiny, I observe, is simply pulsating with magic, fate and other supernatural elements. And I know somebody who is extremely knowledgeable about such matters and will certainly help us.'

'Ah,' Dandelion said, delighted. 'Who's that? Where are they? Far from here?'

'Closer than the capital of Nilfgaard. In actual fact, really quite close. In Angren. On this bank of the Yaruga. I'm talking about the Druids' Circle, which has its seat in the forests of Caed Dhu.'

'Let's go without delay!'

'Don't any of you,' Geralt said, annoyed, 'think you should ask me my opinion?'

'You?' Dandelion said, turning around. 'But you haven't got a clue what you're doing. You even owe the soup you gobbled down to us. Were it not for us, you'd be hungry. We would be too, had we waited for you to act. That cauldron of soup was the result of cooperation. Of teamwork. The joint efforts of a fellowship united by a common goal. Get it, friend?'

'How could he get it?' Milva said, grimacing. 'He's just "me, me, by myself, all alone". A lone wolf! But you can see he's no hunter, that he's a stranger to the forest. Wolves don't hunt alone! Never! A lone wolf, ha, what twaddle, foolish townie nonsense. But he doesn't understand that!'

'Oh, he does, he does,' Regis cut in, smiling through pursed lips, as was his custom.

'He only looks stupid,' Dandelion confirmed. 'But I do keep hoping he'll finally decide to strain his grey matter. Perhaps he'll come to some useful conclusions. Perhaps he'll realise the only activity that's worth doing alone is wanking.'

Cahir Mawr Dyffryn aep Ceallach remained tactfully silent.

'The hell with all of you,' the Witcher finally said, sticking his spoon into his bootleg. 'The hell with all of you, you cooperative fellowship of idiots, united by a common goal which none of you understand. And the hell with me too.'

This time the others, following Cahir's example, also remained tactfully silent. Dandelion, Maria Barring, also known as Milva, and Emiel Regis Rohellec Terzieff-Godefroy.

'What a company I ended up with,' Geralt continued, shaking his head. 'Brothers in arms! A team of heroes! What have I done to deserve it? A poetaster with a lute. A wild and lippy half-dryad, half-woman. A vampire, who's about to notch up his fifth century. And a bloody Nilfgaardian who insists he isn't a Nilfgaardian.'

'And leading the party is the Witcher, who suffers from pangs of conscience, impotence and the inability to take decisions,' Regis finished calmly. 'I suggest we travel incognito, to avoid arousing suspicion.'

'Or raising a laugh,' Milva added.

The queen replied: 'Ask not me for mercy, but those whom you wronged with your magic. You had the courage to commit those deeds, now have courage when your pursuers and justice are close at hand. It is not in my power to pardon your sins.' Then the witch hissed like a cat and her sinister eyes flashed. 'My end is nigh,' she shrieked, 'but yours is too, O Queen. You shall remember Lara Dorren and her curse in the hour of your dreadful death. And know this: my curse will hound your descendants unto the tenth generation.' Seeing, however, that a doughty heart was beating in the queen's breast, the evil elven witch ceased to malign her, or try to frighten her with the curse, but began instead to whine for help and mercy like a bitch dog . . .

The Tale of Lara Dorren,
as told by the humans

. . . but her begging softened not the stony hearts of the Dh'oine, the merciless, cruel humans. So when Lara, now not begging for mercy for herself, but for her unborn child, caught hold of the carriage door, on the order of the queen the thuggish executioner struck with a sword and hacked off her fingers. And when a severe frost descended in the night, Lara breathed her last on the forested hilltop, giving birth to a tiny daughter, whom she protected with the remains of the warmth still flickering in her. And though she was surrounded by the blizzard, the night and the winter, spring suddenly bloomed on the hilltop and feainnewedd flowers blossomed. Even today do those flowers bloom in only two places: in Dol Blathanna and on the hilltop where Lara Dorren aep Shiadhal perished.

The Tale of Lara Dorren,
as told by the elves

CHAPTER SIX

'I asked you,' Ciri, who was lying on her back, snapped angrily. 'I asked you not to touch me.'

Mistle withdrew her hand and the blade of grass she had been tickling Ciri's neck with, stretched out beside her and gazed up at the sky, placing both hands under her shaven neck.

'You've been acting strangely of late, Young Falcon.'

'I just want you to stop touching me!'

'It's just for fun.'

'I know,' Ciri said through pursed lips. 'Just for fun. It's always been "just for fun". But I've stopped enjoying it, do you see? For me it's no fun any more!'

Mistle was silent for a long while, lying on her back and staring at the blue sky riven with ragged streaks of cloud. A hawk circled high above the trees.

'Your dreams,' she finally said. 'It's because of your dreams, isn't it? You wake almost every night screaming. What you once lived through now returns in your dreams. I'm no stranger to such things myself.'

Ciri did not answer.

'You've never told me anything about yourself,' Mistle said, breaking the silence once again. 'About what you've been through. Or where you're from. Or if you've left anyone behind . . .'

Ciri brought a hand up swiftly to her neck, but this time it was only a ladybird.

'There were a few people,' she said quietly, not looking at her companion. 'I mean, I thought there were . . . People who would find me even here, at the end of the world, if they only wanted to . . . Or if they were still alive. Oh, what do you want of me, Mistle? Do you want me to unbosom myself?'

'You don't have to.'

'Good. Because, surely, it'd just be for fun. Like everything else we share.'

'I don't understand,' Mistle said, turning her head away, 'why you don't leave, if being with me is so awful.'

'I don't want to be alone.'

'Is that all?'

'That is a lot.'

Mistle bit her lip. But before she had time to say anything, there was a whistle. They both sprang to their feet, brushing off pine needles, and ran to their horses.

'The fun's about to begin,' said Mistle, leaping into the saddle and drawing her sword. 'The fun you've come to enjoy more than anything, Falka. Don't think I haven't noticed.'

Ciri angrily kicked her horse with her heels. They hurtled along the side of a ravine at breakneck speed, already hearing the wild whooping of the remaining Rats rushing out of a thicket on the other side of the highway. The pincers of the ambush were closing.

The private audience was over. Vattier de Rideaux, Viscount of Eiddon, head of Imperator Emhyr var Emreis's military intelligence, left the library, bowing to the Queen of the Valley of Flowers even more politely than courtly protocol demanded. At the same time his bow was very cautious, and his movements deliberate and guarded; the imperial spy's eyes never left the two ocelots stretched out at the feet of the elven queen. The golden-eyed cats looked languorous and drowsy, but Vattier knew they weren't cuddly mascots but vigilant guards, ever ready to reduce anyone to a bloody pulp if they tried to come closer to the queen than protocol decreed.

Francesca Findabair, also called Enid an Gleanna, the Daisy of the Valleys, waited until the door was closed behind Vattier, and stroked the ocelots.

'Very well, Ida,' she said.

Ida Emean aep Sivney, elven sorceress, one of the free Aen Seidhe from the Blue Mountains, during the audience shrouded by an invisibility spell, materialised in a corner of the library, and smoothed down her dress and vermilion-red hair. The ocelots only reacted with a slight widening of their eyes. Like all cats, they could see what was invisible and could not be deceived by a simple spell.

'This parade of spies is beginning to annoy me,' Francesca said with a sneer, finding a more comfortable position on the ebony chair. 'Henselt of Kaedwen sent me a "consul" not long ago. Dijkstra dispatched a "trade mission" to Dol Blathanna. And now the arch-spy Vattier de Rideaux himself! Oh, and some time ago Stephan Skellen, the Grand Imperial Nobody, was creeping around too. But I didn't give him an audience. I'm the queen and Skellen's a nobody. He may hold a position, but he's a nobody nonetheless.'

'Stephan Skellen,' Ida Emean said slowly, 'visited us too, and was more fortunate. He spoke with Filavandrel and Vanadain.'

'And like Vattier with me, did he enquire about Vilgefortz, Yennefer, Rience and Cahir Mawr Dyffryn aep Ceallach?'

'Among other things. It may surprise you, but he was more interested in the original version of Ithlinne Aegli aep Aevenien's prophecy, particularly the parts about Aen Hen Ichaer, the Elder Blood. He was also curious about Tor Lara, the Tower of Gulls, and the legendary portal which once connected the Tower of Gulls to Tor Zireael, the Tower of Swallows. How typical of humans, Enid. To expect that, at a single nod, we shall unravel enigmas and mysteries for them which we have been endeavouring to solve for centuries.'

Francesca raised her hand and examined the rings adorning it.

'I wonder,' she said, 'whether Philippa knows about the strange preoccupation of Skellen and Vattier. And of Emhyr var Emreis, whom they both serve.'

'It would be risky to assume she doesn't,' Ida Emean replied, looking keenly at the queen, 'and to withhold what we know from Philippa and the entire lodge at the council in Montecalvo. It wouldn't show us in a very favourable light . . . And we want the lodge to come into being. We want to be trusted – we, elven sorceresses – and not to be suspected of playing a double game.'

'But we *are* playing a double game, Ida. And playing with fire: with the White Flame of Nilfgaard . . .'

'Fire burns,' Ida Emean said, raising her heavily made-up eyes at the queen, 'but it also purifies. It must be passed through. Risks have to be taken, Enid. The lodge ought to exist, ought to begin functioning. At full strength. Twelve sorceresses, including the one mentioned in the prophecy. Even if it is a game, let us rely on trust.'

'And if it's an entrapment?'

'You know the individuals involved better than I do.'

Enid an Gleanna thought for a while.

'Sheala de Tancarville,' she finally said, 'is a secretive recluse, without any loyalties. Triss Merigold and Keira Metz were loyal but they are now both emigrants, since King Foltest drove all the mages from Temeria. Margarita Laux-Antille cares for her school and nothing besides. Of course, at this moment the last three are heavily under Philippa's sway, and Philippa is an enigma. Sabrina Glevissig will not give up the political influence she has in Kaedwen, but will not betray the lodge either. She is too attracted by the power it can give her.'

'And what about Assire var Anahid? And the other Nilfgaardian, whom we shall meet in Montecalvo?'

'I know little about them.' Francesca smiled faintly. 'But once I see them I shall know more. As soon as I see how they are dressed.'

Ida Emean lowered her painted eyelids, but refrained from asking a question.

'This leaves us with the jade statuette,' she said a moment later. 'The still dubious and enigmatic jade figurine mentioned in the Ithlinnespeath, Ithlinne's Prophecy. I now deem it's time to allow her to express herself. And to tell her what she may expect. Shall I help you with the decompression?'

'No, I shall do it myself. You are familiar with reactions to unpacking. The fewer the witnesses, the less painful a blow it will be to her pride.'

Francesca Findabair checked one more time that the entire courtyard was thoroughly isolated from the rest of the palace by a protective field, which hid it from view and muffled its sounds. She lit three black candles planted in candlesticks equipped with parabolic mirrors. The candlesticks stood at points marked out by a circular mosaic pavement depicting the eight signs of Vicca, the elven zodiac, on the symbols indicating Belleteyn, Lammas and Yule. Inside the zodiac circle, the mosaic formed another, smaller circle, dotted with magic symbols and enclosing a pentagram. Francesca placed small, iron tripods on three symbols of the smaller circle, and then on each of them she carefully mounted three crystals. The cut of the crystals' bases corresponded to the form of the tripods' tops, which meant their placement could be nothing other than precise, but even so Francesca checked everything several times. She didn't want to leave anything to chance.

A fountain was trickling nearby, the water gushing from a marble jug held by a marble naiad. It fell into the pool in four streams and made the water lilies, between which goldfish darted, quiver.

Francesca opened a jewellery case, removed a small, waxy jade figurine from it, and placed it precisely at the centre of the pentagram. She withdrew, glanced once again at the grimoire lying on a table, took a deep breath, raised her hands and chanted a spell.

The candles burst into bright flame, the crystals' facets lit up and sparkled with streaks of light. Those streaks of light shot towards the figurine, which immediately changed colour from green to gold, and a moment later became transparent. The air shimmered with magical energy, which struck against the protective field. Sparks flew from one of the candles, shadows played on the floor, the mosaic came alive and the shapes in it transformed. Francesca did not lower her hands or interrupt the incantation.

The statuette grew at lightning speed, pulsating and throbbing, its structure and shape changing like a cloud of smoke crawling across the floor. The light shining from the crystals pierced the air; movement and congealing matter appeared in the streams of light. A moment later a human body suddenly manifested in the centre of the magical circles. It was the figure of a black-haired woman, lying inertly on the floor.

The candles bloomed with ribbons of smoke and the crystals went out. Francesca lowered her arms, relaxed her fingers and wiped the sweat from her forehead.

The black-haired woman on the floor curled up in a ball and began to scream.

'What is your name?' Francesca asked in a breathy voice.

The woman convulsed and howled, both hands clutching her belly.

'What is your name?'

'Ye . . . Yennef . . . Yennefeerrr!!! Aaaaaagh . . .'

The elf sighed with relief. The woman continued to squirm and howl, banging her fists against the floor and retching. Francesca waited patiently. And calmly. The woman – a moment earlier a jade figurine – was suffering, that was obvious. And normal. But her mind was undamaged.

'Well, Yennefer,' she said after a long pause, interrupting the groans. 'That ought to do, oughtn't it?'

Yennefer raised herself onto her hands and knees with obvious effort, wiped her nose with her wrist and looked around vacantly. Her gaze flitted over Francesca, as though the she-elf wasn't even in the courtyard, then came to rest – and brightened – at the sight of the fountain gushing water. Having crawled up to it with immense difficulty, Yennefer hauled herself over the lip and flopped into the pool with a splash. She choked, began to splutter, cough and spit, until finally, parting the water lilies, she waded to the marble naiad and sat down, leaning back against the pedestal of the statue. The water came up to her breasts.

'Francesca . . .' she mumbled, touching the obsidian star hanging from her neck and looking at the she-elf with a slightly clearer gaze. 'It's you . . .'

'It's me. What do you recall?'

'You packed me up . . . Hell's teeth, you packed me up, didn't you!'

'I packed you up and then unpacked you. What do you recall?'

'Garstang . . . Elves. Ciri. You. And the fifty tons suddenly landing on my head . . . Now I know what it was. Artefact compression . . .'

'Your memory's working. Good.'

Yennefer lowered her head and looked between her thighs, over which goldfish were darting.

'The water in the pool will need changing, Enid,' she mumbled. 'I just peed in it.'

'No matter.' Francesca smiled. 'But just see if there's any blood in the water. Compression has been known to damage the kidneys.'

'Only the kidneys?' Yennefer said, taking a cautious breath. 'I don't think there's a single undamaged organ in my body . . . At least that's how I feel. Hell's teeth, Enid, I really don't know what I did to deserve this . . .'

'Get out of the pool.'

'No. I like it here.'

'I know. It's called dehydration.'

'Degradation. Depredation! Why did you do it to me?'

'Get out, Yennefer.'

The sorceress stood up with difficulty, holding onto the marble naiad with both hands. She shook off the water lilies, with a sharp tug tore away her dripping dress and stood naked before the fountain, under the gushing streams. After rinsing herself down and drinking deeply, she stepped out of the pool, sat down on the edge, wrung out her hair and looked around.

'Where am I?'

'In Dol Blathanna.'

Yennefer wiped her nose.

'Do the hostilities on Thanedd continue?'

'No. They ended a month and a half ago.'

'I must have wronged you greatly,' Yennefer said a moment later. 'I must really have got under your skin, Enid. But you can consider us even. You've exacted a full revenge, if a little too sadistic. Couldn't you have just cut my throat?'

'Don't talk nonsense,' the elf said, making a face. 'I packed you up and got you out of Garstang to save your life. We'll come back to that, but a little later. Here, have this towel. And this sheet. You'll get a new dress after you've bathed – in a suitable place, in a tub full of warm water. You've done enough damage to my goldfish.'

*

Ida Emean and Francesca were drinking wine. Yennefer was drinking sugar water and carrot juice. In huge quantities.

'To sum up,' she said, after hearing Francesca's account. 'Nilfgaard has defeated Lyria, in an alliance with Kaedwen has dismantled Aedirn, burnt down Vengerberg, subjugated Verden, and is crushing Brugge and Sodden at this very moment. Vilgefortz has disappeared without a trace. Tissaia de Vries has committed suicide, and you've become queen of the Valley of Flowers. Imperator Emhyr has rewarded you with a crown and sceptre in exchange for my Ciri, whom he was hunting for so long, and whom he now has in his power and is using as he sees fit. You packed me up and have kept me in a box as a jade statuette for a month and a half. And no doubt expect me to thank you for it.'

'It would be polite,' Francesca Findabair replied coldly. 'On Thanedd there was a certain Rience, who had made it a point of honour to submit you to a slow and cruel death, and Vilgefortz offered to expedite it. Rience pursued you all over Garstang. But he didn't find you, because you were already a jade figurine safe in my cleavage.'

'And I was that figurine for forty-seven days.'

'Yes. While I, if asked, could always reply that Yennefer of Vengerberg was not in Dol Blathanna. Because the question referred to Yennefer, not a statuette.'

'What changed to induce you finally to unpack me?'

'A great deal changed. I shall explain forthwith.'

'First explain something else to me: the Witcher was also on Thanedd. Geralt. Remember, I introduced him to you in Aretuza. How is he?'

'Please remain calm. He's alive.'

'I *am* calm. Tell me, Enid.'

'In the space of an hour,' Francesca said, 'your Witcher did more than some manage in their entire lives. Put succinctly: he broke Dijkstra's leg, beheaded Artaud Terranova and slew ten Scoia'tael. Oh, I almost forgot: he also aroused Keira Metz's unhealthy passions.'

'Dreadful,' Yennefer said with a grimace. 'But Keira will have got over it by now, I imagine. I hope she doesn't hold a grudge against him. The fact that he didn't fuck her after inflaming her desire certainly resulted from lack of time, not lack of respect. Please put her mind at ease for me.'

'You'll have the chance to do that yourself,' the Daisy of the Valleys said coldly. 'And quite soon. Let's go back, though, to the issues about which you are lamely feigning indifference. Your Witcher was so fervid in his defence of Ciri that he acted very rashly. He attacked Vilgefortz. And Vilgefortz gave him a sound thrashing. The fact that he didn't kill him certainly resulted from lack of time, not lack of effort. Well? Are you still going to pretend you don't care?'

'No,' Yennefer said, her grimace no longer expressing scorn. 'No, Enid. I do care. Some people will soon learn how much. You can take my word for it.'

Francesca was no more concerned by Yennefer's threat than she had been by her mockery.

'Triss Merigold teleported what was left of the Witcher to Brokilon,' she stated. 'As far as I know, the dryads are still healing him. He is said to be recovering now, but it would be better if he didn't venture out of the forest. He's being tracked by Dijkstra's spies and the military intelligence services of all the kings. So are you, for that matter.'

'What did I do to deserve such attention? I didn't break anything of Dijkstra's . . . Oh, keep quiet and let me guess. I vanished without a trace from Thanedd. No one suspects I ended up in your pocket, shrunken down and packed up. Everybody is convinced I escaped to Nilfgaard with my fellow conspirators. Everybody apart from the real conspirators, naturally, but they won't be correcting that error. For a war is raging, and disinformation is a weapon whose blade must always be kept sharp. And now, forty-seven days later, comes your moment to use that weapon. My house in Vengerberg is burnt to the ground, and I'm being hunted. There's nothing left to do but join a Scoia'tael commando. Or join the fight for the elves' freedom in some other way.'

Yennefer sipped her carrot juice, and stared into the eyes of Ida Emean aep Sivney, who still remained peaceful and silent.

'Well, Mistress Ida, free lady of the Aen Seidhe from the Blue Mountains, have I correctly guessed what's in store for me? Why are you so tight-lipped?'

'Because I, Mistress Yennefer,' the red-headed she-elf answered, 'say nothing when I have nothing sensible to say. It's always better than to make unfounded speculations and disguise one's anxiety with idle talk. Enid, get to the point. Tell Mistress Yennefer what this is all about.'

'You have my undivided attention,' Yennefer said, touching the obsidian star hanging from its velvet ribbon. 'Speak, Francesca.'

The Daisy of the Valleys rested her chin on her interlocked hands.

'Today,' she announced, 'is the second night of the full moon. In a short while, we shall be teleporting to Montecalvo Castle, the seat of Philippa Eilhart. We shall be taking part in a session of an organisation that ought to interest you. After all, you were always of the opinion that magic represents the utmost value, superior to all disputes, conflicts, political choices, personal interests, grudges, sentiments and animosities. It will no doubt gladden you to hear that not long ago the foundations of an institution were laid down. Something like a secret lodge, brought into being exclusively to defend the interests of magic, meant to ensure that magic occupies the place it deserves in the hierarchy of the world. Exercising my privilege to recommend new members to this lodge, I took the liberty of proposing two candidates: Ida Emean aep Sivney and you.'

'What an unexpected honour,' Yennefer sneered. 'From magical oblivion straight to a secret, elite and omnipotent lodge, which stands above personal grudges and resentments. But am I suitable? Will I find sufficient strength of character to rid myself of my grudges against the people who took Ciri from me, cruelly beat a man who is dear to me, and packed—'

'I am certain,' the she-elf interrupted, 'that you will find sufficient strength of character, Yennefer. I know you and know you are not lacking in strength of that kind. Neither are you lacking in ambition, which ought to dispel your doubts about the honour and the advancement which has come your way. If you want, though, I'll tell you frankly: I'm recommending you to the lodge, because I consider

246

you a person who deserves it and who may render the cause a significant service.'

'Thank you,' Yennefer responded, the scornful smirk in no hurry to disappear from her lips. 'Thank you, Enid. I truly feel the ambition, hubris and self-adoration filling me up. I'm ready to explode at any moment. And that's before I even begin wondering why you aren't recommending one more elf from Dol Blathanna or a she-elf from the Blue Mountains instead of me.'

'You will find out why in Montecalvo,' Francesca replied coldly.

'I'd rather find out now.'

'Tell her,' Ida Emean muttered.

'It's because of Ciri,' Francesca said after a moment's thought, raising her inscrutable eyes towards Yennefer. 'The lodge is interested in her, and no one knows the girl as well as you. You'll learn the rest when we get there.'

'Agreed,' Yennefer said, vigorously scratching a shoulder blade. Her skin, dried out by the compression, was still itching intolerably. 'Now tell me the names of the other members. Apart from you and Philippa.'

'Margarita Laux-Antille, Triss Merigold and Keira Metz. Sheala de Tancarville of Kovir. Sabrina Glevissig. And two sorceresses from Nilfgaard.'

'An international women's republic?'

'Let's say.'

'They must still think I'm an accomplice of Vilgefortz. Will they accept me?'

'They accepted me. The rest I leave to you. You will be asked to give an account of your relationship with Ciri. From the very beginning, which – thanks to your witcher – was fifteen years ago in Cintra, and right up until the events of a month and a half ago. Frankness and honesty will be absolutely paramount. And will confirm your loyalty to the lodge.'

'Who said there's anything to confirm? Isn't it too early to talk of loyalty? I'm not even familiar with the statute or programme of this new institution . . .'

'Yennefer,' the she-elf interjected, frowning slightly. 'I'm recommending you to the lodge. But I have no intention of forcing you to do anything. Particularly not to be loyal. You have a choice.'

'I think I know what it is.'

'And you would be right. But it is still a free choice. Speaking for myself, I still heartily encourage you to choose the lodge. Trust me; by doing so you'll be helping Ciri much more effectively than by plunging headlong into a whirl of events, which, I'm guessing, you would love to do. Ciri's life is in danger. Only our combined efforts can save her. When you have heard what is said in Montecalvo, you'll realise I was speaking the truth . . . Yennefer, I don't like the gleam in your eyes. Give me your word you will not try to escape.'

'No.' Yennefer shook her head, covering the star on the velvet ribbon with her hand. 'No, I will not, Francesca.'

'I must warn you, my dear. All Montecalvo's stationary portals have a distorting blockade. Anyone who tries to enter or leave without Philippa's permission will end up in a dungeon lined with dimeritium. You'll be unable to open your own teleportal without the appropriate components. I don't want to confiscate your star, because you have to be in full possession of your faculties. But if you try any tricks . . . Yennefer, I cannot allow— The lodge won't allow you to launch an insane, one-woman attempt to rescue Ciri and seek vengeance. I still have your matrix and the spell's algorithm. I'll shrink you and pack you into a jade statuette again. For several months this time. Or years, if necessary.'

'Thank you for the warning. But I still will not give you my word.'

Fringilla Vigo was putting on a brave face, but she was anxious and stressed. She herself had often reprimanded young Nilfgaardian mages for uncritically yielding to stereotypical opinions and notions. She herself had regularly ridiculed the crude image painted by gossip and propaganda of the typical sorceress from the North: artificially beautiful, arrogant, vain and spoiled to the limits of perversion, and often beyond them. Right now, though, the closer the sequence of teleportals brought her to Montecalvo Castle, the greater she was racked by uncertainty about what she would find when she arrived at the secret lodge meeting. And about what awaited her. Her untrammelled imagination offered up images of impossibly gorgeous women with diamond necklaces resting on naked breasts with rouged nipples, women with moist lips and eyes glistening from the effects of alcohol and narcotics. In her mind's eye Fringilla could already see the gathering becoming a wild and depraved orgy accompanied by frenzied music, aphrodisiacs, and slaves of both sexes using exotic accessories.

The final teleportal left her standing between two black marble columns, with dry lips, her eyes watering from the magic wind and her hand tightly clenching her emerald necklace, which filled the square neckline. Beside her materialised Assire var Anahid, also visibly agitated. Nevertheless, Fringilla had reason to suppose her friend was feeling uncomfortable owing to her new and unfamiliar outfit: a plain, but very elegant hyacinth dress, complemented with a small, modest alexandrite necklace.

Her anxiety was dispelled at once. It was cool and quiet in the large hall, which was lit by magical lanterns. There was no naked slave beating a drum, nor girls with sequinned pubic mounds dancing on the table. Neither was there the scent of hashish or Spanish fly in the air. Instead the Nilfgaardian enchantresses were welcomed by Philippa Eilhart, the lady of the castle; tastefully dressed, grave, courteous and businesslike. The others approached and introduced themselves and Fringilla sighed with relief. The sorceresses from the North were beautiful, colourful, and sparkled with jewellery, but there was no trace of intoxicating substances or nymphomania in their eyes, which were accentuated by understated make-up. Nor did any of them have naked breasts. Quite the opposite. Two of them had extremely modest gowns, fastened up to the neck: the severe Sheala de Tancarville, dressed in black, and the young Triss Merigold with her blue eyes and exquisite auburn hair. The dark-haired Sabrina Glevissig and the blondes Margarita Laux-Antille and Keira Metz all had low-cut necklines, only slightly more revealing than Fringilla's.

The wait for other participants was filled by polite conversation, during which all of them had the opportunity to say something about themselves. Philippa Eilhart's tactful comments and observations swiftly and adroitly broke the ice, although the only ice in the vicinity was on the food table, which was piled high with a mountain of oysters. No other ice could be discerned. Sheala de Tancarville, a scholar, immediately found a great deal of common ground with the scholar Assire var Anahid, while Fringilla quickly warmed towards the bubbly Triss Merigold. The conversation was accompanied by the greedy consumption of oysters. The only person not eating was Sabrina Glevissig, a true daughter of the Kaedwen forests, who took the liberty of expressing a scornful opinion about 'that slimy filth' and a yen for a slice of cold venison with plums. Philippa Eilhart, instead of reacting to the insult with haughty coolness, tugged on the bell pull and a moment later meat was brought in inconspicuously and noiselessly. Fringilla's astonishment was immense. *Well*, she thought, *it takes all sorts*.

The teleportal between the columns flared up and vibrated audibly. Utter amazement was painted on Sabrina Glevissig's face. Keira Metz dropped an oyster and a knife onto the ice. Triss stifled a gasp.

Three sorceresses emerged from the portal. Three she-elves. One with hair the colour of dark gold, one of vermilion and the third of raven black.

'Welcome, Francesca,' Philippa said. In her voice was none of the emotion being expressed by her eyes, which, though, she quickly narrowed. 'Welcome, Yennefer.'

'I was given the privilege of filling two seats,' the golden-haired newcomer addressed as Francesca said melodiously, undoubtedly noticing Philippa's astonishment. 'Here are my candidates. Yennefer of Vengerberg, who needs no introduction. And Mistress Ida Emean aep Sivney, an Aen Saevherne from the Blue Mountains.'

Ida Emean slightly inclined her head and her mass of red curls and rustled her floating daffodil-yellow dress.

'May I assume,' Francesca said, looking around, 'that we are all here now?'

'Only Vilgefortz is missing,' Sabrina Glevissig hissed quietly, but with unfeigned anger, looking askance at Yennefer.

'And the Scoia'tael hiding in the cellars,' Keira Metz muttered. Triss froze her with a look.

Philippa made the introductions. Fringilla watched Francesca Findabair with curiosity – Enid an Gleanna, the Daisy of the Valleys, the illustrious Queen of Dol Blathanna, the queen of the elves, who had not long before recovered their country. *The rumours about Francesca's beauty were not exaggerated*, thought Fringilla.

The red-headed and large-eyed Ida Emean clearly aroused everybody's interest, including both sorceresses from Nilfgaard. The free elves from the Blue Mountains maintained contact neither with humans nor with their own kind living closer to humans. The few Aen Saevherne – or Sages – among the free elves were an almost legendary enigma. Few – even among elves – could boast of a close relationship with the Aen Saevherne. Ida did not only stand out in the group by the colour of hair. There was not a single ounce of metal nor a carat of stone in her jewellery; she wore only pearls, coral and amber.

However, the source of the greatest emotions was, unsurprisingly, the third of the new arrivals: Yennefer, dressed in black and white and with raven-black hair, who was no elf despite first impressions. Her arrival in Montecalvo must have been an immense surprise, and a not entirely pleasant one. Fringilla felt an aura of antipathy and hostility emanating from some of the sorceresses.

While the Nilfgaardian sorceresses were being introduced to her, Yennefer let her violet eyes rest on Fringilla. They were tired and had dark circles around them, which even her make-up was unable to hide.

'We know each other,' she said, touching the obsidian star hanging from its velvet ribbon.

A heavy silence, pregnant with anticipation, suddenly descended on the chamber.

'We've already met,' Yennefer spoke again.

'I don't recall,' Fringilla said without looking away.

'I'm not surprised. But I have a good memory for faces and figures. I saw you from Sodden Hill.'

'In which case there can be no mistake,' Fringilla Vigo said and raised her head proudly, sweeping her eyes over all those present. 'I was at the Battle of Sodden.'

Philippa Eilhart forestalled a response.

'I was there too,' she said. 'And I also have many recollections. I don't think, however, that excessive straining of the memory or unnecessary rummaging around in it will bring us any benefit here, in this chamber. What we plan to undertake here will be better served by forgetting, forgiving and being reconciled with each other. Do you agree, Yennefer?'

The black-haired sorceress tossed her curly locks away from her forehead.

'When I finally learn what you're trying to do here,' she replied, 'I'll tell you what I agree with, Philippa. And what I don't agree with.'

'In that case it would be best if we began without delay. Please, would you take your places, ladies.'

The seats at the round table – apart from one – had place cards. Fringilla sat down beside Assire var Anahid, with the unnamed seat on her right separating her from Sheala de Tancarville, beyond whom Sabina Glevissig and Keira Metz took their places. On Assire's left sat Ida Emean, Francesca Findabair and Yennefer. Philippa Eilhart occupied the place exactly opposite Assire, with Margarita Laux-Antille on her right, and Triss Merigold on her left.

All of the chairs had armrests carved in the shape of sphinxes.

Philippa began. She repeated the welcome and immediately got down to business. Fringilla, to whom Assire had given a detailed report of the lodge's previous meeting, learned nothing new from the introduction. Neither was she surprised by the declarations made by all the sorceresses to join the lodge, nor the first contributions to the discussion. She was somewhat disconcerted, however, that those first voices related to the war the Empire was waging with the Nordlings, and in particular the operation in Sodden and Brugge which had been begun a short time before, during which the imperial forces had clashed with the Temerian Army. In spite of the lodge's statutory political neutrality, the sorceresses were unable to hide their views. Some were clearly anxious about the close proximity of

Nilfgaard. Fringilla had mixed feelings. She had assumed that such educated people would understand that the Empire was bringing culture, prosperity, order and political stability to the North. On the other hand, though, she didn't know how she would have reacted herself, were foreign armies approaching her home.

However, Philippa Eilhart had clearly heard enough discussion about military matters.

'No one is capable of predicting the outcome of this war,' she said. 'What is more, predictions of that kind are pointless. It's time we looked at this matter with a dispassionate eye. Firstly, war is not such a great evil. I'd be more afraid of the consequences of over-population, which at this stage of the growth of agriculture and industry would lead to famine. Secondly, war is an extension of the kings' politics. How many of those who are reigning now will be alive in a hundred years? None of them, that's obvious. How many dynasties will last? There's no way of predicting. In a hundred years, today's territorial and dynastic conflicts, today's ambitions and hopes will be dust in the history books. But if we don't protect ourselves, if we allow ourselves to be drawn into the war, nothing but dust will remain of us too. If, however, we look a little beyond the battle flags, if we close our ears to the cries of war and patriotism, we shall survive. And we must survive. We must, because we bear responsibility. Not towards kings and their local interests, focused on the concerns of one kingdom. We are responsible for the whole world. For progress. For the changes which accompany this progress. We are responsible for the future.'

'Tissaia de Vries would have expressed it differently,' Francesca Findabair said. 'She was always concerned with responsibility towards the common man. Not in the future, but here and now.'

'Tissaia de Vries is dead. Were she alive, she would be here among us.'

'No doubt,' the Daisy of the Valleys smiled. 'But I don't think she would have agreed with the theory that war is a remedy for famine and overpopulation. Pay attention to the language used here, honourable sisters. We are debating using the Common Speech, which is meant to ease understanding. But for me it's a foreign language;

one becoming more and more foreign. In the language of my mother the expression "the common man" does not exist, and "the common elf" would be a coinage. The late, lamented Tissaia de Vries was concerned with the fate of ordinary humans. To me, the fate of ordinary elves is no less important. I'd gladly applaud the idea of looking ahead and treating today as ephemera. But I'm sorry to state that today paves the way for tomorrow, and without tomorrow there won't be any future. For you, humans, perhaps the tears I shed over a lilac shrub burnt to ash during the turmoil of war are ridiculous. After all, there will always be lilac shrubs; if not that one, then another. And if there are no more lilac shrubs, well, there'll be acacia trees. Forgive my botanical metaphors. But kindly note that what is a matter of politics to you humans is a matter of physical survival to the elves.'

'Politics don't interest me,' Margarita Laux-Antille, the rectoress of the academy of magic, announced loudly. 'I simply do not wish my girls, whose education I've dedicated myself to, to be used as mercenaries, pulling the wool over their eyes with slogans about love for one's homeland. The homeland of those girls is magic; that's what I teach them. If someone involves my girls in a war, stands them on a new Sodden Hill, they will be lost, irrespective of the result on that battlefield. I understand your reservations, Enid, but we're here to discuss the future of magic, not issues of race.'

'We are here to discuss the future of magic,' Sabrina Glevissig repeated. 'But the future of magic is determined by the status of sorcerers. Our status. Our importance. The role we play in society. Trust, respect and credibility, general faith in our usefulness, faith that magic is indispensable. The alternative we face seems simple: either a loss of status and isolation in ivory towers, or service. Service even on the hills of Sodden, even as mercenaries . . .'

'Or as servants and errand girls?' Triss Merigold cut in, tossing her beautiful hair off her shoulder. 'With bent backs, ready to leap into action at every wag of the imperial finger? For that's the role we will be assigned by the *Pax Nilfgaardiana*, should Nilfgaard conquer us all.'

'If it does,' Philippa said with emphasis. 'Anyhow we won't have much choice. For we have to serve. But serve magic. Not kings or imperators, not their present politics. Not matters of racial integration, because they are also subject to today's political goals. Our lodge, my dear ladies, was not brought into being for us to adapt to today's politics and daily changes on the front line. Or to feverishly search for solutions appropriate to the situation at hand, changing the colour of our skin like chameleons. Our lodge must be active, but its assigned role should be quite the opposite. And carried out using all the means we have at our disposal.'

'If I understand correctly,' Sheala de Tancarville said, raising her head, 'you are persuading us to actively influence the course of events. By fair means or foul? Including illegal measures?'

'What laws do you speak of? The ones governing the rabble? The ones written in the codices, which we drew up and dictated to the royal jurists? We are only bound by one law. Our own!'

'I see.' The sorceress from Kovir smiled. 'We, then, shall actively influence the course of events. Should the kings' politics not be to our liking, we'll simply change it. Correct, Philippa? Or perhaps it's better to overthrow all those crowned asses at once; dethrone them and drive them out. And seize power at once?'

'In the past we crowned kings who were convenient to us. Unfortunately we did not put magic on the throne. We have never given magic absolute power. It's time we corrected that mistake.'

'You have yourself in mind, of course?' Sabrina Glevissig said, leaning across the table. 'On the Redanian throne, naturally? Her Majesty Philippa the First? With Dijkstra as prince consort?'

'I was not thinking about myself. Nor was I thinking about the Kingdom of Redania. I have in mind the Kingdom of the North, which the Kingdom of Kovir is today evolving into. An empire whose power will be equal to Nilfgaard's, thanks to which the currently oscillating scales of the world will finally come to rest in equilibrium. An empire ruled by magic, which we shall raise to the throne by marrying the Kovirian crown prince to a sorceress. Yes, you heard correctly, dear sisters; you are looking in the right direction. Yes, here, at this table, in this vacant seat, we shall place the lodge's twelfth sorceress. And then we shall put her on the throne.'

The silence that fell was broken by Sheala de Tancarville.

'An ambitious project indeed,' she said with a hint of derision in her voice. 'Truly worthy of us all, here seated. It absolutely justifies establishing a lodge of this kind. After all, less lofty tasks, even ones that are tottering on the brink of reality and feasibility, would be an affront to us. That would be like using an astrolabe to hammer in nails. No, no, it is best to set ourselves an utterly impossible task from the start.'

'Why call it impossible?'

'Have mercy, Philippa.' Sabrina Glevissig sighed. 'No king would ever wed a sorceress. No society would accept a sorceress on the throne. An ancient custom stands in the way. A foolish one, perhaps, but it is there nevertheless.'

'There also exist,' Margarita Laux-Antille added, 'obstacles of what I would call a technical nature. The sorceress who joined the House of Kovir would have to comply with a large number of conditions, both from our point of view and that of the House of Kovir. Those conditions are mutually exclusive, they contradict each other in obvious ways. Don't you see that, Philippa? For us this person ought to be schooled in magic, utterly dedicated to magic, comprehending her role and capable of playing it deftly, imperceptibly and without arousing suspicion. Without direction or prompt, without any grey eminences standing in the shadows, against whom rebels always first direct their anger in a revolution. And Kovir itself, without any apparent pressure from us, must also choose her as the wife of the heir to the throne.'

'That is obvious.'

'So who do you think Kovir would select, given a free choice? A girl from a royal family, whose royal blood flows back many generations. A very young woman, suitable for a young prince. A girl who is fertile, because this is about a dynasty. Such prerequisites rule you out, Philippa. Rule me out, rule out Keira and Triss even, the youngest among us. They also rule out all the novices at my school, who are anyhow of little interest to us; they are but buds, the colour of whose petals are still unknown. It's unthinkable that any of them could occupy the twelfth, empty seat at this table. In other words, were Kovir to be afflicted with insanity and willing to marry their prince to a sorceress, we couldn't find a suitable woman. Who, then, is to be this Queen of the North?'

'A girl from a royal family,' Philippa calmly replied, 'in whose veins flows royal blood, the blood of several great dynasties. Very young and capable of producing offspring. A girl with exceptional magical and prophetic abilities, a carrier of the Elder Blood as the prophecies have heralded. A girl who will play her role with great aplomb without direction, prompt, sycophants or grey eminences, because that is what her destiny demands. A girl, whose true abilities are and will be known only to us: Cirilla, daughter of Princess Pavetta of Cintra, the granddaughter of the Queen Calanthe called the Lioness of Cintra. The Elder Blood, the Icy Flame of the North, the Destroyer and Restorer, whose coming was prophesied centuries ago. Ciri of Cintra, the Queen of the North. And her blood, from which will be born the Queen of the World.'

At the sight of the Rats bursting out of the ambush, two of the horsemen escorting the carriage immediately turned tail and sped away. But they didn't stand a chance. Giselher, helped by Reef and Iskra, cut off their escape and after a short fight hacked them to pieces. Kayleigh, Asse and Mistle fell on the other two, who were prepared to defend the carriage, and the four spotted horses harnessed to it, desperately. Ciri felt disappointment and overwhelming anger. They hadn't left anyone for her. It looked as though she would have no one to kill.

But there was still one horseman, riding in front of the carriage as an outrider, lightly armed, on a swift horse. He could have escaped, but hadn't. He turned back, swung his sword and dashed straight at Ciri.

She let him approach, even somewhat slowing her horse. When he struck, rising up in the stirrups, she leant far out from the saddle, skilfully ducking under his blade, then sat back up, pushing off hard against the stirrups. The horseman was quick and agile and managed to strike again. This time she parried obliquely, and when the sword slid away she struck the horseman in the hand from below

257

with a short lunge, then swung her sword in a feint towards his face. He involuntarily covered his head with his left hand and she deftly turned the sword around in her hand and slashed him in the armpit, a cut she had practised for hours at Kaer Morhen. The Nilfgaardian slid from his saddle, fell to the ground, lifted himself up onto his knees, and howled like an animal, desperately trying to staunch the blood gushing from his severed arteries. Ciri watched him for a moment, as usual fascinated by the sight of a man fiercely fighting death with all his strength. She waited for him to bleed out. Then she rode off without looking back.

The ambush was over. The escort had been dispatched. Asse and Reef stopped the carriage, seizing the reins of the lead pair. The postilion, a young boy in colourful livery, having been pushed from the right lead horse, knelt on the ground, crying and begging for mercy. The coachman threw down the reins and also begged for his life, his hands placed together as though in prayer. Giselher, Iskra and Mistle cantered over to the carriage, and Kayleigh jumped off and jerked the door open. Ciri rode up and dismounted, still holding her blood-covered sword.

In the carriage sat a fat matron in an old-fashioned gown and bonnet, clutching a young and terribly pale girl in a black dress fastened up to the neck with a guipure lace collar. Ciri noticed she had a brooch pinned to her dress. A very pretty brooch.

'Oh, spotted horses!' Iskra called, looking at the rig. 'What beauties! We'll get a few florins for this four!'

'And the coachman and postilion,' Kayleigh said, grinning at the woman and the girl, 'will pull the carriage to town, once we've harnessed them up. And when we come to a hill, these two fine ladies will help!'

'Highwaymen, sirs!' the matron in the old-fashioned gown whimpered, clearly more horrified by Kayleigh's hideous smile than the bloody steel in Ciri's hand. 'I appeal to your honour! You surely will not outrage this young maiden.'

'Hey, Mistle,' Kayleigh called, smiling derisively, 'your honour's being appealed to!'

'Shut your gob.' Giselher grimaced, still mounted. 'Your jokes don't make anyone laugh. And you, woman, calm down. We're the Rats. We don't fight women and we don't harm them. Reef, Iskra. Unharness the ponies! Mistle, catch our mounts; we're leaving!'

'We Rats don't fight with women.' Kayleigh grinned once more, staring at the ashen face of the girl in the black dress. 'We just have some fun with them occasionally, if they have a yen. Well, do you, young lady? You haven't got an itch between your legs, have you? Please don't be shy. Just nod your little head.'

'Show some respect!' the lady in the old-fashioned gown screamed, her voice faltering. 'How dare you talk like that to the Much Honoured Baron's daughter, brigand!'

Kayleigh roared with laughter, then bowed extravagantly.

'I beg for forgiveness. I didn't wish to offend. What, mayn't I even ask?'

'Kayleigh!' Iskra called. 'Come here and stop dallying! Help us unharness these horses! Falka! Move it!'

Ciri couldn't tear her eyes away from the coat of arms on the carriage doors: a silver unicorn on a black field. *A unicorn*, she thought. *I once saw a unicorn like that . . . When? In another life? Or perhaps it was only a dream.*

'Falka! What's the matter?'

I am Falka. But I wasn't always. Not always.

She gathered herself and pursed her lips. *I was unkind to Mistle*, she thought. *I upset her. I have to apologise somehow.*

She placed a foot on the carriage steps, staring at the brooch on the pale girl's dress.

'Hand it over,' she said bluntly.

'How dare you?' the matron choked. 'Do you know who you are speaking to? She is the noble-born daughter of the Baron of Casadei!'

Ciri looked around, making sure no one was listening.

'A Baron's daughter?' she hissed. 'A petty title. And even if the snot were a countess, she ought to curtsy before me, arse close to the ground and head low. Give me the brooch! What are you waiting for? Should I tear it off along with the bodice?'

*

The silence which fell at the table after Philippa's declaration was quickly replaced by an uproar. The sorceresses vied with each other to voice their astonishment and disbelief, demanding explanations. Some of them undoubtedly knew a great deal about the prophesied Queen of the North – Cirilla or Ciri – while for others the name was less familiar. Fringilla Vigo didn't know anything, but she had her suspicions and was lost in conjecture, mainly centred on a certain lock of hair. However, when she asked Assire in hushed tones, the sorceress said nothing and instructed her to remain silent too. Meanwhile, Philippa Eilhart took the floor once again.

'Most of us saw Ciri on Thanedd, where she delivered prophecy in a trance and caused a great deal of confusion. Some of us are close – or even very close – to her. I have you in mind, in particular, Yennefer. It's your turn to speak.'

When Yennefer was telling the assembly about Ciri, Triss Merigold looked attentively at her. Yennefer spoke calmly and without emotion, but Triss knew her too well and had known her for too long to be fooled. She had seen her in many situations, including stressful ones, which had exhausted her and led her to the verge of sickness, and occasionally into it. Now, without doubt, Yennefer found herself in such a situation again. She looked distressed, weary and ill.

The sorceress talked, and Triss, who knew both the story and the person it concerned, discreetly observed the audience. Particularly the two sorceresses from Nilfgaard. The utterly transformed Assire var Anahid, now dressed up but still feeling uncertain in her make-up and fashionable dress. And Fringilla Vigo, the younger, friendly, naturally graceful and modestly elegant one, with green eyes and hair as black as Yennefer's but less luxuriant, cut shorter and brushed down smoothly.

Neither of the Nilfgaardians gave the impression of being lost among the complexities of Ciri's story, even though Yennefer's account was lengthy and tangled, beginning with the infamous love affair between Pavetta of Cintra and the young man magically transformed into Urcheon. She recounted Geralt's role and the Law of Surprise, and the destiny linking the Witcher and Ciri. Yennefer talked about Ciri and Geralt meeting in Brokilon, about the war, about her being lost and found, and about Kaer Morhen. About Rience and the Nilfgaardian agents hunting the girl. About her education in the Temple of Melitele, and about Ciri's mysterious abilities.

They're listening with such inscrutable expressions, Triss thought, looking at Assire and Fringilla. *Like sphinxes. But they are clearly hiding something. I wonder what. Their astonishment? Since they couldn't have known who Emhyr had brought to Nilfgaard. Or is it that they've known all this for a long time, perhaps even better than we do? Yennefer will soon reach Ciri's arrival on Thanedd, and the prophecy she gave while in a trance, which sowed so much confusion. About the bloody fighting in Garstang, which left Geralt severely beaten and Ciri abducted.*

Then the dissembling will be over, Triss thought, *and the masks will fall. Everyone knows that Nilfgaard was behind the events on Thanedd. And when all eyes turn towards you, Nilfgaardians, you won't have a choice, you'll have to talk. And then certain matters will be explained and perhaps I shall find out more. Like how Yennefer managed to vanish from Thanedd, and why she suddenly appeared here, in Montecalvo, with Francesca. Who is Ida Emean, she-elf, Aen Saevherne from the Blue Mountains, and what role is she playing here? Why do I have the impression Philippa Eilhart reveals less than she knows, even though she declares her devotion and loyalty to magic, and not to Dijkstra . . . with whom she remains in unceasing contact?*

And perhaps I'll finally learn who Ciri really is. Ciri; the Queen of the North to them, but the flaxen-haired witcher-girl of Kaer Morhen to me. A girl I still think of as a younger sister.

Fringilla Vigo had heard something about witchers: individuals who earned their keep by killing monsters and beasts. She listened attentively to Yennefer's story and to the sound of her voice, and observed her face. She didn't let herself be deceived. The strong emotional relationship between Yennefer and Ciri – whom everyone found so fascinating – was clear as day. Interestingly enough, the relationship between the sorceress and the Witcher she had mentioned was equally clear and equally strong. Fringilla began to reflect on this, but was interrupted by raised voices.

She had already worked out that some of the assembled company had been in opposing camps during the rebellion on Thanedd, so was not at all surprised by the antipathy expressed in the form of biting comments, directed at Yennefer as she spoke. Just as an argument seemed inevitable, Philippa Eilhart cut it short by unceremoniously slapping the table, which made the cups jingle.

'Enough!' she shouted. 'Be quiet, Sabrina! Don't let her goad you, Francesca! That's quite enough about Thanedd and Garstang. It's history!'

History, Fringilla thought, with an astonishing sense of hurt. *But history, which they – even though they belonged to different camps – had a hand in. They made their mark. They knew what they were doing and why. And we, imperial sorceresses, don't know anything. We really are like errand girls, who know what they are being sent to do, but don't know why. It's good that this lodge is coming into being,* she deemed. *The devil only knows how it will end, but at least it's beginning, here and now.*

'Yennefer, continue,' Philippa summoned.

'I don't have anything else to say,' the black-haired sorceress answered through pursed lips. 'I repeat: Tissaia de Vries ordered me to bring Ciri to Garstang.'

'It's easy to blame the dead,' Sabrina Glevissig snarled, but Philippa quietened her with a sharp gesture.

'I didn't want to meddle in Aretuza's business,' Yennefer said, pale and clearly disturbed. 'I wanted to take Ciri and escape Thanedd. But Tissaia convinced me that the girl's appearance in Garstang would be a shock to many and that her prophecy would pour oil on troubled waters. I'm not blaming her, however, because I agreed with her then. Both of us made a mistake. Mine was greater, though. Had I left Ciri in Rita's care . . .'

'What's done cannot be undone,' Philippa interrupted. 'Anyone can make a mistake. Even Tissaia de Vries. When did Tissaia see Ciri for the first time?'

'Three days before the conclave began,' Margarita Laux-Antille replied. 'In Gors Velen. I also made her acquaintance then. And I knew she was a remarkable individual the moment I saw her!'

'Extremely remarkable,' said the previously silent Ida Emean aep Sivney. 'For the legacy of remarkable blood is concentrated in her. Hen Ichaer, the Elder Blood. Genetic material determining the carrier's uncommon abilities. Determining the great role she will play. That she *must* play.'

'Because that is what elven legends, myths and prophecies demand?' Sabrina Glevissig asked with a sneer. 'Since the very beginning, this whole matter has smacked of fairy-tales and fantasies! Now I have no doubts. My dear ladies, I suggest we discuss something important, rational and real for a change.'

'I bow before sober rationality; the power and source of your race's great superiority,' Ida Emean said, smiling faintly. 'Nonetheless, here, in the company of individuals capable of using a power which does not always lend itself to rational analysis or explanations, it seems somewhat improper to disregard the elves' prophecies. Neither our race nor our power draws its strength from rationality. In spite of that it has endured for tens of thousands of years.'

'The genetic material called the Elder Blood, of which we are talking, turned out to be a little less hardy, however,' Sheala de Tancarville observed. 'Even elven legends and prophecies, which I in no way disregard, consider the Elder Blood to be utterly atrophied. Extinct. Am I right, Mistress Ida? There is no more Elder Blood in the world. The last person in whose veins it flowed was Lara Dorren aep Shiadhal, and we all know the legend of Lara Dorren and Cregennan of Lod.'

'Not all of us,' Assire var Anahid said, speaking for the first time. 'I only studied your mythology cursorily and have never come across that legend.'

'It is not a legend,' Philippa Eilhart said, 'but a true story. And there is one among us who not only knows the tale of Lara and Cregennan very well, but also what came after, which will certainly interest you all. Would you take up the story, Francesca?'

'From what you say' – the queen of the elves smiled – 'it would seem you know this tale no less thoroughly than I do.'

'Quite possibly. But I would nonetheless ask you to tell it.'

'In order to test my honesty and loyalty to the lodge,' Enid an Gleanna said, nodding. 'Very well. I would ask you all to make yourselves comfortable, for the story will not be a short one.'

'The story of Lara and Cregennan is a true story, although today it is so overgrown with fairy-tale ornamentation it is difficult to recognise. There is also enormous variance between the legend's human and elven versions; chauvinism and racial hatred can be heard in both of them, though. Thus I shall refrain from embellishments and limit myself to dry facts. Cregennan of Lod was a sorcerer. Lara Dorren aep Shiadhal was an elven sorceress, an Aen Saevherne, a Sage, one of the carriers of the Elder Blood, which is even mysterious to we elves. The friendship – and later romance – between the two of them was at first joyfully acknowledged by both races, but there soon appeared opponents to their union. Sworn enemies to the idea of melding human and elven magic, who regarded it as betrayal. With the wisdom of hindsight, there were also feuds of a personal nature at work: jealousy and envy. Put simply: Cregennan was assassinated and Lara Dorren, hounded and hunted, died of exhaustion in a wilderness after giving birth to a daughter. The baby was saved by a miracle. She was taken in by Cerro, the Queen of Redania—'

'Only because she was terrified of the curse Lara cast when she refused to help and drove Lara out into the cold of winter,' Keira Metz said, butting in. 'Had Cerro not adopted the child, terrible calamities would have fallen on her and her entire family—'

'Those are precisely the fantastic ornaments Francesca has dispensed with,' Philippa Eilhart interrupted. 'Let us stick to facts.'

'The prophetic abilities of the Sages of the Elder Blood are facts,' Ida Emean said, raising her eyes towards Philippa. 'And the evocative motif of prophecy which appears in every version of the legend is food for thought.'

'It is now, and it was in the past,' Francesca confirmed. 'The rumours of Lara's curse never died away, and were even recalled seventeen years later when Riannon – the little girl Cerro had adopted – grew into a young woman whose beauty eclipsed even her mother's legendary looks. She bore the official title of Princess of Redania, and many ruling houses were interested in making a match with her. When Riannon finally chose Goidemar, the young King of Temeria, from among many suitors, it would not have taken much for rumours of the curse to thwart the marriage. However, the rumours only became common knowledge three years after their wedding. During the Falka Rebellion.'

Fringilla, who had never heard of Falka or the rebellion, raised her eyebrows. Francesca noticed it.

'For the northern kingdoms,' she explained, 'these are tragic and bloody events, which live on in the memory, though more than a century has passed. In Nilfgaard, with whom the North had almost no contact at that time, the matter is probably not known so I will take the liberty of briefly restating certain facts. Falka was the daughter of Vridank, the King of Redania, and the issue of a marriage he dissolved when he took a fancy to the beautiful Cerro – the same Cerro who later adopted Lara's child. A document survives, lengthily and circuitously stating the reasons for the divorce, but a surviving miniature of Vridank's first wife, an undoubtedly half-elf Kovirian noblewoman with predominantly human traits, says a lot more. It depicts her with the eyes of a deranged hermit, the hair of a drowned corpse and the mouth of a lizard. To cut a long story short: an ugly woman was sent back to Kovir with her year-old daughter, Falka. And soon after, the one and the other were both forgotten.'

'Falka,' Enid an Gleanna picked up after a while, 'gave cause to be remembered five-and-twenty years later, when she launched an uprising and murdered her own father, Cerro and two of her stepbrothers, allegedly with her own hands. The armed rebellion initially broke out as an attempt by the legally firstborn daughter, supported by some of the Temerian and Kovirian nobility, to gain the throne which was rightly hers. But it was soon transformed into a peasants' revolt of immense proportions. Both sides committed gruesome atrocities. Falka passed into legend as a bloodthirsty demon, although actually it is more likely she simply lost control of the situation and of the slogans displayed on the insurrectionary standards. "Death To Kings"; "Death To Sorcerers"; "Death To

Priests, Nobility, Gentry and Anybody Well-To-Do"; and soon after: "Death To Everyone and Everything", for it became impossible to curb the blood-drenched evil mob. Then the rebellion began to spread to other countries . . .'

'Nilfgaardian historians have written about that,' Sabrina Glevissig interrupted with a distinct sneer. 'And Mistresses Assire and Vigo have undoubtedly read it. Keep it brief, Francesca. Move on to Riannon and the Houtborg triplets.'

'But of course. Riannon, issue of Lara Dorren, adopted daughter of Cerro, now the wife of Goidemar, King of Temeria, was accidentally seized by Falka's rebels and imprisoned in Houtborg Castle. She was pregnant at the time of her capture. The castle was still under siege long after the rebellion had been suppressed and Falka executed, but Goidemar finally took it by storm and rescued his wife. And three children: two little girls, who were already walking, and a boy, who was learning to. Riannon had been driven insane. The furious Goidemar put all the captives on the rack and from the shreds of their testimonies, interspersed with groans, constructed a plausible picture.

'Falka, who had inherited her looks more from her elven grandmother than her mother, had generously bestowed her charms on all her officers in command, from the noblemen to ordinary captains and thugs; by so doing ensuring their faithfulness and loyalty to her. She finally fell pregnant and gave birth to a child, precisely at the same moment that Riannon – who was imprisoned in Houtborg – had twins. Falka ordered her infant to be raised with Riannon's children. As she was later alleged to have said, only queens were worthy of the honour of being wet nurses to her bastards, and a similar fate would await every queen and princess in the new order Falka would build following her victory.

'The problem was that no one, not even Riannon, knew which of the "triplets" was Falka's. It was surmised that it was most likely one of the girls, because Riannon had reputedly given birth to a girl and a boy. I repeat, most likely, since in spite of Falka's boast the children were suckled by ordinary, peasant wet nurses. Riannon could hardly remember anything when her insanity was finally cured. Yes, she gave birth. Yes, the triplets were occasionally brought to her bed and shown to her. But nothing more.

'Sorcerers were summoned to examine the triplets and establish which was which. Goidemar was so unwavering that he intended – after ascertaining which was Falka's bastard – to publicly execute the child. We could not allow it. After the uprising's suppression, unspeakable brutality had been inflicted on the captured rebels, and it was time to put an end to it. The execution of a child before its second birthday? Can you imagine? What legends would have sprung up! And anyway it had already been rumoured that Falka herself had been born a monster as a result of Lara Dorren's curse. Nonsense, of course, since Falka had been born before Lara had even met Cregennan. But few people could be bothered to count the years. Pamphlets and other ridiculous documents were written about it and published clandestinely in Oxenfurt Academy. But I will return to the examination Goidemar ordered us to carry out—'

'Us?' Yennefer asked, looking up. 'Who precisely was that?'

'Tissaia de Vries, Augusta Wagner, Leticia Charbonneau and Hen Gedymdeith,' Francesca said calmly. 'I was later added to that body. I was a young sorceress, but a pureblood elf. And my father . . . my biological father, who disowned me . . . he was a Sage. I knew what the Elder Blood gene was.'

'And that gene was found in Riannon, when you examined her and the king before studying the children,' Sheala de Tancarville stated. 'And in two of the children – although to different extents – which allowed Falka's bastard to be identified. How did you save the child from the king's wrath?'

'Very simply,' the she-elf smiled. 'By feigning ignorance. We told the king that the matter was complicated, that we were still doing tests, but that tests of that kind demanded time . . . A great deal of time. Goidemar, an irascible but fundamentally good and noble man, quickly cooled down and put no pressure on us while the triplets were growing and running around the palace, bringing joy to the royal couple and the entire court. Amavet, Fiona and Adela. The triplets were as alike as three sparrows. They were watched attentively, of course, and there were frequent suspicions, particularly if one of the children was getting up to mischief. Fiona once tipped the contents of a chamber pot from a window right onto the Great Constable. He called her "a demonic bastard" and kissed goodbye to his post. Sometime later Amavet smeared tallow on the stairs, and then, when a splint was put on the arm of a certain lady-in-waiting, she groaned something about "accursed blood" and soon afterwards said farewell to the court. More lowborn loudmouths made the acquaintance of the whipping post and the horsewhip. Thus everyone swiftly learned to hold their tongues. There was even a baron from an ancient family, who Adela shot in the backside with an arrow, who confined himself to—'

'That's enough about the children's pranks,' Philippa Eilhart interjected. 'When was Goidemar finally told the truth?'

'He was never told. He never asked, which suited us.'

'But you knew which of the children was Falka's bastard?'

'Of course. It was Adela.'

'Not Fiona?'

'No. Adela. She died of the plague. The demonic bastard, the accursed blood, the daughter of the diabolical Falka helped the priests in the infirmary beyond the castle walls during an epidemic – in spite of the king's protests. She caught the plague from the sick children she was treating and died. She was seventeen. A year later her pseudo-brother Amavet became romantically involved with Countess Anna Kameny and was murdered by assassins hired by her husband. The same year Riannon died, distraught and inconsolable after the death of two of her beloved children. Then Goidemar summoned us once more. For the King of Cintra, Coram, was showing an interest in the last of the famous triplets: Princess Fiona. He wanted her to marry his son, also Coram, but knew of the rumours and didn't want to go ahead with the match in case Fiona was indeed Falka's bastard. We staked our reputation on the fact that Fiona was a legitimate child. I don't know if he believed us, but the young couple grew to like each other and thus Riannon's daughter, Ciri's great-great-great-grandmother, became the Queen of Cintra.'

'Introducing your celebrated gene to the Coram dynasty.'

'Fiona,' Enid an Gleanna said calmly, 'was not a carrier of the Elder Blood gene, which we had begun to call the Lara gene.'

'What do you mean exactly?'

'Well, Amavet carried the Lara gene, so our experiment went on. For Anna Kameny, who inadvertently caused the death of both her lover and husband, gave birth to twins while still in mourning. A boy and a girl. Their father must have been Amavet, for the baby girl was a carrier. She was named Muriel.'

'Muriel the Impure?' Sheala de Tancarville asked in astonishment.

'She became that much later.' Francesca smiled. 'At first she was Muriel the Delightful. Indeed, she was a sweet, charming child. When she was fourteen they were already calling her Doe-Eyed Muriel. Many men drowned in those eyes. She was finally given in marriage to Robert, Count of Garramone.'

'And the boy?'

'Crispin. He wasn't a carrier, so he was of no interest to us. If my memory serves, he fell in combat somewhere, for his passion was warfare.'

'Just a moment,' Sabrina said, ruffling her hair vigorously. 'Wasn't Muriel the Impure the mother of Adalia the Seer?'

'Indeed,' Francesca confirmed. 'An interesting one, was Adalia. A powerful Source, excellent material for a sorceress. But she didn't want to be one, unfortunately. She preferred to be a queen.'

'And the gene?' Assire var Anahid asked. 'Did she bear it?'

'Interestingly not.'

'As I thought,' Assire said, nodding. 'Lara's gene can only be passed on inviolately down the female line. If the carrier is a man, the gene disappears in the second, or – at most – the third generation.'

'But wait—'

'It activates later, however,' Philippa Eilhart broke in. 'After all, Adalia, who didn't have the gene, was Calanthe's mother, and Calanthe, Ciri's grandmother, carried the Lara gene.'

'She was the first carrier after Riannon,' Sheala de Tancarville said, suddenly joining the discussion. 'You made a mistake, Francesca. There were two genes. One, the true gene, was latent, quiescent.

You were beguiled by Amavet's powerful, distinct gene. However, what Amavet had wasn't a gene, but an activator. Mistress Assire is right. The activator travelling down the male line was so faint in Adalia you didn't identify it at all. Adalia was Muriel's first child; her later-born definitely didn't have even a trace of the activator. Fiona's latent gene would probably also have vanished in her male descendants at most in the third generation. But it didn't, and I know why.'

'Bloody hell,' Yennefer hissed through her teeth.

'I'm lost,' Sabrina Glevissig declared. 'In this tangle of genetics and genealogy.'

Francesca drew a fruit bowl towards herself, held out a hand and murmured a spell.

'I apologise for this vulgar display of psychokinesis,' she said with a smile, making a red apple rise high above the table. 'But the fruit will help me demonstrate your mistake. Red apples are the Lara gene, the Elder Blood. Green apples represent the latent gene. Pomegranates are the pseudo-gene, the activator. Let us begin. This is Riannon, the red apple. Her son, Amavet, is the pomegranate. Amavet's daughter, Muriel, and his granddaughter, Adalia, are still pomegranates, the last of which is very faint. And here is Fiona's line, Riannon's daughter: a green apple. Her son, Corbett, the King of Cintra, is green. Dagorad, Corbett and Elen of Kaedwen's son, is green too. As you have observed, in two successive generations there are exclusively male descendants. The gene is very weak, and vanishes. So at the very bottom, here, we finish with a pomegranate and a green apple; Adalia, the Princess of Maribor, and Dagorad, the King of Cintra. And the couple's daughter was Calanthe. A red apple. The revived, powerful Lara gene.'

'Fiona's latent gene' – Margarita Laux-Antille nodded – 'met Amavet's activator gene through marital incest. Did no one notice their kinship? Did none of the royal heraldists or chroniclers pay any attention to this blatant incest?'

'It wasn't as blatant as it seems. After all, Anna Kameny didn't advertise that her twins were bastards, because her husband's family would have deprived her and her children of their coat of arms, titles and fortune. Of course there were persistent rumours, and not just among the peasantry. That's why they had to search for a husband for Calanthe, who was contaminated by incest, in distant Ebbing, beyond the rumours' reach.'

'Add two more red apples to your pyramid, Enid,' Margarita said. 'Now, as Mistress Assire has astutely indicated, we can see the reborn Lara gene moving smoothly down the female line.'

'Yes. Here is Pavetta, Calanthe's daughter. And Pavetta's daughter, Cirilla, the sole inheritor of the Elder Blood, carrier of the Lara gene.'

'The sole inheritor?' Sheala de Tancarville asked abruptly. 'You're very confident, Enid.'

'What do you mean by that?'

Sheala suddenly stood up, snapped her beringed fingers towards the fruit bowl and made the remaining fruit levitate, disrupting Francesca's model and transforming it into a multi-coloured confusion.

'This is what I mean,' she said coldly, pointing at the jumble of fruit. 'Here we have all of the possible genetic combinations and permutations. And we know as much as we can see here. Namely nothing. Your mistake backfired, Francesca, and it caused an avalanche of errors. The gene only reappeared by accident after a century, during which time we have no idea what may have occurred. Secret, hidden, hushed-up events. Premarital children, extramarital children, adoptive children – even changelings. Incest. The crossbreeding of races, the blood of forgotten ancestors returning in later generations. In short: a hundred years ago you had the gene within arm's reach, even in your hands. And it gave you the slip. That was a mistake, Enid, a terrible mistake! Too much confusion, too many accidents. Too little control, too little interference in the randomness of it all.'

'We weren't dealing,' Enid an Gleanna said through pursed lips, 'with rabbits, which we could pair off and put in a hutch.'

Fringilla, following Triss Merigold's gaze, noticed Yennefer's hands suddenly clenching her chair's carved armrests.

*

So this is what Yennefer and Francesca have in common, Triss thought feverishly, still avoiding her close friend's gaze. *Cynical duplicity. For, after all, pairing off and breeding turned out to be unavoidable. Indeed, their plans for Ciri and the Prince of Kovir, although apparently improbable, are actually quite realistic. They've done it before. They've placed whoever they wanted on thrones, created the marriages and dynasties they desired and which were convenient for them. Spells, aphrodisiacs and elixirs were all used. Queens and princesses suddenly entered bizarre – often morganatic – marriages, contrary to all plans, intentions and agreements. And later those who wanted children, but ought not to have them, were secretly given contraceptive agents. Those who didn't want children, but ought to have them, were given placebos of liquorice water instead of the promised agents. Which resulted in all of those improbable connections: Calanthe, Pavetta . . . and now Ciri. Yennefer was involved in this. And now she regrets it. She's right to. Damn it, were Geralt to find out . . .*

Sphinxes, Fringilla Vigo thought. *The sphinxes carved on the chairs' armrests. Yes, they ought to be the lodge's emblem. Wise, mysterious, silent. They are all sphinxes. They will easily achieve what they want. It's a trifle for them to marry Kovir off to that Ciri of theirs. They have the power to. They have the expertise. And the means. The diamond necklace around Sabrina Glevissig's neck is probably worth almost as much as the entire income of forested, rocky Kaedwen. They could easily carry out their plans. But there is one snag . . .*

Aha, Triss Merigold thought, *at last we've reached the topic we should have started with: the sobering and discouraging fact that Ciri is in Nilfgaard, in Emhyr's clutches. Far away from the plans being hatched here . . .*

'There is no question that Emhyr had been hunting for Cirilla for many years,' Philippa continued. 'Everyone assumed his goal was a political union with Cintra and control of the fiefdom which is her legal heritage. However, one cannot rule out that rather than politics it concerns the gene of the Elder Blood, which Emhyr wants to introduce to the imperial line. If Emhyr knows what we do, he may want the prophecy to manifest itself in his dynasty, and the future Queen of the World to be born in Nilfgaard.'

'A correction,' Sabrina Glevissig interrupted. 'It's not Emhyr who wants it, but the Nilfgaardian sorcerers. They alone were capable of tracking down the gene and making Emhyr aware of its significance. I'm sure the Nilfgaardian ladies here present will want to confirm that and explain their role in the intrigue.'

'I am astonished,' Fringilla burst out, 'by your tendency to search for the threads of intrigue in distant Nilfgaard, while the evidence requires us to search for conspirators and traitors much closer to you.'

'An observation as blunt as it is apt,' Sheala de Tancarville said, silencing with a glance Sabrina, who was preparing a riposte. 'All the evidence suggests that the facts about the Elder Blood were leaked to Nilfgaard from us. Is it possible you've forgotten about Vilgefortz, ladies?'

'Not I,' Sabrina said, a flame of hatred flaring in her black eyes for a second. 'I have not forgotten!'

'All in good time,' Keira Metz said, flashing her teeth malevolently. 'But for the moment it's not about him, but about the fact that Emhyr var Emreis, Imperator of Nilfgaard, has Ciri – and thus the Elder Blood that is so important to us – in his grasp.'

'The Imperator,' Assire declared calmly, glancing at Fringilla, 'doesn't have anything in his grasp. The girl being held in Darn Rowan is not the carrier of any extraordinary gene. She's ordinary to the point of commonness. Beyond a shadow of doubt she is not Ciri of Cintra. She is not the girl the Imperator was seeking. For he was clearly seeking a girl who carries the gene; he even had some of her hair. I examined it and found something I didn't understand; now I do.'

'So Ciri isn't in Nilfgaard,' Yennefer said softly. 'She's not there.'

'She's not there,' Philippa Eilhart repeated gravely. 'Emhyr was tricked; a double was planted on him. I've known as much since yesterday. However, I'm pleased by Mistress Assire's disclosure. It confirms that our lodge is now functioning.'

Yennefer had great difficulty controlling the trembling of her hands and mouth. *Keep calm*, she told herself. *Keep calm; don't reveal anything; wait for an opportunity. Keep listening. Collect information. A sphinx. Be a sphinx.*

'So it was Vilgefortz,' Sabrina said, slamming her fist down on the table. 'Not Emhyr, but Vilgefortz. That charmer, that handsome scoundrel! He duped Emhyr and us!'

Yennefer calmed herself by breathing deeply. Assire var Anahid, the Nilfgaardian sorceress, feeling understandably uncomfortable in her tight-fitting dress, was talking about a young Nilfgaardian nobleman. Yennefer knew who it was and involuntarily clenched her fists. A black knight in a winged helmet, the nightmare from Ciri's hallucinations . . . She sensed Francesca and Philippa's eyes on her. However, Triss – whose gaze she was trying to attract – was avoiding her eyes. *Bloody hell*, Yennefer thought, trying hard to remain impassive, *I've landed myself in it. What bloody predicament have I tangled the girl up in? Shit, how will I ever be able to look the Witcher in the eye . . . ?*

'Thus, we'll have a perfect opportunity,' Keira Metz called in an excited voice, 'to rescue Ciri and strike at Vilgefortz at the same time. We'll scorch the ground beneath the rascal's arse!'

'Any scorching of ground must be preceded by the discovery of Vilgefortz's whereabouts,' Sheala de Tancarville, the sorceress from Kovir whom Yennefer had never felt much affection for, said mockingly. 'And no one's managed it so far. Not even some of the ladies sitting at this table, who have devoted both their time and their extraordinary abilities to looking for it.'

'Two of Vilgefortz's numerous hideouts have already been found,' Philippa Eilhart responded coldly. 'Dijkstra is searching intensively for the remaining ones, and I wouldn't write him off. Sometimes spies and informers succeed where magic fails.'

One of the agents accompanying Dijkstra looked into the dungeon, stepped back sharply, leant against the wall and went as white as a sheet, looking as though he would faint at any moment. Dijkstra made a mental note to transfer the milksop to office work. But when he looked into the cell himself, he changed his mind. He felt his bile rising. He couldn't embarrass himself in front of his subordinates, however. He unhurriedly removed a perfumed handkerchief from his pocket, held it against his nose and mouth, and leant over the naked corpse lying on the stone floor.

'Belly and womb cut open,' he diagnosed, struggling to maintain his calm and a cold tone. 'Very skilfully, as if by a surgeon's hand. The foetus was removed from the girl. She was alive when they did it, but it was not done here. Are all of them like that? Lennep, I'm talking to you.'

'No . . .' the agent said with a shudder, tearing his eyes away from the corpse. 'The others had been garrotted. They weren't pregnant . . . But we shall perform post-mortems . . .'

'How many were found, in total?'

'Apart from this one, four. We haven't managed to identify any of them.'

'That's not true,' Dijkstra countered from behind his handkerchief. 'I've already managed to identify this one. It's Jolie, the youngest daughter of Count Lanier. The girl who disappeared without a trace a year ago. I'll take a glance at the other ones.'

'Some of them are partially burnt,' Lennep said. 'They will be difficult to identify . . . But, sire, apart from this . . . we found . . .'

'Speak. Don't stammer.'

'There are bones in that well,' the agent said, pointing at a hole gaping in the floor. 'A large quantity of bones. We have not removed or examined them, but we can be sure they all belonged to young women. Were we to ask sorcerers for aid we might be able to identify them . . . and inform those parents who are still looking for their missing daughters . . .'

'Under no circumstances,' Dijkstra said, swinging around. 'Not a word about what's been found here. To anyone. Particularly not to any mages. I'm beginning to lose faith in them after what I've seen here. Lennep, have the upper levels been thoroughly searched? Has nothing been found that might help us in our quest?'

'Nothing, sire,' Lennep said and lowered his head. 'As soon as we received word, we rushed to the castle. But we arrived too late. Everything had burnt down. Consumed by a fearful conflagration.

Magical, without any doubt. Only here, in the dungeons, did the spell not destroy everything. I don't know why . . .'

'But I do. The fuse wasn't lit by Vilgefortz, but by Rience or another of the sorcerer's factotums. Vilgefortz wouldn't have made such a mistake, he wouldn't have left anything but the soot on the walls. Oh yes, he knows that fire purifies . . . and covers tracks.'

'Indeed it does,' Lennep muttered. 'There isn't even any evidence that Vilgefortz was here at all . . .'

'Then fabricate some,' Dijkstra said, removing the handkerchief from his face. 'Must I teach you how it's done? I know that Vilgefortz was here. Did anything else survive in the dungeons apart from the corpses? What's behind that iron door?'

'Step this way, sire,' the agent said, taking a torch from one of the assistants. 'I will show you.'

There was no doubt that the magical spark which had been meant to turn everything in the dungeon to ashes had been placed right there, in the spacious chamber behind the iron door. An error in the spell had largely thwarted the plan, but the fire had still been powerful and fierce. The flames had charred the shelves occupying one of the walls, destroyed and fused the glass vessels, turning everything into a stinking mass. The only thing left unaffected in the chamber was a table with a metal top and two curious chairs set into the floor. Curious, but leaving no doubt as to their function.

'They are constructed,' Lennep said swallowing, and pointing at the chairs and the clasps attached to them, 'so as to hold . . . the legs . . . apart. Wide apart.'

'Bastard,' Dijkstra snapped through clenched teeth. 'Damned bastard . . .'

'We found traces of blood, faeces and urine in the gutter beneath the wooden chair,' the agent continued softly. 'The steel one is brand new, most probably unused. I don't know what to make of it . . .'

'I do,' Dijkstra said. 'The steel one was constructed for somebody special. Someone that Vilgefortz suspected of special abilities.'

*

'In no way do I disregard Dijkstra or his secret service,' Sheala de Tancarville said. 'I know that finding Vilgefortz is only a matter of time. However, passing over the motif of personal vengeance which seems to fascinate some of you, I'll take the liberty of observing that it is not at all certain that Vilgefortz has Ciri.'

'If it's not Vilgefortz, then who? She was on the island. None of us, as far as I know, teleported her away from there. Neither Dijkstra nor any of the kings have her, we know that for sure. And her body wasn't found in the ruins of the Tower of Gulls.'

'Tor Lara,' Ida Emean said slowly, 'once concealed a very powerful teleportal. Could the girl have escaped Thanedd through that portal?'

Yennefer veiled her eyes with her eyelashes and dug her nails into the heads of the sphinxes on the chair's armrests. *Keep calm*, she thought. *Just keep calm*. She felt Margarita's eyes on her, but did not raise her head.

'If Ciri entered the teleportal in the Tower of Gulls,' the rectoress of Aretuza said in a slightly altered voice, 'I fear we can forget our plans and projects. We may never see Ciri again. The now-destroyed portal of Tor Lara was damaged. It's warped. Lethal.'

'What are we talking about here?' Sabrina exploded. 'In order to uncover the teleportal in the tower, in order to see it at all, would require fourth-level magic! And the abilities of a grandmaster would be necessary to activate the portal! I don't know if Vilgefortz is capable of that, never mind a fifteen-year-old filly. How can you even imagine something like that? Who is this girl, in your opinion? What potential does she hold?'

'Is it so important,' Stephan Skellen, also called Tawny Owl, the Coroner of Imperator Emhyr var Emreis said, stretching, 'what potential she holds, Master Bonhart? Or even if any? I'd rather she wasn't around at all. And I'm paying you a hundred florins to make my wish come true. If you want, examine her – after killing her or before, up to you. Either way the fee won't change, I give you my solemn word.'

'And were I to supply her alive?'

'It still won't.'

The man called Bonhart twisted his grey whiskers. He was of immense height, but as bony as a skeleton. His other hand rested on his sword the entire time, as though he wanted to hide the ornate pommel of the hilt from Skellen's eyes.

'Am I to bring you her head?'

'No,' Tawny Owl said, wincing. 'Why would I want her head? To preserve in honey?'

'As proof.'

'I'll take you at your word. You are well known for your reliability, Bonhart.'

'Thank you for the recognition,' the bounty hunter said, and smiled. At the sight of his smile, Skellen, who had twenty armed men waiting outside the tavern, felt a shiver running down his spine. 'Rarely received, although well deserved. I have to bring the barons and the lords Varnhagens the heads of all the Rats I catch or they won't pay. If you have no need of Falka's head, you won't, I imagine, have anything against my adding it to the set.'

'To claim the other reward? What about your professional ethics?'

'Honoured sir,' Bonhart said, narrowing his eyes, 'I am not paid for killing, but for the service I render by killing. A service I'll be rendering both you and the Varnhagens.'

'Fair enough,' Tawny Owl agreed. 'Do whatever you think's right. When can I expect you to collect the bounty money?'

'Soon.'

'Meaning?'

'The Rats are heading for the Bandit's Trail, with plans to winter in the mountains. I'll cut off their route. Twenty days, no more.'

'Are you certain of the route they're taking?'

'They've been seen near Fen Aspra, where they robbed a convoy and two merchants. They've been prowling near Tyffi. Then they stopped off at Druigh for one night, to dance at a village fair. They finally ended up in Loredo, where your Falka hacked a fellow to pieces, in such a fashion that they're still talking about it through chattering teeth. Which is why I asked what there is to this Falka.'

'Perhaps you and she are very much alike,' Stephan Skellen

mocked. 'But no, forgive me. After all, you don't take money for killing, but for services rendered. You're a true craftsman, Bonhart, a genuine professional. A trade, like any other? A job to be done? They pay for it, and everyone has to make a living? Eh?'

The bounty hunter looked at him long and hard. Until Tawny Owl's smirk finally vanished.

'Indeed,' he said. 'Everyone has to make a living. Some earn money doing what they've learned. Others do what they have to. But not many craftsmen have been as lucky in life as I am: they pay me for a trade I truly and honestly enjoy. Not even whores can say that.'

Yennefer welcomed Philippa's suggestion of a break for a bite to eat and to moisten throats dried out by speaking with relief, delight and hope. It soon turned out, however, that her hopes were in vain. Philippa quickly dragged away Margarita – who clearly wanted to talk to Yennefer – to the other end of the room, and Triss Merigold, who had drawn closer to her, was accompanied by Francesca. The she-elf unceremoniously controlled the conversation. Yennefer saw anxiety in Triss's cornflower-blue eyes, however, and was certain that even without witnesses it would have been futile to ask for help. Triss was undoubtedly already committed, heart and soul, to the lodge. And doubtlessly sensed that Yennefer's loyalty was still wavering.

Triss tried to cheer her up by assuring her that Geralt, safe in Brokilon, was returning to health thanks to the dryads' efforts. As usual, she blushed at the mention of his name. *He must have pleased her back then*, Yennefer thought, not without malice. *She had never known anyone like him before and she won't forget him in a hurry. And a good thing too.*

She dismissed the revelations with an apparently indifferent shrug of her shoulders. She wasn't concerned by the fact that neither Triss nor Francesca believed her indifference. She wanted to be alone, and wanted them to see that.

They did just that.

She stood at the far end of the food table, devoting herself to oysters. She ate cautiously, still in pain from her compression. She was reluctant to drink wine, not knowing how she might react.

'Yennefer?'

She turned around. Fringilla Vigo smiled faintly, looking down at the short knife Yennefer was gripping tightly.

'I can see and sense,' she said, 'that you'd rather prise me open than that oyster. Still no love lost?'

'The lodge,' Yennefer replied coolly, 'demands mutual loyalty. Friendship is not compulsory.'

'It isn't and shouldn't be,' the Nilfgaardian sorceress said, and looked around the chamber. 'Friendship is either the result of a lengthy process or is spontaneous.'

'The same goes for enmity,' Yennefer said, opening the oyster and swallowing the contents along with some seawater. 'Occasionally one happens to see another person for only a split second, right before going blind, and one takes a dislike to them instantly.'

'Oh, enmity is considerably more complicated,' Fringilla said, squinting. 'Imagine someone you don't know at all standing at the top of a hill, and ripping a friend of yours to shreds in front of your eyes. You neither saw them nor know them at all, but you still don't like them.'

'So it goes,' Yennefer said, shrugging. 'Fate has a way of playing tricks on you.'

'Fate,' Fringilla said quietly, 'is unpredictable indeed, like a mischievous child. Friends sometimes turn their backs on us, while an enemy comes in useful. You can, for example, talk to them face to face. No one tries to interfere, no one interrupts or eavesdrops. Everyone wonders what the two enemies could possibly be talking about. About nothing important. Why, they're mouthing platitudes and twisting the occasional barb.'

'No doubt,' Yennefer said, nodding, 'that's what everyone thinks. And they're absolutely right.'

'Which means it'll be even easier,' Fringilla said, quite relaxed, 'to bring up a particularly important and remarkable matter.'

'What matter would that be?'

'That of the escape attempt you're planning.'

Yennefer, who was opening another oyster, almost cut her finger. She looked around furtively, and then glanced at the Nilfgaardian from under her eyelashes. Fringilla Vigo smiled slightly.

'Be so kind as to lend me the knife. To open an oyster. Your oysters are excellent. It's not easy for us to get such good ones in the south. Particularly not now, during the wartime blockade ... A blockade is a very bad thing, isn't it?'

Yennefer gave a slight cough.

'I've noticed,' Fringilla said, swallowing the oyster and reaching for another. 'Yes, Philippa's looking at us. Assire too, probably worrying about my loyalty to the lodge. My endangered loyalty. She's liable to think I'll yield to sympathy. Let us see ... Your sweetheart was seriously injured. The girl you treat as a daughter has disappeared, is possibly being imprisoned ... perhaps her life's in danger. Or perhaps she'll just be played as a card in a rigged game? I swear, I couldn't stand it. I'd flee at once. Please, take the knife back. That's enough oysters, I have to watch my figure.'

'A blockade, as you have deigned to observe,' Yennefer whispered, looking into the Nilfgaardian sorceress's eyes, 'is a very bad thing. Simply beastly. It doesn't allow one to do what one wants. But a blockade can be overcome, if one has ... the means. Which I don't.'

'Do you expect me to give the means to you?' the Nilfgaardian asked, examining the rough shell of the oyster, which she was still holding. 'Oh no, not a chance. I'm loyal to the lodge, and the lodge, naturally, doesn't wish you to hurry to the aid of your loved ones. Furthermore, I'm your enemy. How could you forget that, Yennefer?'

'Indeed. How could I?'

'I would warn a friend,' Fringilla said quietly, 'that even if she were in possession of the components for teleportation spells, she wouldn't be able to break the blockade undetected. An operation of that kind demands time and is too conspicuous. An unobtrusive but energetic attractor is a little better. I repeat: a *little* better. Teleportation using an improvised attractor, as you are no doubt aware, is very risky. I would try to dissuade a friend from taking such a risk. But you aren't a friend.'

Fringilla spilt a sprinkling of seawater from the shell she was holding onto the table.

'And on that note, we'll end our banal conversation,' she said. 'The lodge demands mutual loyalty from us. Friendship, fortunately, isn't compulsory.'

'She teleported,' Francesca Findabair stated coldly and unemotionally, when the confusion caused by Yennefer's disappearance had calmed down. 'There's nothing to get het up about, ladies. And there's nothing we can do about it now. She's too far away. It's my mistake. I suspected her obsidian star masked the echo of spells—'

'How did she bloody do it?' Philippa yelled. 'She could muffle an echo, that isn't difficult. But how did she manage to open the portal? Montecalvo has a blockade!'

'I've never liked her,' Sheala de Tancarville said, shrugging her shoulders. 'I've never approved of her lifestyle. But I've never questioned her abilities.'

'She'll tell them everything!' Sabrina Glevissig yelled. 'Everything about the lodge! She'll fly straight to—'

'Nonsense,' Triss Merigold interrupted animatedly, looking at Francesca and Ida Emean. 'Yennefer won't betray us. She didn't escape to betray us.'

'Triss is right,' Margarita Laux-Antille added, backing her up. 'I know why she escaped and who she wants to rescue. I've seen them, she and Ciri, together. And I understand.'

'But I don't understand any of this!' Sabrina yelled and everything became heated again.

Assire var Anahid leant towards her friend.

'I won't ask why you did it,' she whispered. 'I won't ask how you did it. I'll only ask: where is she headed?'

Fringilla Vigo smiled faintly, stroking the carved head of the sphinx on the chair's armrest with her fingers.

'And how could I possibly know,' she whispered back, 'which coast these oysters came from?'

Ithlina, actually *Ithlinne Aegli: daughter of Aevenien, the legendary elven healer, astrologist and soothsayer, famous for her predictions and prophecies, of which Aen Ithlinnespeath, Ithlina's Prophecy, is the best known. It has been written down many times and published in numerous forms. The Prophecy enjoyed great popularity at certain moments, and the commentaries, clues and clarifications appended to it adapted the text to contemporary events, which strengthened convictions about its great clairvoyance. In particular it is believed* **I.** *predicted the Northern Wars (1239– 1268), the Great Plagues (1268, 1272 and 1294), the bloody War of the Two Unicorns (1309–1318) and the Haak Invasion (1350).* **I.** *was also supposed to have prophesied the climatic changes observed from the end of the thirteenth century, known as the Great Frost, which superstition always claimed was a sign of the end of the world and linked to the prophesied coming of the Destroyer (q.v.). This passage from* **I.'s** *Prophecy gave rise to the infamous witch hunts (1272–76) and contributed to the deaths of many women and unfortunate girls mistaken for the incarnation of the Destroyer. Today* **I.** *is regarded by many scholars as a legendary figure and her 'prophecies' as very recently fabricated apocrypha, and a cunning literary fraud.*

Effenberg and Talbot,
Encyclopaedia Maxima Mundi, Volume X

CHAPTER SEVEN

The children gathered in a ring around the wandering storyteller Stribog showed their disapproval by making a dreadful, riotous uproar. Finally Connor, the blacksmith's son, the oldest, strongest and bravest of the children, and also the one who brought the storyteller a pot full of cabbage soup and potatoes sprinkled with scraps of fried bacon, stepped forward as the spokesman and exponent of the general opinion.

'How's that?' he yelled. 'What do you mean "that's your lot"? Is it fair to end the tale there? To leave us hungry for more? We want to know what happened next! We can't wait till you visit our village again, for it might be in six months or a whole year! Go on with the story!'

'The sun's gone down,' the old man replied. 'It's time for bed, young 'uns. When you start to yawn and grumble over your chores tomorrow, what will your parents say? I know what they'll say: "Old Stribog was telling them tales till past midnight, wearying the children's heads with songs, and didn't let them get to bed. So when he wends his way to the village again, don't give him nothing; no kasha, no dumplings, no bacon. Just drive him off, the old gimmer, because nothing comes from his tales but woe and trouble—"'

'They won't say that!' the children all shouted. 'Tell us more! Pleeease!'

'Mmm,' the old man mumbled, looking at the sun disappearing behind the treetops on the far bank of the Yaruga. 'Very well then. But here's the bargain: one of you's to hurry over to the cottage and fetch some buttermilk for me to moisten my throat. The rest of you, meanwhile, are to decide whose story I'll tell, for I shan't tell everyone's tale today, even were I to spin yarns till morning. You have to decide: who do I tell of now, and who another time.'

The children began to yell again, each trying to outshout the others.

'Silence!' Stribog roared, brandishing his stick. 'I told you to choose, not shriek like jays: skaak-skaak-skaak! What'll it be? Whose story shall I tell?'

'Yennefer's,' Nimue squeaked. She was the youngest in the audience, nicknamed 'Squirt' owing to her height, and was stroking a kitten that was asleep on her lap. 'Tell us what happened to the sorceress afterwards. How she used magic to flee from the cov-cov-coven on Bald Mountain to rescue Ciri. I'd love to hear that. I want to be a sorceress when I grow up!'

'No chance!' shouted Bronik, the miller's son. 'Wipe your nose first, Squirt. They don't take snot-noses for sorcerers' apprentices! And you, old man, don't talk about Yennefer, but about Ciri and the Rats, when they went a-robbing and beat up—'

'Quiet,' Connor said, glum and pensive. 'You're all stupid, and that's that. If we're to hear one thing more tonight, let there be some order. Tell us about the Witcher and his band, when the company set off from the Yaruga—'

'I want to hear about Yennefer,' Nimue squealed.

'Me too,' Orla, her elder sister, joined in. 'I want to hear about her love for the Witcher. How they doted on each other. But be sure it's a happy ending! Nowt about fighting, oh no!'

'Quiet, you silly thing, who cares about love? We want war and fighting!'

'And the Witcher's sword!'

'No, Ciri and the Rats!'

'Shut your traps,' Connor said and looked around fiercely. 'Or I'll get a stick and give you a thrashing, you little snots! I said: let there be some order. Let him carry on about the Witcher, when he was travelling with Dandelion and Milva—'

'Yes!' Nimue squealed again. 'I want to hear about Milva, about Milva! Because if the sorceresses don't take me, I'm going to be an archer!'

'So we've decided,' Connor said. 'Look at him nodding, nose dipping like a corncrake's . . . Hey, old man! Wake up! Tell us about the Witcher, about Geralt the Witcher, I mean. When he formed his fellowship on the bank of the Yaruga.'

'But first,' Bronik interrupted, 'to salve our curiosity, tell us a little about the others. About what happened to them. Then it'll be easier for us to wait till you come back and continue the story. Just a little about Yennefer and Ciri. Please.'

'Yennefer' – Stribog giggled – 'flew from the enchanted castle, which was called Bald Mountain, using a spell. And she plopped straight into the ocean. Into the rough seas, among cruel rocks. But don't be afeared, it was a trifle for the enchantress. She didn't drown. She landed up on the Skellige Islands and found allies there. For you must know that a great fury arose in her against the Wizard Vilgefortz. Convinced he had kidnapped Ciri, she vowed to track him down, exact a terrible vengeance and free Ciri. And that's that. I'll tell you more another time.'

'And Ciri?'

'Ciri was still prowling with the Rats, calling herself "Falka". She had gained a taste for the robbers' life. For though no one knew it then, there was fury and cruelty in that girl. The worst of everything that hides in a person emerged from her and slowly got the upper hand. Oh, the witchers of Kaer Morhen made a great mistake by teaching her how to kill! And Ciri herself – dealing out death – didn't even suspect that the Grim Reaper was hot on her trail. For the terrible Bonhart was tracking her, hunting her. The meeting of these two, Bonhart and Ciri, was meant to be. But I shall recount their tale another time. For tonight you shall hear the tale of the Witcher.'

The children calmed down and crowded around the old man in a tight circle. They listened. Night was falling. The hemp shrubs, the raspberry bushes and hollyhocks growing near the cottage – friendly during the day – were suddenly transformed into an extraordinary, sinister forest. What was rustling there? Was it a mouse, or a terrible, fiery-eyed elf? Or perhaps a striga or a witch, hungry for children's flesh? Was it an ox stamping in the cowshed, or the hooves of cruel invaders' warhorses, crossing the Yaruga as they had a century before? Was that a nightjar flitting above the thatched roof, or perhaps a vampire, thirsty for blood? Or perhaps a beautiful sorceress, flying towards the distant sea with the aid of a magic spell?

'Geralt the Witcher,' the storyteller began, 'set out with his company towards the bogs and forests of Angren. And you must know that in those days there were truly wild forests in Angren, oh my, not like now, there aren't any forests like that left, unless in Brokilon . . . The company trekked eastwards, up the Yaruga, towards the wildernesses of the Black Forest. Things went well at first, but later, oh my . . . you'll learn what happened later . . .'

The tale of long-past, forgotten times unravelled and flowed. And the children listened.

The Witcher sat on a log at the top of a cliff from which unfolded a view over the wetlands and reed beds lining the bank of the Yaruga. The sun was sinking. Cranes soared up from the marshes, whooping, flying in a skein.

Everything's gone to pot, the Witcher thought, looking at the ruins of a woodman's shack and the thin ribbon of smoke rising from Milva's campfire. *Everything's fallen through. And it was going so well. My companions were strange, but at least they stood by me. We had a goal to achieve; close at hand, realistic, defined. Eastwards through Angren, towards Caed Dhu. It was going pretty well. But it had to get fucked up. Was it bad luck, or fate?*

The cranes sounded their bugle call.

Emiel Regis Rohellec Terzieff-Godefroy led the way, riding a Nilfgaardian bay captured by the Witcher near Armeria. The horse, although at first somewhat tetchy with the vampire and his herby smell, quickly became accustomed to him and didn't cause any more problems than Roach, who was walking alongside and was capable of bucking wildly if stung by a horsefly. Dandelion followed behind Regis and Geralt on Pegasus, with a bandaged head and a warlike mien. As he rode, the poet composed a heroic ballad, in whose melody and rhymes could be heard his recollections of their recent adventures. The song clearly implied that the author and performer had been the bravest of the brave during the adventures. Milva and Cahir Mawr Dyffryn aep Ceallach brought up the rear. Cahir was riding his recovered chestnut, pulling the grey laden with some of their modest accoutrement.

They finally left the riverside marshes, heading towards higher and drier, hilly terrain from which they could see the sparkling ribbon of the Great Yaruga to the south, and to the north the high, rocky approaches to the distant Mahakam massif. The weather was splendid, the sun was warm, and the mosquitoes had stopped biting and buzzing around their ears. Their boots and trousers had dried out. On the sunny slope brambles were black with fruit and the horses found grass to eat. The streams tumbling down from the hills flowed with crystal-clear water and were full of trout. When night fell, they were able to make a fire and even lie beside it. In short, everything was wonderful and their moods ought to have improved right away. But they didn't. The reason why became apparent at one of the first camps.

'Wait a moment, Geralt,' the poet began, looking around and clearing his throat. 'Don't rush back to the camp. Milva and I would like to talk to you in private. It's about . . . you know . . . Regis.'

'Ah,' the Witcher said, laying a handful of brushwood on the ground. 'So now you're afraid? It's a bit late for that.'

'Stop that,' Dandelion said with a grimace. 'We've accepted him as a companion; he's offered to help us search for Ciri. He saved my neck from the noose, which I shall never forget. But hell's bells, we are feeling something like fear. Does that surprise you? You've spent your entire life hunting and killing his like.'

'I did not kill him. And I'm not planning to. Does that declaration suffice? If it doesn't, even though my heart's brimming with sorrow for you, I can't cure you of your anxieties. Paradoxically, Regis is the only one among us capable of curing anything.'

'Stop that,' the troubadour repeated, annoyed. 'You aren't talking to Yennefer; you can drop the tortuous eloquence. Give us a simple answer to a simple question.'

'Then ask it. Without any tortuous eloquence.'

'Regis is a vampire. It's no secret what vampires feed on. What will happen when he gets seriously hungry? Yes, yes, we saw him eating fish soup, and since then he's been eating and drinking with us, as normal as anyone. But . . . will he be able to control his craving . . . Geralt, do I have to spell it out to you?'

'He controlled his blood lust, when gore was pouring from your head. He didn't even lick his fingers after he'd finished applying the dressing. And during the full moon, when we'd been drinking his mandrake moonshine and were sleeping in his shack, he had the perfect opportunity to get his hands on us. Have you checked for puncture marks on your swanlike neck?'

'Don't take the piss, Witcher,' Milva growled. 'You know more about vampires than we do. You're mocking Dandelion, so tell me. I was raised in the forest, I didn't go to school. I'm ignorant. But it's no fault of mine. It's not right to mock. I – I'm ashamed to say – am also a bit afraid of . . . Regis.'

'Not unreasonably,' Geralt said, nodding. 'He's a so-called higher vampire. He's extremely dangerous. Were he our enemy, I'd be afraid of him too. But, bloody hell, for reasons unknown to me, he's our companion. Right now, he's leading us to Caed Dhu, to the druids, who may be able to help me get information about Ciri. I'm desperate, so I want to seize the chance and certainly not give up on it. Which is why I've agreed to his vampiric company.'

'Only because of that?'

'No,' he answered, with a trace of reluctance. Then he finally decided to be frank. 'Not just that. He . . . he behaves decently. He didn't hesitate to act during that girl's trial at the camp by the Chotla. Although he knew it would unmask him.'

'He took that red-hot horseshoe from the fire,' Dandelion recalled. 'Why, he held it in his hand for a good few seconds without even flinching. None of us would be able to repeat that trick; not even with a roast potato.'

'He's invulnerable to fire.'

'What else is he capable of?'

'He can become invisible if he wishes. He can bewitch with his gaze, and put someone in a deep sleep. He did that to the guards in Vissegerd's camp. He can assume the form of a bat and fly. I presume he can only do those things at night, during a full moon, but I could be wrong. He's already surprised me a few times, so he might still have something up his sleeve. I suspect he's quite remarkable even among vampires. He imitates humans perfectly, and has done so for years. He baffles horses and dogs – which can sense his true nature – using the smell of the herbs he keeps with him at all times. Though my medallion doesn't react to him either, and it ought to. I tell you; he defies easy classification. Talk to him if you want to know more. He's our companion. There should be nothing left unsaid between us, particularly not mutual mistrust or fear. Let's get back to the camp. Help me with this brushwood.'

'Geralt?'

'Yes, Dandelion.'

'If . . . and I'm asking purely theoretically . . . If . . .'

'I don't know,' the Witcher replied honestly and frankly. 'I don't know if I'd be capable of killing him. I truly would prefer not to be forced to try.'

Dandelion took the Witcher's advice to heart, deciding to clear up the uncertainty and dispel their doubts. He began as soon as they set off. With his usual tact.

'Milva!' he suddenly called as they were riding, sneaking a glance at the vampire. 'Why don't you ride on ahead with your bow, and bring down a fawn or wild boar. I've had enough of damned black-berries and mushrooms, fish and mussels. I fancy eating a hunk of real meat for a change. How about you, Regis?'

'I beg your pardon?' the vampire said, lifting his head from the horse's neck.

'Meat!' the poet repeated emphatically. 'I'm trying to persuade Milva to go hunting. Fancy some fresh meat?'

'Yes, I do.'

'And blood. Would you like some fresh blood?'

'Blood?' Regis asked, swallowing. 'No. I'll decline the blood. But, if you have a taste for some, feel free.'

Geralt, Milva and Cahir observed an awkward, sepulchral silence.

'I know what this is about, Dandelion,' Regis said slowly. 'And let me reassure you. I'm a vampire, but I don't drink blood.'

The silence became as heavy as lead. But Dandelion wouldn't have been Dandelion if he had remained silent.

'You must have misunderstood me,' he said seemingly light-heartedly. 'I didn't mean . . .'

'I don't drink blood,' Regis interrupted. 'Haven't for many years. I gave it up.'

'What do you mean, gave it up?'

'Just that.'

'I really don't understand . . .'

'Forgive me. It's a personal matter.'

'But . . .'

'Dandelion,' the Witcher burst out, turning around in the saddle. 'Regis just told you to fuck off. He just said it more politely. Be so good as to shut your trap.'

However, the seeds of anxiety and doubts that had been sown now germinated and sprouted. When they stopped for the night, the ambience was still heavy and tense, which even Milva shooting down a plump barnacle goose by the river couldn't relieve. They covered the catch in clay, roasted and ate it, gnawing even the tiniest bones clean. They had sated their hunger, but the anxiety remained. The conversation was awkward despite Dandelion's titanic efforts. The poet's chatter became a monologue, so obviously apparent that even he finally noticed it and stopped talking. Only the sound of the horses crunching their hay disturbed the deathly silence around the campfire.

In spite of the late hour no one seemed to be getting ready for bed. Milva was boiling water in a pot above the fire and straightening the crumpled fletchings of her arrows in the steam. Cahir was repairing a torn boot buckle. Geralt was whittling a piece of wood. And Regis swept his eyes over all of them in turn.

'Very well,' he said at last. 'I see it is inevitable. It would appear I ought to have explained a few things to you long ago . . .'

'No one expects it of you,' Geralt said. He threw the stick he had been lengthily and enthusiastically carving into the fire and looked up. 'I don't need explanations. I'm the old-fashioned type. When I hold my hand out to someone and accept him as a comrade, it means more to me than a contract signed in the presence of a notary.'

'I'm old-fashioned too,' Cahir said, still bent over his boot.

'I don't know any other custom,' Milva said drily, placing another arrow in the steam rising up from the pot.

'Don't worry about Dandelion's chatter,' the Witcher added. 'He can't help it. And you don't have to confide in us or explain anything. We haven't confided in you either.'

'I nonetheless think' – the vampire smiled faintly – 'that you'd like to hear what I have to say, even though no one's forcing you to. I feel the need for openness towards the individuals I extend a hand to and accept as my comrades.'

This time no one said anything.

'I ought to begin by saying,' Regis said a moment later, 'that all fears linked to my vampiric nature are groundless. I won't attack anybody, nor will I creep around at night trying to sink my teeth into somebody's neck. And this does not merely concern my comrades, to whom my relationship is no less old-fashioned than theirs is to me. I don't touch blood. Not at all and never. I stopped drinking it when it became a problem for me. A serious problem, which I had difficulty solving.

'In fact, the problem arose and acquired negative characteristics in true textbook style,' he continued a moment later. 'Even during my youth I enjoyed . . . er . . . the pleasures of good company, in which respect I was no different to the majority of my peers. You know what it's like; you were young too. With humans, however, there exists a system of rules and restrictions: parental authority, guardians, superiors and elders – morals, ultimately. We have nothing like that. Youngsters have complete freedom and exploit it. They create their own patterns of behaviour. Stupid ones, you understand. It's real youthful foolishness. "Don't fancy a drink? And you call yourself a vampire?" "He doesn't drink? Don't invite him, he'll spoil the party!" I didn't want to spoil the party, and the thought of losing social approval terrified me. So I partied. Revelries and frolics, shindigs and booze-ups; every full moon we'd fly to a village and drink from anyone we found. The foulest, the worst class of . . . er . . . fluid. It made no difference to us whose it was, as long as there was . . . er . . . haemoglobin . . . It can't be a party without blood, after all! And I was terribly shy with vampire girls, too, until I'd had a drop.'

Regis fell silent, lost in thought. No one responded. Geralt felt a terrible urge to have a drink himself.

'It got rowdier and rowdier,' the vampire continued. 'And worse and worse as time went on. Occasionally I went on such benders that I didn't return to the crypt for three or four nights in a row. A tiny amount of fluid and I lost control, which, of course, didn't stop me from continuing the party. My friends? Well, you know what they're like. Some of them tried to make me see reason, so I took offence. Others were a bad influence, and dragged me out of the crypt to revels. Why, they even set me up with . . . er . . . playthings. And they enjoyed themselves at my expense.'

Milva, still busy restoring her arrows' flattened fletchings, murmured angrily. Cahir had finished repairing his boot and seemed to be asleep.

'Later on,' Regis continued, 'more alarming symptoms appeared. Parties and company began to play an absolutely secondary role. I noticed I could manage without them. Blood was all I needed, was all that mattered, even when it was . . .'

'Just you and your shadow?' Dandelion interjected.

'Worse than that,' Regis answered calmly. 'I don't even cast one.'

He was silent for a while.

'Then I met a special vampire girl. It might have been – I think it was – serious. I settled down. But not for long. She left me. So I began to double my intake. Despair and grief, as you know, are perfect excuses. Everyone thinks they understand. Even I thought I understood. But I was merely applying theory to practice. Am I boring you? I'll try to make it short. I finally began to do absolutely unacceptable things, the kind of things no vampire does. I flew under the influence. One night the boys sent me to the village to fetch some blood, and I missed my target: a girl who was walking to the well. I smashed straight into the well at top speed . . . The villagers almost beat me to death, but fortunately they didn't know how to go about it . . . They punctured me with stakes, chopped my head off, poured holy water all over me and buried me. Can you imagine how I felt when I woke up?'

'We can,' Milva said, examining an arrow. Everyone looked at her strangely. The archer coughed and looked away. Regis smiled faintly.

'I won't be long now,' he said. 'In the grave I had plenty of time to rethink things . . .'

'Plenty?' Geralt asked. 'How much?'

Regis looked at him.

'Professional curiosity? Around fifty years. After I'd regenerated I decided to pull myself together. It wasn't easy, but I did it. And I haven't drunk since.'

'Not at all?' Dandelion said, and stuttered. But his curiosity got the better of him. 'Not at all? Never? But . . . ?'

'Dandelion,' Geralt said, slightly raising his eyebrows. 'Get a grip and think. In silence.'

'I beg your pardon,' the poet grunted.

'Don't apologise,' the vampire said placatingly. 'And, Geralt, don't chasten him. I understand his curiosity. I – by which I mean I and my myth – personify all his human fears. One cannot expect a human to rid himself of them. Fear plays a no less important role in the human psyche than all the other emotions. A psyche without fears would be crippled.'

'But,' Dandelion said, regaining his poise, 'you don't frighten me. Does that make me a cripple?'

For a moment Geralt expected Regis to show his fangs and cure Dandelion of his supposed disability, but he was wrong. The vampire wasn't inclined towards theatrical gestures.

'I was talking about fears deeply lodged in the consciousness and the subconscious,' he explained calmly. 'Please don't be hurt by this metaphor, but a crow isn't afraid of a hat and coat hung on a stick, after it has overcome that fear and alighted on them. But when the wind jerks the scarecrow, the bird flees.'

'The crow's behaviour might be seen as a struggle for life,' Cahir observed from the darkness.

'Struggle, schmuggle.' Milva snorted. 'The crow isn't afraid of the scarecrow. It's afraid of men, because men throw stones and shoot at it.'

'A struggle for life.' Geralt nodded. 'But in human – not corvine – terms. Thank you for the explanation, Regis, we accept it whole-heartedly. But don't go rooting about in the depths of the human subconscious. Milva's right. The reasons people react in panic-stricken horror at the sight of a thirsty vampire aren't irrational, they are a result of the will to survive.'

'Thus speaks an expert,' the vampire said, bowing slightly towards him. 'An expert whose professional pride would not allow him to take money for fighting imaginary fears. The self-respecting witcher who only hires himself out to fight real, unequivocally dangerous evil. This professional will probably want to explain why a vampire is a greater threat than a dragon or a wolf. They have fangs too, don't forget.'

'Perhaps because the latter two use their fangs to stave off hunger or in self-defence, but never for fun or for breaking the ice or over-coming shyness towards the opposite sex.'

'People know nothing about that,' riposted Regis. 'You have known it for some time, but the rest of our company have only just discovered the truth. The remaining majority are deeply convinced that vampires do not drink for fun but feed on blood, and nothing but blood. Needless to say, human blood. Blood is a life-giving fluid; its loss results in the weakening of the body, the seeping away of a vital force. You reason thus: a creature that spills our blood is our deadly enemy. And a creature that attacks us for our blood, because it lives on it, is doubly evil. It grows in vital force at the expense of ours. For its species to thrive, ours must fade away. Ultimately a creature like that is repellent to you humans, for although you are aware of blood's life-giving qualities, it is disgusting to you. Would any of you drink blood? I doubt it. And there are people who grow weak or even faint at the sight of blood. In some societies women are con-sidered unclean for a few days every month and they are isolated—'

'Among savages, perhaps,' Cahir interrupted. 'And I think only Nordlings grow faint at the sight of blood.'

'We've strayed,' the Witcher said, looking up. 'We've deviated from a straight path into a tangle of dubious philosophy. Do you think, Regis, that it would make a difference to humans were they to know you don't treat them as prey, but as a watering hole? Where do you see the irrationality of fears here? Vampires drink human blood; that particular fact cannot be challenged. A human treated by a vampire as a demijohn of vodka loses his strength, that's also clear. A totally drained human – so to speak – loses his vitality definitively. He dies. Forgive me, but the fear of death can't be lumped together with an aversion to blood. Menstrual or otherwise.'

'Your talk's so clever it makes my head spin,' Milva snorted. 'And all your wisdom comes down to what's under a woman's skirt. Woeful philosophers.'

'Let's cast aside the symbolism of blood for a moment,' Regis said. 'For here the myths really do have certain grounds in facts. Let's focus on those universally accepted myths with no grounds in fact. After all, everyone knows that if someone is bitten by a vampire and survives they must become a vampire themselves. Right?'

'Right,' Dandelion said. 'There's even a ballad—'

'Do you understand basic arithmetic?'

'I've studied all seven liberal arts, and was awarded a degree summa cum laude.'

'After the Conjunction of the Spheres there remained approximately one thousand two hundred higher vampires in your world. The number of teetotallers – because there is a considerable number of them – balances the number who drink excessively, as I did in my day. Generally, the statistically average vampire drinks during every full moon, for the full moon is a holy day for us, which we usually . . . er . . . celebrate with a drink. Applying the matter to the human calendar and assuming there are twelve full moons a year gives us the theoretical sum of fourteen thousand four hundred humans bitten annually. Since the Conjunction – once again calculating according to your reckoning – one thousand five hundred years have passed. A simple calculation will show that at the present moment, twenty-one million six hundred thousand vampires ought to exist in the world. If that figure is augmented by exponential growth . . .'

'That'll do.' Dandelion sighed. 'I don't have an abacus, but I can imagine the number. Actually I can't imagine it, and you're saying that infection from a bite is nonsense and a fabrication.'

'Thank you,' Regis said, bowing. 'Let's move on to the next myth, which states that a vampire is a human being who has died – but not completely. He doesn't rot or crumble to dust in the grave. He lies there as fresh as a daisy and ruddy-faced, ready to go forth and bite a victim. Where does that myth come from, if not from your subconscious and irrational aversion to your dearly departed? You surround the dead with veneration and memory, you dream of immortality, and in your myths and legends there's always someone being resurrected, conquering death. But were your esteemed late great-grandfather really to suddenly rise from the grave and order a beer, panic would ensue. And it doesn't surprise me. Organic matter, in which the vital processes have ceased, succumbs to degradation, which manifests itself very unpleasantly. The corpse stinks and dissolves into slime. The immortal soul, an indispensable element of your myths, abandons the stinking carcass in disgust and spirits away, forgive the pun. The soul is pure, and one can easily venerate it. But then you invented a revolting kind of spirit, which doesn't soar, doesn't abandon the cadaver, why, it doesn't even stink. That's repulsive and unnatural! For you, the living dead is the most revolting of revolting anomalies. Some moron even coined the term "the undead", which you're ever so keen to bestow on us.'

'Humans,' Geralt said, smiling slightly, 'are a primitive and superstitious race. They find it difficult to fully understand and appropriately name a creature that resurrects, even though it's had stakes pushed through it, had its head removed and been buried in the ground for fifty years.'

'Yes, indeed,' said the vampire, impervious to the derision. 'Your mutated race is capable of regenerating its fingernails, toenails, hair and epidermis, but is unable to accept the fact that other races are more advanced in that respect. That inability is not the result of your primitiveness. Quite the opposite: it's a result of egotism and a conviction in your own perfection. Anything that is more perfect than you must be a repulsive aberration. And repulsive aberrations are consigned to myths, for sociological reasons.'

'I don't understand fuck all,' Milva announced calmly, brushing the hair from her forehead with an arrow tip. 'I hear you're talking about fairy-tales, and even I know fairy-tales, though I'm a foolish wench from the forest. So it astonishes me that you aren't afraid of the sun, Regis. In fairy-tales sunlight burns a vampire to ash. Should I lump it together with the other fairy-tales?'

'Of course you should,' Regis confirmed. 'You believe a vampire is only dangerous at night, that the first rays of the sun turn him into ash. At the root of this myth, invented around primeval campfires, lies your heliophilia, by which I mean love of warmth; the circadian rhythm, which relies upon diurnal activity. For you the night is cold, dark, sinister, menacing, and full of danger. The sunrise, however, represents another victory in the fight for life, a new day, the continuation of existence. Sunlight carries with it light and the sun; and the sun's rays, which are invigorating for you, bring with them the destruction of hostile monsters. A vampire turns to ash, a troll succumbs to petrifaction, a werewolf turns back into a human, and a goblin flees, covering his eyes. Nocturnal predators return to their lairs and cease to be a threat. The world belongs to you until sunset. I repeat and stress: this myth arose around ancient campfires. Today it is only a myth, for now you light and heat your dwelling places. Even though you are still governed by the solar rhythm, you have managed to appropriate the night. We, higher vampires, have also moved some way from our primeval crypts. We have appropriated the day. The analogy is complete. Does this explanation satisfy you, my dear Milva?'

'Not in the slightest,' the archer replied, throwing the arrow away. 'But I think I've got it. I'm learning. I'll be learned one day. Sociolation, petrificology, werewolfation, crap-ology. In schools they lecture and birch you. It's more pleasant learning with you lot. My head hurts a bit, but my arse is still in one piece.'

'One thing is beyond question and is easy to observe,' Dandelion said. 'The sun's rays don't turn you into ash, Regis. The sun's warmth has as much effect on you as that red-hot horseshoe you so nimbly removed from the fire with your bare hands. Returning, however, to your analogies, for us humans the day will always remain the natural time for activity, and the night the natural time for rest. That is our physical structure. During the day, for example, we see better than at night. Except Geralt, who sees just as well at all times, but he's a mutant. Was it also a question of mutation among vampires?'

'One could call it that,' Regis agreed. 'Although I would argue that when mutation is spread over a sufficiently long period it ceases to be mutation and becomes evolution. But what you said about physical structure is apt. Adapting to sunlight was an unpleasant necessity for us. In order to survive, we had to become like humans in that respect. Mimicry, I'd call it. Which had its consequences. To use a metaphor: we lay down in the sick man's bed.'

'I beg your pardon?'

'There are reasons to believe that sunlight is lethal in the long run. There's a theory that in about five thousand years, at a conservative estimate, this world will only be inhabited by lunar creatures, which are active at night.'

'I'm glad I won't be around that long.' Cahir sighed, then yawned widely. 'I don't know about you, but the intensive diurnal activity is reminding me of the need for nocturnal sleep.'

'Me too,' the Witcher said, stretching. 'And there are only a few hours left until the dawning of the murderous sun. But before sleep overcomes us . . . Regis, in the name of science and the spread of knowledge, puncture some other myths about vampirism. Because I bet you've still got at least one.'

'Indeed.' The vampire nodded. 'I have one more. It's the last, but in no sense any less important. It is the myth behind your sexual phobias.'

Cahir snorted softly.

'I left this myth until the end,' Regis said, looking him up and down. 'I would have tactfully passed over it, but since Geralt has challenged me, I won't spare you. Humans are most powerfully influenced by fears with a sexual origin. The virgin fainting in the embrace of a vampire who drinks her blood. The young man falling prey to the vile practices of a female vampire running her lips over his body. That's how you imagine it. Oral rape. Vampires paralyse their victims with fear and force them to have oral sex. Or rather, a revolting parody of oral sex. And there is something disgusting about sex like that, which, after all, rules out procreation.'

'Speak for yourself,' the Witcher muttered.

'An act crowned not by procreation, but by sensual delight and death,' Regis continued. 'You have turned it into a baleful myth. You unconsciously dream of something like it, but shy away from offering it to your lovers. So it's done for you by the mythological vampire, who as a result swells to become a fascinating symbol of evil.'

'Didn't I say it?' Milva yelled, as soon as Dandelion had finished explaining to her what Regis had been talking about. 'It's all they ever have on their minds! It starts off brainy, but always comes back to humping!'

The distant trumpeting of cranes slowly died away.

The next day, the Witcher recalled, *we set off in much better humour. And then, utterly unexpectedly, war caught up with us again.*

They travelled through a practically deserted and strategically unimportant country covered in huge, dense forests, unappealing to invaders. Although Nilfgaard was close at last, and they were only separated from the imperial lands by the broad waters of the Great Yaruga, it was difficult terrain to cover. Their astonishment was all the greater because of that.

War appeared in a less spectacular way than it had in Brugge and Sodden, where the horizon had glowed with fires at night, and during the day columns of black smoke had slashed the blue sky. It was not so picturesque here in Angren. It was much worse. They suddenly saw a murder of crows circling over the forest with a horrible cawing, and soon after they happened upon some corpses. Although the bodies had been stripped of their clothing and were impossible to identify, they bore the infallible and clear marks of violent death. Those people had been killed in combat. And not just killed. Most of the corpses were lying in the undergrowth, but some, cruelly mutilated, hung from trees by their arms or legs, lay sprawled on burnt-out pyres, or were impaled on stakes. And they stank. The whole of Angren had suddenly begun to reek with the monstrous, repulsive stench of barbarity.

It wasn't long before they had to hide in ravines and thick undergrowth, for to their left and right, and in front and behind them, the earth shook with cavalry horses' hooves, and more and more units passed their hideout, stirring up dust.

'Once again,' Dandelion said, shaking his head, 'once again we don't know who's fighting who and why. Once again we don't know who's behind us or who's ahead of us, or what direction they're headed. Who's attacking and who's retreating. The pox take it all. I don't know if I've ever told you, but I see it like this: war is no different to a whorehouse with a fire raging through it—'

'You have,' Geralt interrupted. 'A hundred times.'

'What are they fighting over?' the poet asked, spitting violently. 'Juniper bushes and sand? I mean, this exquisite country hasn't got anything else to offer.'

'There were elves among the bodies in the bushes,' Milva said. 'Scoia'tael commandos march this way, they always have. This is the route volunteers from Dol Blathanna and the Blue Mountains take when they head for Temeria. Someone wants to block their path. That's what I think.'

'It's likely,' Regis admitted, 'that the Temerian Army would try to ambush the Squirrels here. But I'd say there are too many soldiers in the area. I surmise the Nilfgaardians have crossed the Yaruga.'

'I surmise the same,' the Witcher said, grimacing a little as he looked at Cahir's stony countenance. 'The bodies we saw this morning carried the marks of Nilfgaardian combat methods.'

'They're all as bad as each other,' Milva snapped, unexpectedly taking the side of the young Nilfgaardian. 'And don't look daggers at Cahir, because now you're bound by the same, bizarre fate. He dies if he falls into the Blacks' clutches, and you escaped a Temerian

302

noose a while back. So it's no use trying to find out which army is in front of us and which behind, who are our comrades, who are our enemies, who's good and who's evil. Now they're all our common foes, no matter what colours they're wearing.'

'You're right.'

'Strange,' Dandelion said, when the next day they had to hide in another ravine and wait for another cavalcade to pass. 'The army are rumbling over the hills, and yet woodmen are felling trees by the Yaruga as if nothing was happening. Can you hear it?'

'Perhaps they aren't woodmen,' Cahir wondered. 'Perhaps it's the army, and they're sappers.'

'No, they're woodmen,' Regis said. 'It's clear nothing is capable of interrupting the mining of Angren gold.'

'What gold?'

'Take a closer look at those trees,' the vampire said, once again assuming the tone of an all-knowing, patronising sage instructing mere mortals or the simple-minded. He often acquired that tone, which Geralt found somewhat irritating. 'Those trees,' Regis repeated, 'are cedars, sycamores and Angren pines. Very valuable material. There are timber ports all around here, from which logs are floated downstream. They're felling trees everywhere and axes are thudding away day and night. The war we can see and hear is beginning to make sense. Nilfgaard, as you know, has captured the mouth of the Yaruga, Cintra and Verden, as well as Upper Sodden. At this moment probably also Brugge and part of Lower Sodden. That means that the timber being floated from Angren is already supplying the imperial sawmills and shipyards. The northern kingdoms are trying to halt the process, while the Nilfgaardians, on the contrary, want to fell and float as much as possible.'

'And we, as usual, have found ourselves in a tight spot,' Dandelion said, nodding. 'Seeing as we have to get to Caed Dhu, right through the very centre of Angren and this timber war. Isn't there another bloody way?'

*

I asked Regis the same question, the Witcher recalled, staring at the sun setting over the Yaruga, *as soon as the thudding of hooves had faded into the distance, things had calmed down and we were finally able to continue our journey.*

'Another way to Caed Dhu?' the vampire pondered. 'Which avoids the hills and keeps out of the soldiers' way? Indeed, there is such a way. Not very comfortable and not very safe. And it's longer too. But I guarantee we won't meet any soldiers there.'

'Go on.'

'We can turn south and try to get across a low point in one of the Yaruga's meanders. Across Ysgith. Do you know Ysgith, Witcher?'

'Yes.'

'Have you ever ridden through those forests?'

'Of course.'

'The calm in your voice,' the vampire said, clearing his throat, 'would seem to signify you accept the idea. Well, there are five of us, including a witcher, a warrior and an archer. Experience, two swords and a bow. Too little to take on a Nilfgaardian raiding party, but it ought to be sufficient for Ysgith.'

Ysgith, the Witcher thought. *More than thirty square miles of bogs and mud, dotted with tarns. And murky forests full of weird trees dividing up the bogs. Some have trunks covered in scales. At the base they're as bulbous as onions, thinning towards the top, ending in dense, flat crowns. Others are low and misshapen, crouching on piles of roots twisted like octopuses, with beards of moss and shrivelled bog lichen hanging on their bare branches. Those beards sway, not from the wind though, but from poisonous swamp gas. Ysgith means mud hole. 'Stink hole' would be more appropriate.*

And the mud and bogs, the tarns and lakes overgrown with duck-weed and pondweed teem with life. Ysgith isn't just inhabited by beavers, frogs, tortoises and water birds. It is swarming with much more dangerous creatures, armed with pincers, tentacles and prehensile limbs, which they use to catch, mutilate, drown and tear apart their prey. There are so many of these creatures that no one has ever been able to identify and classify them all. Not even witchers. Geralt himself had rarely hunted in Ysgith and never in Lower Angren. The land was sparsely populated, and the few humans who lived on the fringes of the bogs were accustomed to treating the monsters as part of the landscape. They kept their distance, but it rarely occurred to them to hire a witcher to exterminate the monstrosities. Rarely, however, did not mean never. So Geralt knew Ysgith and its dangers.

Two swords and a bow, he thought. *And experience, my witcher's expertise. We ought to manage in a group. Especially when I'll be riding in the vanguard and keeping close watch on everything. On the rotten tree trunks, piles of weed, scrub, tussocks of grass; and the plants, orchids included. For in Ysgith even the orchids sometimes only look like plants, but are actually venomous crab spiders. I'll have to keep Dandelion on a short leash, and make sure he doesn't touch anything. Particularly since there's no shortage of plant life which likes to supplement its chlorophyll diet with morsels of meat. Plants whose shoots are as deadly as a crab spider's venom when they come into contact with skin. And the gas, of course. Not to mention poisonous fumes. We shall have to find a way to cover our mouths and noses . . .*

'Well?' Regis asked, pulling him out of his reverie. 'Do you accept the plan?'

'Yes, I do. Let's go.'

Something finally prompted me, the Witcher recalled, *not to talk to the rest of the company about the plan to cross Ysgith. And to ask Regis not to mention it either. I don't know why I was reluctant. Today, when everything is absolutely and totally screwed up, I might claim to have been aware of Milva's behaviour. Of the problems she was having. Of her obvious symptoms. But it wouldn't be true; I didn't notice anything, and what I did notice I ignored. Like a blockhead. So we continued eastwards, reluctant to turn towards the bogs.*

On the other hand it was good that we lingered, he thought, drawing his sword and running his thumb over the razor-sharp blade. *Had we headed straight for Ysgith then, I wouldn't have this weapon today.*

*

They hadn't seen or heard any soldiers since dawn. Milva led the way, riding far ahead of the rest of the company. Regis, Dandelion and Cahir were talking.

'I just hope those druids will deign to help us find Ciri,' the poet said worriedly. 'I've met druids and, believe me, they are uncooperative, tight-lipped, unfriendly, eccentric recluses. They might not talk to us at all, far less use magic to help us.'

'Regis knows one of the druids from Caed Dhu,' the Witcher reminded them.

'Are you sure the friendship doesn't go back three or four centuries?'

'It's considerably more recent than that,' the vampire assured them with a mysterious smile. 'Anyhow, druids enjoy longevity. They're always out in the open, in the bosom of primordial and unpolluted nature, which has a marvellous effect on the health. Breathe deeply, Dandelion, fill your lungs with forest air and you'll be healthy too.'

'I'll soon grow fur in this bloody wilderness,' Dandelion said sneeringly. 'When I sleep, I dream of inns, drinks and bathhouses. A primordial pox on this primordial nature. I really have my doubts about its miraculous effect on the health, particularly mental health. The said druids are the best example, because they're eccentric madmen. They're fanatical about nature and protecting it. I've witnessed them petitioning the authorities more times than I care to remember. Don't hunt, don't cut down trees, don't empty cesspits into rivers and other similar codswallop. And the height of idiocy was the visit of a delegation all arrayed in mistletoe wreathes to the court of King Ethain in Cidaris. I happened to be there . . .'

'What did they want?' Geralt asked, curious.

'Cidaris, as you know, is a kingdom where most people make a living from fishing. The druids demanded that the king order the use of nets with mesh of a specific size, and harshly punish anyone who used finer nets than instructed. Ethain's jaw dropped, and the mistletoers explained that limiting the size of mesh was the only way to protect fish stocks from depletion. The king led them out onto the terrace, pointed to the sea and told them how his bravest sailor had once sailed westwards for two months and only returned because supplies of fresh water had run out on his vessel, and there still wasn't a sign of land on the horizon. Could the druids, he asked, imagine the fish stocks in a sea like that being exhausted? By all means, the mistletoers confirmed. For though there was no doubt sea fishery would endure the longest as a means of acquiring food directly from nature, the time would come when fish would run out and hunger would stare them all in the face. Then it would be absolutely necessary to fish using nets with large mesh, to only catch fully grown specimens, and protect the small fry. Ethain asked when, in the druids' opinion, this dreadful time of hunger would occur, and they said in about two thousand years, according to their forecasts. The king bade them a courteous farewell and requested that they drop by in around a thousand years, when he would think it over. The mistletoers didn't get the joke and began to protest, so they were thrown out.'

'They're like that, those druids,' Cahir agreed. 'Back home, in Nilfgaard—'

'Got you!' Dandelion cried triumphantly. 'Back home, in Nilfgaard! Only yesterday, when I called you a Nilfgaardian, you leapt up as though you'd been stung by a hornet! Perhaps you could finally decide who you are, Cahir.'

'To you,' Cahir said, shrugging, 'I have to be a Nilfgaardian, for as I see nothing will convince you otherwise. However, for the sake of precision please know that in the Empire such a title is reserved exclusively for indigenous residents of the capital and its closest environs, lying by the lower reaches of the Alba. My family originates in Vicovaro, and thus—'

'Shut your traps!' Milva commanded abruptly and not very politely from the vanguard.

They all immediately fell silent and reined in their horses, having learned by now that it was a sign the girl had seen, heard or instinctively sensed something edible, provided it could be stalked and shot with an arrow. Milva had indeed raised her bow to shoot, but had not dismounted. That meant it was not about food. Geralt approached her cautiously.

'Smoke,' she said bluntly.

'I can't see it.'

'Sniff it then.'

The archer's sense of smell had not deceived her, even though the scent of smoke was faint. It couldn't have been the smoke from the conflagration behind them.

This smoke, Geralt observed, *smells nice. It's coming from a camp-fire on which something is being roasted.*

'Do we steer clear of it?' Milva asked quietly.

'After we've taken a look,' he replied, dismounting from his mare and handing the reins to Dandelion. 'It would be good to know what we're steering clear of. And who we have behind us. Come with me, Maria. The rest of you stay in your saddles. Be vigilant.'

From the brush at the edge of the forest unfolded a view of a vast clearing with logs piled up in even cords of wood. A very thin ribbon of smoke rose from between the woodpiles. Geralt calmed down somewhat, as nothing was moving in his field of vision and there was too little space between the woodpiles for a large group to be hiding there. Milva shared his opinion.

'No horses,' she whispered. 'They aren't soldiers. Woodmen, I'd say.'

'Me too. But I'll go and check. Cover me.'

When he approached, cautiously picking his way around the piles of logs, he heard voices. He came closer. And was absolutely amazed. But his ears hadn't let him down.

'Half a contract in diamonds!'

'Small slam in diamonds!'

'Barrel!'

'Pass. Your lead! Show your hand! Cards on the table! What the . . . ?'

'Ha-ha-ha! Just the knave and some low numbers. Got you right where it hurts! I'll make you suffer, before you get a small slam!'

'We'll see about that. My knave. What? It's been taken? Hey, Yazon, you really got fucked over!'

'Why didn't you play the lady, shithead? Pshaw, I ought to take my rod to you . . .'

The Witcher, perhaps, might still have been cautious; after all, various different individuals could have been playing Barrel, and many people might have been called Yazon. However, a familiar hoarse squawking interrupted the card players' excited voices.

''Uuuckkk . . . me!'

'Hello, boys,' Geralt said, emerging from behind the woodpile. 'I'm delighted to see you. Particularly as you're at full force again, including the parrot.'

'Bloody hell!' Zoltan Chivay said, dropping his cards in astonishment, then quickly leaping to his feet, so suddenly that Field Marshal Windbag, who was sitting on his shoulder, fluttered his wings and shrieked in alarm. 'The Witcher, as I live and breathe! Or is it a mirage? Percival, do you see what I see?'

Percival Schuttenbach, Munro Bruys, Yazon Varda and Figgis Merluzzo surrounded Geralt and seriously strained his right hand with their iron-hard grips. And when the rest of the company emerged from behind the logs, the shouts of joy increased accordingly.

'Milva! Regis!' Zoltan shouted, embracing them all. 'Dandelion, alive and kicking, even if your skull's bandaged! And what do you say, you bloody busker, about this latest melodramatic banality? Life, it turns out, isn't poetry! And do you know why? Because it's so resistant to criticism!'

'Where's Caleb Stratton?' Dandelion asked, looking around.

Zoltan and the others fell silent and grew solemn.

'Caleb,' the dwarf finally said, sniffing, 'is sleeping in a birch wood, far from his beloved peaks and Mount Carbon. When the Blacks overwhelmed us by the Ina, his legs were too slow and he didn't make it to the forest . . . He caught a sword across the head and when he fell they dispatched him with bear spears. But come on, cheer up, we've already mourned him and that'll do. We ought to be cheerful. After all, you got out of the madness in the camp in one piece. Why, the company's even grown, I see.'

Cahir inclined his head a little under the dwarf's sharp gaze, but said nothing.

'Come on, sit you down,' Zoltan invited. 'We're roasting a lamb here. We happened upon it a few days ago, lonely and sad. We stopped it from dying a miserable death from hunger or in a wolf's maw by slaughtering it mercifully and turning it into food. Sit down. And I'd like a few words with you, Regis. And Geralt, if you would.'

Two women were sitting behind the woodpile. One of them, who was suckling an infant, turned away in embarrassment at the sight of them approaching. Nearby, a young woman with an arm wrapped in none too clean rags was playing with two children on the sand. As soon as she raised her misty, blank eyes to him the Witcher recognised her.

'We untied her from the wagon, which was already in flames,' the dwarf explained. 'It almost finished the way that priest wanted. You know, the one who was after her blood. She passed through a baptism of fire, nonetheless. The flames were licking at her, scorching her to the raw flesh. We dressed her wounds as well as we could. We covered her in lard, but it's a bit messy. Barber-surgeon, if you would . . . ?'

'Right away.'

When Regis tried to peel off the dressing the girl whimpered, retreating and covering her face with her good hand. Geralt approached to hold her still, but the vampire gestured him to stop. He looked deeply into the girl's vacant eyes, and she immediately calmed down and relaxed. Her head drooped gently on her chest. She didn't even flinch when Regis carefully peeled off the dirty rag and smeared an intense and strange smelling ointment on her burnt arm.

Geralt turned his head, pointed with his chin at the two women and the two children, and then bored his eyes into the dwarf. Zoltan cleared his throat.

'We came across the two young 'uns and the women here in Angren,' he explained in hushed tones. 'They'd got lost during their escape. They were alone, fearful and hungry, so we took them on board, and we're looking after them. It just seemed to happen.'

'It just seemed to happen,' Geralt echoed, smiling faintly. 'You're an incorrigible altruist, Zoltan Chivay.'

'We all have our faults. I mean, you're still determined to rescue your girl.'

'Indeed. Although it's become more complicated than that . . . .'

'Because of that Nilfgaardian, who was tracking you and has now joined the company?'

'Partly. Zoltan, where are those fugitives from? Who were they fleeing? Nilfgaard or the Squirrels?'

'Hard to say. The kids know bugger all, the women aren't too talkative and get upset for no reason at all. If you swear near them or fart they go as red as beetroots . . . Never mind. But we've met other fugitives – woodmen – and they say the Nilfgaardians are prowling around here. It's our old friends, probably, the troop that came from the west, from across the Ina. But apparently there are also units here that arrived from the south. From across the Yaruga.'

'And who are they fighting?'

'It's a mystery. The woodmen talked of an army being commanded by a White Queen or some such. That queen's fighting the Blacks. It's said she and her army are even venturing onto the far bank of the Yaruga, taking fire and sword to imperial lands.'

'What army could that be?'

'No idea,' Zoltan said and scratched an ear. 'See, every day some company or other comes through, messing up the tracks with their hooves. We don't ask who they are, we just hide in the bushes . . .'

Regis, who was dealing with the burns on the girl's arm, interrupted their conversation.

'The dressing must be changed daily,' he said to the dwarf. 'I'll leave you the ointment and some gauze which won't stick to the burns.'

'Thank you, barber-surgeon.'

'Her arm will heal,' the vampire said softly, looking at the Witcher. 'With time the scar will even vanish from her young skin. What's happening in the poor girl's head is worse, though. My ointments can't cure that.'

Geralt said nothing. Regis wiped his hands on a rag.

'It's a curse,' he said in hushed tones, 'to be able to sense a sickness – the entire essence of it – in the blood, but not be able to treat it . . .'

'Indeed.' Zoltan sighed. 'Patching up the skin is one thing, but when the mind's addled, you're helpless. All you can do is give a damn and look after them. . . Thank you for your aid, barber-surgeon. I see you've also joined the Witcher's company.'

'It just seemed to happen.'

'Mmm,' Zoltan said and stroked his beard. 'And which way will you head in search of Ciri?'

'We're heading east, to Caed Dhu, to the druids' circle. We're counting on the druids' help . . .'

'No help,' said the girl with the bandaged arm in a ringing, metallic voice. 'No help. Only blood. And a baptism of fire. Fire purifies. But also kills.'

Zoltan was dumbfounded. Regis gripped his arm tightly and gestured him to remain silent. Geralt, who could recognise a hypnotic trance, said nothing and did not move.

'He who has spilt blood and he who has drunk blood,' the girl said, her head still lowered, 'shall pay in blood. Within three days one shall die in the other, and something shall die in each. They shall die inch by inch, piece by piece . . . And when finally the iron-shod clogs wear out and the tears dry, then the last shreds will pass. Even that which never dies shall die.'

'Speak on,' Regis said softly and gently. 'What can you see?'

'Fog. A tower in the fog. It is the Tower of Swallows . . . on a lake bound by ice.'

'What else do you see?'

'Fog.'

'What do you feel?'

'Pain . . .'

Regis had no time to ask another question. The girl jerked her head, screamed wildly, and whimpered. When she raised her eyes there really was nothing but fog in them.

Zoltan, Geralt recalled, still running his fingers over the rune-covered blade, *started to respect Regis more after that incident, altogether dropping the familiar tone he normally used in conversations with the barber-surgeon.*

Regis requested they did not say a single word to the others about the strange incident. The Witcher was not too concerned about it.

He had seen similar trances in the past and tended towards the view that the ravings of people under hypnosis were not prophecy but the regurgitation of thoughts they had intercepted and the suggestions of the hypnotist. Of course in this case it was not hypnosis but a vampire spell, and Geralt mused over what else the girl might have picked up from Regis's mind, had the trance lasted any longer.

They marched with the dwarves and their charges for half a day. Then Zoltan Chivay stopped the procession and took the Witcher aside.

'It is time to part company,' he declared briefly. 'We have made a decision, Geralt. Mahakam is looming up to the north, and this valley leads straight to the mountains. We've had enough adventures. We're going back home. To Mount Carbon.'

'I understand.'

'It's nice that you want to understand. I wish you and your company luck. It's a strange company, if you don't mind me saying so.'

'They want to help,' the Witcher said softly. 'That's something new for me. Which is why I've decided not to enquire into their motives.'

'That's wise,' Zoltan said, removing the dwarven sihil in its lacquered scabbard, wrapped in catskins, from his back. 'Here you go, take it. Before we go our separate ways.'

'Zoltan . . .'

'Don't say anything, just take it. We'll sit out the war in the mountains. We have no need of hardware. But it'll be pleasant to recall, from time to time, that this Mahakam-forged sihil is in safe hands and whistles in a just cause. That it won't bring shame on itself. And when you use the blade to slaughter your Ciri's persecutors, take one down for Caleb Stratton. And remember Zoltan Chivay and the dwarven forges.'

'You can be certain I will,' Geralt said, taking the sword and slinging it across his back. 'You can be certain I'll remember. In this rotten world, Zoltan Chivay, goodness, honesty and integrity become deeply engraved in the memory.'

'That is true,' the dwarf said, narrowing his eyes. 'Which is why I won't forget about you and the marauders in the forest clearing, nor about Regis and the horseshoe in the coals. While we're talking about reciprocity . . .'

He broke off, coughed, hawked and spat.

'Geralt, we robbed a merchant near Dillingen. A wealthy man, who'd got rich as a hawker. We waylaid him after he'd loaded his gold and jewels onto a wagon and fled the city. He defended his property like a lion and was yelling for help, so he took a few blows of an axe butt to the pate and became as quiet as a lamb. Do you remember the chest we lugged along, then carried on the wagon, and finally buried in the earth by the River O? Well, it contained his goods. Stolen loot, which we intend to build our future on.'

'Why are you telling me this, Zoltan?'

'Because I reckon you were still being misled by false appearances not so long ago. What you took for goodness and integrity was rottenness hidden under a pretty mask. You're easy to deceive, Witcher, because you don't look into motives. But I don't want to deceive you. So don't look at those women and children . . . don't take the dwarf who's standing in front of you as virtuous and noble. Before you stands a thief, a robber and possibly even a murderer. Because I can't be certain the hawker we roughed up didn't die in the ditch by the Dillingen highway.'

A lengthy silence followed, as they both looked northwards at the distant mountains enveloped in clouds.

'Farewell, Zoltan,' Geralt finally said. 'Perhaps the forces, the existence of which I'm slowly becoming convinced about, will permit us to meet again one day. I hope our paths cross again. I'd like to introduce Ciri to you, I'd like her to meet you. But even if it never happens, know that I won't forget you. Farewell, dwarf.'

'Will you shake my hand? Me, a thief and a thug?'

'Without hesitation. Because I'm not as easy to deceive as I once was. Although I don't enquire into people's motives, I'm slowly learning the art of looking beneath masks.'

Geralt swung the sihil and bisected a moth that was flying past.

After parting with Zoltan and his group, he recalled, *we happened upon a group of wandering peasants in the forest. Some of them took flight on seeing us, but Milva stopped a few by threatening them with her bow. The peasants, it turned out, had been captives of the Nilfgaardians not long before. They had been forced to fell cedar trees, but a few days ago their guards had been attacked and overcome by a unit of soldiers who freed them. Now they were going home. Dandelion insisted they describe their liberators. He pushed them aggressively and asked sharp questions.*

'Those soldiers,' the peasant repeated, 'they serve the White Queen. They're giving the Black infantry a proper hiding! They said they're carrying out baboon attacks on the enemy's rear lines.'

'What?'

'I'm telling you, aren't I? Baboon attacks.'

'Bollocks to those baboons,' Dandelion said, grimacing and waving a hand. 'Good people . . . I asked you what banners the army were bearing.'

'Divers ones, sire. Mainly cavalry. And the infantry were wearing something crimson.'

The peasant picked up a stick and described a rhombus in the sand.

'A lozenge,' Dandelion, who was well versed in heraldry, said in astonishment. 'Not the Temerian lily, but a lozenge. Rivia's coat of arms. Interesting. It's two hundred miles from here to Rivia. Not to mention the fact that the armies of Lyria and Rivia were utterly annihilated during the fighting in Dol Angra and at Aldersberg, and Nilfgaard has since occupied the country. I don't understand any of this!'

'That's normal,' the Witcher interrupted. 'Enough talking. We need to go.'

'Ha!' the poet cried. He had been pondering and analysing the information extracted from the peasants the whole time. 'I've got it! Not baboons – guerrillas! Partisans! Do you see?'

'We see.' Cahir nodded. 'In other words, a Nordling partisan troop is operating in the area. A few units, probably formed from the remains of the Lyrian and Rivian armies, which were defeated

315

at Aldersberg in the middle of July. I heard about that battle while I was with the Squirrels.'

'I consider the news heartening,' Dandelion declared, proud he had been able to solve the mystery of the baboons. 'Even if the peasants had confused the heraldic emblems, we don't seem to be dealing with the Temerian Army. And I don't think news has reached the Rivian guerrillas about the two spies who recently cheated Marshal Vissegerd's gallows. Should we happen upon those partisans we have a chance to lie our way out of it.'

'Yes, we have a chance . . .,' Geralt agreed, calming the frolicking Roach. 'But, to be honest, I'd prefer not to try our luck.'

'But they're your countrymen, Witcher,' Regis said. 'I mean, they call you Geralt of Rivia.'

'A slight correction,' he replied coldly. 'I call myself that to make my name sound fancier. It's an addition that inspires more trust in my clients.'

'I see,' the vampire said, smiling. 'And why exactly did you choose Rivia?'

'I drew sticks, marked with various grand-sounding names. My witcher preceptor suggested that method to me, although not initially. Only after I'd insisted on adopting the name Geralt Roger Eric du Haute-Bellegarde. Vesemir thought it was ridiculous; pretentious and idiotic. I dare say he was right.'

Dandelion snorted loudly, looking meaningfully at the vampire and the Nilfgaardian.

'My full name,' Regis said, a little piqued by the look, 'is authentic. And in keeping with vampire tradition.'

'Mine too,' Cahir hurried to explain. 'Mawr is my mother's given name, and Dyffryn my great-grandfather's. And there's nothing ridiculous about it, poet. And what's your name, by the way? Dandelion must be a pseudonym.'

'I can neither use nor betray my real name,' the bard replied mysteriously, proudly putting on airs. 'It's too celebrated.'

'It always sorely annoyed me,' added Milva, who after being silent and gloomy for a long while had suddenly joined in the conversation, 'when I was called pet names like Maya, Manya or Marilka.

When someone hears a name like that they always think they can pinch a girl's behind.'

It grew dark. The cranes flew off and their trumpeting faded into the distance. The breeze blowing from the hills subsided. The Witcher sheathed the sihil.

It was only this morning. This morning. And all hell broke loose in the afternoon.

We should have suspected earlier, he thought. *But which of us, apart from Regis, knew anything about this kind of thing? Naturally everyone noticed that Milva often vomited at dawn. But we all ate grub that turned our stomachs. Dandelion puked once or twice too, and on one occasion Cahir got the runs so badly he feared it was dysentery. And the fact that the girl kept dismounting and going into the bushes, well I took it as a bladder infection . . .*

I was an ass.

I think Regis realised the truth. But he kept quiet. He kept quiet until he couldn't keep quiet any longer. When we stopped to make camp in a deserted woodmen's shack, Milva led him into the forest, spoke to him at length and at times in quite a loud voice. The vampire returned from the forest alone. He brewed up and mixed some herbs, and then abruptly summoned us all to the shack. He began rather vaguely, in his annoying patronising manner.

'I'm addressing all of you,' Regis said. 'We are, after all, a fellowship and bear collective responsibility. The fact that the one who bears ultimate responsibility . . . direct responsibility, so to speak . . . is probably not with us doesn't change anything.'

'Spit it out,' Dandelion said, irritated. 'Fellowship, responsibility. . . What's the matter with Milva? What's she suffering from?'

'She's not suffering from anything,' Cahir said softly.

'At least not strictly speaking,' Regis added. 'Milva's pregnant.'

Cahir nodded to show it was as he suspected. Dandelion, however, was dumbstruck. Geralt bit his lip.

'How far gone is she?'

'She declined, quite rudely, to give any dates at all, including the date of her last period. But I'm something of an expert. The tenth week.'

'Then refrain from your pompous appeals to direct responsibility,' Geralt said sombrely. 'It's not one of us. If you had any doubts at all in this regard, I hereby dispel them. You were absolutely right, however, to talk about collective responsibility. She's with us now. We have suddenly been promoted to the role of husbands and fathers. So let's listen carefully to what the physician says.'

'Wholesome, regular meals,' Regis began to list. 'No stress. Sufficient sleep. And soon the end of horseback riding.'

They were all quiet for a long time.

'We hear you, Regis,' Dandelion finally said. 'My fellow husbands and fathers, we have a problem.'

'It's a bigger problem than you think,' the vampire said. 'Or a lesser one. It all depends on one's point of view.'

'I don't understand.'

'Well you ought to,' Cahir muttered.

'She demanded,' Regis began a short while later, 'that I prepare and give her a strong and powerful . . . medicament. She considers it a remedy for the problem. Her mind is made up.'

'And have you?'

Regis smiled.

'Without talking to the other fathers?'

'The medicine she's requesting,' Cahir said quietly, 'isn't a miraculous panacea. I have three sisters, so I know what I'm talking about. She thinks, it seems to me, that she'll drink the decoction in the evening, and the next morning she'll ride on with us. Not a bit of it. For about ten days there won't be a chance of her even sitting on a horse. Before you give her that medicine, Regis, you have to tell her that. And we can only give her the medicine after we've found a bed for her. A clean bed.'

'I see,' Regis said, nodding. 'One voice in favour. What about you, Geralt?'

'What about me?'

'Gentlemen.' The vampire swept across them with his dark eyes. 'Don't pretend you don't understand.'

318

'In Nilfgaard,' Cahir said, blushing and lowering his head, 'the woman decides. No one has the right to influence her decision. Regis said that Milva is certain she wants the . . . medicament. Only for that reason, absolutely only for that reason, have I begun – in spite of myself – to think of it as an established fact. And to think about the consequences. But I'm a foreigner, who doesn't know . . . I ought not to get involved. I apologise.'

'What for?' the troubadour asked, surprised. 'Do you think we're savages, Nilfgaardian? Primitive tribes, obeying some sort of shamanic taboo? It's obvious that only the woman can make a decision like that. It's her inalienable right. If Milva decides to—'

'Shut up, Dandelion,' the Witcher snapped. 'Please shut up.'

'You don't agree?' the poet said, losing his temper. 'Are you planning to forbid her or—'

'Shut your bloody mouth, or I won't be answerable for my actions! Regis, you seem to be conducting something like a poll among us. Why? You're the physician. The agent she's asking for . . . yes, the agent. The word medicament doesn't suit me somehow . . . Only you can prepare and give her this agent. And you'll do it should she ask you for it again. You won't refuse.'

'I've already prepared the agent,' Regis said, showing them all a little bottle made of dark glass. 'Should she ask again, I shall not refuse. Should she ask again,' he repeated with force.

'What's this all about then? Unanimity? Total agreement? Is that what you're expecting?'

'You know very well what it's about,' the vampire answered. 'You sense perfectly what ought to be done. But since you ask, I shall tell you. Yes, Geralt, that's precisely what it's about. Yes, that's precisely what ought to be done. And no, it's not me that's expecting it.'

'Could you be clearer?'

'No, Dandelion,' the vampire snapped. 'I can't be any clearer. Particularly since there's no need. Right, Geralt?'

'Right,' the Witcher said, resting his forehead on his clasped hands. 'Yes, too bloody right. But why are you looking at me? You want me to do it? I don't know how. I can't. I'm not suited for this role at all . . . Not at all, get it?'

'No,' Dandelion interjected. 'I don't get it at all. Cahir? Do you get it?'

The Nilfgaardian looked at Regis and then at Geralt.

'I think I do,' he said slowly. 'I think so.'

'Ah,' the troubadour said, nodding. 'Ah. Geralt understood right away and Cahir thinks he understands. I, naturally, demand to be enlightened, but first I'm told to be quiet, and then I hear there's no need for me to understand. Thank you. Twenty years in the service of poetry, long enough to know there are things you either understand at once, even without words; or you'll never understand them.'

The vampire smiled.

'I don't know anyone,' he said, 'who could have put it more elegantly.'

It was totally dark. The Witcher got to his feet.

It's now or never, he thought. *I can't run away from it. There's no point putting it off. It's got to be done. And that's an end to it.*

Milva sat alone by the tiny fire she had started in the forest, in a pit left by a fallen tree, away from the woodmen's shack where the rest of the company were sleeping. She didn't move when she heard his footsteps. It was as though she was expecting him. She just shifted along, making space for him on the fallen tree trunk.

'Well?' she said harshly, not waiting for him to say anything. 'We're in a fix, aren't we, eh?'

He didn't answer.

'You didn't expect this when we set off, did you? When you let me join the company? You thought: "So what if she's a peasant; a foolish, country wench?" You let me join. "I won't be able to talk to her about brainy things on the road," you thought, "but she might come in useful. She's a healthy, sturdy lass. She shoots a straight arrow, she won't get a sore arse from the saddle, and if it gets nasty she won't shit her britches. She'll come in useful." And it turns out she's no use, just a hindrance. A millstone. A typical bloody woman!'

'Why did you come after me?' he asked softly. 'Why didn't you stay in Brokilon? You must have known . . .'

'I did,' she interrupted. 'I mean, I was with the dryads, they always know what's wrong with a girl; you can't keep anything secret from them. They realised quicker than me . . . But I never thought I'd start feeling poorly so soon. I thought I'd drink some ergot or some other decoction, and you wouldn't even notice, wouldn't even guess . . .'

'It's not that simple.'

'I know. The vampire told me. I spent too long dragging my feet, meditating, hesitating. Now it won't be so easy . . .'

'That's not what I meant.'

'Bollocks,' she said a moment later. 'Imagine this. I had more than one string to my bow . . . I saw how Dandelion puts on a brave face; but thought him weak, soft, not used to hardship. I was just waiting for him to give up and then we'd have to offload him. I thought if it got hard I'd go back with Dandelion . . . Now just look: Dandelion's the hero, and I'm . . .'

Her voice suddenly cracked. Geralt embraced her. And he knew at once it was the gesture she had been waiting for, which she needed more than anything else. The roughness and hardness of the Brokilon archer disappeared just like that, and what remained was the trembling, gentle softness of a frightened girl. But it was she who interrupted the lengthening silence.

'And that's what you told me . . . in Brokilon. That I would need a . . . a shoulder to lean on. That I would call out, in the darkness . . . You're here, I can feel your arm next to mine . . . And I still want to scream . . . Oh dear, oh dear . . . Why are you trembling?'

'It's nothing. A memory.'

'What will become of me?'

He didn't answer. The question wasn't meant for him.

'Daddy once showed me . . . Where I come from there's a black wasp that lives by the river and lays its eggs in a live caterpillar. The young wasps hatch and eat the caterpillar alive . . . from the inside. . . Something like that's in me now. In me, inside me, in my own belly. It's growing, it keeps growing and it's going to eat me alive . . .'

'Milva—'

'Maria. I'm Maria, not Milva. What kind of Red Kite am I? A mother hen with an egg, not a Kite . . . Milva laughed with the dryads on the battleground, pulled arrows from bloodied corpses. Waste of a good arrow shaft or a good arrowhead! And if someone was still breathing, a knife across the throat! Milva was treacherous, she led those people to their fate and laughed . . . Now their blood calls. That blood, like a wasp's venom, is devouring Maria from the inside. Maria is paying for Milva.'

He remained silent. Mainly because he didn't know what to say. The girl snuggled up closer against his shoulder.

'I was guiding a commando to Brokilon,' she said softly. 'It was in Burnt Stump, in June, on the Sunday before summer solstice. We were chased, there was a fight, seven of us escaped on horseback. Five elves, one she-elf and me. About half a mile to the Ribbon, but the cavalry were behind us and in front of us, darkness all around, swamps, bogs . . . At night we hid in the willows, we had to let ourselves and the horses rest. Then the she-elf undressed without a word, lay down . . . and the first elf lay with her . . . It froze me, I didn't know what to do . . . Move away, or pretend I couldn't see? The blood was pounding in my temples, but I heard it when she said: "Who knows what tomorrow will bring? Who will cross the Ribbon and who will perish? *En'ca minne.*" *En'ca minne*, a little love. Only this way, she said, can death be overcome. Death or fear. They were afraid, she was afraid, I was afraid . . . So I undressed too and lay down nearby. I placed a blanket under my back . . . When the first one embraced me I clenched my teeth, for I wasn't ready, I was terrified and dry . . . But he was wise – an elf, after all – he only seemed young . . . wise . . . tender . . . He smelled of moss, grass and dew . . . I held my arms out towards the second one myself . . . desiring . . . a little love? The devil only knows how much love there was in it and how much fear, but I'm certain there was more fear . . . For the love was fake. Perhaps well faked, but fake even so, like a pantomime, where if the actors are skilled you soon forget what's playacting and what's the truth. But there was fear. There was real fear.'

Geralt remained silent.

'Nor did we manage to defeat death. They killed two of them at dawn, before we reached the bank of the Ribbon. Of the three who survived I never saw any of them again. My mother always told me a wench knows whose fruit she's bearing . . . But I don't know. I didn't even know the names of those elves, so how could I tell? How?'

He said nothing. He let his arm speak for him.

'And anyway, why do I need to know? The vampire will soon have the draft ready . . . The time will come for me to be left in some village or other . . . No, don't say a word; be silent. I know what you're like. You won't even give up that skittish mare, you won't leave her, you won't exchange her for another, even though you keep threatening to. You aren't the kind that leaves others behind. But now you have no choice. After I drink it I won't be able to sit in the saddle. But know this; when I've recovered I'll set off after you. For I would like you to find your Ciri, Witcher. To find her and get her back, with my help.'

'So that's why you rode after me,' he said, wiping his forehead. 'That's why.'

She lowered her head.

'That's why you rode after me,' he repeated. 'You set off to help rescue someone else's child. You wanted to pay; to pay off a debt, that you intended to incur even when you set off . . . Someone else's child for your own, a life for a life. And I promised to help you should you be in need. But, Milva, I can't help you. Believe me, I cannot.'

This time she remained silent. But he could not. He felt compelled to speak.

'Back there, in Brokilon, I became indebted to you and swore I'd repay you. Unwisely. Stupidly. You offered me help in a moment when I needed help very much. There's no way of paying off a debt like that. It's impossible to repay something that has no price. Some say everything in the world – everything, with no exception – has a price. It's not true. There are things with no price, things that are priceless. But you realise it belatedly: when you lose them, you lose them forever and nothing can get them back for you. I have lost many such things. Which is why I can't help you today.'

'But you have helped me,' she replied, very calmly. 'You don't even know how you've helped me. Now go, please. Leave me alone. Go away, Witcher. Go, before you destroy my whole world.'

When they set off again at dawn, Milva rode at the head, calm and smiling. And when Dandelion, who was riding behind her, began to strum away on his lute, she whistled the melody.

Geralt and Regis brought up the rear. At a certain moment the vampire glanced at the Witcher, smiled, and nodded in acknowledgement and admiration. Without a word. Then he took a small bottle of dark glass out of his medical bag and showed it to Geralt. Regis smiled again and threw the bottle into the bushes.

The Witcher said nothing.

When they stopped to water the horses, Geralt led Regis away to a secluded place.

'A change of plans,' he informed briefly. 'We aren't going through Ysgith.'

The vampire remained silent for a moment, boring into him with his black eyes.

'Had I not known,' he finally said, 'that as a witcher you are only afraid of real hazards, I should have thought you were worried by the preposterous chatter of a deranged girl.'

'But you do know. And you're sure to be guided by logic.'

'Indeed. However, I should like to draw your attention to two matters. Firstly, Milva's condition, which is neither an illness nor a disability. The girl must, of course, take care of herself, but she is utterly healthy and physically fit. I would even say more than fit. The hormones—'

'Drop the patronising, superior tone,' Geralt interrupted, 'because it's getting on my nerves.'

'That was the first matter of the two I intended to bring up,' Regis continued. 'Here's the second: when Milva notices your overprotectiveness, when she realises you're making a fuss and mollycoddling her, she'll be furious. And then she'll feel stressed; which is absolutely inadvisable for her. Geralt, I don't want to be patronising. I want to be rational.'

Geralt did not answer.

'There's also a third matter,' Regis added, still watching the Witcher carefully. 'We aren't being compelled to go through Ysgith by enthusiasm or the lust for adventure, but by necessity. Soldiers are roaming the hills, and we have to make it to the druids in Caed Dhu. I understood it was urgent. That it was important for you to acquire the information and set off to rescue your Ciri as quickly as possible.'

'It is,' Geralt said, looking away. 'It's very important to me. I want to rescue Ciri and get her back. Until recently I thought I'd do it at any price. But no. I won't pay that price, I won't consent to taking that risk. We won't go through Ysgith.'

'The alternative?'

'The far bank of the Yaruga. We'll go upstream, far beyond the swamps. And we'll cross the Yaruga again near Caed Dhu. If it turns out to be difficult, only the two of us will meet the druids. I'll swim across and you'll fly over as a bat. Why are you staring at me like that? I mean, rivers being obstacles to vampires is another myth and superstition. Or perhaps I'm wrong.'

'No, you are not wrong. But I can only fly during a full moon, not at any other time.'

'That's only two weeks away. When we reach the right place it'll almost be full moon.'

'Geralt,' the vampire said, still not taking his eyes away from the Witcher. 'You're a strange man. To make myself clear, I wasn't being critical. Right, then. We give up on Ysgith, which is dangerous for a woman with child. We cross to the far bank of the Yaruga, which you consider safer.'

'I'm capable of assessing the level of risk.'

'I don't doubt it.'

'Not a word to Milva or the others. Should they ask, it's part of our plan.'

'Of course. Let us begin to look for a boat.'

They didn't have to look for long, and the result of their search surpassed their expectations. They didn't find just a boat, but a ferryboat. Hidden among the willows, craftily camouflaged with branches and bunches of bulrushes, it was betrayed by the painter connecting it to the left bank.

The ferryman was also found. While they were approaching he quickly hid in the bushes, but Milva spotted him and dragged him from the undergrowth by the collar. She also flushed out his helper, a powerfully built fellow with the shoulders of an ogre and the face of an utter simpleton. The ferryman shook with fear, and his eyes darted around like a couple of mice in an empty granary.

'To the far bank?' he whined, when he found out what they wanted. 'Not a chance! That's Nilfgaardian territory and there's a war on! They'll catch us and stick us on a spike! I'm not going! You can kill me, but I'm not going!'

'We can kill you,' Milva said, grinding her teeth. 'We can also beat you up first. Open your trap again and you'll see what we can do.'

'I'm sure the fact there's a war on,' the vampire said, boring his eyes into the ferryman, 'doesn't interfere with smuggling, does it, my good man? Which is what your ferry is for, after all, craftily positioned as it is far from the royal and Nilfgaardian toll collectors. Am I right? Go on, push it into the water.'

'That would be wise,' Cahir added, stroking his sword hilt. 'Should you hesitate, we shall cross the river ourselves, without you, and your ferry will remain on the far bank. To get it back you'll have to swim across doing the breaststroke. This way you ferry us across and return. An hour of fear and then you can forget all about it.'

'But if you resist, you halfwit,' Milva snapped, 'I'll give you such a beating you won't forget us till next winter!'

The ferryman yielded in the face of these hard, indisputable arguments, and soon the entire company was on the ferry. Some of the horses, particularly Roach, resisted and refused to go aboard, but the ferryman and his dopey helper used twitches made of sticks and rope. The skill with which they calmed the animals proved it was not the first time they had smuggled stolen mounts across the Yaruga. The giant simpleton got down to turning the wheel which drove the ferry, and the crossing began.

When they reached the peaceful waters and felt the gentle breeze, their moods improved. Crossing the Yaruga was something new, a clear milestone, marking progress in their trek. In front of them was the Nilfgaardian bank, the frontier, the border. They all suddenly cheered up. It even affected the ferryman's foolish helper, who began to whistle an inane tune. Even Geralt was strangely euphoric, as though Ciri would emerge at any moment from the alder grove on the far bank and shout out joyfully on seeing him.

Instead of that the ferryman began shouting. And not joyfully in the least.

'By the Gods! We're done for!'

Geralt looked towards where he was pointing and cursed. Suits of armour flashed and hooves thudded among the alders on the high bank. A moment later the jetty on the left bank was teeming with horsemen.

'Black Riders!' the ferryman screamed, paling and releasing the wheel. 'Nilfgaardians! Death! Gods, save us!'

'Hold the horses, Dandelion!' Milva yelled, trying to remove her bow from her saddle with one hand. 'Hold the horses!'

'They aren't imperial forces,' Cahir said. 'I don't think . . .'

His voice was drowned out by the shouts of the horsemen on the jetty and the ferryman's yelling. Urged on by the yelling, the daft helper seized a hatchet, swung it and brought the blade down powerfully on the rope. The ferryman came forward to help him with another hatchet. The horsemen on the jetty noticed it and also began to yell. Several of them rode into the water, to seize the rope. Others began swimming towards the ferry.

'Leave that rope alone!' Dandelion shouted. 'It's not Nilfgaard! Don't cut it—'

It was too late, however. The loose end of the rope sank heavily into the water, the ferry turned a little and began to float downstream. The horsemen on the bank started yelling.

'Dandelion's right,' Cahir said grimly. 'They aren't imperial forces . . . They're on the Nilfgaardian bank, but it isn't Nilfgaard.'

'Of course they aren't!' Dandelion called. 'I recognise their livery! Eagles and lozenges! It's Lyria's coat of arms! They're the Lyrian guerrillas! Hey, you men . . .'

327

'Get down, you idiot!'

The poet, as usual, rather than listen to the warning, wanted to know what it was all about. And right then arrows whistled through the air. Some of them thudded into the side of the ferry, some of them flew over the deck and splashed into the water. Two flew straight for Dandelion, but the Witcher already had his sword in his hand, leapt forward and deflected both of them with swift blows.

'By the Great Sun,' Cahir grunted. 'He deflected two arrows! Remarkable! I've never seen anything like it . . .'

'And you never will again! That's the first time I've ever managed two in a row! Now get down, will you!'

However, the soldiers by the jetty had stopped shooting, seeing the current pushing the drifting ferryboat straight towards their bank. Water foamed beside the horses which had been driven into the river. The ferry station was filling up with more horsemen. There were at least two hundred of them.

'Help!' the ferryman yelled. 'Seize the poles, m'lords! We're being carried to the bank!'

They understood at once, and fortunately there were plenty of poles. Regis and Dandelion held the horses, and Milva, Cahir and the Witcher aided the efforts of the ferryman and his duffer of an assistant. Pushed off by five poles, the ferryboat turned and began to move more quickly, clearly heading towards the midstream. The soldiers on the bank started yelling again, and took up their bows once again. Again, several arrows whistled past and one of their horses neighed wildly. The ferryboat, carried away by a more powerful current, was fortunately travelling quickly and began to move further from the bank, beyond the range of an effective arrow shot.

They were now floating in the middle of the river, on calm waters. The ferryboat was spinning like a turd in an ice hole and the horses stamped and whinnied, tugging at the reins, which were being held by Dandelion and the vampire. The horsemen on the bank yelled and shook their fists at them. Geralt suddenly noticed a rider on a white steed among them, who was waving a sword and issuing orders. A moment later the cavalcade withdrew into the forest and galloped along the edge of the high bank. Their armour flashed among the riverside undergrowth.

'They aren't letting us go,' the ferryman groaned. 'They know that the rapids round the corner will push us over towards the bank again . . . Keep those poles at the ready, m'lords! When it turns towards the right bank, we'll have to help the old tub get the better of the current and land . . . Else we're doomed . . .'

They floated, turning, drifting slightly towards the right bank; a steep, high bluff, bristling with crooked pine trees. The left bank, the one that was moving away from them, had become flat and jutted into the river in a semi-circular, sandy spit. Horsemen galloped onto the spit, their momentum taking them into the water. By the spit there was clearly a sand-bank channel, a shallow, and before the water had reached the height of the horses' bellies, the horsemen had ridden quite far into the river.

'We're in arrow range,' Milva judged grimly. 'Get down.'

Arrows began whistling again and some of them thumped into the planks. But the current, pushing them away from the channel, quickly carried the ferryboat towards a sharp bend on the right.

'To the poles!' the trembling ferryman ordered. 'With a will. Let's land before the rapids carry us away!'

It wasn't so easy. The current was swift, the water deep and the ferryboat large, heavy and cumbersome. At first it did not react to their efforts at all, but finally the poles found more purchase on the riverbed. It looked as though they might succeed, when Milva suddenly dropped her pole and pointed wordlessly at the right bank.

'This time . . .' Cahir said, wiping sweat from his brow. 'This time it's definitely Nilfgaard.'

Geralt saw it too. The horsemen who had suddenly appeared on the right bank were wearing black and green cloaks, and the horses had typical Nilfgaardian blinders. There were at least a hundred of them.

'Now we're done for . . .' the ferryman whimpered. 'Mother of mine, it's the Black Riders!'

'To the poles!' the Witcher roared. 'To the poles and into the current! Away from the bank!'

Once again it turned out to be a difficult task. The current by the right bank was powerful and pushed the ferryboat straight under the high bluff, from which the shouts of the Nilfgaardians could be heard. A moment later, when Geralt, who was leaning on his pole, looked upwards, he saw pine branches above his head. An arrow shot from the top of the bluff penetrated the ferryboat's deck almost vertically, two feet from him. He deflected another, which was heading for Cahir, with a blow of his sword.

Milva, Cahir, the ferryman and his assistant pushed away – not from the riverbed, but from the bank where the bluff was. Geralt dropped his sword, caught up a pole and helped them, and the ferryboat began to drift towards the calm waters again. But they were still dangerously close to the right bank and to their pursuers galloping along the edge of it. Before they could move away, the bluff ended and Nilfgaardians flooded onto the flat, reedy bank. Fletchings screamed through the air.

'Get down!'

The ferryman's helper suddenly coughed strangely, dropping his pole into the water. Geralt saw a bloodied arrowhead and four inches of shaft sticking out of his back. Cahir's chestnut reared, neighed in pain, jerking its penetrated neck, knocked Dandelion down and leaped overboard. The remaining horses also neighed and thrashed, and the ferryboat shook from the impact of their hooves.

'Hold the horses!' the vampire yelled. 'Three—'

He suddenly broke off, fell backwards against the planks, and sat down with his head lolling. A black-feathered arrow was sticking out of his chest.

Milva saw it too. She screamed with fury, picked up her bow, knelt and emptied the quiver of arrows right on the deck. Then she began to shoot. Quickly. Arrow after arrow. Not one missed its target.

There was confusion on the bank, the Nilfgaardians retreating into the forest, leaving their dead and wounded in the reeds. Hidden in the undergrowth they continued to shoot, but their arrows were barely reaching the ferryboat, which was being carried towards the midstream by the swift current. The distance was too great for the Nilfgaardian archers to shoot accurately. But not too great for Milva.

Among the Nilfgaardians suddenly appeared an officer in a black cape and a helmet with raven's wings flapping on it. He was yelling, brandishing a mace and pointing downstream. Milva stood, took a broader stance, pulled the bowstring to her ear and quickly took aim. The arrow hissed in the air, and the officer bent backwards in his saddle and sagged in the arms of the soldiers holding him up. Milva drew her bow again and released her fingers from the bowstring. One of the Nilfgaardians holding up the officer screamed piercingly and lurched back off his horse. The others disappeared into the forest.

'Masterful shots,' Regis said calmly from behind the Witcher's back. 'But it'd be better if you grabbed the poles. We're still too close to the bank and we're being carried into the shallows.'

The archer and Geralt turned around.

'Aren't you dead?' they asked in in chorus.

'Did you think,' the vampire said, showing them the black-fletched shaft, 'I could be harmed by any old bit of wood?'

There was no time to be surprised. The ferryboat was once again turning around in the current and moving along the calm waters. But on the bend in the river another beach appeared, a sandbank and shallow channel, and the bank teemed with black-clad Nilfgaardians again. Some of them were riding into the river and preparing to shoot. Everyone, including Dandelion, rushed for the poles, which soon could not reach the bottom as – owing to the combined effort – the current finally carried the ferryboat towards swifter water.

'Good,' Milva panted, dropping her pole. 'Now they won't be able to reach us . . .'

'One of them's made it to the sandbank!' Dandelion cried. 'He's going to shoot! Get out of sight!'

'He'll miss,' Milva said coldly.

The arrow splashed into the water two yards from the ferryboat's bow.

'He's doing it again!' the troubadour yelled, peeping out from above the saxboard. 'Look out!'

'He'll miss,' Milva repeated, straightening the bracer on her left forearm. 'He's got a good bow, but he's as much an archer as my old grannie. He's overexcited. After he releases, he trembles and shakes like a woman with a slug wriggling up her arse. Hold onto the horses, so I don't get knocked over.'

This time the Nilfgaardian shot too high and the arrow whistled over the ferryboat. Milva raised her bow, her stance firm, quickly pulled the bowstring to her cheek and released it gently, not changing her position by even a fraction of an inch. The Nilfgaardian tumbled into the water as though struck by lightning and began to float with the current. His black cape billowed out like a balloon.

'That's how it's done,' Milva said and lowered her bow. 'But it's too late for him to learn.'

'The others are galloping after us,' Cahir said, pointing towards the right bank. 'And I vouch they won't stop chasing us. Not now that Milva's shot their officer. The river's meandering and the current will carry us towards their bank again on the next bend. They know it and they'll be waiting . . .'

'Right now we have another worry,' the ferryman moaned, getting up from his knees and throwing off his dead helper. 'We're being pushed straight for the left bank . . . By the Gods, we're caught between two fires . . . And all because of you, m'lords! The blood will fall on your heads . . .'

'Shut your trap and grab a pole!'

The flat, left bank, which was now nearer, was teeming with horsemen, identified by Dandelion as Lyrian partisans. They were yelling and waving their arms. Geralt noticed a rider on a white horse among them. He wasn't certain, but he thought the rider was a woman. A fair-haired woman in armour, but without a helmet.

'What are they yelling?' Dandelion said, straining to listen. 'Something about a queen, is it?'

The shouting on the left bank intensified. They could also hear the clanging of steel distinctly now.

'It's a battle,' Cahir said bluntly. 'Look. Those are imperial forces running out of the forest. The Nordlings were fleeing from them, and now they've been caught in a trap.'

'The way out of the trap,' Geralt said, spitting into the water, 'was the ferry. I think they wanted to save at least their queen and their officers by ferrying them onto the other bank. And we hijacked the ferry. Oh, they won't like us now, no, no . . .'

'But they ought to!' Dandelion said. 'The ferry wouldn't have saved anyone, just carried them straight into the clutches of the Nilfgaardians on the right bank. Let's avoid the right bank too. We can parley with the Lyrians, but the Blacks will beat us to death without a second thought . . .'

'It's carrying us quicker and quicker,' Milva said, spitting into the water too and watching her saliva drift away. 'And right down the centre of the run. They can kiss our arses, both armies. The bends are gentle, the banks are level and overgrown with willows. We're heading down the Yaruga and they won't catch up with us. They'll soon get bored.'

'Bullshit,' the ferryman groaned. 'The Red Port is ahead of us . . . There's a bridge there! And shallows! The ferry will get stuck . . . If they overtake us, they'll be waiting for us . . .'

'The Nordlings won't overtake us,' Regis said, pointing at the left bank from the stern. 'They have their own worries.'

Indeed, a fierce battle was raging on the right bank. Most of the fighting took place in the forest and only betrayed itself by battle cries, but here and there the black and colourfully uniformed horsemen were delivering blows to each other in the water near the bank. Bodies were splashing into the Yaruga. The tumult and clang of steel quietened, and the ferryboat majestically, but quite quickly, headed downstream.

Finally no soldiers could be seen on the overgrown banks, and no sounds of their pursuers could be heard. Only when Geralt was starting to hope everything would end well did they see a wooden bridge spanning the two banks. The river flowed beneath the bridge, past sandbars and islands, the largest of which supported the bridge's piers. On the right bank lay the timber port; they could see thousands of logs piled up there.

'It's shallow all around,' the ferryman panted. 'We can only get through the middle, to the right of the island. The current is carrying us there now, but grab the poles, they might help if we get stuck . . .'

'There are soldiers on the bridge,' Cahir said, shielding his eyes with his hand. 'On the bridge and in the port . . .'

They could all see the soldiers. And they all saw the band of horsemen in black and green cloaks flooding out of the forest behind the port. They were even close enough to hear the noise of battle.

'Nilfgaard,' Cahir confirmed drily. 'The men who were pursuing us. So the men in the port are Nordlings . . .'

'To the poles!' the ferryman yelled. 'Maybe we'll sneak through while they're fighting!'

They did not manage to. They were very close to the bridge when it suddenly began to shake from the boots of running soldiers. The footmen were wearing white tunics, decorated with red lozenges over their hauberks. Most of them had crossbows, which they rested on the railing and aimed at the ferryboat approaching the bridge.

'Don't shoot, boys!' Dandelion yelled at the top of his voice. 'Don't shoot! We're with you!'

The soldiers did not hear, or did not want to hear.

The salvo of quarrels turned out to have tragic results. The only human to be hit was the ferryman, who was still trying to steer with his pole. A bolt pierced him right through. Cahir, Milva and Regis ducked down behind the side in time. Geralt seized his sword and deflected one quarrel, but there were too many of them. By an inexplicable miracle Dandelion, who was still yelling and waving his arms, was not hit. However, the hail of missiles caused real carnage among the horses. The grey slumped to its knees, struck by three quarrels. Milva's black fell, kicking. Regis's bay too. Roach, shot in the withers, reared and leaped overboard.

'Don't shoot!' Dandelion bellowed. 'We're with you!'

This time it worked.

The ferryboat, carried by the current, ploughed into a sandbank with a grinding sound and came to rest. They all jumped onto the island or into the water, escaping the hooves of the agonised, thrashing horses. Milva was the last, for her movements had suddenly become horrifyingly slow. *She's been hit,* the Witcher thought, seeing the girl clambering clumsily over the side and dropping inertly on the sand. He leapt towards her, but the vampire was quicker.

'Something's broken off in me,' the girl said very slowly. And very unnaturally. And then she pressed her hands to her womb. Geralt saw the leg of her woollen trousers darkening with blood.

'Pour that over my hands,' Regis said, handing Geralt a small bottle he had removed from his bag. 'Pour that over my hands, quickly.'

'What is it?'

'She's miscarrying. Give me a knife. I have to cut open her clothes. And go away.'

'No,' Milva said. 'I want him to stay . . .'

A tear trickled down her cheek.

The bridge above them thundered with soldiers' boots.

'Geralt!' Dandelion yelled.

The Witcher, seeing what the vampire was doing to Milva, turned his head away in embarrassment. He noticed soldiers in white tunics rushing across the bridge at great speed. An uproar could still be heard from the right bank and the timber port.

'They're running away,' Dandelion panted, running to him and tugging his sleeve. 'The Nilfgaardians are already on the right bridgehead! The battle is still raging there, but most of the army are fleeing to the left bank! Do you hear? We have to flee too!'

'We can't,' he said through clenched teeth. 'Milva's miscarried. She can't walk.'

Dandelion swore.

'We'll have to carry her then,' he declared. 'It's our only chance . . .'

'Not our only one,' Cahir said. 'Geralt, onto the bridge.'

'What do you mean?'

'We'll hold back their flight. If those Nordlings can hold the right bridgehead long enough, perhaps we'll be able to escape by the left one.'

'How do you plan to do it?'

'I'm an officer, don't forget. Climb up that pier and onto the bridge!'

On the bridge, Cahir demonstrated that he was indeed experienced at bringing panicked soldiers under control.

'Where are you going, scum? Where are you going, bastards?' he yelled. Each roar was accompanied by a punch, as he knocked a fleeing soldier down onto the bridge's boards. 'Stop! Stop, you fucking swine!'

Some – but far from all – of the fleeing soldiers stopped, terrified by the roaring and flashing of the sword Cahir was whirling dramatically. Others tried to sneak behind his back. But Geralt had already drawn his sword and joined the spectacle.

'Where are you going?' he shouted, catching one of the soldiers in his tracks in a powerful grip. 'Where? Stand fast! Get back there!'

'Nilfgaard, sire!' the soldier screamed. 'It's a bloodbath! Let me go!'

'Cowards!' Dandelion roared in a voice Geralt had never heard, as he clambered onto the bridge. 'Base cowards! Chickenhearts! Would you flee to save your skins? To live out your days in ignominy, you varlets?'

'They are too many, Sir Knight! We stand no chance!'

'The centurion's fallen . . .' another of them moaned. 'The decurions have taken flight! Death is coming!'

'We must run!'

'Your comrades,' Cahir yelled, brandishing his sword, 'are still fighting on the bridgehead and at the port! They are still fighting! Dishonour will be his who does not go to their aid! Follow me!'

'Dandelion,' the Witcher hissed. 'Get down onto the island. You and Regis will have to get Milva onto the left bank somehow. Well, what are you waiting for?'

'Follow me, boys!' Cahir repeated, whirling his sword. 'Follow me if the Gods are dear to you! To the timber port! Death to the dogs!'

About a dozen soldiers shook their weapons and took up the cry, their voices expressing very varied degrees of conviction. About a dozen of the men who had already run away turned back in shame and joined the ragtag army on the bridge. An army which was suddenly being led by the Witcher and the Nilfgaardian.

They might really have set off for the timber port, but the bridgehead was suddenly black with the cavalrymen's cloaks. The

Nilfgaardians broke through the defence and forced their way onto the bridge. Horseshoes thudded on the planking. Some of the soldiers who had been stopped darted away, others stood indecisively. Cahir cursed. In Nilfgaardian. But no one apart from the Witcher paid any attention to it.

'What has been started must be finished,' Geralt snapped, gripping his sword tightly. 'Let's get them! We have to spur our men into action.'

'Geralt,' Cahir said, stopping and looking at him uncertainly. 'Do you want me to . . . to kill my own? I can't . . .'

'I don't give a shit about this war,' the Witcher said, grinding his teeth. 'This is about Milva. You joined the company, so make a choice. Follow me or join the black cloaks. But do it quickly.'

'I'm coming with you.'

And so it was that a witcher and a Nilfgaardian roared savagely, whirled their swords and leapt forward together without a second thought – two brothers in arms, two allies and comrades – in an encounter with their common foe, in an uneven battle. And that was their baptism of fire. A baptism of shared fighting, fury, madness and death. They were going to their deaths, the two of them. Or so they thought. For they could not know that they would not die that day, on that bridge over the River Yaruga. They did not know that they were both destined for other deaths, in other places and times.

The Nilfgaardians had silver scorpions embroidered on their sleeves. Cahir slashed two of them with quick blows of his long sword, and Geralt cut up two more with blows of his sihil. Then he jumped onto the bridge's railing, running along it to attack the rest. He was a witcher and keeping his balance was a trifle to him, but his acrobatic feat astonished the attackers. And amazed they died, from blows of his dwarven blade, which cut through their hauberks as though they were made of wool, their blood splashing the bridge's polished timbers.

Seeing their commanders' valour the now larger army on the bridge raised a cheer, a roar which expressed returning morale and a growing fighting spirit. And so it was that the previously panicked fugitives attacked the Nilfgaardians like fierce wolves, slashing with

swords and battle-axes, stabbing with spears and halberds and striking with clubs and maces. The railing broke and horses plunged into
the river with their black-cloaked riders. The roaring army hurtled
onto the bridgehead, pushing their chance commanders ahead of
them, not letting Geralt and Cahir do what they wanted to do. For
they wanted to withdraw quietly, return to help Milva and flee to
the left bank.

A battle was still raging at the timber port. The Nilfgaardians had
surrounded and cut off the soldiers – who had not yet fled – from
the bridge. Those in turn were defending themselves ferociously
behind barricades built from cedar and pine logs. At the sight of the
reinforcements the handful of soldiers raised a joyful cry. A little
too hastily, however. The tight wedge of reinforcements swept the
Nilfgaardians off the bridge. But now a flanking cavalry counter-
attack began on the bridgehead. Had it not been for the barricades
and timber port's woodpiles, which inhibited both escape and the
cavalry's momentum, the infantry would have been scattered in an
instant. Pressed against the woodpiles, the soldiers took up a fierce
fight.

For Geralt it was something he did not know, a completely new
kind of fighting. Swordsmanship was out of the question, it was
simply a chaotic melee; a ceaseless parrying of blows falling from
every direction. However, he continued to take advantage of the
rather undeserved privilege of being the commander; the soldiers
crowded around him covering his flanks, protected his back and
cleared the area in front of him, creating space for him to strike and
mortally wound. But it was becoming more and more cramped.
The Witcher and his army found themselves fighting shoulder to
shoulder with the bloody and exhausted handful of soldiers – mainly
dwarven mercenaries – defending the barricade. They fought,
surrounded on all sides.

And then came fire.

One side of the barricade, located between the timber port and
the bridge, had been a huge pile of pine branches, as spiky as a
hedgehog, an unsurmountable obstacle to horses and infantry. Now
that pile was on fire; someone had thrown a burning brand into it.

The defenders retreated, assaulted by flames and smoke. Crowded together, blinded, hampering each other, they began to die under the blows of the attacking Nilfgaardians.

Cahir saved the day. Making use of his military experience, he did not allow the soldiers gathering around him on the barricade to be surrounded. He had been cut off from Geralt's group, but was now returning. He had even managed to acquire a horse in a black caparison, and now, hacking in all directions with his sword, he charged at the flank. Behind him, yelling wildly, halberdiers and spearmen in red-lozenged tunics forced their way into the gap.

Geralt put his fingers together and struck the burning pile with the Aard Sign. He did not expect any great effect, since he had been forced to make do without his witcher elixirs for several weeks. But he succeeded nonetheless. The pile of branches exploded and fell apart, showering sparks around.

'Follow me!' he roared, slashing a Nilfgaardian's temple when the man was trying to push his way onto the barricade. 'Follow me! Through the fire!'

And so they set off, scattering the still-burning pyre with their spears, throwing the flaming brands they had picked up with their bare hands at the Nilfgaardian horses.

A baptism of fire, the Witcher thought, furiously striking and parrying blows. *I was meant to pass through fire for Ciri. And I'm passing through fire in a battle which is of no interest to me at all. Which I don't understand in any way. The fire that was meant to purify me is just scorching my hair and face.*

The blood he was splattered with hissed and steamed.

'Onward, comrades! Cahir! To me!'

'Geralt!' Cahir shouted, sweeping another Nilfgaardian from the saddle. 'To the bridge! Force your way through to the bridge! We'll close ranks . . .'

He did not finish, for a cavalryman in a black breastplate, without a helmet, with flowing, bloodied hair, galloped at him. Cahir parried a blow of the rider's long sword, but was thrown from his horse, which sat down on its haunches. The Nilfgaardian leant over to pin him to the ground with his sword. But he did not. He stayed his thrust. The silver scorpion on his breastplate flashed.

'Cahir!' he cried in astonishment. 'Cahir aep Ceallach!'

'Morteisen . . .' no less astonishment could be heard in the voice of Cahir, spread-eagled on the ground.

A dwarven mercenary running alongside Geralt in a blackened and charred tunic with a red lozenge didn't waste time being astonished by anything. He plunged his bear spear powerfully into the Nilfgaardian's belly, unseating the enemy with the impetus of the blow. Another leapt forward, stamping on the fallen cavalryman's black breastplate with a heavy boot, and thrust his spear's blade straight into his throat. The Nilfgaardian wheezed, puking blood and raking the sand with his spurs.

At the same moment the Witcher received a blow in the base of his spine with something very heavy and very hard. His knees buckled beneath him. Falling, he heard a great, triumphant roar. He saw the horsemen in black cloaks fleeing into the trees. He heard the bridge thundering beneath the hooves of the cavalry arriving from the left bank, carrying a banner with an eagle surrounded by red lozenges.

And thus, for Geralt, ended the great battle for the bridge on the Yaruga. A battle which later chroniclers did not, of course, even mention.

'Don't worry, my lord,' the field surgeon said, tapping and feeling the Witcher's back. 'The bridge is down. We aren't in danger of being attacked from the other bank. Your comrades and the woman are also safe. Is she your wife?'

'No.'

'Oh, and I thought . . . For it's always dreadful, sire, when pregnant women suffer in wars . . .'

'Be silent. Not a word about it. What are those banners?'

'Don't you know who you were fighting for? Who would have thought such a thing were possible . . . That's the Lyrian Army. See, the black Lyrian eagle and the red Rivian lozenges. Good, I'm done here. It was only a bump. Your back will hurt a little, but it's nothing. You'll recover.'

'Thanks.'

'I should be thanking you. Had you not held the bridge, Nilfgaard would have slaughtered us on the far bank, forcing us back into the water. We wouldn't have been able to flee from them . . . You saved the queen! Well, farewell, sire. I have to go, others need me to tend to their wounds.'

'Thanks.'

He sat on a log in the port, weary, sore and apathetic. Alone. Cahir had disappeared somewhere. The golden-green Yaruga flowed between the piers of the ruined bridge, sparkling in the light of the sun, which was setting in the west.

He raised his head, hearing steps, the clatter of horseshoes and the clanking of armour.

'This is he, Your Majesty. Let me help you dismount . . .'

'Thtay away.'

Geralt lifted up his eyes. Before him stood a woman in a suit of armour, a woman with very pale hair, almost as pale as his own. He saw that the hair was not fair, but grey, although the woman's face did not bear the marks of old age. A mature age, indeed. But not old age.

The woman pressed a batiste handkerchief with lace hems to her lips. The handkerchief was heavily blood-stained.

'Rise, sire,' one of the knights standing alongside whispered to Geralt. 'And pay homage. It is the Queen.'

The Witcher stood up. And bowed, overcoming the pain in his lower back.

'Did you thafeguard the bridge?'

'I beg your pardon?'

The woman took the handkerchief away from her mouth and spat blood. Several red drops fell on her ornamented breastplate.

'Her Royal Highness Meve, Queen of Lyria and Rivia,' said a knight in a purple cloak decorated with gold embroidery, standing beside the woman, 'is asking if you led the heroic defence of the bridge on the Yaruga?'

'It just seemed to happen.'

'Theemed to happen?' the queen said, trying to laugh, but not

341

having much success. She scowled, swore foully but indistinctly, and spat again. Before she had time to cover her mouth he saw a nasty wound, and noticed she lacked several teeth. She caught his eye.

'Yes,' she said behind her handkerchief, looking him in the eye. 'Thome thon-of-a-bitch thmacked me right in the fathe. A trifle.'

'Queen Meve,' the knight in the purple cloak announced, 'fought in the front line, like a man, like a knight, opposing the superior forces of Nilfgaard! The wound hurts, but does not shame her! And you saved her and our corps. After some traitors had captured and hijacked the ferryboat, that bridge became our only hope. And you defended it valiantly . . .'

'Thtop, Odo. What ith your name, hero?'

'Mine?'

'Certainly,' the knight in purple said, looking at him menacingly. 'What is the matter with you? Are you wounded? Injured? Were you struck in the head?'

'No.'

'Then answer the Queen! You see, do you not, that she is wounded in the mouth and has difficulty speaking!'

'Thtop that, Odo.'

The purple knight bowed and then glanced at Geralt.

'Your name?'

Very well, he thought. *I've had enough of this. I will not lie.*

'Geralt.'

'Geralt from where?'

'From nowhere.'

'Has no one bethtowed a knighthood on you?' Meve asked, once more decorating the sand beneath her feet with a red splash of saliva mixed with blood.

'I beg your pardon? No, no. Nobody has. Your Majesty.'

Meve drew her sword.

'Kneel.'

He obeyed, still unable to believe what was happening. He was still thinking of Milva and the route he had chosen for her, fearing the swamps of Ysgith.

342

The queen turned to the Purple Knight.

'You will thpeak the formula. I am toothleth.'

'For outstanding valour in the fight for a just cause,' the Purple Knight recited with emphasis. 'For showing proof of virtue, honour and loyalty to the Crown, I, Meve, by grace of the Gods the Queen of Lyria and Rivia, by my power, right and privilege dub you a knight. Serve us faithfully. Bear this blow, shirk not away from pain.'

Geralt felt the touch of the blade on his shoulder. He looked into the queen's pale green eyes. Meve spat thick red gore, pressed the handkerchief to her face, and winked at him over the lace.

The Purple Knight walked over to her and whispered something. The Witcher heard the words: 'predicate', 'Rivian lozenges', 'banner' and 'virtue'.

'That ith tho,' Meve said, nodding. She spoke more and more clearly, overcoming the pain and sticking her tongue in the gap left by missing teeth. 'You held the bridge with tholdierth of Rivia, valiant Geralt of nowhere. It jutht theemed to happen, ha, ha. Well, it hath come to me to give you a predicate for that deed: Geralt of Rivia. Ha, ha.'

'Bow, sir knight,' the Purple Knight hissed.

The freshly dubbed knight, Geralt of Rivia, bowed low, so that Queen Meve, his suzerain, would not see the smile – the bitter smile – that he was unable to resist.

ABOUT GOLLANCZ

Gollancz is the oldest SF publishing imprint in the world. Since being founded in 1927 Gollancz has continued to publish a focused selection of bestselling and award-winning authors. The front-list includes **Ben Aaronovitch**, **Joe Abercrombie**, **Charlaine Harris**, **Joanne Harris**, **Joe Hill**, **Alastair Reynolds**, **Patrick Rothfuss**, **Nalini Singh** and **Brandon Sanderson**.

As one of the largest Science Fiction and Fantasy imprints in the UK it is no surprise we have one of the most extensive backlists in the world. Find high-quality SF on Gateway written by such authors as **Philip K. Dick**, **Ursula Le Guin**, **Connie Willis**, **Sir Arthur C. Clarke**, **Pat Cadigan**, **Michael Moorcock** and **George R.R. Martin**.

We also have a strand of publishing in translation, which includes French, Polish and Russian authors. Gollancz is home to more award-winning authors than any other imprint, with names including **Aliette de Bodard**, **M. John Harrison**, **Paul McAuley**, **Sarah Pinborough**, **Pierre Pevel**, **Justina Robson** and many more.

The SF Gateway
More than 3,000 classic, rare and previously out-of-print SF novels at your fingertips.
www.sfgateway.com

The Gollancz Blog
Bringing you news from our worlds to yours. Stories, interviews, articles and exclusive extracts just for you!
www.gollancz.co.uk

GOLLANCZ
LONDON